T
Danny McGee

"Grim's novel is mostly a quiet, slow-moving reflection on second chances, the ethics of cloning, the privileges of the rich, and what it means to be human. The story's perspective alternates between that of Sam and Logan, exploring the experiences of the campers and the counselors, by turns. There's a tinge of unreliability to their narration that gives the tale a compelling, evocative, and uneasy feel. The author also cleverly weaves in the ever changing story of a ghost who supposedly haunts the camp—the eponymous Danny McGee—adding an extra layer to the story in which everybody's repeatedly told to 'Stay on the trails.'

"Quietly insightful speculative fiction that will appeal to fans of *Westworld* and *Black Mirror*."

KIRKUS REVIEWS

"Twisted, sinister, and wildly inventive, Quinlan Grim delivers a chilling campfire story that will keep you up past lights out."

MARY McCOY
AUTHOR OF CAMP SO-AND-SO

"A great near-future science-fiction premise, an all-American summer camp, crystal clear storytelling, a possible murderer and his victim make this a perfect book to read in sunshine."

IMRAAN COOVADIA
AUTHOR OF A SPY IN TIME AND TALES OF THE METRIC SYSTEM

REACTIONS FROM NETGALLEY

"I absolutely loved this! It was so well written and engaging whereas the plot was unique. I can't wait to recommend this to friends."

•••

"I never wanted this book to end. It felt like I was at Camp Phoenix. This would be a great summer read and I definitely plan on rereading it when it comes out."

The Ghost of
Danny McGee

The Ghost of Danny McGee

QUINLAN GRIM

A CALIFORNIA COLDBLOOD BOOK
LOS ANGELES, CALIF.

THIS IS A GENUINE CALIFORNIA COLDBLOOD BOOK
Los Angeles, Calif.

californiacoldblood.com

Set in Minion
Cover design by Dale Halvorsen

Printed in the United States

Publisher's Cataloging-in-Publication Data

Names: Grim, Quinlan, author.

Title: The ghost of Danny McGee / by Quinlan Grim.

Description: Los Angeles, CA: California Coldblood Books, 2022.

Identifiers: ISBN: 978-1-955085-10-6 Subjects: LCSH Camps--Fiction. |
Identity (Psychology)--Fiction. | Murder--Fiction. | Psychological fiction.
| Science fiction. | Thrillers (Fiction) | BISAC FICTION / Science Fiction
/ General | FICTION / Psychological | FICTION / Thriller / General
Classification: LCC PS3607 .R5548 G46 2022 | DDC 813.6--dc23

DEDICATION

For Charlie.

week one

Sam

THE HAT ON THE DASHBOARD is crumpled and dusty. It sits against the corner of the windshield, the visor facing out, frowning at her. Sam frowns back at it. She lets the car idle in the parking space and chews on her lip. Even here, with her eyes on the hat, her head is still in Paris.

It's the first day of June, and the sky is a hard, suburban blue. People loiter in the lot around her in cargo shorts and sundresses, leaning up against their pickups, clutching their canvas bags of barbecue supplies. A pack of kids parades by on scooters and roller blades. Sam shuts off her engine and reaches for the hat in the windshield. She fished it out from under the back seat of her car this morning, where it has been stuffed, forgotten, for nearly a year. The insignia on the front is stained, stitched in white over sun-faded green: two crossed pine branches, topped with a bird's nest.

Hesitantly, Sam puts on the hat. She nods at her reflection in the mirror, tugging the visor down over her eyes. Then she grunts, tosses the hat back onto the dashboard, and pushes herself out of her car.

She mumbles through her packing list as she crosses the grocery store parking lot. Sunscreen, toothpaste, disposable razors. Socks—last summer, she always ran out of socks between laundry days. Sunscreen. The good kind: the lotion, not the spray. She juggles a growing mound of toiletries through the aisles. As she stands under the fluorescent lights and air-conditioning, her feet in sandals, hair in a ponytail, it strikes Sam that she hardly left at all.

If she'd had it her way—if the scholarship extension had been granted to her—she would still be in Paris. She had a summer internship in mind, an apartment of her own, mornings spent sipping coffee and smiling at strangers in sunny cafés. In Paris, she was a real adult. The scholarship board asked if she had access to a summer job at home, and she had to answer honestly: yes. Now, browsing the cosmetics aisle of her old neighborhood market, she is just a kid again.

It's only temporary, Sam tells herself. Eleven weeks at Camp, then she'll be back in Paris. It's just a summer job. She thinks again of the hat in her car, the dusty smell of it, and her stomach squirms in a funny way. Bug repellent, she remembers suddenly, turning on her heel and dashing back down the aisle.

In no hurry to drive back to her parents' house, where her bedroom has been remodeled to a home office and her little sister has grown a nasty attitude, Sam lingers in the parking lot. She leans against the hood of her car and lights a cigarette. In Paris, smoking was an appealing, sexy habit—one she never quite got the hang of. Here, it's a satisfying act of rebellion. As she puffs on the cigarette, she jangles her keys in her fist and stares down at her legs. She wonders how long it has been since she last wore shorts in public, and when, exactly, she got so pale.

"Sam Red!"

Sam blinks up, squinting into the flat sunshine. It seems inevitable; a childhood friend has spotted her from across the parking lot and now charges toward her, arms spread wide. She drops her cigarette, realizing she doesn't actually want to get caught. "Hi."

They haven't seen each other in years. He was a few grades ahead of her in school, an awkward, lisping boy. Once, bored at a neighborhood barbecue, she was dared to kiss him. He has a full sleeve of tattoos now and a grimy toddler in tow. "Wow." He smiles at her. "You look great."

Sam nods. She tilts her chin in a practiced way, letting his look run over her. The past year has made her thinner, sharper. Her hair is longer and darker than it used to be, the baby fat drained from her freckled cheeks. She knows her own charm as she sees it in those up-and-down glances.

"Where have you been, again? England?"

"France."

"France? What made you run off to France?"

Sam eyes the kid at his knees, who has begun to pout and pick at scabs. His little hands are streaked with dirt. Unease rises in her chest. Not waiting for an answer, her old friend carries on, telling her all about his job and his truck and his new craftsman home.

"Hey, I'm really sorry, Danny," Sam cuts him off after some time. "I kind of have to get going. It was great seeing you."

"Well, how long are you here for? You want to—I mean, are you twenty-one yet?"

"I'm leaving in a couple of days, actually. I have a job. At a camp."

"A camp." His eyes widen. "Oh. I heard about that. You're going back there?"

Sam nods again and, with a few awkward pleasantries, manages to detangle herself from the conversation. She ducks into her car, fumbling with the keys.

"What's it like?" he asks, leaning on his arm over her open window. "Do they actually look like . . . you know, like kids? Do you get to see it all happen? How do they do it?"

The radio blares when the engine turns over. Sam flashes him a vapid smile and nods. "It was great to see you!" she calls over the music. At the exit to the parking lot, she glances back through the rearview mirror.

In Paris, no one asked her about Camp Phoenix. She looks at the hat on the dashboard and thinks anxiously of scabs, and sunburns, and small, dirt-streaked hands. She has a long summer ahead of her.

Socks, Sam remembers with a groan, hitting her blinker. She'll have to go to another store for socks.

Logan

LOGAN'S FINGERTIP HOVERS OVER THE screen. She hesitates, sighs, and lets it fall to *replay* again.

It begins with a shot of a boy in swim trunks running across a broad green lawn. His hair flops back on the breeze, his face screwed into a fierce, determined look.

Do you remember what it felt like to run? To climb? To fight? To play?

The scene changes with each suggestion to a slow-motion clip of children engaging in the named activity. The setting is sunny and natural. The children are pretty boys and girls, peppered with token diversity. Low music swells behind the narrator's voice.

To laugh freely? To cry openly? To be loved—(here, a shot of a young woman holding a little girl on her lap, their faces both thrown back in laughter)— *unconditionally?*

The tone of the video shifts. Traffic, office windows. A couple arguing soundlessly. A lock of white hair brushed back by a wrinkled hand.

Do you remember being carefree? Do you remember the life you once had? Do you ever think . . . The narration pauses over a woman staring solemnly at a framed photograph. . . . *about going back?*

The video fades to black, and the familiar bird's nest insignia melts into view on Logan's screen. *Camp Phoenix*, she reads, in bold white text. *Go Back.* Again, her finger leaps to *replay*.

Logan pauses, shakes her head, and lowers her hand. She pushes herself back from her desk, blinking some of the bleariness from her eyes. She doesn't need to watch the promotion again. It isn't exactly good—clichéd, even. Still, something about it coos to her. *Go Back.* They make it sound so simple.

"Mrs. Gill?"

She lifts her head from her screen. "Adler-Gill," she corrects the intern in her doorway. It's a recent change. She has to correct people more often than not. She hears the whispered rumors in the hallways, murmurs of divorce, of her descent into spinsterhood. Why hyphenate, they mutter, when she's just going to drop her husband's name entirely? The change has nothing to do with her husband, of course—it's a little thing, only for herself.

"Sorry." The girl blushes. A pause stretches before she gets to what she needs, stammering through her question. Afterward, she lingers at the door for a moment until Logan looks expectantly back up.

"Something else?"

"Did, umm . . . did you hear the news today?"

Logan laughs, although there is nothing really funny about it. Whatever else may be happening in the world, Hugo Baker is all anyone ever wants to talk about. "Yes, I did." She shrugs, all too aware of the stiffness in her shoulders. "You know, just being out on bond doesn't mean he won't be convicted."

A gossipy smile creeps over the intern's mouth. "You don't think he's innocent, do you?"

"I've never heard of an innocent man paying his own bail."

The girl gives a surprised snicker, and Logan smiles. She smooths down her blouse and wonders absently, with a nudge of her old self-consciousness, what she thinks of her.

"Close the door behind you, hon."

It's a chilly evening, for early summer, and growing dark by the time Logan can leave her office. She clutches the collar of her jacket tight to her throat as she hurries to her car. There is a lot on her mind; only a few more days until they leave, and too much to be done before then.

She'll miss Emma's bedtime if she stops at the co-op. Money has been tighter since they paid their Camp tuitions, though, and she can't justify the delivery fee just for oat milk and Merlot. Standing in line at the register, her eyes drift to the community corkboard on the wall. There, tacked alongside the lost puppies and garage sale announcements, is the same poster she has seen all over the city in the past few weeks. A beaming Hollywood headshot, darkened, with a single word scrawled across the eyes in oozing red. *Murderer.*

"Did you hear the news?" the cashier asks her. Logan nods.

She gets home after dark. The nanny sits on the sofa watching a music video show on low volume. Vintage, Logan notes with a chuckle. She thanks the nanny and sends her home, swallowing her guilt, again, about being so late. In her daughter's room, about a ream of white cardstock has been scattered across the floor. Each sheet is a canvas for sparse rainbows and loopy flowers and bloated, stork-legged people floating in space. Logan takes a moment to study the pictures. It's funny—*Mommy* and *Daddy* always seem to be drawn in red and blue crayon, respectively, but Emma depicts herself in a whole spectrum of colors, constantly changing.

Her little girl is fast asleep beneath the comforter, mouth open. Logan crouches at the edge of the bed and wrestles the urge to wake her up. She wants to know what she is dreaming about. Instead, she leans down and leaves a kiss on her temple, lingering there, measuring the steady pulse against her lips.

Downstairs, she fills a wineglass and disintegrates into the sofa. The TV is still on. Logan stares blankly at the old music video. She must have been about the nanny's age when this song came out, she thinks, watching Poppy Warbler strut across the screen in leopard-print spandex. She wasn't exactly a fan at the time. Bad music is like that, though—it only gets better with age and nostalgia. She bobs her head along to the tune. The empty house is lonely at night, even a little spooky.

Her husband is across the city. They aren't supposed to have any contact in the weeks leading up to the consciousness transfer. The idea, supposedly, is to weaken their memories of each other, to avoid any sense of familiarity when they first meet at Camp Phoenix. Logan thought it was ridiculous at first. Now, she is alarmed by how rapidly the details of her spouse's features are fading from her mind's eye. She can't quite place the freckle on his throat, the scar at his hairline, the rings of gold in his irises. Memory is a fragile, terrifying thing.

The glass in her hand is half empty when he calls.

"Hey, Loges." He sounds tired. They shouldn't be speaking, technically, but at the pace of their lives, it's simply impossible.

"Hi. You're a little late. I just put her to bed."

"Did you see the news?" His tone is hard and heavy, leaning forward.

Logan laughs, somewhat clunkily. "Are you talking about what I think you're talking about?"

A long sigh fills her ear. "This isn't right. We should call someone, see if they'll reconsider. I don't think we should support them now."

"Wait, what?"

Again, he sighs. "Are you in the living room? Look."

Logan watches the TV screen. The sentimental music video cuts out, and the clip he has sent her appears. She looks at the same handsome headshot she saw in the co-op, now undefaced. Open collar, silver hair, notorious smile. Logan adjusts the volume skeptically. It's a talk show—a gossip show, really, not the kind of thing either of them would normally watch. A snide, excited debate carries out across the image.

. . . innocent until proven guilty. In this country, someone is innocent until they are proven guilty.

Logan scoffs.

I agree, and I'm not saying he's guilty. We can't know yet. But just because he might be innocent, should that mean that he gets to just drop out of reality while he's out on bond? I mean, by letting him into that place, the execs at Phoenix Genetics are really showing us there's nothing money can't buy . . .

"What?" Logan breathes aloud. The image on the talk show shifts, from Hugo Baker's photo to a sunny forest, a rustic log cabin, a child-sized pair of muddy sneakers on a porch. Next is another headshot of another smiling, gray-haired man.

. . . and listen, we couldn't get Byron on the phone tonight, but if you ask me, he's just looking at Baker as another paying client. We're talking about the ethics of a man who manufactures human children, for God's sake . . .

She forgot she was still holding her phone to her ear. His voice, when he speaks up again, makes her jump. "He's going to be there, Logan. He's going to be there with us."

Sam

EARLY IN THE MORNING, ON the third of June, Sam leaves for Camp Phoenix.

She pulls out of her parents' driveway just before sunrise. The drive will take about ten winding hours, but she doesn't mind—a week of sitting still in suburbia has left her twitchy and restless. She sings along with the radio as she merges onto the freeway, happy just to be moving again. By noon, the landscape has flattened around her, and the road ahead is clear. Her high spirits slowly give way to nerves.

A year ago, when she made this drive for the first time, she had no idea what she was heading toward. They found her online. She was exactly the sort of person Camp Phoenix was looking for, the message in her inbox said: a college student, driven and enthusiastic, good with kids—Would she be interested in a unique, high-paying summer job? Sam assumed it had to be a scam. Camp Phoenix was an international scandal in her childhood, a millionaire's unethical playground; there was no way they recruited their staff through social media. Desperate to afford her exchange program in Paris, she sent the application on a whim, anyway. Six weeks later, she was driving up this freeway with a single backpack and a head full of wild expectations.

The summer was intense. Sam's memories of it now are vibrant and somewhat painful, but vaguely distant, as if she watched it all happen through a screen. She swore, back in August, that she wouldn't come back. Now, she wonders what it will be like to see the place again, to see her friends. She wonders if they have all grown as much as she believes she has.

As the sun peaks overhead, Sam turns off the freeway and picks up speed along an all-but-empty highway, over open plains brown and dry with drought. Tiny towns and dilapidated barns fly by. She rolls down the windows to let in the dry air and the stink of cows. The day is getting hotter. At a gas station, she looks back at her little black sedan to find it turned a muted gray, coated in a thick layer of dust. It will look like that until the summer ends.

The highway shoots her upward, into green mountains, and dwindles to a winding country road. The air cools. Houses thin and then vanish entirely from the scenery, aside from the occasional wilting, suspicious-looking shed. Poverty turns to wilderness. Sam's last glimpse of human society is a tiny child standing on a mobile home porch, dirty and diapered, holding a plastic jug. She shudders.

Tall pines tower over the road on either side. The sun is sinking behind them when at last she turns onto a paved private road and spends the last hour of her drive in nervous silence through a dense, darkening forest. The smell of the air here is so distinct that she jolts and lifts her head when it reaches her; it's the smell of rich dirt and crushed pine needles and something sickly sweet, like rot. Nature and decay. Some way along that final stretch of the drive, Sam feels a *pop* deep within her ears, and for a moment her vision blurs. She nearly drives off the road. When the fuzziness clears, she is offset, dissociated. She turns up the stereo and rolls the windows down again.

At last, the car breaks out of the trees onto a bald ridgetop, and Sam realizes she has made it. To one side, the world stretches below her, endless and green. To the other, the ridge drops steeply into a thumbprint lake basin. Straight ahead is a tiny town. A wooden sign greets her:

Welcome to Smith's Ridge!
Elevation: 4,856'
Private property of Phoenix Genetics, Inc.

There is no indicator of population on the sign. Smith's Ridge is undeniably charming, alien but somehow nostalgic, like the set of a treasured childhood movie. Clapboard cabins and a few pastel storefronts line the single, one-lane road cutting along the ridgetop. At its end, slightly obscured by the pines, is a tremendous log mansion. High glass windows wink through the trees.

Sam turns in the center of town and twists downward toward the lake and Camp on the other side, crossing a high bridge beside the dam. Old Hatchery Bridge, it's called. As the story goes, there was once a fish hatchery at the foot of the dam. Its crumbling remains are still there: a squat, gargoyle-ish concrete shack. A black ribbon of lake water tumbles over the spillway, down the face of the dam and into a shallow pool. From there, the stream flows through the old hatchery's foundations and sputters out on the other side, rushing down the mountain.

Across the bridge, pavement gives way to hard-packed red dirt beneath Sam's tires. She bounces her way through the trees parallel to the lakeshore. In the gaps between trunks and boulders she sees green water, flat and reflective under the late-afternoon sun.

The dusty parking lot is already full of cars, each as dirty and dented as her own. Sam parks among them, feeling buoyant and surreal. She is late and figures she can blame that on traffic—silly as it sounds now. Traffic and freeways are already a world away. She shoulders her backpack and leaves her keys on the dashboard. A rocky trail carries her through the pines into the heart of Camp.

The place is beautiful, bizarre, eerie as a painting in its emptiness. Open cabin doors creak in the breeze and branches shush and rustle around her. The trail delivers her straight onto the main lawn, a groomed green plateau overlooking the lake. To one side the land cuts up in a sharp dirt rise; a wood-plank staircase carved into it leads to a great old lodge with a tented tin roof. Near the base of the hill, before the lawn, a semicircular cement patio curves around a bell tower. The tower is built of stacked stones and concrete and rises up to twice Sam's height. It looks like something medieval, an ancient relic. The sight of that bell tower, more so than anything else, twists an anxious knot in Sam's gut.

Sprawled along the set of splintery benches on the patio, where the whole Camp will sit for daily announcements once the summer starts, are about two dozen people in tired T-shirts and ball caps and ponytails. In the scattered excitement of their conversation, it takes some time for anyone to notice Sam crossing the lawn. She has nearly reached the announcement benches when a high shriek shatters the air. A little figure comes springing away from the group, sprints across the grass, and takes a flying leap into Sam's arms, nearly toppling her.

Rosie—tiny and dark, built like a bullet. Her cheek pressed to Sam's smells like spearmint and sunscreen. Sam squeals as she drops her bag, spinning with her. Behind them, a gangly blond boy lopes across the lawn, shouting. Elias pulls her into a stiff hug. The edge of his sunglasses knocks against her temple, and Sam laughs. Here they are, she thinks in a rush, exactly as she remembered them.

"I thought you weren't coming!" Rosie gasps. Two long braids fall over her shoulders, swaying as she dances in place. "You said you were going to Paris."

"I did." Sam grins, overwhelmed. "I'm back."

Elias gives her a crooked smile. "Couldn't stay away," he says, in a voice Sam remembers all too well, a lazy, affected drawl. "I knew it." He turns to Rosie. "I told you."

"You did not." Rosie snatches the sunglasses off his face. Sam tousles his hair, snickering, and they walk together to the announcement benches.

She isn't the last to arrive, but close to it. Everyone is back. One year older and none the wiser, they boast new facial hair and fresh tattoos, stories of school and travel and corporate internships. Sam sinks joyfully into the crowd, bouncing from one smiling face to the next. Jeremy looks like he has grown a foot. Jaeden is as stoically handsome as ever; Sadie, still round-cheeked and eager. Dane and Katie seem to have reignited their longstanding on-again, off-again relationship. They haven't had long to catch up before the bell at the top of the tower sounds with a great resounding chime, and they all rise instinctively, ready to get back to work.

The counselors sit down for a hasty, chattery dinner in the mess hall. There is no ceremony tonight, beyond a few words from their director and the older staff members. Formality and instructions will come later in the week. The air buzzes with excitement, and no one is able to sit still for long. At the ancient piano in the back of the dining room, Elias and his older brother, Nick, bicker their way through a trickling ballad as the rest of the group sings tunelessly along.

Gus Campbell, the director of Camp Phoenix, is broad-faced and kind. He wears wire-rimmed glasses and doesn't own a single item of clothing, to the extent of Sam's knowledge, not made of khaki or promoting his children's various high school sports teams. *Emerson High Junior Varsity Lacrosse,* his T-shirt reads. *Go Dragons!* He putters around the room with his plate in hand, smiling over them. "Sam Red!" He tosses her into a gruff, back-clapping hug when he sees her. "Good to see you, kid! Good to have you back!"

In all the chaos of greetings and clattering dishes, Sam, Elias, and Rosie manage to sneak away from the crowd. They duck out of the mess hall and hurry down the slippery plank steps, across the lawn and downhill toward the lakeshore, where they sit at the water's edge and bury their toes in the mud. The lake is frigid, soberingly cold so early in the summer.

"I can't believe we're all here again." Elias laughs. "I mean, didn't you both say you weren't coming back, at the end of last summer?"

Sam looks out across the water. The sun has fallen below the ridge on the other side of the lake, and the blue of the sky is growing richer. She can see the glint of the windows high on the ridgetop, through the trees. A breeze billows tiny ripples over the lake's mirrored surface.

She does remember the end of last summer. She remembers how tired she was, how sick she felt. How she swore that she would get as far away as she possibly could. Still, she somehow forgot how beautiful the lake is after dinner, when the sun drops behind the ridge and the hues of the sky melt together.

Rosie laughs and wiggles her feet in the water. "I don't think we even believed it when we said it. There's no way I'm turning down this paycheck."

Elias shakes his head. "It's not just about the money."

He has filled out some over the past year, Sam notices. His shoulders are a little broader, his face less boyish, even now, flushed with the heat and excitement of the day. They are comic opposites, he and Rosie: pale against tan, soft against sharp. She has a narrow nose and a cutting jaw and piercing, speculative eyes.

The three of them were the only new hires added to the Camp Phoenix staff last summer. They hated each other from the start. Rosie was too opinionated, Sam too pretentious, and Elias had a grating flare for the dramatic. It took some time and a few drunken mishaps, naturally, but they grew to love each other in a way only people forced into such close circumstances can. Now, here they are again. Rosie lives in Los Angeles; she's on an all-female mixed martial arts team and takes women's studies classes at night. Elias studies theater in New York on his parents' funds. Sam lives in Paris. There isn't a shred of sense to their friendship.

"It's not just about the money," Sam agrees quietly. She squishes the silt between her toes.

"You guys know about the murderer?"

"Yup," they chime together and giggle at each other.

"So?"

"So, what? Do I think he's guilty?" Rosie squints at him, her face pinched into a hard, imposing frown. "Yes. It's disgusting they're letting him come."

"How long until they get here, again?"

"Eight days. Wait . . ." Elias counts his fingers and nods to himself. "Yup. Eight days."

Sam looks again toward the facility on the ridge. She lets out a long rush of breath and sinks back onto the coarse sand, on her elbows, her chin wedged gracelessly to her chest. Soon there will be meetings, and training, and cabin assignments. Then there will be campers. A hundred grown-up souls in tiny bodies, running around under their strained and incompetent care.

It was all very hazy, trapped behind fogged glass, until she saw the lake and the trees, until she was struck by the dirty, decaying smell of the forest. Now she remembers exactly how raw and exciting and busy it all is. It will be hard. Tonight, though, she can't see any reason not to be happy she is back.

A chime rings from the bell tower, and the three of them hop to their feet.

Logan

THEY COME FOR HER AT seven a.m. A dark SUV pulls into the drive, and Logan steps out of her house exactly as she is: no phone, no keys, no wallet. As if she is going to be right back.

Her husband will be flying from another airport to maintain their separation. Their daughter is already settled with Logan's parents for the summer. Ten weeks is a long time for a kid so young. Every time Logan wrestles with her guilt over it, she returns to the same conclusion: the best thing for Emma, in the long run, is to have happy, healthy parents. Parents who love each other.

The driver takes her to the airport, straight onto the tarmac, where a little white jet sits shrouded in the morning mist. Onboard are four or five men about twice her age. Logan takes her seat and orders a coffee, and they're in the air before long. She sits back and closes her eyes. Home and life fall away below her.

The flight is quick. They touch down on a tiny landing strip in the middle of a flat, dusty nowhere. From there, they are shuttled into private cars and driven another two and a half hours, deep into the mountains. Their destination is about as far away from anything as a place can get—isolation, total separation from reality, is the goal. The ridgetop town appears all at once, like a mirage in the thick wilderness. Just past it, the road leads them up to a grand log cabin structure, six stories high and warmly welcoming. Carved bears and tulips wave them up the front steps. It might be a ritzy ski lodge or a summer resort, a billionaire's vacation home. There is no sign out front, no name on the door. Nothing to indicate what happens here.

"Mrs. Gill?" they greet her, all smiles at reception.

"Adler-Gill." Logan nods.

The interior of the building is cool and softly lit. Wood floors and high ceiling beams give it an air of rustic elegance, tinged with the sanitary gleam of a hospital. Staff in pale blue scrubs bustle through the halls. Logan's room is on the fifth floor, small and dorm-like. A sliding glass door opens up to a narrow balcony, a view of the mountains. The paintings on the walls mirror the landscape outside.

As directed, she goes straight into the bathroom and undresses. She takes a shower, then puts on the clothes left in neat stacks for her—loose, plain white cotton. With her hair still dripping, she steps out onto her balcony. Below her, a carpet of bristling treetops stretches down toward a green lake, its surface still and calm. On the distant horizon are blue-gray peaks. One floor down, she can see a man standing on his own balcony. Judging by the top of his head, he is not her husband. He probably isn't Hugo Baker, either. A chill mountain breeze touches her wet scalp, raising goosebumps over her arms. Carried on it is the scent of pine trees and earth and lake water. The sounds of the forest, a trilling bird call and rustling needles, echo faintly in her memory.

A series of vivid images rushes her. Scraped knees, sunburnt shoulders. Cool, murky water rolling on her skin. Dirty clothes ripe with campfire smoke, greasy food on a plastic plate, drifting to sleep on a grown-up's warm lap. Logan blinks and wavers. The memories are happy, soothing, but they never sit quite right. Even here. They don't feel like her own; they are borrowed from someone who never really existed.

Logan has been to Camp Phoenix once before, five years ago. She was seven. Everything they say about the experience is true: it is pure, and renewing, and life-changing. It becomes harder to remember as time passes, though, and adulthood takes its toll again.

An attendant comes by the room to take her weight and temperature. He gives her a few injections and leaves a tidy handful of pink pills to be taken over the next few hours. They are doping her up, preparing her body for the long weeks of suspension ahead. "A nice, long nap," the attendant jokes, tastelessly.

Next is a psychologist with a binder full of details. "Good afternoon, Mrs. Gill. Let's go over your summer goals again, shall we?"

"It's Adler-Gill."

"Of course." He winks at her. "Soon to be just Adler, right?"

The whole day is a headache of drugs and wavers and paperwork. It's a dreary, painfully grown-up process, considering the purpose of it all. Maybe there is something deliberate about that, Logan thinks. A final push before release.

The next morning, she is scheduled to meet with the Camp's owner. She approaches an intimidating dark oak door at the end of a long hall on the ground floor of the facility. For a moment she hesitates, like a schoolkid at the principal's office, deliberating over whether to knock or to sit and wait. Just as she raises her fist, the door swings inward, and Logan swallows a yelp of surprise. She blinks, then gawks at the face staring dully back at her.

It's another client, a woman about her own age. From her appearance, she might be much older—but Logan knows exactly who this is. Her hair is yellow and stringy, her face sallow, lips turned down. Her eyes are bloodshot and empty. Still, her face is iconic, unmistakable, and Logan's heart flutters despite herself. She chokes out an unclear apology as they edge by each other, trading places in the doorway. The door falls shut, and she is left looking across a polished wood floor at a man behind a long, sleek desk. Morning sunlight pours through a wall of high windows to her right, flooding the space between them.

Richard Byron stands and moves around his desk to extend a hand to her. His shirt is untucked, his sleeves cuffed, wrists and fingers bare. He wears a close gray beard and a glimmering smile. "Mrs. Gill," he greets her warmly. His handshake is firm and jaunty.

Logan does not correct him. He has probably met with Mr. Gill already; the mistake is understandable. They settle at opposite sides of the desk. The leather of the chair is still warm from its last occupant. Unable to help herself, Logan points vaguely over her head, toward the door. "Am I wrong, or was that . . . ?"

He laughs out loud. It's a delighted, somewhat private laugh. Although they are the only two people in the room, that laugh somehow excludes her. "I know," he says, shaking his head. "She's looked better, hasn't she?"

Logan nods and permits herself a small smile.

His hair is too long for his age and esteem, swooped playfully back from his brow. He runs a hand through it as he looks her over. Logan shifts in her seat, suddenly uncomfortable in the shapeless white hospital garb.

"Glad to have you back, Mrs. Gill." He speaks in a low, drifting voice. His attention shifts to the screen on his desk—skimming over her personal data, she imagines. "This will be your second summer, that correct?"

"Yes."

"Well, what's it been? Five years?" Richard Byron reads swiftly over his screen. "Why the long gap?"

"Oh. Well, adult life, you know. I've had a lot on my plate, professionally. And I became a mother."

"Of course. Adopted a little girl, right?"

"Yes."

"That's sweet." He nods, and his tone shifts upward toward business. "Now, you didn't come alone this year, right?"

"Right."

"Right. And he's never been to Camp before, has he?"

"No, this will be his first summer."

"Right." Byron nods. "So, we're digging into the past to fix the present, huh?"

Logan stiffens in her seat, unsure whether or not to be embarrassed. She supposes not. They have talked about it with their advisors over the course of a year, written their goals down in detail. To the man behind the whole process, it must be just another order of business. She nods.

"Well, that's what we do here. One way or another." He gives her a warm smile. "You two have made a great decision, doing this together. There's no true bond like a bond formed in childhood, you know. I think you'll be surprised what you learn this summer. If everything goes according to plan."

Logan frowns. "I don't think we have much of a *plan*."

Again, it's as if he is laughing at a joke she missed, something whispered in his ear while she was looking away. "No, of course not. No one does. There's never a set plan here. That's really the beauty of the whole thing, isn't it? No—what I mean is, if the camper cooperates with all the goals you've laid out. I mean, if her experience this summer is everything you want it to be."

Logan folds her hands in her lap. The stream of daylight falling over her through the windows seems altogether too harsh; she is very much aware of the paleness of her own skin, the fine creases and slack. "Her," she repeats with a breathy laugh through her nose. "That's funny."

"What's that?"

"It's just, I think you're the first person I've talked to who refers to *her*. Not *me*."

He scoffs, waving a dismissive hand in the air. "You'll have to forgive me. You know, this time of year, I'm spending more time with the campers than with the clients. Sometimes I forget all about *you*, to be honest." He chuckles to himself.

The conversation carries on for some time. Byron is charming, for all his digressions and off-putting smiles—the quirks of a mad genius, allegedly. Logan is surprised when he brings up the subject of Hugo Baker. Surprised, but finds it admirable. He wants to know if she is uncomfortable with the news, if it played into her decision to come back. She tells him honestly: it was her husband who was really upset. He talked a lot about getting their money back, about taking the moral high ground. The reality, she knows, is that he was scared. He was never sure about the summer to begin with. Baker's presence was just a fair excuse to raise a stink. She stops short of saying as much to Richard Byron.

He nods, and his gaze is set in a firm line, adamant, when he says: "You have to know, Mrs. Gill, that if I—if anyone with Phoenix Gen—thought that he could be a danger to any of our clients, we would not have accepted his application to the program. I mean that. The truth is, if he is guilty of what they're accusing him of, or not—" Here, he holds up two defensive palms and frowns evenly, as if to clarify that he is not trying to pass judgment one way or the other. Logan knows that gesture well. It's a gesture men his age are fond of, a blanketing shrug to smother debate. "The truth is, on the other side of that lake, it doesn't matter. Once the consciousness transfer goes through, he won't be guilty, or innocent, of anything. Any more than you will be. A kid is just a kid. Does that make sense?"

Logan looks toward the windows. She can see the taut surface of the lake through the trees and, if she squints, the edges of a groomed lawn far on the other side. "Yes." She nods. "It does."

She imagines, for a moment, the notorious filmmaker sitting in this same leather seat. How differently their conversation must have gone.

"You seem agitated. If you have any other questions, about any of it, please go ahead and ask." Byron folds his hands on his desk, thumbs twiddling. "That's what this meeting is for."

Logan shakes her head. A stray lock has fallen from her bun; she tucks it habitually behind her ear. "No. No, I don't think I have anything to ask. It's just a little overwhelming at this point. Even the second time around. I'm still thinking about *her*, I guess."

"Well, that is perfectly understandable. I can't blame you." He leans back in his chair. A tiny, mischievous grin blooms on his lips. "Would you like to meet her?"

Logan freezes, hovering on the edge of her next thought. "Are you serious? I thought that wasn't allowed."

He laughs heartily, shaking his head. Then he shifts forward to type something into his desktop. "It can be a little much for some people to handle," he explains carefully. "But since this is your second summer, and you seem to have a reasonable head on your shoulders, Logan, if you don't mind my saying . . ." He clicks his tongue, then looks up from his screen and bobs his chin at her. "Ready?"

Logan cannot say that she is, but she nods. Her hands twist in her lap as she slides forward on the leather seat. He swivels the screen to face her.

It appears to be live footage. Logan looks down into a small, tidy room, at a white-sheeted hospital bed. An attendant leans over the body on the bed; when they move aside, she and Byron have full view of the girl. Logan's breath catches in her throat.

She knows that girl. There are those boyish round cheeks. She knows that sloping nose, those downy brows. The thin, mousy hair tucked neatly behind her ears. The skinny arms and legs, the mole above her knee, the scarcely protruding points of her chest.

"Oh," she breathes.

"Pretty incredible, isn't it? That's her."

The girl's eyes are closed, her face blank. Her breath rises and falls in a perfect, shallow rhythm. Something cold and heavy sinks into Logan's chest. A cry of protest, of horror, lodges deep in her stomach. She is naked, exposed; she wants to rush into that room and cover her up. "That's . . . me."

"No," Byron corrects her. "Now, that's the critical point. *You* are you. That is no one. But, in a couple of days, when the transfer goes through, that will be you. And you will be no one."

After a pause, he brings his hand to his desktop. With a light *clack*, the girl is gone. He swivels the screen away from her view again. Logan realizes she has nearly slid off the front of her chair.

"So, what do you think? Did we do all right on her?"

"Perfect." Logan swallows a deep breath. The heaviness in her chest dissipates, rising into an ethereal joy. "Perfect, just . . . Well, I'm sure it's taken care of already."

"What is it?"

"The glasses. It's really important to me that she—that I—wear those glasses."

"The red ones, right?"

Logan nods, taken aback. It's impressive for a man of his stature to remember such a small detail. "Yes, exactly. The red ones." Big and owlish, scarlet frames. She hid behind those glasses until high school.

Richard Byron assures her it will be taken care of. He wishes her a perfect summer as he ushers her out the door. Logan is still shaken and nearly asks for another look at the girl. She holds it back. She will see her again, soon.

week two

Sam

EVERYONE IS GIVEN A NEW wardrobe. The clothes are plain, generically American, all denim, khaki, and flannel. White and gray, forest green, and garish, Christmas red. They could belong to any generation. Anything personal the counselors brought with them is scrutinized by Campbell and the assistant directors. If it has a drastic cut or a commercial logo, it has to go.

"Come on," Elias groans in front of the mess hall one morning, peeling off his T-shirt to toss into Nick's waiting hand. "I won't wear it in front of the kids!"

"Then you shouldn't wear it at all," Nick says. He folds the shirt before Sam can read the slogan on the front.

Hair is cut, dye washed out. Tattoos must be small and coverable. Piercings are restricted to female earlobes. On their second morning at Camp, the counselors line up to trade in their phones for wristwatches—clunky and burdensome, each with the same sickly green digital face. That afternoon, they sit through a lecture with a language coach, who teaches them to check their slang and adjust their vocabulary, to speak neutrally and properly once the campers arrive.

"Fuck this," Rosie hisses under her breath, making Sam snort with laughter. "Grammar is so elitist."

The point of the training isn't for them to have good grammar, Sam knows, but to strip them of the telltale signs of their generation, of any generation. Camp Phoenix is meant to resemble anyone's childhood, and at the same time, no one's. It is a time and space entirely of its own. In another afternoon training, they discuss the process that brings the campers to Camp. Not in detail—just the basics, as much as the counselors need to understand. They go over the policies regarding their relationship to Phoenix Genetics and its clients. Psychologists from the facility teach them how to instill a sense of normalcy, to establish a routine, to build a secure environment the campers will have no need to question.

They have to memorize the terms of their work contracts before they sign them.

Counselors will not take photographs of clients while Camp is in Session. Counselors will not discuss clients' personal matters outside of Camp. Counselors will not have contact with those outside of Phoenix Genetics' employment while Camp is in session. Counselors will never, under any circumstances, reveal the nature of the Camp program nor details of clients' lives to campers.

There are other, simpler rules, most of them unspoken. Stay on the trails. Don't break curfew. Wear your sunscreen.

In the mornings, the counselors are put to work setting up Camp, getting the place ready for the campers' arrival. The chores are exhausting and poorly supervised, and they muddle through them clumsily, drunk on sunshine and each other's company.

"Why do we have to do this, again?" Jeremy grunts, slopping a shovelful of barnyard mud over his shoulder.

It's Saturday morning, and they're supposed to be setting fenceposts around the goats' pen. Sam sits against the barn wall in a sliver of shade, watching the boys work. The day is getting hotter. She wipes her lips with the back of her hand, tastes grit and salty sweat.

"Goats have to live somewhere, buddy." The boy working between Jeremy and Elias has an elfish face and a cheeky, childish grin. He drums his fingers along the fencepost he's holding, constantly tapping, the nervous habit that earned him his nickname.

"Give me that, Taps." Elias tugs the post from his fidgeting hands. He measures it against the hole Jeremy dug, frowning. "Gotta be deeper."

Jeremy shakes his head. He was allowed to keep his floppy hair for the summer—every generation has its deadbeats, Sam supposes. "You know what I mean," he says. "Why do *we* have to do this?" Not waiting for an answer, he takes the fencepost from Elias and wedges it between his legs, swiveling his hips to hit them with it.

"Oh, is that accurate?"

"Almost."

Sam grunts at them from the barn wall: "If someone else did this, what would they do with us?"

Elias squints at her. He picks up his shovel and tosses a scoop of mud in her direction—it falls just short of her boots. "Hey, thanks for your contribution, Sam. What are you doing over there?"

"I'm supervising." Sam nudges her sunglasses up her nose. Her head is pounding. "The hole needs to be deeper."

Her hangover has only gotten worse since breakfast. There is a ritual to this pre-Camp week: work, train, drink. At night, they are cut loose to wander the empty property. They light the campfire and skinny dip in the lake, test each other's boundaries. Friendships and flings, new and reignited, settle into place. The nights are as important as the days. A strong bond between the counselors is crucial, the assistant directors tell them, for an authentic summer—for the next ten weeks, they are the only people in the world. Last night's bonding was particularly aggressive. Sam woke up at dawn in a floating rowboat. It was punishment, apparently, for her bitter loss in their elaborate tournament of drinking games.

Taps picks up another fencepost from the pile and holds it like Jeremy, between his legs. "Hey, Germ!" he crows across the mud. "Let's joust!"

When the boys eventually give up on the fenceposts, they all retreat into the cool shade of the barn. It's a massive building of graying wood slats, designed to look decrepit beyond its years, the floor paved in a decade's worth of straw and grime. Against the far back wall is a rickety ladder. They scamper up it one by one, shoving and bickering, into the barn loft.

The shallow, dusty room at the top of the ladder is called the Nest. Mismatched couches and loveseats and old floral rugs are littered haphazardly over the rotting floorboards. Hazy light streams through the window over the barn doorway. They have a water cooler, a humming refrigerator, a bare overhead bulb, and a bookshelf stacked with board games and loose cards and old smut novels. In the center of the room, a worn rope ladder leads up to a crawlspace tucked into the peak of the ceiling beams. Someone is up there now; Sam can hear two voices. One is Rosie's.

"Hello!" Taps bellows upward. Jeremy opens the fridge door and tosses beer cans over his shoulder at them. Sam catches hers before she has a chance to protest—they'll tease her again about the rowboat if she does.

Rosie's head appears in the crawlspace. "Hi. What are you doing?"

"Taking a break. What are *you* doing?"

"Campbell wanted us to count the extra riding boots up here. See if he needs to order more." Rosie climbs agilely down the ladder. Behind her is Phoebe, a new hire this summer they've all taken a liking to; a tall, awkward girl with an endearing lisp.

Jeremy flops onto a couch, raising a puff of dust—from his clothes or the cushions, no one could guess. He flashes an awkward smile at Rosie, which Elias must catch, because he grins knowingly at Sam.

"We keep boots in the shagging attic?"

"Yup. Do you have to call it that?"

"I guess I can think of something better."

"Smash pad," Taps suggests, cracking the tab on his beer can. "The hook-up nook."

"Hook-up-don't-look-up," says Elias, peering up the rope ladder as Phoebe lands on the floor slats. Sam snorts.

The Nest is stifling and smelly in the heat of the day, but it's their place, the only place on Camp property not polished to perfect authenticity for the campers. They settle onto couches, beers in hand, and talk. The conversation turns quickly to cabin assignments. Everyone will be given their group lists this afternoon. They're all nervous, anxious to see the names and ages.

"Hummingbirds," says Rosie. "Or Chickadees. There's less drama with the little ones."

"More boogers," Sam points out.

Elias holds his cold beer to his forehead, flushing from the heat. "No way. I had the Wrens last summer, remember? You know how many times I got woken up because someone peed the bed? Older is the way to go."

"It's so weird," Phoebe says slowly. She leans against the back of Elias's couch, scratching at a blistered palm. "I mean, they're all up there now, right?" She nods in the direction of the lake. "And we're sitting here, talking about them . . . peeing the bed."

Sam nods. She felt the same way a year ago—she still does. "It won't feel as weird when they get here. They're just like kids. You forget everything else."

"Yeah," Jeremy laughs. "Except, today is the weirdest. Just wait 'til you see the names on your list."

"Dane said there's some big ones this year." Elias says. He shoots Rosie an irritated look as she opens her mouth to protest, cutting her off with a wave of his hand. "I'm not just talking about him. There's more. Henry Owens, the Olympic diver. That Chinese guy that owns the space tech company—I can't remember his name, but he's stupid rich. Katie was talking about some famous author. Oh, and Oscar Delario—remember him? That senator with the whole dirty pictures scandal?"

"Yuck." Rosie rolls her eyes. "I'll let that kid drown in the lake if I get the chance."

Phoebe frowns down at Elias over the back of the couch. "Wait. Why don't you know your group list already? Couldn't Nick tell you?"

The rest of them laugh, and Elias shakes his head in a huffy, well-rehearsed way. "My brother and I aren't exactly friends at Camp."

"No one's Nicky's *friend*," Jeremy adds snidely. "We're all his inferiors."

"That's a little harsh," says Rosie. "He's a nice enough guy. He's just . . ."

". . . Too serious about his job to ever take the stick out of his ass," Elias finishes for her. "Not that I mind. I'll always have a job here, once he runs the place."

Sam sits up on her couch, suddenly conscious of all their eyes on her. She runs a thumb over the chill, sweating wall of her beer can. "You think that's going to happen?" she asks Elias. "You think Nick wants to run Camp?"

Elias shrugs. "I don't see why not. If Campbell ever retires, I don't know who else Chard would pick. Not Gabe. Definitely not Dane."

"He wouldn't hire another director?" Phoebe asks. "From, like, outside?"

"Outside?" Rosie smiles, gesturing for the beer in Elias's hand. He passes it to her reluctantly. After a long, heavy gulp, she says: "It's not really like that. No one gets into Camp Phoenix from outside unless you're coming through a consciousness transfer. It's a closed ecosystem. Cooks, maintenance—everyone here has some kind of tie to Phoenix Gen. Except for us."

"Oh." Phoebe chews a fingernail thoughtfully. Then, quieter, asks: "So, why do they hire us?"

For a moment, the Nest is quiet. Sam shrugs to herself. Taps, drumming on his kneecaps, is the first to speak. "Chard has his methods," he tells the new girl. "Listen, don't go down that road. If you start thinking too much about stuff, you won't survive the summer. We're here to wipe their butts and get paid. That's it." He tilts his head to drain his beer, tapping against the bottom of the can. "Germ," he says through a belch. "Toss me another."

Phoebe's expression gives her away. Her eyes shift around the Nest, glancing at them all in turn, overwhelmed. Sam can hardly blame her.

After lunch that afternoon, they move the tables in the mess hall aside to form a circle of folding cafeteria chairs. The stagnant air smells like sweat and sunscreen and the mud caked on the hems of their jeans. Counselors and assistant directors chatter in their seats, folding their hands, crossing and uncrossing their legs in anticipation. Sam sits between Rosie and Elias with a buzzing in her ears.

"Chard's here," says Rosie, nudging her.

Sam looks up. Three men enter the dining room through the kitchen, steaming coffee mugs in hand. They speak quietly to each other as their eyes scan the room. Sure enough, one of them is Richard Byron.

Between Campbell and Nick, Byron strides like a man who owns the world. He *does* own the world, as they all know it. Sam can't help but notice the way he and Nick hold their chipped mugs in the exact same manner: left-handed, elbow at a perfect ninety-degree angle, thumb on the rim. Byron smiles and pats Nick's shoulder briskly. Whatever they were talking about seems to have been resolved to his satisfaction.

The elder Borowitz brother is wiry and angular. Like a negative copy of Elias, his hair is dark, his eyes unnervingly pale. He gazes over the other assistant directors and nods to himself before settling into his seat. Across the circle, Sam briefly meets his eyes. He scratches his head; she turns her attention to her hands in her lap.

"All right, all right." Campbell claps his hands together. The resounding *smack* kills the rabble in the room. He clears his throat and begins with a few announcements: the belaying harnesses need to be moved to the ropes course, the horses will be arriving at the stables tomorrow morning, the shifter on the ski boat has been sticking—don't jam it too hard. He cracks a few jokes that fall over the room with the same satisfying dry *smack* as his hand clap. Then Richard Byron speaks to them, for the first time this summer. His voice is low and soothing, and Sam, dreary with her hangover and the weight of the beers from earlier, finds herself absent for most of his speech. What she does catch, she remembers from last year.

"These people have chosen to have this experience for a lot of reasons. Some of them had wonderful childhoods, and they want to revisit that time. Some of them are looking for a childhood they never really had. All of them want to live out their own story this summer. A story unique to them that they can take back to their ordinary lives. Your job . . ." Byron looks slowly around the room. When his gaze lands on Sam, she is sure his lips curl up into a tiny, private smile. ". . . Is just to treat each of them like any other kid. Because that's what they are when they're here. Regardless of who they are out in the world." He delivers this final sentence firmly, each word deliberate.

There is no pause for questions. It would not be their place to ask, anyway. Their place is cabin chore charts and mealtime etiquette and campfire skits. The thorny reality—celebrities, digital consciousness transfers, genetically engineered bodies—has to exist outside of their understanding for the summer to make sense. Richard Byron is the only person in the lake basin with a foot in each world.

Having said what he needs to say, Byron settles back into his chair. A quiet tension breaks with his nod, and Campbell and Nick rise to begin passing out the group lists. They give each counselor a bulky binder—green covers, the Camp Phoenix insignia etched in white. As the counselors take their binders and flip through them greedily, the din in the mess hall rises.

"Falcons!" Elias whoops when he snatches his binder from his brother's hand. "Nice!"

"Chickadees," says Rosie. She smiles brightly, flipping through her list.

Sam takes her binder wordlessly from Nick. Behind the front cover she finds her own name and the name of her intended cabin group. "Hummingbirds," she reads aloud. Her heart sinks. "Hummingbirds?"

Inside the binder are the profiles of every camper in the group. Each profile holds two pictures: one of the adult client, and another of the camper they will soon become. The smiling camper photos are just slightly unnatural, near-perfect digital constructions set against a plain white backdrop. Sam flips through her binder disdainfully, a sour taste on her tongue. She told Campbell when she resubmitted her application that she wanted older campers; last year she had the Sparrows, ten-year-olds, and thought her hands were full enough.

Debra Fitzgerald, she reads the page on her lap. *Age: 53. Camper age: 7. Previous summers: 0.* She skims over Debra Fitzgerald's summer goals, which go on for three pages in excruciating detail: she would like to reconnect with her youth, to form an intimate bond with nature, to overcome her childhood stage fright, and, in doing so, to lay the foundations for confidence in her professional life. Sam flips on. *Maggie Geranimo*, she reads. *Age: 67. Camper age: 7. Lucille Summers. Camper age: 7. Margaret Fredricks. Camper age: 6. Paula Warbler. Camper age: 6.*

Sam's eyes catch on that name. She holds her breath, thoughts whirring.

"Hey, at least we're going to be neighbors," Rosie says, studying her own list. "We can cover each other's cabins when we're—" Sam reaches out to smack her with the back of her hand, stopping her mid-sentence. "—Ow! What?"

"Look." She shoves the open profile at her. Rosie blinks, then squints at the page, and the look on her face melts from annoyance, to disbelief, to reverence. The woman in the picture is blond and familiar, wearing an iconic pout.

"Oh my God." Rosie gasps. "Oh my God. Dude, that's *Poppy* Warbler. El, look!" She thrusts a flapping hand across Sam's lap. "Sam has Poppy Warbler!"

Elias seems to have vanished into himself. He stares at his open binder, chewing on his lip. As counselors shove back their chairs and dash to compare group lists around them, he looks up. "I have Hugo Baker," he says. A hush falls over the three of them.

Logan

LOGAN IS AWAKE.

She's not sure how long she has been awake, exactly, and she can't quite say when she fell asleep. She only knows that she is awake, and sounds, shapes, colors are settling into place around her.

Her belly aches with a stabbing fear. She must have been having a nightmare. It was black and suffocating, like being squeezed through a dark tunnel. She couldn't breathe, couldn't scream. Now it's over, and she is washed in a tremendous, sleepy laziness, warm and safe and bright like Sunday morning.

She hears voices. People in blurry blue are moving around her. They have been talking to her for some time. She has to get up, Logan thinks. She is going to be late, late for . . . something.

She is up, she realizes. She is sitting. She can move. Time is sticky and thick as syrup.

"Logan." Fingers snap in her ear. "Logan. Come on, now."

She wiggles in place on a crunchy sheet of paper. The walls around her are covered in bright pictures. A woman in a white coat bends to look at her, examining her. She writes on her clipboard. "Logan," she says again. "Let me hear that voice."

Logan locates her hands and brings them to her face. She is so heavy. Her lips move first, and her voice comes after. "Glasses."

"What's that?"

"Glasses," she rasps. "Where are my glasses?"

A friendly weight settles onto her nose. Suddenly, everything is clear. Logan blinks in surprise. The doctor gives her a paper cup of cool water to drink. She asks her questions as she shuffles around her.

"Can you tell me your name?"

"Logan."

"Your full name?"

"Logan Marie Adler."

"Excellent." The doctor takes her temperature. The metal of the rolling thermometer is cold against her forehead. "How old are you, Logan?"

Logan thumbs the waxy brim of the cup in her hands. It crumples satisfyingly to her touch. "Twelve."

"Do you know where you are?"

What a weird question. Of course she does.

"You're on your way to Camp, remember?"

"Yeah."

"Camp Phoenix."

"Yeah."

"Your parents just dropped you off. We have to give you a checkup, just to make sure you're healthy, before you get on the bus."

Logan nods. Mom hugged her tight. Dad ruffled her hair so hard, she had to redo her ponytail in the reflection of the car window. Her baby brother is still too little to come to Camp. He sat in his booster seat, pouting.

"Yeah." She squeezes and releases the paper cup in her hand. It moves like a gabbing mouth. It's funny. "So, am I healthy?"

"Yes, sweet girl. You're perfectly healthy."

She is outside under a hot, bright sun. It feels nice on her shoulders and the top of her head. She sees dirt under her feet and trees all around, tastes a sticky grape sucker in her mouth. The world is brown and green and blue and yellow, in that order, bottom to top. She is wearing white sneakers and denim shorts and a plain red T-shirt—it's her favorite color, the same bright scarlet as the frames of her glasses. The sucker makes her saliva syrupy and sweet. She spits on the ground and sees purple.

There are other kids around her. Eight or ten of them. Most of them are boys, and most of them are littler than her. Adults guide them toward a little white bus stained with red dirt. Painted on the side of the bus in dark green is a picture of two straight tree branches, crossed in an *X*, with a round bird's nest on top. On either side of the nest are the letters *C* and *P*.

Logan remembers that picture. She has been to Camp Phoenix before. It was a long time ago, and she can't remember much about it.

"Come on, Logan. Time to go."

She sits on a squishy bus seat next to a little boy with watery red eyes. He sniffles.

"What's your name?" Logan asks him.

"Oscar."

"Hi, Oscar. My name's Logan."

Oscar sniffs and turns his puffy eyes on her, frowning like she said something mean to him. "That's a boy's name," he says.

The bus goes down a winding road, through the forest. They come out on a bridge. Out the window, Logan can see a mossy gray wall of concrete and the lake behind it. Water runs down the face of the wall like a stream of drool into a black pool far below them. She shivers—she doesn't like heights. When they get to Camp, people come running to greet them. Pretty, tan people in matching green T-shirts. Logan likes them immediately. They smile and laugh and pull on each other's arms like they're all best friends. "This guy," they say to the campers. "Don't listen to *this* guy, he picks his nose."

Her own counselor is named Sadie. She has a round face and long blond braids that swing over a very round chest. She hugs Logan tight around the shoulders, barely an inch taller than her. "We're so happy you're here, Logan! Come on, I have *so* much to show you."

It's beautiful. The forest is green and flowering. Tiny birds twitter and flutter from branch to bush. The lake is huge, deep green, and welcoming, shining in the spaces between tree trunks. Dust kicks up in rusty brown clouds at their feet. Sadie takes Logan along a trail, away from the parking lot and through the trees. They pass the barnyard, a muddy spat of land level with the lakeshore, and the stables just behind. Four or five horses are out grazing in the yard. Logan squeals at the sight of them, their chestnut and black and speckled coats, sleek and shiny in the sunlight. They nicker and flick their manes and twitch their tails at flies.

"You like horses, right?" Sadie asks her with a smile.

Logan nods. "I really do. Last time I came to Camp, I went on the trail rides every day. I think."

The girls' cabins are uphill from the barn and stables. Their trail weaves around stumps and boulders and patches of shrubby grass. "You have to stay on the trails," Sadie tells her, huffing as they walk. "That's the number-one rule at Camp. Always stay on the trails."

"Why?"

"Because it is."

High up the hill, almost at the tippy-top, is Logan's cabin: the Ravens. They're the second oldest at Camp, Sadie says. Their cabin is squat and friendly, with a green metal roof and a wide porch out front. Three girls are sitting on the porch already. Their names are Donna and Joy and Liz. They all have tired faces and wear plain-colored T-shirts like Logan's: orange, hot pink, and cotton candy blue.

Inside the cabin is a single shady room. Bunk beds line the walls, with tall wooden lockers between them. Windows with four panes let in the green world. The bathroom is outside, under an awning, closed off by half-walls. There are two toilet stalls, a shower with a plastic curtain, and a row of toothbrushes in colorful plastic cups. Logan spots a scarlet cup, and orange, hot pink, and cotton candy blue.

Sadie shows her to her bunk.

"Top?" Logan looks worriedly up at it, chewing her lip. A stacked set of sheets and a rolled flannel sleeping bag sit waiting on the bare mattress. "Can I trade?"

"No, sweetie. We don't do trades. Look, all your clothes are already here, and your journal, your flashlight . . ." Sadie gestures at the locker against the wall.

"But I'm scared of heights."

Before Sadie can answer, a raspy laugh rings at their knees. Logan is surprised to notice someone stretched out on the bottom bunk already. "You're scared of the top bunk? It's not *that* high!"

"Logan, this is Milly," the counselor says. She glances out the door of the cabin, suddenly irritated. "I have to go meet our next camper, girls. Milly, hon, why don't you help Logan get her bed set up?"

Sadie leaves Logan standing sheepishly next to the bed. Milly sits up on her mattress. She has a bony, skeptical face and a royal purple T-shirt. Her hair is short, almost like a boy's, in tidy dreadlocks just long enough to tuck behind her ears.

"Hi."

"Hi." They size each other up. Then Milly stands and gestures to the locker shelves. "The bottom two are mine. Those top two are yours. We split that one in the middle—Sadie says that's our books and binoculars and stuff." She points to a low cubby at the foot of the bunk. "Those are our shoes."

Logan looks. She sees two pairs of strappy sandals, two pairs of sneakers, two pairs of hiking boots. "How do I know which ones are mine?"

"The ones that fit you, I guess." Milly shrugs, then flops back onto her mattress. Logan stares at her springy hair. She wants to touch it. She knows better than to ask. Milly looks up at her with squinty eyes. "Are you really scared of heights?"

"Umm. Yeah."

"Well, you know they have a tightrope at the ropes course that's, like, fifty feet high?"

"Yeah, I know. I'm gonna do it this summer." Logan knows this exactly as she says it.

Milly laughs again. She has a breathless, gravelly laugh, like an old lady. "Seriously? You're too scared to sleep on the top bunk, but you want to do the fifty-foot tightrope?"

Logan frowns. "It's different."

"Why?"

"I don't know." She turns to look through the clothes on her shelves. There are wool socks, T-shirts, pullovers, and hats. Swimsuits, both one-piece and two-piece. Even a few thin cotton bras. Logan twists her lips as she runs the fabric between her fingers. She doesn't wear a bra. The girls on the porch look like they might; the fact that they're in her locker means girls her age are expected to.

Milly doesn't look like she wears bras, either. She's scrawny and smaller than Logan. "Sorry for making fun of you," she says plainly. "I'm scared of sharks, so . . . you know. You want help setting up your bunk?"

They work together to stretch the starchy sheet over the mattress corners. The mattress has a plastic coating that crinkles as they move. Logan sits, with a hand on each side rail like she's in a boat, and looks around the cabin. There is hardly any space between the bunks, no privacy at all. Panic begins to set in through her tiredness—she is suddenly, intensely aware that she will have to change, and towel off, and poop, in this tiny cabin with all the other girls around. She nudges her glasses into place on her nose.

Milly faces her on the mattress, crisscrossed. She picks at her fingernails. "How old are you?"

"Twelve."

"Me too. I think."

"You think?"

"Yeah. I'm really tired."

Logan nods. A flash of confusion passes through her head, but it's gone when she blinks, replaced by another rush of embarrassment as she looks back toward the front window, the other girls on the porch. "Yeah. Me too." She smiles nervously at her new bunkmate. Milly smiles back.

There are seven Ravens in total. Annie arrives next—she's as little as Milly. After her is Mei, who came all the way from Japan. Sadie tours them around in their line of seven. She shows them their table in the mess hall, their bench at announcements, and their log at campfire. She tells them about the swimming dock rules and the qualifications at the ropes course. Logan catches Donna and Joy rolling their eyes at each other when the counselor isn't looking. Milly doesn't roll her eyes, but she doesn't pay Sadie much attention, either. In the reeds at the fishing dock, she catches a snake and hands it to Logan. It winds around her wrist, cool and smooth against her skin. Logan laughs with glee at the tiny, beady eyes, the flicking tongue.

Dinner—crusty lasagna, garlic bread, lemonade in a dingy plastic pitcher—is over before she knows it. Night falls, and then Sadie leads them to the first campfire. They sit on a semicircle of flat log benches. Flames dance and flicker in a rusted metal ring. Every so often there is a loud *crack*, and a smatter of sparks shoots upward, up toward a fading sky, shades of painted blue blurring to black. The stage is a bare wood platform behind the fire. The counselors standing on it tell them a story about a magical lake in the wilderness, where there used to be a fish hatchery.

Mr. Campbell is bald and smiley. He tells them to stay on the trails, and Logan isn't sure what else. Her world is spinning on its axis, day and night blurring, head swimming, sparks trailing up into stars. Someone plays a guitar and sings a soft song on the stage. Her glasses slip down her nose, and she can't seem to lift a hand to fix them. She slumps against Sadie's side and lets her hug her.

At the end of the song, the whole Camp stands. The fire has burnt low and red. The counselors sing in a low, swaying tune, and Logan remembers the words; she is singing along.

> *Look up to the moon, moon, moon,*
> *Remember the sunshine bright.*
> *Breathe in the mountain air, my friend,*
> *Before we say good night.*
> *Look up to the moon, moon, moon,*
> *Hug every rock and tree,*

> *I will take care of you, my friend,*
> *If you take care of me.*

Silence falls with the last note. Brand-new stars glint overhead, glitter tossed over black ink. A single chime rings low and clear from the bell tower. It crosses Camp and thrums over the lake and resonates right through Logan's core.

When she finally crawls into her sleeping bag, she isn't thinking about the height of the bunk. She isn't thinking about anything. The crinkly mattress is a bed of feathers.

Sam

IT'S EASY TO GET THE campers to bed on the first night. The little things are exhausted, still dizzy with drugs and muddled memories, and they pass out on top of their sleeping bags, some of them with their shoes still on. A dense quiet settles over the Hummingbirds' cabin. Sam sighs with relief. She sits on the edge of her bunk and leans heavily over her knees. It was a long day.

When the first busload of campers arrived from the facility this morning, most of the staff still had boozy breath and bloodshot eyes behind their sunglasses. They all wore their matching T-shirts: counselors in green, assistant directors in gray, and Campbell in white. Sam zips her jacket over her green T-shirt now. She can smell the sweat and sunscreen caked into it, but the energy to change is beyond her. A sleeping bag rustles, and she pauses to look down the rows of bunks.

To think of the profiles in her binder now is absurd. When Sam was in high school, she wrote a biographical essay about Rachel Settler, a pioneering political journalist. Today she met Rachel Meyersburg, age seven, who cried through the tour and wet her pants at dinner. Daria Petrovsky, a seventy-five-year-old former diplomat a day ago, didn't say a word all afternoon until she blinked at Sam and mumbled, "Mama?"

They aren't kids to her yet, exactly—only little things. Little aliens, wide-eyed and confused. Camp will mold them into their own people as they settle into the routine.

At a tap on the cabin window behind her, Sam looks up. Rosie nudges the door open and peers through the crack. "Still awake?" she mouths.

"Them, or me?"

"Both."

"Neither."

Rosie leans around the door, craning her neck to look at the bottom bunk closest to Sam's. A head of tangled blond hair lies motionless on the pillow. She nods at the camper with a geeky grin, and Sam grimaces.

Paula Warbler arrived in a bright pink T-shirt and pigtails. She didn't step off the bus so much as leap, arms raised and toes pointed, a trail of blood running down her shin from a fresh scrape on her knee. A wide, chubby-cheeked smile revealed a missing front tooth. "My name's not *Paula*," she said when Sam greeted her, "it's *Poppy*. Everybody calls me Poppy." Hardly an hour later, she hurled herself into a tantrum over being assigned to a bottom bunk, screaming loud enough to shake spiders from the ceiling beams, scaring the other girls. Poor Deb ran crying to the bathroom with her hands clamped over her ears.

"I'll meet you down there," Sam whispers to Rosie. "Campbell wants to talk to me."

"What about?"

"I don't know. Maybe I'm fired."

Rosie laughs. "Wishful thinking," she teases, then pulls the cabin door shut behind her. Sam listens to her footsteps creak away on the porch.

Campbell asked her to come to the Camp office as soon as her campers were asleep. Sam walks alone over the trails, following her flashlight beam, hugging her jacket close against the night chill. The little A-frame cabin sits nestled between the trees above the mess hall. Inside is a single, gray-carpeted room, two desks overloaded by ancient computer monitors. The shabbiness of the space, the curly-corded landlines and chugging printers and smudged whiteboards, gives it an innocent, vaguely authoritative feel, like a parents' workplace in a childhood memory. Sam steps cautiously through the open screen door.

Dane and Nick nod to her from the spiral staircase in the back of the cabin. They're coming down from their bunk room, both still wearing their gray opening-day T-shirts. "Hanging in there, Red?" Dane teases her, and Sam realizes she must look more frazzled than she thinks. She runs a hand over the frayed hairs beneath her beanie.

Campbell sits at his desk, distracted by something on his bulbous monitor screen. "Come on in." He waves at her.

Sam settles onto the chair at the other desk. Nick, to her surprise, joins them, standing over her chair with folded arms. He clears his throat. They both watch Campbell drag his attention from the screen in silence.

"We, uh . . ." he begins slowly, then swivels in his seat, blinking at her. "We've got a job for you, kid. If you're interested."

"A job?" Sam repeats. In a flash, she imagines herself up at dawn to work in the kitchen or haul manure—she must have complained a little too loudly over her cabin assignment.

"We're looking for someone to shadow Nick this summer. It'll be in the mornings, mostly. You'd help him put the schedule together, learn a little about his job. Run some errands for me. Help us wrangle the rest of the chuckleheads." Campbell bobs his head at the screen door, gesturing vaguely toward the barnyard, where Sam knows bottles have already been cracked and green shirts abandoned on the Nest floor.

"Oh." She glances up at Nick, who nods and offers her a thin smile. "Like an assistant?"

"Well, a shadow. But that's the basic idea, yeah. This would replace your regular morning activity."

"Okay. Why do you want me to do it?"

The two of them share a look. Sam catches a whiff of embarrassment in the air, of something unspoken. Campbell clears his throat before saying: "We had you pegged for it by the end of last summer, actually. You're a good fit."

Dane, filling his water bottle at the sink in the back of the room, turns to her with a plain, unblinking look. "Sam. Remember how Amy shadowed me last year?"

She nods, her head reeling to catch up. Amy followed Dane around Camp all summer, to his girlfriend's chagrin. Now she is an assistant director. His insinuation doesn't answer her question, though—Why, of all the counselors, would they pick her to wedge into leadership? Again, Sam looks up at Nick. A glaring answer occurs to her, and she quickly drops her eyes, mortified.

"Listen," says Campbell, "it's up to you. If you want to be on the regular activity schedule, that's fine. If you do this, though, we'll want you to take it seriously." He smiles at her, friendly and fatherly, then stands to stretch his back with a grunt. "Take the night to think about it, okay?"

"Okay," Sam says. She waits, swiveling in the desk chair, for more information, more answers, but nothing comes. She is dismissed. Campbell, Nick, and Dane gather in the back of the office, and Sam leaves. Their low voices trail like shadows behind her as she crosses the cabin porch.

Now that Camp has officially started, the counselors' free time is restricted. Between the hours of ten and two, a rotating patrol schedule covers the cabins: two male counselors stay behind on the boys' side of Camp, and two female counselors on the girls'. Everyone else is left to their own whims.

The rules are simple, passed down year after year from one generation of staff to the next. Campbell turns a deliberately ignorant eye to their free hours as long as the routine is never disrupted. The campers can't be woken up. No evidence can be left out the next morning. Everyone must wake up in their own beds. Curfew is strict, and working hours resume as soon as the patrols are relieved. These rules are their mantra, adhered to with a sort of religious reverence, and while the assistant directors are technically in charge whenever Campbell is off the property, the counselors manage to govern themselves under the threat of losing their post-bedtime freedom. As long as they stick to the rules, their nights make the summer days livable.

In later weeks they'll leave Camp to build a fire somewhere in the forest, or to hang out behind the Smith's Ridge market, pretend they're anywhere else in the world. Tonight, they are tired. They cluster in the Nest on the sofas and floor, the barn ceiling beams groaning beneath their weight. Sam stretches out on a scratchy rug. Nursing a warm beer, she feels the day stretching out behind her, the weight of it tugging at her eyelids. They talk about the campers.

"I used to have a Poppy Warbler poster over my bed," Phoebe says, "when I was little."

"I was her for Halloween once. Twice, actually." Rosie smiles. There is vodka in the coffee mug at her knees, and Jeremy's hand is on her lower back, creeping up her shirt, both of them sprawled sloppily against the foot of a couch. They're drunk enough, Sam can tell, to think they're being subtle.

"You?" He laughs at her.

"Yes, me. Something wrong with that?"

"No. Just, Poppy's not . . ."

"What?" She reels back from him, her face hardened. "Short? Puerto Rican? Go ahead, Germ."

". . . Brunette," Jeremy finishes weakly, and Rosie rolls her eyes. She pushes herself to her feet and walks off pointedly to refill her mug. He grunts, then wilts against the couch behind him. "Goddamn. Can't make a joke around that one."

Phoebe leans over her crossed legs on the rug. "You don't have to cover it up by calling it a joke," she says. "Just think before you say stuff."

Sam snickers. Jeremy shrugs and flicks his hair from his eyes, swallowing a belch. Their conversation drifts, and Rosie doesn't come back to the circle. Sam glances over her shoulder to see her talking with Elias, both leaning against the back of an armchair.

Phoebe's eyes, too, linger on Elias. She clears her throat, picking at the label of her beer bottle, then says quietly, "Did you see him?"

Sam nods. She looks down at her own hands, the splinter in the pad of her pinky, black dirt crusted beneath her fingernails. There will be dirt beneath her fingernails for the next ten weeks, no matter how often she scrapes them clean. "I think so," she says. "Yellow shirt, right?"

"Yeah. He looked so normal. Cute." Phoebe twists her lips thoughtfully toward the rug. "She was his girlfriend, wasn't she?"

"Yup. His mistress. They're calling it a crime of passion." Jeremy holds up both open palms and glances between the two of them, eyebrows raised. "*If* he did it," he adds. It's a challenge to debate that both Sam and Phoebe let flare and die in front of them. If Rosie had heard him, she would not have ignored it.

Sam doesn't want to talk about Hugo Baker anymore, or Poppy Warbler. A little overwhelmed, she excuses herself from the conversation and stands up. Rosie and Elias have fallen into a snippy argument. Taps is asleep on the couch and Sadie wavers in the corner of the room, looking like she might vomit. Sam feels along the top of the fridge for her stashed pack of cigarettes and heads for the ladder, chased by their jeers. The barn below is bigger at night, shadowy and cavernous. Chickens mutter and rustle in their coop. She stands in the broad doorway, looking up, listening to the laughter overhead. Just as she lifts the cigarette to her lips, she hears someone cross the creaking floor slats behind her.

"Hey, Red."

Sam turns. Nick holds an unlit cigarette between his fingers. He gestures for the lighter in her hand and she offers it to him with a nod. "I don't know whose that is. It was on the fridge."

He laughs behind the spark and glow in his palms. "It's mine."

"Ah. Shit."

They lean against opposite sides of the doorframe, smoking and looking up. The moon overhead is half full. Pine boughs cast in pale silver shift and rustle in the breeze. The mountain nights here are as cold as the days are hot; Sam shivers and pulls her wool beanie down over her ears. She casts a sideways glance at Nick. His profile is framed in the dim barn light, highlighting the ridge of his nose, the flat plane of a cheek, scraggly curls at the nape of his neck.

"Listen," he begins, and Sam's heart clenches in her chest.

"We don't have to do that," she says quickly.

"It's about the shadowing thing."

"Oh. Okay." Sam shrugs. In the flurry of the day, she nearly forgot.

"We talked about it last summer. It was Chard's idea, actually. He was saying we should pick a counselor, someone younger, to put on a leadership path. I brought up your name, and he said he liked you. That was before . . ." Nick stiffly flicks the hand holding his cigarette, a flat gesture toward the end of his sentence.

Sam shifts. Feeling suddenly heavy, she can't think of anything but the awkward way she has been holding her arms.

It was the last night of the summer. They stumbled into each other at the bell tower—she'd wanted one last look at the moonlit lake below the lawn. Everyone else had already coupled up and disappeared. He asked if she was too drunk, but he could barely stand in place, and his shoes were on the wrong feet. They woke up to angry sunlight on her bunk in the empty Sparrows' cabin. Sam hasn't told anyone. Nick is practically their boss, and Elias's brother—and her friendship with Elias wasn't strictly platonic last summer, either. The whole thing was too bizarre to be real. She wishes he hadn't brought it up.

Nick straightens in the doorway, one hand in his pocket. "I just want you to know it's not because of that," he says.

"Then why?" Sam asks. The earnestness of the question makes them both laugh in awkward, breathy puffs. "Why me?"

"Like I said. Chard likes you. So does Gus." He turns to look at her, and his face is entirely unreadable. "You're good at your job. Do you not realize that?"

Sam frowns. Of all the things she knows she is good at—French, algebra, boys—a job has never been one of them. Her cigarette, abandoned, burns near her fingertips. "I don't really understand what it takes to be good at this job."

For a moment, she thinks he isn't going to say anything. Then Nick shakes his head. "You're smart. Confident. People like you."

"The kids don't listen to me."

"It's not so much about who they listen to. It's who they want to be like." He crouches to ash his cigarette in the mud at their feet. When he stands again, he asks: "What's Paris like?"

"Oh. Great, actually." Sam squints across the barnyard, trying to count the days since she left Paris. "It's so much more real there."

"Real?"

"Yeah. You know, like, if you go to the store and buy a pack of eggs, they're all brown. Not white. And people never have to smile at each other. We're always smiling in the States, for no reason."

Nick nods steadily. If he finds her half-drunk musings on Parisian eggs ridiculous, he doesn't show it. They stub out their cigarettes, and he offers to throw her butt away for her. His fingertips are freezing and calloused against hers when she passes it to him.

"Thanks."

"No problem." He stands in the barn doorway, waiting, allowing Sam to walk toward the trail ahead of him so they aren't stuck crossing Camp together in the silent moonlight. Chivalrous of him, she thinks. "See you tomorrow, Sam. Stay on the trails."

Sam snorts as she starts across the mud. "Yeah. Stay on the trails."

She shuts off her flashlight when she reaches the Hummingbirds' porch and lets the darkness chase her to the door. Inside, the smell of clean sheets and new rubber shoes and the beer on her breath paints a funny picture of the day. Her bunk is just below the front window, as if she is expected to defend her campers from whatever might come slinking in. Sam slides off her shoes and hat and whispers their names to herself as she tiptoes down the row of beds, toward the bathroom.

"Poppy . . . Deb . . . Lucy . . . Maggie G. . . . Rachel . . . Maggie F. . . . Daria."

They are so small, hunkered in their sleeping bags, and Sam is all alone. If a mountain lion came leaping through the window, if a ceiling beam fell or the place suddenly caught on fire, it would be just her with these seven tiny people.

She brushes her teeth in the outdoor bathroom and tiptoes back to her bunk. Poppy stirs in her sleeping bag. Sam lies on her side and watches her. Her stumpy little fingers twitch on the pillow; her breath catches and releases in her nose. She looks remarkably normal, lying there. Sam can't help but wonder. Across the lake is a grown-up Poppy Warbler, unconscious in another bed. Are her fingers twitching, too? Does her knee ache where Poppy scraped it? Did her blood rush to her face when Poppy shrieked about the bottom bunk?

She wonders where exactly Poppy is now, while she sleeps. Here, or there, or somewhere in between. She imagines her suspended high over the lake, a shimmering sliver of human life, caught between two bodies. Is that all Poppy Warbler is—just a sliver, a stream of consciousness? Or is she the grubby kid in the next bunk over? Or the woman in the poster tacked over Phoebe's childhood bed?

Sam decides not to wonder. She is tired enough that she can choose not to think about it. That, after all, is the real magic of Camp Phoenix. She rolls onto her back and looks up at the stars through the window. She thinks, instead, about the smell of barnyard mud and cigarette smoke, and calloused fingertips, and brown eggs in Paris. Then she is asleep.

week three

Logan

THE WAKE-UP BELL CHIMES WHEN the light through the window is more yellow than blue. The glass is fogged by the cold outside. Logan lies on her stomach, hugging her pillow under her chin, watching the condensation gather and fall in trailing teardrops. *Dong . . . dong . . . dong . . .* the bell sings from the center of Camp.

She hears a burst of stifled giggles and reaches for her glasses on the top of her locker. Donna, Joy, and Mei are gathered around Sadie's bunk in the back of the cabin. The counselor is a heavy sleeper, especially in the mornings. They take turns dangling a loose scrap of yarn from a God's eye over her open mouth. When she breathes in, the string sucks to her lips and sticks there, then shoots upward again with an ugly snore. The girls hold their hands over their mouths and crinkle up their faces in mean laughter.

Logan rolls to her back and looks up at the ceiling beams. Today is Saturday. Nearly a week of Camp has gone by already.

The mornings are always cold. They have to wear long pants and sweatshirts and beanies to breakfast. Logan's sweatshirt still smells like campfire when she pulls it over her head. She watches the other Ravens through the sides of her eyes. They change quickly and daintily, with their locker doors propped open in the bunk aisles. They tie up their hair in ponytails and braids and crowd each other in the bathroom mirror, smearing on lotion like makeup. When they giggle over each other's outfits, Logan feels her cheeks burn, like she can't quite get the joke.

The first thing she has learned at Camp is that she is missing something. She can't move the way they move, or see things the way they do, or talk to them the way they talk to each other. The rest of the Ravens have something she must have been born without, some instinct that tells them how to do these things. Milly has it, too—in her own way. She has it, but she doesn't use it. She wears her pajamas to breakfast and rolls her eyes as she pushes through them to get to the toilet.

When the bell rings again, they leave the cabin and flood toward the main lawn to wait for breakfast. The area below the mess hall becomes a jungle before mealtimes. It's divided into three clear sections: lawn, bell tower, announcement benches. These areas have strict borders, and campers have established territory within them. Logan and Milly like to sit halfway up the mess hall steps and watch everything play out.

Younger kids play on the lawn. The littlest, the Hummingbirds and Chickadees, Finches and Wrens, stick to the edge of the dewy grass, closer to the counselors. Girls build pinecone houses and fill their shirts with acorns. Boys dig for worms. They crawl on their hands and knees and bark like dogs or whinny like horses. Farther out on the lawn the kids are older: Bluebirds, Sparrows, and Magpies; Blackbirds, Pigeons, Crows. They have big, active games, games with names and serious rules. They play Blob Tag and Mafia and sometimes cards, if someone swipes a deck from the game room. They push and shove and stick out their tongues. Boys punch each other and girls pick on each other.

"I'm rubber and you're glue," they recite back and forth. "Whatever you say bounces off me and sticks to you!"

Or: "Sticks and stones might break my bones, but words will never hurt me!"

Some girls stay away from the games. They sit on the ground, under the trees, and weave their friendship bracelets. They talk quietly and seriously, more like grown-ups than the counselors.

The counselors themselves always gather around the two wooden picnic benches at the base of the bell tower. They hold their coffee cups in both hands while they talk. Sometimes they are hushed, sometimes loud and excited. Behind the bell tower, where they can't see, is where the oldest kids hang out. Ravens and Eagles, Hawks and Falcons. They sit on the announcement benches in nuclear clusters. Girls with girls and boys with boys. Sometimes they crane their necks to talk across the clusters. They whisper behind their hands, and the way they shout when the secrets touch their ears makes Logan want to hear them, too. Girls weave friendship bracelets and give them to other girls, and sometimes to boys, but for a girl to give a boy a bracelet is a bold and very public event.

If it weren't for Milly, Logan would probably sit on the benches, too. She would sit off to the side of the group and try not to look like she was trying too hard to be a part of things. That's what Annie does. Sometimes she thinks she would like it there, but it's too late now—they're a week into Camp life and everyone's places are set. Her place is glued to Milly's side.

"Look," Milly will say, sweeping her arm out from their perch on the steps. "See, over there they're playing make-believe, and over here, they're doing the same thing. At least the little kids *know* they're pretending."

Milly has a grudge against everyone else their own age. She says she is an old soul. She says a lot of things that Logan can't quite believe, like that her full name is Millipede Meyer, and her mom is an astronaut, and she is raising three orphaned baby squirrels at home. She talks about these things sincerely, without any effort, as if they're no big deal at all. She doesn't seem to mind that she is different from the other girls. As long as she sticks with Milly, Logan doesn't have to mind much, either.

The day is measured in bell chimes. A counselor tugs the rope inside the bell tower, and everybody stops what they're doing to form a trickling line up the steps and into the mess hall. Breakfast is French toast with syrup and powdered sugar, slimy fruit and greasy sausage links. The mess hall is always loud and warm. The walls are covered in faded banners and dusty paintings and black-and-white photos of summers long ago; the counselors say Camp has been around forever, a hundred years, or longer.

After breakfast, they file back down the steps for announcements. The Falcons sit behind the Ravens, poke them in their backs and pull their braids. The day is warming up. Logan slides her beanie off but then, worried about her hair, puts it back on. She hopes no one noticed.

Back at the cabin, they put on their sunscreen and do their chores. The bell sends them out to morning activity. They get to choose their activity in the afternoon, but in the mornings, they go to assigned activities as a group. Today they have a nature walk with the Hawks. The Hawks' counselor leads them. Logan likes him—curly hair, dimpled cheeks, enormous smiles. Sometimes she catches herself looking for him under the bell tower before meals. He says his name is Christian, but the counselors and his cabin call him Taps.

They start out at the gold-panning claim, way up above the ropes course. Taps leads them along the creek on a bumpy trail. He points out anthills and coyote tracks and termite paths in bark, different species of moss and mushroom and even a raggedy crawfish claw, which he fishes out of the creek and places on the top of Donna's head while she is distracted, talking. She screams like bloody murder when she realizes. Milly laughs so hard tears run down her cheeks, earning her a glare from Donna and the others.

"You see," says the counselor, "that's why we always have to be alert when we're out in nature. You never know what's going to jump out and get you."

Logan imagines detached crawfish claws stalking through the trees, jumping out at them, and she laughs, too—not as obviously as Milly.

They follow the creek up the mountainside as the sun climbs higher and higher. Around the middle of the activity period, they stop in a clearing beside the water. Taps shows them a rocky mound where they can climb up to see the view of Camp below. Anyone who doesn't feel comfortable climbing, he tells them, should stay on the ground. Logan certainly does not feel comfortable. Her stomach turns just looking at the pebbles that come tumbling down under Taps's boots. The Hawks all follow him up, and so does Milly.

Logan crouches at the edge of the creek, watching for scuttling critters down in the stones. She reaches in and lets the cold water run through her fingers. It feels nice. The air is always so hot and dry at Camp. Her lips are chapped and sore, and she left her lip balm in the cabin. She would like to fling her whole body in and let the creek flow over her. Instead, she cups the icy water in her hands and raises it to her mouth, hoping to soothe her splitting lips.

"You probably shouldn't drink that."

Logan twitches and lets the water fall from her hands. It splatters down the front of her shirt. A boy—apparently the only one who didn't climb the rocks—has sat down on the bank of the creek behind her.

"I wasn't drinking it." She nudges her glasses up on her nose. "That'd be gross."

"Then what are you doing?"

"My lips are chapped. I was trying to cool them down."

The boy reaches into the pocket of his baggy shorts. He's a chubby kid, with rich, reddish-tan skin and heavy eyebrows. His hair is black and unwashed and hangs drearily over his forehead. After some fishing, he pulls out a roll of lip balm and offers it to her silently.

Logan hesitates. She glances toward the rest of the Ravens, sitting on a log in the clearing, chatting. From the top of the rock mound, she can hear everyone else's voices. "Sure," she says and stands to take the lip balm from him. Not thinking much about it, she removes the lid and spreads it twice over her top and bottom lips. Before she can thank the boy, an excited squeal pierces through the woods.

"Oh my God, Logan!"

Logan looks up. Donna is staring and pointing right at her.

"Did you just use that kid's lip balm? That's disgusting!"

She looks at the little tube in her hand. Disgusting? Why?

Joy and Liz and Mei laugh, their noses crinkled behind their hands. Mortified, Logan caps the tube and thrusts it back at the boy.

"Ew, Logan, you basically just *made out* with him."

"And why are you all wet?" Liz adds.

Logan looks down at her splattered shirt and can't see who is speaking. Whoever it is, they say it quietly, just for the other girls but still loud enough for her to hear. "Oh my God, she's so weird."

When she looks up again, they are all rolling their eyes and nodding in agreement. They go back to whatever they were talking about before.

The boy walks away quickly without saying anything. Logan plops onto the creek bank. *So weird*, she hears in her head, on repeat like a skipping song. *So weird, so weird, so weird.*

She mouths the words to herself until they lose their meaning and sound like nonsense. Gravity has gotten stronger, pulling her downward, the treetops threatening to timber over on top of her. She wishes Milly would come back down from the lookout. Camp is horrible, she thinks in a rush, and everything is ugly. She wants to go home.

Sam

SHE STEPS ONTO HER PORCH in wool socks and sandals and a smoky-smelling flannel shirt. The morning light is soft and dewy. Birds twitter busily in the trees. Blinking, her eyes still heavy with sleep, Sam shuts the door behind her. She crosses the trails in solitary silence toward the mess hall, where she hikes up the steps and sneaks into the kitchen for a cup of coffee. It comes from an industrial carafe, burnt and bitter. The cooks have been at work for hours already. They greet her through the sizzle and steam and banter over their blaring music.

As a part of her new shadowing role in the office, Sam's job is to walk up the creek to the Camp gold-panning claim every morning, before the wake-up bell, and plant fake gold in the water. It's a long walk, coming off a few sparse hours of sleep, but she is starting to enjoy it. In the quiet mornings, the forest breathes with life. She watches for squirrels and deer along the trail. Sometimes she spooks herself, catching leering shapes in the dappled shadows, listening to her own crunching footsteps.

A hand-painted sign marks their imaginary gold-panning claim, where the water in the creek pools deep and slow. The pyrite is hidden in a molding cardboard box, stashed in a burrow under the pine needles. Sam selects a sparkling chunk, places it on a flat rock and brings another rock down hard on top of it, dusting herself with glitter and grime. She scatters the pieces across the pool and watches them sink down into the stones and scum. Later today, greedy little fingers will snatch them up in disbelief. There is something satisfying about the morning chore.

Crossing the lawn on her way back, Sam pauses and looks out over the lake. The water is still as glass, reflecting the pines and the new blue sky. Dew soaks her toes. Birds chatter. A harsh, vibrant and aesthetic loneliness washes over her. At the Hummingbirds' porch, she steps loudly and slowly and listens to the clamor of frantic feet inside.

"She's back! Hurry, get back in bed!"

Sam opens the door to find them tucked tight in their sleeping bags, eyes screwed shut.

The Hummingbirds' cabin is connected to the Chickadees' next door by their bathroom, a shielded concrete patio under a narrow awning. They share a set of child-sized toilet stalls, tin sinks, and rusting showerheads. Sam meets Rosie here as a matter of ritual every morning; they shower in side-by-side stalls and discuss the previous night over the splatter of hot water on concrete.

"Did you hook up with Jaeden?" Rosie asks her through the curtain.

"No."

"Are you going to?"

Sam scrubs her face in the stream. The water around her toes runs murky brown. "I don't know."

When the wake-up bell rings, Sam and Rosie let the girls scamper ahead of them down the trail. Sam refills her coffee, and they join the rest of the counselors clustered around the picnic tables below the bell tower. Bitter steam rises from the mugs in their grasp. Campers shout and run around them, largely unsupervised.

"That's the thing," Taps is saying as Sam and Rosie take their places in the group. His hands are pattering out a steady *ta-da, ta-da, ta-da* rhythm on the surface of the table. "He has no clue who she is. But, like, what if he does? What if they recognize each other, you know, subconsciously?"

"What's that?" Sam asks from behind her mug.

Elias, in his sunglasses already—still drunk, for all they know—answers her: "Taps has this kid in his cabin. Came here with his wife."

"Weird."

"Yup. They're both here. Same age. No idea."

A pair of boys playing tag dashes by the tables. One brushes against Sam's hip, splattering her coffee. Oblivious to the grown-ups and their droning gossip, they run on. Sam grumbles, wiping her arms clean on the front of her shirt.

"They did it on purpose, apparently," Taps adds. "It was in his profile. They thought, like, if they catch a crush on each other as kids, it'll save their marriage or something."

Rosie bursts with laughter. She combs her fingers through Elias's hair, trying to pick out a clump of sap to his mumbled disgruntlement. "Hold *still*, I'm trying to help. That's the worst idea I've ever heard," she says to Taps.

"People really do some ridiculous things when they're bored and rich, don't they?"

"Yeah, well, that's what we're here for." Taps shrugs. "Anyway, don't try telling Sadie that. She has the girl, and she thinks it's just *so* romantic. She keeps cornering me and trying to scheme ways we can, you know, shove them together."

Jeremy's face lights up in a malicious grin. Before he can get through his joke, he is distracted by a camper out on the grass. "Hey, Brooker!" he shouts. "Get your hand out of your pants, man, come on! Jesus." His voice drops again, disdainful. "That dude owns my bank, you know that? One of the world's richest CEOs. Look at him—now he's sniffing his fingers."

They all turn to look at the Pigeon in question. The boy has one shoe untied and his sweatshirt is inside out.

A sharp whistle from the mess hall steps tears their attention away. "Hey!" Nick waves his watch at them, indignant. "It's two past eight! Who's ringing the bell today?"

"Shit." Elias shoves himself upright and sprints for the bell tower, hair and sunglasses askew. The rest of them scatter to herd the campers into line.

Sam counts the Hummingbirds as they enter the mess hall. Sometimes they don't all make it to a meal—every once in a while, someone will be lost, still wandering around on the lawn or back at the cabin. The room sings with stomping feet and high laughter and the clatter of cheap cutlery banged over plastic plates. Tacked on the wall beside their table, Sam keeps a tally of spills. If they make it through a week with fewer than ten spills, she promised them, she will personally arrange an ice cream party. Today is Monday, the start of a new week. In the first week, their tally reached twenty-four.

"Two hands," she shouts over the din. "Two hands!" Lucy tips the jug and hot chocolate topples into Maggie F.'s lap. Tears quickly follow.

Morning chores are a bigger challenge. Sam limps across the cabin with Daria clinging to one leg, holding a bottle of sunscreen, begging them to shove their messes back into their lockers. "Push the broom, Deb, don't pull it. Poppy, come here." She catches her by the arm.

"I'm bored!" Poppy squirms as Sam slathers sunscreen over her cheeks.

"Did you make your bed?"

"Yeah. Look, my tooth is wiggly." She opens her mouth and jabs at her single front tooth with a dirty fingertip.

"You didn't make your bed. I'm looking right at it. Daria, stand up, please, you need to get dressed."

"Look at my tooth, Sam!"

Sam sighs. She lifts a hand to rub her eyes, forgetting that her fingers are still coated in sunscreen, and nearly swears out loud at the sting. "Poppy," she winces, squinting through tears, "make your bed."

When they are finally dressed, Sam sends the Hummingbirds out to their morning sailing lesson. Poor, hungover Kyle, she thinks smugly, will be waiting for them at the boathouse. If not for her new job, she would have a morning activity to run, too. Right now, Elias is saddling horses and Rosie is dividing up volleyball teams. Sam takes her time lingering in the empty cabin, sifting through her dirty laundry and humming to herself, before she slowly makes her way back across Camp to the office.

Campbell isn't at his desk. He left a list of chores for her scrawled on the whiteboard in red ink: *Sam, pls type & print out 30 copies of new lifeguard policies. Call Steve @ Craft Depot & order lanyard string (3 crate). Check with Ellen in the kitchen about flour stocks. Ur a rockstar!* The 3 is written over a cloudy smudge; it was a 2 before he changed his mind.

Sam helps herself to a fourth or fifth cup of coffee from the pot in the back of the room and settles at Campbell's desk. His teenage children smile emptily at her from their framed portraits. She wonders, abstractly, where in the world they are. Gus Campbell has a cabin in Smith's Ridge for the summers, but he has never mentioned where his real home is—maybe he isn't supposed to. It's strange to think that he has a life somewhere else. Somewhere he watches movies and cooks dinner, maybe even wears a coat and tie.

Nick comes down from his bunk room to sit at the other desk. They talk lightly behind their coffees. As he draws up the schedule for the week, he narrates his steps out loud to her, distractedly, bare thoughts popping out of him as they come to mind. He isn't much of a mentor. The space between them is comfortable enough, though, and Sam doesn't mind the quiet mornings with him as much as she thought she might.

Around ten thirty a.m., a shrill ring shatters the dull, sleepy air. It's coming from the compact radio in Nick's pocket. He picks it up, still eyeing the dry-erase schedule board on his desk.

"Yeah?"

Amy's voice comes crackling through the static. *"Hey, Nick. You at the office?"*

"Yeah."

"Can you come down to ropes? We've got a hurt camper here."

Sam looks up from Campbell's monitor, blinking away the haze from the sudden change of light.

"Okay, on my way." Nick releases the receiver. Amy buzzes back.

"Nick?"

"Yeah?"

"I, uh . . . don't know how bad it is. You should bring your keys."

Nick stands in a rush and stuffs the little radio back into his pocket. He frowns. A hand flies to his chest, grasping at something beneath his T-shirt. "Come on, Sam."

"What?" Sam pushes her chair back hesitantly.

"Come on!"

They take off running. The ropes course isn't far from the office, but Sam is in worse shape than she'd like to admit. She falls behind him, huffing. Curious heads turn as they pass on the trail.

When they round the corner onto the ropes course, she is surprised to see the Camp horses, standing calmly in line with campers still mounted. Trail rides don't normally come this way, as a rule. The campers who are supposed to be climbing are gathered in a nervous bunch, still in their harnesses and helmets, their faces blanched and frightened. Elias, Phoebe, and Amy crouch over someone on the ground. Amy wears a belaying harness; Elias and Phoebe are in riding boots and jeans. Sam takes in the scene, panting, as Nick rushes to the counselors.

"Is he conscious?"

Elias has blood on his arms, Sam realizes. Her heart pounds in her throat. She lifts her hands, not quite sure what to do with them.

"I don't know. I didn't want to move him. The nurse is coming."

"Get the kids off their horses. Keep them all together, talk to them. Sam—come here."

She approaches on heavy feet, head spinning. The edge in his voice is all wrong. As she steps up behind Nick's crouched back, she sees a boy on the ground, an older camper, splayed over the rocky dirt where he fell. His face and shirt are splattered with blood. His chest heaves, eyes closed. Not far away, between the pines that support the high tightrope, a rider-less mare watches them placidly.

"What happened?" Sam whispers.

Phoebe's face is pale. Her voice trembles with choked tears. "His horse . . . It got scared by the ropes, I guess."

"There's a reason we don't take the rides through here," says Nick swiftly. He looks up at Amy and again reaches for something at his chest. He nods. With an anxious glance at Sam, Amy grasps Phoebe by the shoulders and tugs her away.

"Come here, Sam. Hold his head."

Sam does as she is told. She kneels over the camper and braces his head between her hands. She recognizes him: a quiet, stout boy, heavy-browed and solemn. His left arm sits across his stomach at a funny, crooked angle. The blood streaming from his nose and brow strikes her as unrealistically red, vivid, as if it has leached the color from everything else around them.

Nick tugs something over his head: a long, looped black lanyard with a keyring on the end. Hanging among the keys is a little black tube about the size of a thumb. This he clasps between his fingers. He holds it to his side, his arm stiff. The keys jangle.

"What is that?" Sam asks him. Behind Nick's back, Elias and Amy help campers off their horses, talking to them in loud, blanketing tones. The kids' faces strain toward the excitement. The boy's head jerks between Sam's hands; she looks down to see his eyelids flutter.

"Stay still, stay still," she whispers frantically to him.

Nick is crouched, poised with the black tube in his hand. It might be a roll of lip balm, or a laser pointer. He holds it like a weapon.

"Nick, what is that?"

Then, all at once, the splayed body on the ground regains life. He twists and sputters, spraying the blood that has trickled between his lips. "Ow," he gasps, blinking up at Sam.

"It's okay!" She lifts a hand to his forehead. "It's okay, you're okay."

Nick sighs. His eyes fall closed for a moment. "You're okay, buddy. Nurse May's coming. Look at me, look at me. How many fingers?" With one hand he holds up three steady fingers. With the other, he hangs the lanyard back over his head, tucking it away beneath the neck of his T-shirt.

The nurse arrives in a rickety, open-top cart. She takes Sam's place over the boy's head, and Sam helps the others gather campers and horses out of the way. Phoebe has grown inconsolable, sobbing, scaring the kids. Amy leads her away with an arm around her shoulders. In the middle of the bustle, a doe-eyed girl in large, red-framed glasses tugs at Sam's arm. "It was my fault," she tells her. "I shouted. I scared his horse."

Sam hugs the girl and tells her it was no one's fault, that accidents happen. Even as she does, she looks over her head at the panic in Elias's face, the resignation in Nick's. Accidents should not happen. Not like this.

The injured camper's name is Max. He is twelve, in the Hawks' cabin. Sam helps Nick lift him and carry him to the cart with a good deal of difficulty. "Shock," Nurse May mutters, shaking her head, as they lay him down in the back seat. The blood on his face smudges against Sam's shirt. "He'll be fine. Just shock and a bump on the head."

Max grips his arm and moans. He does look shocked, Sam thinks. Shocked, afraid, and entirely childlike.

When the cart rattles away, a heavy hush falls over the clearing. The whispers from the campers are muted, smothered by the thick silence of the forest around them. Sam turns to Nick. "What now? Should I help Elias?"

"No." His focus is on the campers, eyeing them calculatedly. "You should change your shirt, then go meet Campbell at the office. I'll call him." He pats the radio in his pocket. Then he frowns hesitantly at her. "You okay?"

Sam's eyes fall to the center of his chest. She can see the outline of the lanyard through his T-shirt, the lump of the keyring at his sternum. Her question dies in her throat.

Nick shakes his head. "It could have been worse," he says by way of answering, then turns to help his brother with the campers.

Logan

SPARK IS LOGAN'S FAVORITE HORSE. She's a gorgeous four-year-old Appalachian mare with a speckled coat and a wild streak—that's what Sadie says. Logan loves her. Unfortunately, Elias is leading the trail ride today, and he never lets her ride Spark.

"But *I* know how to handle her," she begs, stomping across the hay and muck of the stables behind him.

"Logan, I already told you. The biggest kids get the biggest horses. That's just how it works." The counselor shakes her off. He has his sunglasses on and his T-shirt sleeves cuffed over his shoulders. He *humphs* as he messes up his hair. The other Ravens have crushes on him, but Logan knows better. Only an idiot would refuse to understand the bond between a girl and her horse.

When the ride finally starts, Logan is riding a fat old mare named Daisy— she can hardly do anything but pull up weeds and follow the butt in front of her—and Spark is saddled with the chubby, tan-skinned boy who offered Logan his lip balm at the creek. She can never seem to get away from that boy. Every time the other girls see him, they make a point of teasing her about it.

"Logan, your *boy*friend's here," Liz says. It's a mean joke because of who he is. If he were a different boy—the kind of boy who wore his Camp Phoenix ball cap backwards and sat on the announcement benches before meals, the kind of boy girls made bracelets for—it would be a different joke. He isn't, though.

There aren't enough horses for all of the Ravens and Hawks, so they split into two groups for the ride. Logan's group goes first. They strap into sweaty helmets and riding boots and the counselors boost them up into the saddles. The horses line up single file. Daisy is behind Spark. Logan simmers, watching the boy in front of her. He tilts awkwardly sideways on Spark's back, her reins loose and lifeless in his hands. A few minutes into the ride, he turns fully around and stares at Logan.

"Hey."

"Hey," she says unsurely.

"I'm sorry you didn't get my horse." He has a low voice. Frog-ish.

"It's fine." Logan glances over her shoulder. The scene she made over Spark in the stables was enough embarrassment for one day; she doesn't want the other Ravens to see her talking to him. "You should really look where you're going."

"Oh, right." The boy swivels in his saddle to face forward. A moment or two later, as their line sways along the trail toward the girls' cabins, he looks back at her again. His helmet is too loose, slipping back on his forehead. "My name's Max," he says.

"My name's Logan."

"Really? Isn't that a boy's name?"

"No," Logan huffs, "it's my name. And you should really look where you're going."

"Oh. Right." He turns forward again.

They ride on through Camp, up and around the mess hall, past the ranges and back down, toward the ropes course. From the back of the line, Elias calls: "Phoebe, stick right!" The other counselor doesn't say anything back. Soon, Logan can hear shouts and the zipping sound of carabiner clips on steel cables. The tops of the trees bounce with the weight of climbing campers. The horses lumber along, and every minute or so Max glances over his shoulder at Logan. He has wide eyes, like he's confused, like he can't quite figure out what she is doing on Daisy's back behind him. Each time he turns around, she grows more irritated.

Their trail takes them right through the center of the ropes course. The Falcons are there with the Blackbirds, climbing the plank walk: a single high board suspended between two trees. The challenge is to climb up a ladder of iron staples in one tree, cross the plank, and then jump from the top, floating back down on a belay rope. Logan watches the boy in the treetops queasily. He has nearly made it all the way across. The space between his feet and the ground is infinite and blurry. Logan's stomach turns and she has to look away—when she does, she sees Max staring back at her again.

"Hey, Logan?"

Logan snaps. "*What?*"

She didn't mean to shout so loud. Her voice startles Spark, who tosses her head with a whinny of alarm. Max drops the reins in a panic. At that exact moment, the boy on the plank walk jumps.

It happens so fast. Spark rears back and takes off at a full, flying gallop. She bolts from the line and runs straight across the clearing, straight for a squat pine with a low-hanging bough. Max screams. The branch hits him square in the face. The loose helmet goes flying. He slumps in the saddle and then Spark bucks—Max flops and falls like a rag doll, lands hard on his front, rolls to his back, and lies still.

With the boy off her back, Spark settles down. She trots calmly back to them, nickers, and shakes out her mane, proud of herself. Logan is stunned.

It's only after the counselors have helped them off their horses, after Nurse May has arrived and crouched at Max's side, that she realizes what really happened. It was all her fault. She shouted loud enough to scare Spark. She set her on edge and made Max drop his reins. A strangling fear grabs ahold of her throat as she watches Elias tug the horse back into line. Logan has read enough books; she knows what happens to horses who become too dangerous for their jobs. She has to tell someone—before it's too late—that it was her fault, not Spark's.

"It was my fault. I shouted too loud. It was *my* fault!"

None of the adults at the scene will listen to her. Spark should have just kept running.

The riders crowd into a huddle with the boys from the climbing activity, who still have harnesses strapped like diapers around their hips. Whispers start. Logan hears them growing, rising in a chorus all around her.

"Did you see him?"

". . . the horse stomped on him . . ."

". . . all that blood . . ."

". . . cracked his skull . . ."

". . . he had a hole in his neck, I saw it . . ."

Logan squeezes her eyes shut. She wants to throw her hands over her ears. *My fault, my fault, my fault* . . . Now Max the Hawk has a cracked skull and a hole in his neck and Spark will surely be executed. She hates Camp. Everything is going wrong. Hot tears pool behind her eyelids and spill through, dribbling down her cheeks. She gulps down a shaky breath.

"Hey!" A clear shout breaks through all the whispers as Logan struggles to get a grip on herself. "Shut up, you guys! Look, you're freaking her out."

Logan opens her eyes. Through her fogging lenses, she sees a boy. One of the Falcons. He steps closer and puts an arm around her shoulders.

"Hey." For a boy so tall, his voice is high and soft. "Don't cry. He's gonna be all right."

"Yeah, don't cry!"

Suddenly, everyone's hands are on her. They pat her shoulders and back and head. Even Donna is hugging her. To Logan's utter embarrassment, she chokes, and a ragged sob comes tearing from her throat. She had no idea she was capable of producing such a sound.

Amy leads them all away from the ropes course to the lawn. The Falcon keeps his arm around her while they walk. He doesn't say anything, just presses her into his side and carries on talking to the other boys, like this is all normal; like they're old friends and everything is okay. As Logan's eyes clear, she looks cautiously up at him. His arms are long and skinny, his T-shirt sleeves cuffed, like Elias's. His hair is dark blond and swooping and curls over the tips of big, protruding ears. When he smiles at her, his cheeks flush pink. There is something funnily familiar about him, Logan thinks.

Milly was with the other half of the group, not on the ride. When the bell rings for lunch, she comes sprinting across the lawn to ask Logan about the accident—apparently, they got to help Elias wrangle the horses back to the stables. Logan has calmed down some. She tells her the story and is about to admit her fears about Spark being put down when she sees the tall Falcon loping back across the grass toward them. He has finally taken off his climbing harness. He carries it like a heavy sack across his shoulder.

"Hey." He stretches one of his long arms out, like he's going to touch her, but doesn't quite reach her. "I forgot to ask. What's your name?"

A squishy weight squirms in Logan's stomach. There is *something* about him—she could swear she has seen him before, somewhere. "Logan," she says.

"Logan," he repeats. "Huh. I think I know a boy named Logan."

"Well, I'm a girl named Logan."

She watches the muscles in his face work, his pink cheeks twitching up and down. She wants him to go away. At the same time, she would very much like to touch his hair, to push it back behind his ears and measure exactly how far they stick out from his head. Milly smirks sideways at her.

"Logan," he says again, like he is examining her name, studying it, holding it up to the light and peering through it. He nods. "That's a cool name." Again, his arm twitches toward her. "Anyway, I hope you're feeling better. I'll see you around. Oh"—he swivels on his heel as he turns away, back toward his friends—"I'm Hugo, by the way."

Logan smiles. His name is even funnier than hers. "See you, Hugo," she mumbles as he runs off. She looks at Milly, and they both start laughing. She can't really say what is so funny.

Sam

SAM STANDS AT THE ENTRANCE to a long hallway stretching out in front of her to a gray dead end. The ceiling is low and curved. The floor is grayish-white tile, tinted yellow in the fluorescent overhead lighting. Bitter chemical cleaner coats her throat, stings her eyes. On either side of the hall are closed doors, uniform in pale blue. Each door bears a tidy copper nameplate. *Martin. McHenry. Meyer. Noonan. Owens.* Sam reads over the doors, her eyes pinging back and forth from one side of the hallway to the other, until she gets near the end: *Warbler.*

The whole place is silent and ominous. There are no buzzing flies, no beeping machines. Nothing but her own tired breath. Sam shudders, shakes her head, and tears herself away. Her footsteps echo across the concrete ceiling as she pads down another hall, turns right, then left, and dashes up a staircase, landing in a wood-paneled waiting area. Nick sits on a low bench against the wall. He leans forward with his forearms flat on his knees and looks up at her.

"You shouldn't be wandering."

"I was curious."

Counselors usually aren't allowed to come into the facility. Sam has never been inside the building. They came here to pick up Max, the Hawk, who is having his broken wrist cast. He comes out of the examination room heavily sedated, his eyes half open, head lolling on his shoulders like a drunk. A facility worker in pale scrubs pushes his wheelchair.

Sam and Nick rise from their seats to follow him out of the waiting area and into the elevator. They leave the facility the same way they came in: through the maze, down another hallway of blue doors, and out through a squat basement entrance. It's dusk, campfire time; blue fades to black over the tips of the pines. The facility attendant—an alien, a citizen of another universe, who looks over their heavy wristwatches and dirt-streaked faces bemusedly—hands off the boy and his X-rays and vanishes back inside the building. Sam and Nick brace the camper and lift him into the old Camp pickup together. In the tiny cab of the truck, they must look like a bad comedy, like two bumbling killers, their hapless victim propped between them.

They park as close to the infirmary as they can to gracelessly carry Max inside. His face is battered and swelling. His wrist is in a navy blue cast up to the elbow. In the infirmary bed he mumbles and groans. His eyes flicker open, unseeing.

The Camp nurse is a sensible old woman with a stern, pinched mouth. "Lucky boy," she says dryly, pulling a blanket up to Max's chest. In her other hand she holds a bottle of sickly pink antacid for the vomiting Pigeon in the next room over.

"Probably not the childhood experience he had in mind," Nick says.

Nurse May waves the pink bottle dismissively at him. "The way they drugged him up, he's barely going to remember it. That cast will just give him a little character."

Sam follows Nick from the room, and they step outside onto the infirmary porch. Night has fallen in full. Two silent figures stand in the buttery half-glow of the windows, their arms crossed, facing outward toward the lake. The singing voices from the campfire float toward them on the night air.

> Look up to the moon, moon, moon,
> Hug every rock and tree,
> I will take care of you, my friend,
> If you take care of me.

The solitary bell chime sounds. In the ringing silence that follows, Sam is struck with a pang of nostalgia tinged with anxiety. Richard Byron and Gus Campbell both shift and unfold their arms as the spell of the song breaks. Campbell turns to Nick, and they begin discussing the camper in low voices.

"Miss Red."

Sam looks up. Byron is smiling down at her. He's a big man, she realizes, standing so close. Tall and imposing. A lock of peppery gray sits at a jaunty angle across his brow.

"Hi." She returns his smile.

There is something undeniably, giddily exciting about standing so close to him. He is a mystery to her, the boss of her boss, shrouded in legend. A genius with a troubled past, they say. An orphan. Mad scientist. Recovered alcoholic—according to some, 'recovered' is a loose term. "He drinks," Elias told Sam once, knowingly. "It's a part of his brand. Everybody loves a self-medicated genius." Elias admires Richard Byron. A lot of people admire him; genius or not, he is wildly successful. Under his gaze, Sam finds herself flustered.

His eyes are bright, as if fighting laughter. "Nicky," he says, "your new shadow's a hell of a lot prettier than you, you know that?"

All three of them chuckle. Sam feels his stare fall over her again. She wipes at her face, expecting to find a glob of toothpaste or sunscreen. He reaches out and lays a warm, broad hand on the back of her neck. The men keep talking, all stern business and throat-clearing, and if it weren't for the hand on the back of Sam's neck, she would be sure this was her time to leave, to go back to her Hummingbirds.

"Phoebe's new. She'd never led a ride on her own before. Elias was supposed to be training her."

"New or not—you don't take the horses through ropes. She should have known that. Someone should have told her that."

"That mare's been skittish since we got her. The owners told us to always saddle her with the heaviest rider."

"Mr. Gill, I take it, was the heaviest in the group?"

"That's what Elias says."

Sam watches this conversation play out, curious. They are gambling, spinning a wheel, guessing at where the blame should land.

"Well, we can't keep that horse in the stables anymore."

"She'll be gone by next week. If they won't take her back, I'll have Dane start digging a hole."

"And what about the counselors responsible?"

Campbell's face twists into a sorry grimace. His expression is lengthened by the shadows, dragging his frown lines downward, exaggerated, cartoonish. "That's your call, Rich," he says. "When it comes down to it, it's always your call."

The hand on the back of Sam's neck lifts and falls in a gentle, affectionate pat. Silence settles on the porch. Not far off, they can hear the stream of sleepy, manic campers headed for bed. The occasional high shout and cackle peppers the buzz.

"Sam?"

She blinks up.

"Can I chat with you for a minute?"

Sam nods. Her mouth has gone chalky. "Sure."

He guides her away from the porch, out of reach of the light. Nick and Campbell's conversation carries on behind them. They follow the trail to a moonlit fork; to the right is the parking lot and the road to Smith's Ridge, and to the left is the center of Camp, the clamoring voices. Byron stands with his hands in his pockets and smiles at her. "How is Poppy Warbler?"

"Poppy?" Sam laughs. It's strange to hear him say her name, strange to think her existence has anything to do with him. "She's, uh . . ."

"A handful, isn't she?"

"Yeah. Yeah, that's a good way to put it."

"Right. I expected as much. Once a rockstar, always a rockstar." He cocks an eyebrow at her. "You know, it says a lot about you, that Gus and Nick knew you could handle that cabin. On top of this little shadowing gig they've got you on. Looks like you're top of the class this summer."

"Oh. I don't know."

"Better not fuck it up, huh?"

Sam stares up at him in the weak light. A joke, she realizes, half a second too late. Byron cracks a smile at her stunned silence, then guffaws, throwing his bearded chin to the moon. Sam lets herself chuckle along.

"Listen," he begins as his booming laugh patters down. He shifts his stance to look at her, and Sam can't help but notice the youthful way he moves, the flex of his biceps beneath flannel sleeves. She has no idea how old the owner of Camp Phoenix is, exactly, but he is certainly in the best health money can buy. "I'm going to need your advice, Miss Red. If you don't mind."

"Okay."

"This is complicated. It's difficult to explain, but there's a tricky balance between the clients and the campers. Keeping them both happy. It's sort of like dealing with children and their parents, if you know what I mean. Kids want to have fun. Parents want their kids to be safe." Byron watches her carefully, as if to make sure she tracks his every word. "So, when something bad happens, something like this, someone needs to be held accountable. For the sake of the client. Do you understand?"

Slowly, unsurely, Sam nods.

"That kid up there." He gestures vaguely behind them, toward the infirmary. "I know it's hard to remember sometimes—that's by design, of course—but he's a grown man. He's a paying client. A client who had some reservations about the program to begin with, I should add. When the consciousness transfer is withdrawn in August, he is going to be upset about what happened to him. He's going to want to know what actions I took to make it right."

"But . . ." Sam bites back the thought, then releases it anyway. "But he's fine, isn't he? It's just a broken wrist."

Byron's smile is proud, as if she has said exactly the right thing. "You're right. He is going to be fine, and he'll be able to enjoy the rest of his summer. But let's say, for the sake of argument, that he wasn't fine. Do you know what would happen then?"

"You mean . . . ?"

"Yes. I mean if he'd hit that branch a little harder. If he'd landed on his neck, instead of his arm. Do you know what happens if one of them dies?"

She isn't sure what to say, if she should know. "They wake up, right?"

He laughs. "Well, yeah. They do wake up. But before they wake up, they *die*. As a child. These kids have no clue what's going on here. They don't know they're going to wake up. They don't know where they're going any more than the rest of us do. Death is death. No one should have to live through death."

Sam glances down at her sandaled toes. Her feet are cold and dirty. She notices the black scab on her pinky toe where she stubbed it on the fishing dock three days ago. She should really wash it out, she thinks; it's starting to look infected.

"I'm not trying to make you uncomfortable, Sam. I just want you to understand. This is a life-and-death scenario. That's why, as much as it kills me, I am going to have to let someone go."

Again, Sam nods, winding her fingers together at her waist.

"I understand you're good friends with both of the counselors involved in the accident." Byron stoops to look her in the eyes. His face has fallen serious. Still, the laughing light is there, just a twinkle, a comedian stuck on the verge of the punchline. "I can't ask Nick about this—it's his brother, you know. And the other ADs don't work as closely with either of them as you do. So, I'm just going to ask you: How can we handle this without impacting the rest of the staff too much?"

When she doesn't answer, he asks again. This time his words are pointed, direct.

"I need your help. I want to handle this delicately. Who is going to leave a smaller void behind them?"

Sam stands still under the moonlight and his smiling eyes for an oddly empty stretch of time. Her thoughts float away from her head, carrying her off across the lake and back to the facility, back down that hallway. This is not real. Finally, her mouth falls open and Phoebe's name falls out of it.

Byron straightens up, nodding. "Yeah, that's about what I thought. It's tough for a new hire to really get integrated, isn't it?" He reaches out and squeezes Sam's shoulder tight. "You do have a future here, I think. Not everyone can see those kinds of things. The big picture."

"I don't understand."

"What's that?"

"I don't understand," she says again, slowly, trying to sort out the muddled question in her head. She didn't mean to speak up, but the words were somehow squeezed out by the hand on her shoulder. "If it's that serious—if it's life-and-death—why are we in charge of them? Why put Elias and Phoebe out there in the first place?"

"Oh." He chuckles. "The really big picture. That's a little bigger than your pay grade, to be honest, Sam, but I'll tell you again: it's complicated. There's a balance. Camp wouldn't be the same without you kids." His hand falls from her shoulder and he steps back, yawning. "You'll learn more about all that next summer, I'm sure. For now, just stay on the trails, all right?"

"All right."

"Good night, sweetheart. Thanks for your help."

When she gets back to the cabin, she finds the Hummingbirds still fluttering through their nighttime routine. Deb is singing in the bathroom, Lucy has toothpaste in her hair, and Daria is lying on the floor in her hiking boots and underpants. Katie, who was watching them through campfire, looks frazzled as she leaves.

"All right, you monsters," Sam rushes them. "Get to bed."

"Sam, tell us a Danny McGee!" Poppy begs. "Just one!"

"Only if you get in bed *now*."

It started as a bedtime story a few days ago. Since then, it has evolved. Danny McGee is an ordinary, clumsy boy who attended Camp Phoenix in some forgotten year when things were still magical. His misadventures always end with him covered in poop or boogers or anything else embarrassing enough to leave the girls howling with laughter. Sam is proud of the stories. She even told a version at evening crafts and passed it on to Elias, who has given Danny his own theatrical spin.

A tap on the front window makes Sam jump. She looks out to see Rosie, bundled in her beanie and windbreaker, shrugging at her watch. *Go ahead*, she mouths to her. She won't meet them all at the Nest tonight.

"Okay, okay." Sam paces along the bunk beds, thinking. As the campers fall quiet in their sleeping bags, she closes her eyes. She can let herself get lost in the nonsense, the silly story. "Once upon a time, a long, long time ago, Danny McGee was a camper here at this Camp, just like all of you . . ."

week four

Sam

THE WORST PART ABOUT LEADING evening gold-panning is the inevitable attendance of at least one snarky, older camper who has only come to show off their skepticism to the littler ones. Today, it's a Sparrow named Elaine. Sam eyes the girl as she turns the pyrite chunks over in her palm, preaching to a wide-eyed Wren. They stand shin-deep in the flowing water.

"See?" Elaine says to the boy. "*Real* gold doesn't crumble like that. If it was real, it would be *impossible* to break it."

Sam rolls her eyes. This is always a tricky line to walk. If she scolds her, it would only confirm her suspicions. On the other hand, if Elaine keeps talking, she is going to ruin the fantasy of the activity for the rest of the campers. Sam decides to feign ignorance. She sits on the needled creek bank, leaning back against a broad tree trunk, guarding the burrow in the ground where she hides the box of fake gold every morning. She lets her head fall back and gazes up to a reddening sky. Campers wade and splash in the water around her.

It's hot, even as the sun sinks low. They should have had a rainstorm by this point in the summer, but the skies are crystal clear and the air is dry. The last of the spring green in the forest is shriveling. Leaves crunch crisply underfoot, and dust hangs free in the air. Campers sport scabby red rings around their mouths from licking their chapped lips. Sam's shoulders are perpetually sunburnt, and the freckles beneath her eyes are spreading and darkening like a rash.

"Even if it *was* real, it wouldn't be this easy to find. Gold doesn't just float around in rivers anymore. Haven't you ever heard of the Gold Rush?"

"Elaine," Sam groans, "that's enough." For a fraction of a second, she wonders who this girl is in her other life, in the real world. A lawyer or political analyst, perhaps a social media profit.

"It's fake, isn't it, Sam? It's just pyrite, isn't it?"

"It's gold," Sam says, shifting her leg to cover the stone that hides the pyrite stash.

When the bell chimes from the center of Camp, the little prospectors pocket their finds, uncuff the sopping hems of their pants, and struggle back into their socks and shoes. Sam leads them along the trail, onto the lawn, and down toward campfire, where they dash off to join their cabins.

The Hummingbirds have their first campfire skits tonight. Poppy is the star, of course. She prances across the creaking stage, swimming in a long prop gown, crying: "Where, oh *where*, are my royal papers? Fetch me my royal papers!" The rest of the girls come on in various costumes, giggling, presenting newspapers and magazines and maps. The queen rejects each of them with increasing fury. Daria appears last, slumped in a hunchback's gait, wielding a roll of toilet paper. "At last!" Poppy tosses her arms upward. "My royal papers!"

For their second act they sing an old, well-worn campfire song.

> *Late last night, while we were all in bed,*
> *Old Lady Leary left the lantern in the shed . . .*

Sam crouches on stage with the girls, prodding them to sing louder. The fire crackles in its metal ring, and the voices rise in unharmonious unison.

. . . *and when the cow kicked it over, she winked her eye and said,*

> *IT'S GONNA BE A HOT TIME, IN THE OLD TOWN, TONIGHT!*
> *FIRE, FIRE, FIRE!*
> *WATER, WATER, WATER!*
> *JUMP, LADY, JUMP!*
> *AAAAH, SPLAT!*

The song ends with a solid, ringing *clap*—the sound of a body smacking the ground. The whole scene is gruesome, cultish; the flames, the stars, the singsong nonsense wailed into the night.

Camp Phoenix has quickly become a universe of its own. By the design of the program, they are completely cut off from the rest of the world— there is no year, no time, no media. No parents or school. They have each other, and their own patched-together culture, their matching wardrobes and friendship bracelets, ghost stories and legends and silly songs. Entire sentences can be strung together with words nobody outside the lake basin would ever understand.

The counselors are just as affected by the isolation as the clients of Camp Phoenix. As two weeks fade into three, they are all rapidly losing touch with the things that used to matter to them. Sam tries to think back to her life in Paris and finds herself coming up with a flat caricature. Lifeless images, like postcard pictures, of the landscape, her apartment, the high ceilings of the classroom where she studied French philosophy, rattle across a drained skull.

She believes she used to speak with sophistication and culture. Now she says: "If Germ thinks he's leaving me to shovel the goat shit in afternoon period again, he can suck my ass."

She has a lit cigarette balanced between her fingers, perched on the tailgate of somebody's truck. It's just past midnight; tonight, they drove down the road from Camp to build a bonfire at Lobster Point, the gravelly campsite near the dam.

"You're at the barn again tomorrow?" Rosie asks her. "I thought we were lifeguarding together."

"Yeah, I don't know. Guess Nick moved me."

They both look across the flickering fire, where the Borowitz brothers sit on rotting stumps, strumming their guitars. Elias has a disarmingly lovely, folksy singing voice. They bumble the chords and laugh at each other and play on. The rest of the staff sits watching them, drunk and entranced. Over the firelit branches, the stars are bright and infinite.

"Aren't you, like, his assistant now? Don't you get a say?"

Sam shrugs. If she does ask Nick to give her a more favorable schedule, people will start to see something between the two of them. There is nothing to see between the two of them—not really—but if people start to believe it, in their tiny world, it becomes as good as true. She can't be the girl who sleeps her way into privileges. There are rules at Camp, lines not to be crossed.

Sam snakes her arms around her knees and watches how the firelight distorts the brothers' features. Nick's face is locked in an absent trance, sleepy-eyed, fingers plucking worriedly away. She wonders about their childhood, about the parents who put guitars into those boys' hands before they could walk. She imagines aging and important aristocrats. Old money, deep pockets for piano lessons and art schools and European vacations. It's a rich jealousy that drives those thoughts.

"Here." Rosie thrusts a bottle of cheap tequila at her. Sam can smell it before it touches her lips. "To Phoebe."

She swigs and gags, and the firelight blurs. "To Phoebe."

They mourn her like she is dead. To them, she might as well be. Phoebe left quietly. She was gone before anyone knew she had been fired. They were confused, then upset, and then anxious; if it happened to her, it could happen to anyone. Sam swallows her lump of guilt with the burning swig. She cannot—will not—tell anyone about her conversation with Richard Byron.

Back at Camp, a drunken party of scavengers tiptoes up the mess hall stairs to raid the kitchen for snacks. They pop out the window screen and scramble in through the back of the building, tripping over toes and shushing each other as they make for the pantry. Sam, Rosie, and Elias are giggling over a box of cream-filled cookies when a massive crash and clatter sends them leaping.

"What was that?"

Everyone pauses in their munching. There is another loud *thump* and the tinny clang of a trash can falling over. Shuffling. It's coming from behind the rear door of the kitchen, by the dumpsters. They wait in silence for a long time, hunched shadows in the pantry, until someone works up the courage to sneak back through the window and look.

The dumpsters have been overturned and rifled through. Trash is scattered, reeking, across the kitchen's back stoop. The group of counselors stands looking at the scene for a moment, swaying on their feet. Then, in a burst of giddy, nervous whispers, they turn and dash away to the mess hall steps.

•••

DEEP INTO THE EARLY HOURS of the morning, Sam stands alone on the Hummingbirds' porch and stares off into the trees. Rosie has gone to bed in the Chickadees' cabin next door. It's past curfew; she should be asleep, but something holds her still in the cold night air. A little drunk, she searches for something in the starlit landscape—whatever went digging through the dumpsters, maybe, or something else. She strains her eyes, her arms crossed tight around her middle.

Sometimes, when she is alone at night or on her early morning walks, she sees a shadow in the trees. Not an animal, but a haunting, human figure, tall and looming and lanky, with branching arms and a craning neck. It's always the same shape, always standing just a yard or two away, like a person watching her. She can never seem to catch it when she is looking for it. Only when she hears a rustle or a twig snap and turns around in childish fright. That must be what she is doing, standing here on the porch, she decides. Hoping to see the ghostly shadow. If she can finally pin it down with her eyes, maybe she can figure out if it's real.

The shadow does not appear. Nothing does. The giggle of someone still out and sneaking around rings through the trees. Sam shivers, turns away, and shuffles off to bed.

Logan

HUGO BAKER IS ALL ANYONE ever wants to talk about. The Ravens are obsessed with him—with his clothes, his face, his swishy hair and pink cheeks. Even the way his ears stick out when he wears a hat.

They track his every movement, follow him around Camp, and report back to each other in serious whispers over the mess hall table. Speaking in code, they call him *Mr. X* (Liz watched him start an X-pattern friendship bracelet by himself in crafts, which is impressive, for a boy), but the rest of the time they say his full name, all in a single drop: *Hugobaker*. Even the counselors use his last name. Hugo Baker is practically a celebrity.

Weirdly enough, Logan is caught up in all the frantic gossip, too. She has found a place in the cabin. Pretending to be in love with *Mr. X* is easy. All she has to do is say that she doesn't like him, and everyone will assume she does.

"Boys are gross," she says, with her cheeks flushed hot, and Liz giggles at her.

"Logan, you love him the most. You're so precious."

"Presh," says Donna, and the rest of them parrot it back.

"Presh!"

"Yeah, so presh!"

The great cavernous trench that used to separate Logan and Milly from the rest of the cabin is shrinking. There is a delicate place between boyish enough to be likable and girlish enough to be like them where Logan is finding her personality. It's a strange new ground that she tiptoes onto, careful and anxious, ready to lose her footing and slip to her doom at any moment.

She is getting older. It makes no sense—she was twelve when she came to Camp, she is twelve now, and she will be twelve when she leaves at the end of the summer. Somehow, though, she is sure she is growing.

Sometimes, during free hour in the afternoons or late at night when she gets up to pee, she will stand in the bathroom and spend a few minutes alone with her reflection, just staring. The girl in the toothpaste-spotted mirror is mesmerizing and repulsive. Her hair is plain, thin and straight. It hangs limply over her shoulders, except on the days Sadie ties it back in twin French braids. Her eyes are plain, milky brown behind her glasses, and her skin is getting tanner under the summer sunshine. Sometimes she thinks the red frames of her glasses are too bright, too noticeable. Too childish. Some days she is horrified by the sheer size and shape of her nose.

Her body is another source of anxiety. She isn't exactly flat as a board, like Milly, but she doesn't have much to fill a bra with, either. Sometimes they hurt. She wishes they would just make up their mind, flatten back down or balloon up all at once. When she gets dressed in the cabin after showering, she keeps her towel wrapped over her shoulders.

She is learning things as the summer goes on. Things about being a girl. Things about boys. Things the other Ravens were apparently born knowing. Nighttime is when she learns the most; at night, Sadie leaves to go to the counselors' loft, and they are left alone with their flashlights and journals, the lights shut off. They have to be quiet, or the patrols outside will hear them. They lie in the dark and whisper about Hugo Baker. Sometimes they say things Logan thinks kids should not be talking about, but she has to listen, anyway, staring out the window, hugging her pillow to her chin.

"No, you guys, it has to be *hard*," says Joy, trying to be serious. Snickers fill the cabin.

"But how does it get hard?"

Donna says: "It gets excited." Giggles.

"What, like it has a brain?"

Milly only speaks up when she has something very funny to say. "It *is* their brain," she says, and the whole cabin laughs until they lose control, until they are all laughing at each other's laughter, and a counselor comes by and knocks on the window to tell them to quiet down.

This is all news to Logan. Terrifying news. Fascinating news.

Time is funny at Camp Phoenix. Every day feels like it lasts a year, but the weeks pass by the minute. It's all too fast and too slow at once; she is growing and changing while she stays the same, while the world of Camp becomes brighter and much more complicated. In Logan's head it feels like a lifetime has passed since the horse accident, but it's only a few days until Max the Hawk is out of the infirmary and back at Camp.

She sees him at breakfast in the morning. His cheeks are puffy and tinged purple. There are stitches in his eyebrow, and his left arm is in a dark blue cast, hanging in a webbed sling across his shoulder. He catches her staring from their table and gives her a tiny, broken smile. Through the thick smell of syrup and grease and the mealtime jabber, Logan smiles back.

Later, on the way to morning activity, they see each other again. He walks with the Hawks, merging onto the trail from the lawn to the lake. The Ravens chatter along just a few feet behind. He pauses for a half second to look back at her. His sandals twist into the red dirt and his lips hang open, like he is going to say something. Logan steps closer. Those stitches in his eyebrow are terrifying. There is something almost monstrous about the way his face has swollen. She wants to look away. To her relief, as the girls reach the back of the boys' mob, Max seems to change his mind about talking to her. He stutter-steps and jerks ahead along the trail to catch up.

Their morning activity is supposed to be a fishing lesson, but the Ravens have decided fishing is cruel and disgusting, so they lie in the sunshine on the grass by the fishing dock. Pedal boats and rowboats parade by on the water, people shouting and splashing from them. The counselor tells them stories. Today, they're with Rosie: short and tan and a little scary when she gets mad. According to the latest gossip, she is going out with Elias—but other people say Elias is going out with Sam, and others swear that Sam is going out with Jeremy. Allegedly, these grown-up mysteries play out at night when they all leave the cabins to meet in the loft above the barn. Everyone Logan knows would give anything to find out what really goes on in that loft.

"Then, when Danny got to the barn," Rosie says, deep into her story, "he saw that it was so full of goat poop, he couldn't even get through the front door."

There are no boys around, so they giggle at the poop jokes.

Logan twists the tall grass blades between her fingers. When they break, they bleed green over her skin and smell rich and fresh and earthy. She turns to Milly and whispers, "Do you think he's mad at me?"

"Why don't you ask him?"

"I can't ask him. That's weird."

Milly tugs a clover up from the ground, roots and all, carefully counts its leaves and runs it across her lips. "So, let's pick the same activity as him today," she decides thoughtfully. "I'll ask him."

Logan rolls her eyes, turning her attention back to Rosie's story. For someone who constantly makes fun of drama, Milly loves to start it. Still, it isn't a bad idea. She needs to get another look at Max, at least, to figure out his funny stare. To find out if he blames her for his accident or not.

During afternoon announcements, they glance sideways down their bench toward where the Hawks sit. Max raises his hand to sign up for air rifles. Milly nudges Logan; they shrug and copy him. Only one other camper signs up for the activity: Hugo Baker himself. He sits directly behind Logan on the benches so his kneecaps touch her shoulders. After they're chosen, he tugs on the tip of her braid.

"See you there, horse girl," he says. The rest of the Ravens eye her ecstatically, and Logan feels her face go up in flames.

The four of them get to the air rifle range before the counselor. They sit on dusty blue mats inside the shed, facing downrange toward their paper targets. When Jeremy gets there, he takes the guns out of the rusty locker and shows them how to load, aim, and fire. Then he sits back in the shade and dozes as they shoot. He doesn't even make them wear the safety glasses. Every trigger pull makes a *pop* that tenses Logan's shoulders. She can't make the BBs from her gun fly straight. Max lies at a crooked angle to keep the weight off his cast arm while Hugo gives him instructions in a patient voice—not exactly like a friend, Logan thinks, but like a big brother.

Milly likes Jeremy. At least, that's what she says—everyone has to pick someone. She flops around on her shooting mat and pesters him with questions.

"Hey, Jeremy. Can you kill a person with an air rifle?"

"If you try hard enough."

"What about a bear?" Milly sits upright, her back to the range. "Hey, is it true there's a bear? Liz said that Kyle told Lilah there's a bear. It's been breaking into Camp and going through the trash."

"There's no bear," says Jeremy dully. He has his eyes closed, his head tilted back against the shed wall. Then he opens one eye, sneakily, and looks at her. "At least, no one knows it's a bear for sure."

"What's that mean?"

"Well, I don't want to scare you guys. But there's always been *something* out there. Might be a bear. Might not. Why do you think we always tell you to stay on the trails?"

Hugo is still focused down the barrel of his air rifle. "I'll shoot a bear right in the face!" he shouts. He mocks firing away at an invisible enemy downrange. "*Pew, pew, pew.*" Max laughs at him. Milly shakes her head. Logan sits up on her mat and watches the counselor, her attention caught.

"What do you mean there's *always* been something?" Milly presses on. "Since when is always?"

"Since always." Jeremy shrugs. "Don't you guys know that story? About that kid . . . the kid that was a camper here?"

"You mean, Danny McGee?" Logan asks.

"Uh-huh, you bet." The counselor nods away. "That's the one. You know how that story really ends, right? He disappeared one night, and all they ever found of him was a pair of bloody shoes in the water under the dam."

Logan hears the breath catch in Milly's nose. Even Hugo puts down his gun to pay attention. Before Jeremy can tell any more of the story, there is a tap at the shed door. He tells them to hold off on shooting and steps outside, the door hinges creaking violently behind him. They can hear muted voices from the other side of the plywood walls. Laughter.

"Germ's full of shit. Don't listen to him," Hugo says lightly, to the girls. He rolls onto his stomach to peer through the scope of his gun again.

Logan twitches the casual swear. He sounds very grown-up. "What if there *is* a bear, though?"

"I told you, I'd shoot a bear right in the face." He grins sideways at her, his head at a tilt on the butt of the gun. Then he reaches out with one arm to poke Milly in the kneecap. "Right, Miley?"

"*Milly*. My name's Milly, short for Millipede."

Logan looks down the line of mats at Max, who sits cross-legged, chewing thoughtfully on his lip. He hitches the strap of his sling up higher on his shoulder. Then he stares hard at her, with that funny look, and she desperately wants to look away, again, from his bruised face. "Logan." He glances toward the closed shed door. "I have to tell you something."

"Okay?"

Hugo and Milly look toward him too, curious. Max frowns. With his good hand, he scratches nervously around the top of his cast. "It's about Spark."

"Spark?"

"Yeah, the horse."

"What about her?"

"Well, I . . . I don't know for sure, but . . ." Max launches into a stuttering story. It's hard to follow. He says he was in a hospital, and then in the infirmary. He was awake in bed and heard voices out the window. Mr. Campbell, he thinks, and somebody else. "I felt like I was dreaming," he says. "You know, because of all the medicine. But I heard someone asking about the horse, and then someone else said back . . . well, I *think* they said—"

"Come on, man!" Milly rushes him, bouncing impatiently on her mat.

Max grunts and fidgets with his sling again. "He said, 'She'll be gone by next week.' Then he said, 'I'll have Dane dig a hole.'" His brown eyes are drilling into Logan, sharp through their frames of puffy bruise. "I just wanted to tell you. I know you really liked her."

"A hole?" Logan repeats, struggling to understand. Then, all at once, she does. A hole. A hole is a grave, for a horse—it's exactly what she was afraid of. Her heart swells. She jumps to her feet in a rush, still clutching her air rifle in one hand. "Next week is now!"

The door hinges shriek again, and Jeremy steps back into the shed. He is still smiling at whatever the person outside said to him and doesn't seem to care that Logan is standing, gun in hand, like she is about to charge out the door to take on the world. She forces herself defeatedly back onto her mat.

The rest of the activity period passes quietly. Milly and Hugo get into an argument about bears, but Logan is too distracted to pay attention to it, fiddling with her air rifle and thinking about what Max said. They leave the shed before dinner with their paper targets full of holes. Logan feels like she has been shot full of holes herself. "Poor Spark," she moans as soon as the counselor is far enough behind them on the trail. "How *could* they?"

Milly stops walking suddenly. Hugo, busy examining his target, runs straight into her back. He grunts, and for a moment they both look like they might start shouting, until Milly says, "Wait."

"What?" Logan jogs a few strides back up the trail to her. Max stops, too, and they all lean in to hear her. Whatever she has to say, judging by the look on her face, must be important.

Milly gives Max a steady look. "You don't think they did it already, do you?"

Max shrugs.

Logan turns to find Hugo's face alarmingly close. His cheeks are flushed, his teeth gritted. He stares at Milly, but not like he wants to shout at her anymore. "I know what you're thinking," he whispers. To Logan's surprise, they smile mischievously at each other.

"We could save her," says Milly.

Logan pushes her glasses into place on her nose. She feels a long arm wrap over her shoulders, pulling her in toward them. The four of them huddle together on the trail. In excited whispers, they begin to craft their plan.

Sam

FREE PERIODS AT CAMP ARE few and far between. Today, for the first time all summer, Sam, Rosie, and Elias have the afternoon off together. They take Sam's car down to Lobster Point to smoke a joint and gossip. Elias drank away his better judgment last night and wound up fooling around with Sadie on the lifeguard dock; to the girls' amusement, he is frantically trying to recall the details.

On their way back from the parking lot, deep in frenzied conversation, Rosie nearly steps in something mountainous.

"Is that a . . . turd?" They gather around it in wonder.

"That's a bear turd," Elias gasps. He crouches in the center of the trail to investigate.

Rosie stoops beside him. "Could be," she says. "Or, we need to be seriously worried about someone here."

Sam laughs out loud at the two of them. Squatting in the dirt like that, focused and prodding at the mound with twigs, they could be lost campers.

For the rest of the day, a quiet debate races through the undertow. The bear exists, that much is clear—the question is whether or not they should be afraid of it. Some people argue that a single, snack-sized camper alone on the trails after campfire could conceivably be snatched. Some—Dane, namely— have cameras and traps in mind. The fact that no one has actually seen the bear, that it lurks somewhere in the trees, haunting them, makes it all that much scarier. In their overworked imaginations, it could be a monster, a killer.

Sam is too preoccupied to worry much about it. Her attention wears thin. Every day with the Hummingbirds presents a new challenge.

The next morning, after breakfast, she is brushing her teeth in the bathroom when she hears a crash and clamor. Racing back inside, she finds the Hummingbirds' cabin has exploded into pandemonium. Poppy Warbler stands in the center of the room, bawling. She looks like she has just crawled out of a train wreck. The laces of her left shoe are untied, her right shoe is missing entirely, and her face has reddened to a deep, purplish plum color as she screams. Within her wailing mouth, her one front tooth is hazardously loose and rimmed with blood. She holds two halves of a broken, sloppy ceramic bowl in her clenched fists.

"I'm sorry, Poppy!" Rachel is crying, too. Other girls run for cover as the tantrum escalates. Daria crouches on the floor with her hands over her ears. They know what to do—this is hardly the first time.

"You . . . did . . . it . . . on . . . *purpose!*" Poppy shrieks, each word a desperate gasp between the sobs.

"No, I didn't! I didn't!"

If Rachel gets too upset, she will wet herself like an overexcited puppy. Sam rushes to her first. Then she turns to Poppy. Her purple shade is darkening, and her ponytail has broken loose in wild, nearly transparent blond sprigs. Tears splatter down the front of her T-shirt, smearing the grease marks from breakfast.

"Poppy. *Poppy.*" Sam reaches out to touch her, but she flinches away. She lifts one arm and throws the ceramic piece onto the cabin floor. She is strong for a six-year-old. The bowl shatters into dusty shards. The other girls squeal.

Something in Sam snaps. She feels it *crack* like a dry twig inside her, and her arm hitches back. She is going to hit her. Instead, she brings her hand down hard and knocks the other piece of clay out of Poppy's grip. It crashes to the floor, and Poppy hardly notices. Snot bubbles burst from her nose and lips. She lifts her empty hands to her face and claws at her own cheeks as she screams, her fingers drawing hard white lines in the red of her skin.

"Stop. Poppy, stop. Hey!" Sam tries to get ahold of her wrists. Poppy wails and scratches. This isn't about the bowl anymore. This is just chaos, flailing desperation for the sake of flailing desperation.

In a rush, Sam reaches out and wraps the entire writhing little body in her arms. She lifts Poppy and carries her, grunting, across the cabin and out to the bathroom, stomps past the toilets, and deposits her on the damp concrete beneath a showerhead, closing the curtain with a rattle behind them. "Look at me. Poppy, look. Calm down, or I'm going to turn the water on."

Poppy shrieks and stomps Sam's toes. Sam closes her eyes and turns the knob. The water hits them both. Poppy gasps. Sam kneels and lets the freezing stream run over them. She clutches her shoulders and shakes her, on the verge of tears herself. "Are you done?"

Drenched and flushed, Poppy sputters. She blinks, as if only now realizing where she is. Three pink claw lines are etched into the skin of her cheek. She looks at Sam, wavering, deliberating, and then she laughs.

Sam's hair is still wet when she gets to the office later in the morning. She has one chore today: to call a man named Russell Eckart of the Gray Mountain Stables, and she is dreading it. She hates the archaic, curly-corded phone receiver and the faceless voices on the other end. When Dane bursts through the screen door to announce he is tracking bear prints behind the mess hall, she leaps up to join him.

Poppy's tantrum haunts her for the rest of the day, through lifeguarding in the afternoon and evening soccer on the lawn. The scratch marks fade from her cheeks, but Sam can still picture them, red and swollen in the cold shower spray. She almost hit her. With just a shred less clarity, she would have done it. She watches Poppy laugh and smack her food through dinner and feels her skin crawl with guilt. Where is the line drawn? At what point is this person, who looks like a child, who laughs like a child, who screams like a child, not a child? If she had hit her, what would that make the both of them?

Sam is not the only one struggling. She can see it in Elias's eyes. His fingers, like hers, are peeled and scabbed around the nails. He twitches his foot and picks at loose threads. He snaps easily. It's Hugo Baker, Sam knows. The Falcon, charming and popular during the day, apparently suffers from night terrors. He wakes up screaming, shrieking, like Poppy. Sometimes it takes an hour and multiple counselors to settle him down. Some nights he will get out of bed and wander, half awake, onto their porch or to another boy's bunk, mumbling incoherently. The behavior would be spooky in any camper—but Hugo Baker is not just any camper, as much as they might try to forget it. Rumor has it that in the throes of one of his fits a few nights ago, the words *I didn't do it* escaped him. That thought alone is a deeper, much more terrifying mystery than any animal or monster in the forest.

Sam hears most of this from Taps, who has the cabin next door. Elias never talks about it. She worries about him. He isn't exactly cold and practical, like his brother; he feels things, he reacts to changes in the air around him. He—like her—is fully capable of complete, blown-out collapse if pushed far enough. Sam has started to wonder which of the two of them might reach that point first.

When she finally gets the Hummingbirds into bed after campfire, she is exhausted. She already has the plot of another silly story in mind and is getting ready to tell it, hoping to make it quick, when Deb squeaks up from her sleeping bag. "Sam?"

"Yeah?"

A wide pair of eyes watches her through the top slats of the bunk, a flop of dirty hair. Her voice trembles. "Did Danny McGee get eaten by a bear?"

It takes longer than usual to turn out the lights. Sam leaves the cabin livid. She huffs, with anger and lack of breath, as she and Rosie climb up through the Nest doorway. "Which one of you assholes killed Danny McGee?" she asks, scrambling to her feet.

Jeremy lies sprawled on a sofa, his knuckles dragging across the rug below him. He flashes her a grin and a limp peace sign.

"Of course." Sam groans. "Dammit, Germ, that was my story. I just spent half an hour trying to get my girls to bed. They're all freaked out because someone told them Danny got eaten by a bear."

"A *bear*?" Katie, prim and proud under Dane's heavy arm, reaches out to smack him across the back of the head. "What is wrong with you?"

Jeremy ducks forward on the cushions, away from her reach. "Who said 'bear'? I never said it was a bear."

"Well, someone did. Stop stealing my story."

"Oh, that story's public property now," says Kyle from the back of the room. "My kids think he fell off the dam."

"Sorry, Sam. Everybody loves a dead camper." Jeremy shrugs.

"He's right," Dane agrees solemnly. "There's one every summer. Dead campers keep them on the trails."

Jeremy hooks his pinky finger around the handle of the plastic vodka jug on the floor. He lifts it daintily to Rosie, who passes it to Sam with a consoling pat between her shoulders. "RIP, Danny McGee," she sighs.

•••

THE GUEST CABIN IS TUCKED into the edge of the forest behind the infirmary. It was built for potential overnight visitors who never come—nobody ever comes to Camp Phoenix, after all, unless they come through a consciousness transfer—and is full of broken mess hall benches and craft supplies, dusty futons, and a locker stacked with odd relics from years past. The assistant directors have keys to the locked front door. From time to time, they break in to drink without the younger staff around.

Tonight, Nick quietly invites Elias, who brings along Sam and Rosie. It's a little shamefully exciting for the three of them, underclassmen breaking rank. The cabin is warmer and brighter than the Nest. They play a few card games and beer pong across a folding plastic table, and as curfew approaches, the room spins around Sam's head. She sits on the floor, leaning back against Rosie's knees. Katie and Dane have locked themselves into the back room of the cabin to fight about something. Tearful shouts and grunts seep through the wall, ignored by the rest of them.

At the border of Sam's attention, Amy lectures Elias. "Listen to me!" She brandishes her beer bottle haphazardly in his face. "You can't just ignore her. Don't be a dick about it."

A tired stereo on the windowsill cuts in and out, streaming the only radio station that reaches them through the mountains: a greasy old rock channel that cycles through the same ten or fifteen staticky songs on repeat. The music is comforting. Sam sways along to it and listens to the conversation bubbling around her. A violent boredom has overcome her; she mulls over an urge to do something reckless, something stupid.

Elias, his cheeks flushed bright red, lies back on the cabin floor with his hands in his hair. "What am I supposed to say?" he whines. "I can't just tell her I don't like her. That'll break her heart."

"That's a cop-out, and you know it," says Rosie. "You're being such a man right now. Just talk to her." *Man*, the way she says it, is a slur. Sam giggles.

Elias lifts his head to glare at her. "Smells like goddamn hypocrisy in here. Like you *talk*. What'd I catch you and Germ doing in the game room the other night, again?"

Rosie smirks, winding the tip of Sam's ponytail around her fingers. "Talking."

Nick sits across the room from Sam on the edge of a futon. She looks up to see him focused on the beer bottle in his hands, determinedly, deliberately peeling away the label one shred at a time. Sam watches him and thinks about reckless and stupid urges. She thinks about Elias and Sadie on the lifeguard dock. They were out past curfew. They could have been caught. She thinks about Richard Byron and his rumored self-medication, his laughing eyes. How much does he know about their free time? Would he fire them, just for breaking curfew? Or does it take something more serious—does a camper need to be hurt for someone to get fired, like Phoebe?

At the thought of Phoebe and the accident, a cold pressure clamps over Sam's chest. She brings her hands to her hair, like Elias. "Horse!" she shouts suddenly, making Rosie jump. "Nick, the horse!"

He looks up at her. "What?"

"I didn't call the guy, the horse guy!"

Russell Eckart of the Gray Mountain Stables. He can take back his horse tomorrow, and only tomorrow; otherwise, they will have to get rid of her any other way. Sam's only chore in the morning was to call him back. She forgot to do it.

She slaps her palms to the sides of her face and peers through her fingers at Nick, pleading. "Can we . . . ?"

"It's one a.m., Sam."

"We can leave him a message, can't we? Please? In the morning it'll be too late." She hears her voice break.

"Worth a shot, Nicky." Gabe frowns. They speak over Sam's head, like she's a hopeless camper. "Gus is pissed it's taking this long already. And you know how bad Dane wants to dig a hole." He glances toward the back room of the cabin, where the shouts have fallen suddenly, questionably silent.

Nick nods, scratching away the last shred of his label. "All right." He shrugs at Sam. "Come on."

They lace up their shoes and zip into their jackets. The rest of the group is crumbling, singing along to the song on the radio as they leave. Cold, brisk air smacks them at the doorway. Sam stumbles on the first step coming down from the guest cabin porch, and Nick catches her by the arm. The walk to the office is long and silent. When Sam looks up, the stars between the branches are wilting, drifting into one another. She drifts, too.

The porch steps creak and the screen door squeals in protest. Inside, the hum and glow of sleeping computer monitors is unsettling. Nick flicks on the desk lamp, flooding the room with a weak orange glow.

"Do you have his number?"

"What?" Sam squints at him. The skin on his nose is peeling with sunburn, shredding away like the label of his beer. "Oh, yeah. It's on a sticky note. On the desk."

She leans back against the surface of Campbell's desk as he rummages around her. At the dull dial tone, she blinks and sees him holding out the receiver to her, his expression as flat as ever. Sam shakes her head. Her tongue is suddenly thick and sticky in her mouth. Nick shrugs.

His voice, speaking into the phone, is spectacularly composed. It sounds unreal in the dim, empty office, like someone has turned on a radio in another room. "Hi, Russell, this is Nick Borowitz, from Camp Phoenix." He carries on.

Sam watches him. A nasty internal voice gnaws at the back of her mind. This is it, it tells her. Three weeks into the summer, and this is where she breaks. Missing phone calls, burying horses, slapping campers. Her throat clenches. The room spins. She feels sick.

". . . And if you're still willing, our director wanted to let you know we'd be able to meet you halfway." Nick looks up at her as he talks, fixated, then alarmed. Sam realizes there are hot tears on her cheeks. Mortified, she turns her face toward the ceiling and swallows hard. "Again, sorry to call you at this time. Hope we'll hear back from you in the morning."

She hears a click, a heavy breath, then a resounding, devastating silence.

Sam shakes her head, feeling the tears roll faster. She can't stop them. She desperately wants to explain, but when she manages to wedge her mouth open, what she says is: "We should probably go back soon, or everyone will think we're hooking up."

In the pause that follows, the sob in her throat breaks free as a hiccup. They look at each other.

"Okay. Here." Blank-faced, Nick digs into the neck of his sweatshirt and drags out his looped keychain. Sam thinks he is going to take it off and offer it to her. Instead, he swivels the clanking keys around to the back of his neck. He lifts a hand. "Look. Like this." He brings his palm down hard against his chest. *Thump.* Then again. *Thump.* The sound is firm, satisfying.

Sam mirrors him, raising her right hand. *Thump.* She smacks herself just below the collarbones. "Why?"

"Feels good. Doesn't it?"

It does. She repeats the motion. *Thump. Thump. Thump.* Each beat resonates, shaking something loose inside her chest. Flaky rust and mold, chunking apart, rattling clean. Like Poppy scratching her own face, there is method to this. Purpose. They stand together, a foot or so of dim orange space between them, and hit themselves in the chest. Their hands fall just out of pace with each other. *Thu-thump. Thu-thump. Thu-thump.* "I can't do this," she says out loud.

"What?"

"All of it. Poppy. The horse. I shouldn't be in charge of any of this. I can't stop screwing it all up."

Nick's hand slows for a moment to a gentle drum. He clears his throat, then picks up the beat again. "I'm going to tell you something."

"Okay?"

"It wasn't always college kids," he begins slowly. "When Camp opened, those first couple summers, they hired psychologists and teachers to be the counselors. Professionals. And it didn't work."

Sam taps steadily against her chest. "What do you mean?"

"The campers didn't like it. They knew something was up—some of them started remembering their consciousness transfers, and that can be really bad. So, Chard started hiring younger counselors. He brought in college kids, let them really get into it, mess around and drink and stuff, and *then* it felt like the real thing. A real camp."

"Oh." Sam watches the tears plop and spread on the front of her jacket. *Thu-thump. Thu-thump. Thu-thump.* "I didn't know that."

"Yeah, no one does. Hey." He bobs his head, urging her to look up at him. Sam meets his eyes and finds them entirely honest. "It's all a part of it. Accidents. Bears. Kids throwing tantrums and getting hurt. That stuff's supposed to happen. We're supposed to be screwing up. Otherwise, it wouldn't be real."

Thu-thump. Thu-thump. Thu-thump.

"Don't tell anyone I told you that, all right?" Nick says. Then he smiles, quick and uncomfortable. "And I don't think anyone thinks we're hooking up. If that's what you're worried about."

"Okay." *Thu-thump. Thu-thump. Thu-thump.*

After some time, dizzy and embarrassed, Sam pushes herself off the desk and leaves the office.

She is awake before the alarm in her watch goes off the next morning. In the bunk beside her, Poppy's dewy, pink face comes slowly into focus. Her lips are parted in a perfect *O*, her body curled to half its size in the sleeping bag.

Bleary-eyed, head pounding, Sam leaves the cabin and stumbles to the mess hall for coffee. The taste makes her gag, but the warmth of the mug in her hands grounds her. She shuffles along through the gray morning mist to the gold-panning claim, where she rests her mug on the bank and kneels to splash her face with cold water. A rustle in the bushes makes her pause and look up. It takes a few seconds to realize what she is looking at. When she does, she inhales sharply, falls back into the creek bed, and topples her scalding coffee with a flailing arm.

The bear sits upright on its hind legs, half hidden in the brush. It watches her. Sam crouches, frozen in astonishment. It sits at about her height, chocolate brown, with a light nose and chest patch. Two button ears twitch curiously. The bear doesn't appear frightened by her, but maybe mildly irritated, as if willing her to go away and leave it to go about its business.

Sam looks at the bear and the bear looks back at Sam. Time pauses indefinitely. The birds chirp and the mist rises from the trickling creek between them. Cool water drips from her cheeks and chin. Eventually, it drops to its front legs and walks off through the bushes. Sam sits in the mud for some time, wishing it would come back, wondering if it was real. As the shock wears away, she smiles.

Logan

THEY AGREE TO DO IT in the morning, before breakfast. Logan knows the horses' feeding schedule. They are let out to graze before the wake-up bell—this way, it will be almost two hours before any adults come down to the stables, giving Spark plenty of time to escape.

When the bell rings, Logan and Milly slip out the cabin door with their sweatshirt hoods pulled over their heads. They dart away in the opposite direction of the lawn and sprint until they are alone on the trails. It's a cool, misty morning. Their breath comes out in puffy clouds. Milly holds her fingers to her lips and blows upward, pretending she's smoking a cigarette. The way the sun shines through the mist makes it look like the air around them is shimmering.

The boys meet them on the trail to the barnyard. Max is wearing his sling. Hugo grins from ear to ear like they are setting off on a grand adventure. The two of them look funny standing next to each other, one dark and broken and the other pale and loping and smiling.

"Are you sure you want to come?" Logan asks Max. He has to be scared of the horses now, she thinks.

He nods. His hair is pasted to his forehead, still damp from a morning shower—such a strange, serious boy. The four of them hurry down the trail. At the base of the hill, they pause. A little red truck is parked in front of the barnyard gate. Logan hears adult voices.

"Crap," Hugo hisses. "I thought you said they already fed them?"

"I thought they did." They creep forward until they can see two people in dark blue T-shirts approaching the truck from inside the yard. Logan feels Hugo's hand on the back of her hoodie; he pulls them all backward, off the trail. They flop down behind an old log—Max with some difficulty. The wood is dry and crumbly with termites. Four hooded heads, four pairs of eyes, peek over the top of the log and wait, listening. Prickly pine needles stab into Logan's belly.

The two maintenance workers reach the gate and latch it shut behind them. One of them tosses a heavy-looking tool bag into the back of the truck, laughing at something the other said.

"Don't know what they think they're gonna do about it." Logan can make out the words.

"The messed-up thing is," the other man says, climbing into the passenger's seat of the truck, "*that's* what's got them all spooked. An animal. As if they don't have Hugo goddamn Baker running around the place."

Logan feels Hugo's body tense against her side. She glances at Milly, who frowns and shrugs in return. The men laugh, then the truck engine grumbles over the rest of their conversation. With a crunch of tires on gravel, the workers drive away.

"Okay, let's go."

They get up, cross the trail cautiously, and let themselves in through the gate. Then they hurry across the muddy barnyard to the stables. The horses are out, unbridled, grazing from piles of hay. There is Spark, with her perfectly speckled coat, lovely and unbothered. Logan sighs at the sight of her. A sudden, bright vision flashes through her heart: she should climb up on the horse, bareback, hug her neck, and gallop off into the misty morning. Leave Camp and life and everything else behind. They could live in the mountains.

"You all heard that too, right?" Hugo asks as they cross the stables. Max veers wide around each grazing horse they pass. "You heard them say *my* name?"

Milly shakes her head. "Yeah, but it didn't make any sense. Must've been a different Hugo Baker."

"I don't know any other Hugo Bakers," says Hugo proudly. "I swear. They were talking about me."

"Why would they be talking about you? I mean, who do you think *you* are?" Milly walks along next to him, leading the group. A little tug of jealousy makes Logan jog to catch up.

They reach Spark and stand around her in a horseshoe shape. She goes on eating. Logan bites her lip and looks the mare up and down—she didn't think about how they are supposed to move her out of the yard.

Hugo reaches out a hand to Spark. He touches her neck; she flicks her ears and huffs at him. "Hugo *goddamn* Baker, that's who," he answers Milly in a whisper.

After some deliberation, they decide to pick up Spark's meal and coax her to follow them. Hugo scoops up as much of the hay as he can in his long arms and Milly and Logan gather the rest. Max trails nervously behind, adjusting the strap of his sling on his shoulder. Now Spark notices them. She sniffs at the hay dust on the ground and shakes her head, irritated.

"Come on, girl. This way."

"C'mon, horsey."

They make slow, backwards progress across the stables and barnyard. Spark walks behind with her neck outstretched toward them. Hugo giggles when her lips reach his arms, prying for the hay. "She wants to kiss me," he laughs. "Don't you, horsey?"

They make it through the gate. Spark doesn't seem to think much of it; she goes on happily grazing at the pile of hay where they drop it, just outside the fence. Logan latches the gate. They all look at each other unsurely.

"Is that it?" Milly asks.

Logan nods. "She'll leave as soon as she finishes eating. I know she will." She thinks again about climbing onto Spark's back and galloping away. It would be impossible, she decides, so she stays right where she is standing on the trail. She swipes at a stray strand of hair and nudges her glasses into place.

Her last look at Spark will stay with her, she is sure, for the rest of forever. She sees the horse lift her head from the hay to take in her surroundings. Max stands in front of her. He reaches out toward her with his one good arm, shaky fingers open, waiting. Spark meets the hand and lets him pat her on the nose. The boy and the horse stand like that for a moment or two as the rest of them look on and the sunny mist evaporates around them, the chickens chatter and the goats bray and the birds chirp in the trees. Max mutters something to Spark, too quiet to hear.

"Max, let's go! It's almost breakfast."

They take off running, back up the hill, past the girls' cabins, and onto the main lawn. Just in time, they file into line at the base of the mess hall steps. No one seems to notice them. The four horse liberators exchange a serious nod, fingers to lips, before they melt into the crowd.

Logan looks over her shoulder in the line. Hugo is busy talking to his friends, his cheeks still pink from their sprint. *Hugo goddamn Baker.* There must be another Hugo Baker somewhere in the world, she decides. His name does ring a faint bell in her head, like something she heard somewhere else, before Camp, before the whispers and gossip.

Then again, it's hard to remember much outside of Camp.

"Ow!"

She has stepped on someone's toes. Logan looks up to see Sam, the Hummingbirds' counselor, holding a little blond girl's hand. She looks angry. "Watch where you're walking," she snaps. As they walk up the steps, the Hummingbird turns around to stick out her tongue at Logan.

Logan and Milly both make faces back. They laugh at each other, and Logan swells with pride. Everyone else at Camp is pretending to be grown-ups, but not them. They know better. It isn't actually so horrible here, she thinks. It might not be so bad to stay at Camp forever and never have to grow up.

week five

Sam

"Oh, perfect. Why don't you take Red with you?"

Sam looks up, blinking, halfway through the office door. Campbell is staring expectantly at her over the frames of his glasses.

"What?"

"The guy called back," Nick explains, addressing her sandals. He leans against the other desk with the truck keys in his hand. "The horse guy. He's on his way, but we have to meet him halfway."

"Halfway?" Sam repeats. They are in the middle of nowhere—halfway between nowhere and anywhere is still nowhere. "Where's halfway?"

"Sardine Flat, I believe he said." Campbell waves a floating hand between the two of them, distracted by his screen. "You two go together. It'll be a good learning experience for you, Sam."

As they step out onto the office porch, Sam feels the dismay roll off of her in waves. She isn't sure what to say to him. Whatever they shared in the dark of the office last night, if not exactly intimate, has her mortified. She wishes she had thrown up, fallen, tried to kiss him—anything would be less humiliating than what it was: a teary, clichéd confession of inadequacy. They start toward the stables in silence.

Oddly enough, they find the speckled mare standing just outside the barnyard fence, on the trail. She swishes her tail and stares despondently back toward her companions in the stables.

"Weird." Nick frowns. "That's the one, isn't it?"

Sam shrugs. "Yeah. Maybe maintenance let her out."

"Maybe."

They speak flatly and get to work. Sam fetches the horse's halter and lead rope while Nick hitches the trailer to the Camp pickup. She looks at the truck uneasily. Rust-red and iconic, older than God; she can't imagine their odds of breaking down in the mountains are all that low.

The horse cooperates reasonably enough, aside from a few playful head bumps as Sam struggles to fasten the halter. Once loaded, they both get in the truck and begin the drive without a word. Sam lets her forehead fall to the cool glass of the window. The bumpy dirt road shakes the entire frame of the truck, rattles her brain and chatters her teeth. They wind uphill, over the bridge, and pull off at the single-pump Smith's Ridge gas station. Nick gets out. When he comes back, Sam is slowly, thoughtlessly beating her head against the window. She looks up to see him offering her a can of ginger ale.

"Oh. Yeah, thanks."

They leave Smith's Ridge and weave through the forest, their faces blinking in the flashing shadows of trees. Stiff, staccato conversations about Camp and campers pepper the silence.

"I had Poppy Warbler in evening music group yesterday," Nick says.

"Oh, yeah?"

"Yeah. She's a fun kid."

"Fun's one way to put it."

"Yeah. Well, she can really sing, too."

No shit, Sam wants to say. She nods and sips at her ginger ale. "Yeah."

By the time they reach the Sardine Flat campgrounds, the day is clear and hot. They drive into a wide-open valley, dead brown grass like a rolling sea all around them. A little old truck not at all unlike their own is parked at the turnoff already. There, a withered man in a cowboy hat and work jeans waits for them, leaning idyllically against his tailgate with one boot propped up on the bumper.

Sam lets Nick do the talking. He shakes the cowboy's hand and exchanges some half-hearted pleasantries, thankful and apologetic like a proper diplomat. Russell Eckart is a caricature of a man, a sketched cowboy stereotype. He has a lip full of tobacco and spits fat smelly globs into the dirt as he talks. He didn't come with a trailer of his own, Sam notices. She wonders if he is going to ride the horse back to his stables.

"Yeah, we always knew she was trouble," he says, nasally, drawling. "Wouldn't have loaned her out to a kid's camp. Too dangerous." He spits and looks at Nick, his bristly lips curling. "But it's not kids you've got out there, anyway, is it?" When Nick doesn't answer, he turns his attention on Sam. She leans against the side of the trailer, looking over the dead valley through her sunglasses. "How 'bout it, freckles?" He smiles at her. "What's your name?"

Sam steps forward to hold out a reluctant hand. "I'm Sam."

"Sam?" Russell Eckart repeats, clasping her hand in both of his own. He looks her over invasively. The smell of chew and dirty sweat strikes her stomach, raising the sour taste of her hangover in the back of her throat. "You're too pretty to be a *Sam*."

"Well." Sam frees her hand from his grasp. "That's my name."

Behind the cowboy's back, Nick laughs silently. It's not the chauvinism he finds funny, Sam knows, but her disgust at it.

They open the doors of the trailer. The horse sniffs at the dry valley air as they lead her out. She eyes them sideways, smug, owning her title of trouble. Sam gives her a pat on the neck and hands her lead rope to her owner, who looks her over with a sort of dissatisfied finality, a look he might give the scraps of a meal he did not particularly enjoy. He hitches the horse to a signpost at the edge of the grass.

"You folks be careful with your campfires out there," Russell Eckart says to them as parting advice. "About to be fire season, you know. They're saying it'll be a bad one." He sniffs, spits. "That's what they're always saying." He opens a tool case mounted in the bed of his truck and begins rifling through it—for what, Sam can only guess.

Nick thanks him again and they latch up the trailer and clamber back into the Camp pickup in a hurry. Before he turns the key in the ignition, Nick hesitates, then sighs. He looks uncomfortable. Something has gone wrong, but Sam can't figure out what, exactly, until they have already pulled out of the campground and driven away. The gunshot makes them both jump.

It takes about an hour to get back to Camp. The air in the cab of the truck is hot and strained and smothering. A few attempts at dark jokes cross Sam's mind, each of them falling flat before they reach her lips. She reaches up to pat herself in the center of the chest, hoping it will make him smile, or at least breach the awkwardness. He doesn't notice.

They park beside the barnyard and sit in the silent cab, neither of them moving to unbuckle. The smell of horse lingers on their clothes. Nick shuts off the engine. Sam checks her watch; it's already well into lunchtime. Camp is empty and quiet.

He sighs again, leaning on his elbow against the window frame, then turns to say something to her. His mouth falls open, eyes focused, and he says, "There's a bug in your hair."

"What?"

"There's a—come here." He leans across the center console toward her. Sam stiffens. Her ponytail sits flopped over one shoulder; a tiny beetle is running up it toward her ear. Nick reaches carefully for it. "Wait, don't move . . ." He catches the bug up gingerly in his fingertips. Still leaning over the console, he squints into his hand. His face falls. "Shit."

"What?"

"I killed it." The speck drops dejectedly from his fingers, vanishing into the crevice below Sam's seat.

She still has her seat belt on. They pause and look at each other. She drifts, a little nudge of gravity, and then he is kissing her. This is perfectly reasonable, she thinks—this might as well happen, now. Nick is salty with sweat and coarse with stubble. One hand tightens above her knee.

After a moment, Sam pulls away. They hover. "Okay," she says, as if in agreement. To what, she isn't sure.

Nick nods, clears his throat. "Okay."

From the heart of Camp, the bell rings for lunch.

Logan

TIME IS MOVING FASTER.

In the fourth week of Camp, the Ravens are getting ready for their second campout. The trip will take them far away from Camp Phoenix, up a distant mountain to Pike Falls. The view is supposed to be incredible. The Eagles have already gone on their trip, and so have the Hawks and the Falcons. Only Max had to stay behind, because of his cast.

On their first campout, they went to a flat little campground just outside of Camp called Lobster Point. They roasted marshmallows over the fire and froze in their sleeping bags all night. Logan spent the whole time shivering, listening to the rush of the water falling over the dam nearby, and thinking about Danny McGee's bloody shoes. The Pike Falls trip, she hopes, will be more fun—more exciting, at least.

Time is moving faster, and she recognizes herself less and less as the days go by. She still spends most of her time with Milly, but slowly, she's starting to toe her way in with the other girls, too. Sometimes she sits cautiously at the edge of the group, on the announcement benches, and lets Liz braid her hair. Sometimes she speaks up into the darkness, at night in the cabin, when the infectious giggles and dirty jokes zing between their bunks.

Saying the right thing is hard. Everything Logan says is spoken with crossed fingers, praying it won't come out wrong. She has taken to biting her nails and lying awake at night after everyone else falls asleep. She plays out scenarios in her head, imagining what they might do if she said this, wore that. Sometimes it spirals out of control. Sometimes she imagines dramatic altercations: Donna will tell her she is *so weird* and then she will say something cutting, something mean, and then she will punch her right in the boob, and the whole cabin will cheer . . .

. . . and then, she thinks, Hugo Baker will be there. He will walk right up to her and put his arms around her. He will say that he never liked Donna, anyway, and then he will look at her like she's the only girl at Camp . . .

Logan's eyes fly open. The cabin is dark, and she has fallen half asleep.

The blackness around her is heavy with sleepy breathing; it must be late. She has been lost in her silly imagination for a long time. Her own thoughts are embarrassing. All the nighttime chatter and gossip is starting to do funny things to the fantasies in her head. She screws her eyes shut again, wishing for sleep, but sleep refuses to come. Instead, she keeps thinking about Hugo Baker. Then she thinks about Max, with his outstretched hand on Spark's nose, his battered face so quiet and calm. She remembers the panic in that same face when the horse took off running, the blood and the shock as he lay on the ground.

She wonders what it was like to hit that branch. To lose consciousness and flop to the dirt. He was gone, for a moment—she saw him with his eyes closed and his shoulders trembling. Then he came back. Where did he go, in between? Where did he come back from? The thought stretches on and on, until Logan's heart is racing. She can't stop wondering where Max went. Where he would still be, if he hadn't come back. Where she might—will—go someday.

Stop, stop, stop! Logan opens her eyes and forces her body upright. The bunk creaks beneath her. These are worse than the embarrassing thoughts about Hugo Baker, much worse. She rubs her eyes and longs for daylight. Dizzy and sick, she climbs down from her top bunk and tiptoes to the bathroom.

Outside, under the flickering light bulb, Logan stares into her reflection in the mirror above the sink. Messy hair, oily face. She looks strange without her glasses. She feels strange. Off, wrong. Like this is a dream. It's a cold, horrible feeling, a greasy black weight in the pit of her stomach. A fat, fluttering bug rams itself into the light bulb over her head again and again. The sound is like a rattling drum. Logan shuts off the light and walks back into the cabin. She is standing still in the dark, at the foot of her bunk, when a sharp whisper cuts straight through to her heart and makes it skip a beat.

"*Logan?*"

It's Milly, hardly a shadow inside her sleeping bag. Logan's mouth is full of dirt and worms. She can't say anything back.

"What are you doing? Are you okay?"

She swallows, finally. "I don't know."

"Are you sick?" The sleeping bag rustles. Milly's shadowy shape sits upright. "I don't know."

A long pause stretches. "Are you scared?" Milly asks, her voice thick and heavy with sleep. "You want to sit down?"

Logan nods and shuffles toward her in the dark. She sits at the edge of the crinkly mattress and Milly shifts her legs to sit beside her. They stay like that, side by side, for a long time. Logan's breaths come out shaky. Her leg is twitching. The bad thoughts are gone, now, but the feeling still lingers, clinging to her like plastic wrap, tight around her chest. "I think I'm going to throw up," she whispers.

"Really?"

"No. I don't know."

Milly's head falls against her shoulder. Her hair is scratchy, tickly on her cheek. A warm, skinny arm wraps around hers. Normally, Milly doesn't like to be touched. This is a little like the conversations they have when Sadie leaves the cabin: something that would never happen in daylight but feels perfectly fine in the dark. Logan leans into her. They listen to the other girls breathing, the crickets chirping outside. The cabin smells like dirt and sunscreen, like daytime. *Remember the sunshine bright,* Logan sings in her head. Her leg quits shaking. Her heart slows.

"It's okay," says Milly. "Sometimes I get scared at night, too."

"Don't tell anyone, okay?"

"Okay."

"Okay." They sit together for a while longer, then Logan stands and climbs back into her own bed. The awful feeling eventually passes, and she falls asleep.

In the morning, everything is normal. The weird, suffocating sensation is gone, and the day is bright and happy. It's Tuesday. Tomorrow, they will pack up their hiking packs and head out to Pike Falls.

The Ravens go to the lake in morning activity period with the Hawks and the Falcons and Eagles. Milly runs off to hunt for snakes in the reeds. Logan sits on the shore in her white cotton shorts and tank top, sweating beneath the sweltering sun. A circle of boys and girls has gathered on the beach around her. They didn't invite her into the group, exactly, but she didn't force her way in, either—she holds her breath and hopes she blends right in, unnoticed.

"Elias," Liz says, and the rest of the group nods seriously.

"Definitely Elias," Donna agrees. She sits between Hugo Baker's spread knees, leaning back against his chest. They're going out. He is the most popular boy in Camp, and she is the most popular girl—it only makes sense. Since they freed Spark last week, Hugo sometimes shoots Logan a cheeky smile across the mess hall or lawn. His smiles feel sneaky, secretive. She pockets each one for careful consideration later.

Donna knows the way she is sitting with him is scandalous, and she is flaunting it. She smiles up at him, then looks right at Logan. "What about you, Logan?"

"Huh?"

"Who do you think is the cutest counselor?"

"Oh." Logan considers. "I like Christian." As soon as the words have left her mouth, she knows she has said the wrong thing.

"You mean Taps? Oh my God, Logan, you *would*."

Hugo looks bored with the conversation. He raises his head over the top of Donna's and shouts to his friend on the dock: "Henry, do a flip!"

Henry flashes him a thumbs-up, sprints, leaps, and tumbles into the water. As soon as he resurfaces, the lifeguard yells at him. Logan looks longingly toward the waves his splash made. She wants to get in the lake, but she isn't wearing her swimsuit. She told Sadie she couldn't find it. The truth is the idea of wearing nothing but a swimsuit in front of everyone, Donna and Hugo and all the rest, makes her stomach hurt. She would rather sweat and suffer on the beach in her clothes. Uncomfortable on the hot sand, she shifts so she sits cross-legged and leans back on her palms.

Everyone in their circle has fallen silent. Logan realizes, with horror, that they are all looking at her. "What?"

No one says anything. Donna smirks and leans her head up to whisper something into Hugo's ear. Logan cannot stand to look at them a second longer, sitting like that, pretending to be grown-ups. "What?" she demands again, louder.

Someone tugs her upward by the arm. It's Max; like her, he is wearing a shirt and sweating. He leads her away along the beach. Behind them, everyone is giggling.

"Come here," Max pleads. "I want to tell you something."

"What is it?" Logan snaps. She pulls her arm away from him. Max wasn't sitting with the group, but awkwardly off to the side, on his own. He has no right to be dragging her out of the circle.

He hesitates, rubbing the dirty fabric that juts out from his cast between his fingers. Then he leans forward and whispers, stammering, into her ear. Logan sways and looks back at him. "I just thought you should know," he says.

Aghast, she looks down. She spreads her legs and tugs the fabric of her shorts forward. Sure enough, there is a tiny, dark red splotch blooming at the white cotton seam. Fear is a cage that falls from the sky; she is trapped like a mouse in it. She begs Max to leave her alone, and he does, nervously. Her panicked eyes scan the lakeshore. Everyone on the beach is watching her—no one is laughing, but everyone is looking.

Time pauses like that for a long and dreadful moment, an eternity, until eventually a counselor notices her frozen in space. She whispers to two Eagles, who swoop in and bundle Logan under their arms. Voices are buzzing louder behind them as they hurry away from the beach. When they get to the infirmary, Logan stands pigeon-toed on the porch, mumbling. Nurse May looks her up and down, then nods. She shoos the Eagles away and ushers her inside.

The linoleum floor is chilly against her bare feet. The old nurse gives Logan a ginger ale to sip, claiming it will calm her nerves. It does not. Her throat is choked with threatening sobs. An air conditioner roars in the window, numbingly loud. Nurse May disappears into the back room of the infirmary and returns with a box of wet wipes, sanitary pads, an enormous, billowing pair of underwear, and gray sweatpants. As she talks, Logan wishes she could sink her head between her shoulders and disappear, like a turtle.

"Do you have any questions, hon?"

"No." She wants to scream.

"You sure?"

"No. I mean, yes. I'm sure."

She shuts herself into the bathroom to change. Despite the grueling list of facts she has just been presented with, she is still not entirely convinced this is something normal. The spot on her underwear doesn't look like blood at all—it's dark and gory, like her guts have fallen out. For all she or Nurse May knows, she might have burst some kind of internal organ. She could be dead by campfire. She could become another Camp legend like Danny McGee; they'll tell horror stories about the girl who popped her kidney and withered away because everyone thought it was just her period.

Logan realizes she would very much prefer this to be a case of a popped kidney instead of what it is. The sweatpants are too big for her. They hang to the bathroom floor, even when she rolls the waistband. She hates them. Shivering, she plops onto the toilet, takes off her glasses, and holds her face in her hands. She shouts into her palms: "Shit! Shit, shit, *shit!*"

•••

SHE HAS TO MISS THE campout. After dinner, Sadie pulls Logan to the counselors' benches beneath the bell tower. She tells her, gently, that she should stay behind and take the trip later in the summer.

"You know, there's a boy in the Hawks group that had to miss his Pike Falls trip because he got hurt," she says in her most sugary voice. "I talked to his counselor today, and we thought you two could go together. Just the two of you! That would be fun, huh?"

"I guess," Logan shrugs. She does not want to go on a trip with Max—especially not after the way he embarrassed her at the beach. In fact, nothing sounds less fun. "It's not really fair, though," she adds, hoping to sound spiteful.

Sadie hugs her. With a heavy hand, she smooths out her ponytail. "I know it doesn't seem fair, hon. But that's just part of being a girl. We have to make sacrifices."

Logan nods. She hates being called *hon*. For a hot flash of a second, she hates Sadie. She would like to hate everyone and everything. It would feel good, just to hate.

"Maybe the two of you will get along. Who knows?"

She nods again and crosses her legs, adjusting to the ugly weight of the pad between them. This isn't fair. She wants to go home. Even in her rage, though, she knows that home is too far away.

The rest of the Ravens leave for Pike Falls the next day, and Logan stays behind. Everyone knows why, but no one says it out loud. Milly gives her a long, sorry, and confused look as she shoulders her hiking pack. It's like they are standing on opposite sides of a high fence; Logan has suddenly crossed a line she didn't know existed.

She spends the night in the infirmary while her group is gone. Nurse May brings her candy and chapter books, and she gets to watch cartoons on a bubbly-faced TV. It's fun for a while—a weird change from the Camp life she has come to know. She sleeps in a big private room by herself.

In the middle of the night, Logan jerks awake and tosses aside the blankets. The bed is too big and too soft, and the infirmary is too quiet. She has gotten used to the snores and murmurs and farts of the cabin. She grabs her glasses from the nightstand and drops down to the cold linoleum floor. Three padding footsteps carry her to the window. She leans on her elbows against the windowsill and gazes out. A breeze comes through the screen; carried on it is the smell of daytime, pine trees and lake water, and the cheerful chirp of crickets. The moon is bright and full. The landscape she knows so well now is like an entirely different universe under the moonlight, all aglow in silver. As Logan's eyes wander along the trail from the infirmary, she catches a sudden, sharp movement.

She squints through the screen. It's under the shadow of a tree, not quite definable, but she is sure she sees the form of a person standing on the trail. She blinks, rubs her eyes, and squints again. The shape beneath the tree shifts in a way that is definitely not caused by the breeze, a quick movement, like a swinging arm. The longer she looks, the surer Logan is that she sees two legs and two arms and a tilted human head. She shudders and stares harder, convincing herself it's real, more than just a trick of her eyes. Then she sees the shadow turn and step forward.

Logan leaps with fright, stumbles, and crawls back into the infirmary bed. She throws the comforter over her head. In her imagination, she hears footsteps approaching outside the window; she sees a shadowy face stopping, turning, peering in through the screen. She can't bring herself to roll over and look. Under the cover of the blanket, she smiles from the thrill.

Sam

ROSIE SHAKES HER HEAD AT the fire. She nudges a pinecone with the tip of her boot into the embers. In the red gleam, the satisfaction on her face when it sparks into flame is nearly menacing. "God," she says, watching the pinecone ignite. "Poor kid."

Taps tips his cup in salute to her. "My point is, you were right. Girls definitely have it worse than boys. Even here."

"I didn't think they could get periods."

"I can't believe it's any of my business, but apparently, they can."

Sam sits between them on the log, listening quietly to Taps's story. She leans forward to poke at the burning pinecone with the butt of her beer bottle. "It's a choice," she says out loud. She has learned a lot in her mornings in the office, hovering behind Nick as he talks to Campbell or Nurse May. She knows more about the practicalities of the campers and consciousness transfers now. More than she would like to know, at times. "Physical milestones. Some people want them as a part of the experience. Like Poppy's teeth." She falls silent, wondering if she has said too much. It's clear that not everything she learns is meant to be repeated to the other counselors, but no one has told her where, exactly, to draw the line.

"Must be nice." Rosie grimaces. "Choosing your milestones."

Taps nods. "Anyway," he says, drawing their attention back to himself. "Poor kid, I know, but it gave me and Sadie the perfect matchmaking plan. Soon as Max gets his cast off, Katie and Dane will take them up to Pike Falls together. They'll hang out, roast some 'mallows, get a little cozy . . . maybe do a little making out, if my boy plays his cards right."

Everyone around the fire chuckles. "Gross, man," Elias snorts. "They're twelve."

"Yup. And they paid a trillion dollars to *be* twelve. Might as well make the most of it, right?" Taps fidgets with the stick in his lap, picking off shreds of bark and tossing them into the flames. "I got to tell Chard about the idea. He called me—and I quote—brilliant. So, you know, I'm basically the new favorite."

"Better watch out, Sammy," Jeremy teases.

Sam feels her cheeks flush with the heat of the fire. Their laughter rattles over her. It's a joke, she knows, but not without some meanness, some smoldering resentment. A few days ago, Richard Byron walked into the mess hall during lunchtime. He gave her a grand slap on the shoulder and loudly praised her work with the Hummingbirds. Sometimes she sits in on the assistant directors' meetings. Some days she carries a radio in case Nick or Campbell needs to contact her. She knows what the counselors are saying. She can hear their whispers about her brown nose behind her back. "Funny," is all she can think to say.

"Wait, wait, wait. Back up." Elias is very obviously drunk—he was pulling from Jeremy's vodka jug before they left the Nest. He angles his guitar down flat in his lap and holds his palms up over it, frowning defensively around the group. "Why are we saying girls have it worse than boys? My boys are in the middle of puberty, too. It sucks just as much for them."

Rosie raises an eyebrow. "One of your boys murdered a woman," she reminds him coldly.

"We don't know that for sure." Elias raises his voice before she can interrupt, his hands still held up to her. "Anyway, you don't know what it's like for boys. They might not get periods, but they're under a lot more pressure."

"Pressure?" Rosie repeats.

"Yeah. Pressure to be a man. Be tough. Kiss girls, say nasty things. Get in fights. It's hard to be a boy."

The fire spits and crackles. Sam watches Rosie's spine straighten, leaning across their log like she's going to swing at him. "Oh, is it? And it's easy to be a girl—having your whole existence sexualized, having grown men hit on you as soon as you look old enough to assault—that's easy, right?"

"Maybe girls wouldn't be as sexualized if boys weren't pressured to be that way."

"Boys wouldn't be pressured to be that way if men hadn't been that way since the beginning of time."

"That's the same point." Sam interrupts them before either can say anything else. The two of them, she knows, will carry on until they're screaming, until everyone else in the circle has grown uncomfortable and wandered off. "You're saying the same thing. It's the culture that's the problem."

For a moment, they're quiet. A log snaps in the fire. Taps fidgets with the plastic cup between his knees, tapping along its rim. Then he lifts it, downs its contents, and belches. "Culture," he grunts, holding the cup upside down over the edge of the fire. Droplets fall and sizzle on the embers. "What's that?"

They put out their fire about an hour before curfew and pile into cars to drive back to Camp. Sam and Elias walk together from the parking lot toward the cabins. Rosie, despite her own lengthy insistence that she wouldn't, has walked off somewhere with Jeremy. It's a cold, clear night and unusually windy. They walk with their hands in their pockets and their eyes on the moon, both quiet, until Elias clears his throat. "It's pretty messed up, isn't it?"

"Hmm?" Sam tears herself from her thoughts.

"That girl. Sadie's kid. And Taps's kid. The whole idea of it. Like, those people have all the money in the world, right? And what they want to do with it is go back to puberty. Make themselves have crushes on each other. Like, that's the most romantic thing they could think of."

Sam considers for a moment, rubbing the cold from her hands. "There is something romantic about it," she says slowly. "Being twelve. Having a crush. Remember? Everything's so new and embarrassing. It's all right on the surface." She mimes swelling emotions at the base of her throat. "I guess they thought they could get that back. Maybe, when you're in your forties, it would feel good to have that back."

They have stopped walking on the trail. Elias cocks his head at her. His hair is silvery in the moonlight, his eyes drifting. "Would you do it?"

It isn't a question she has considered much. The prospect feels too impossible; they are too close to it all. "No. I don't think so." Sam studies her hands. Scratched and peeling, the nails dirty and broken. "But I didn't think I'd come back to work here this summer, either."

He nods, glancing off through the trees, toward the rippling glow on the lake. A gust runs through the branches and makes them shiver. "It's small here," he says. "It's safe."

After a pause, he looks back at her and smiles. He cups her hands in both of his own and blows a hot puff of breath over them, warming them. The gesture is so absurdly intimate that they both snort and giggle. Elias peers at her over his knuckles.

The two of them shared a few messy, drunken moments last summer. There was some flirting, some fumbling in the back of parked cars. It was easy. They are young and attractive, and their world is small, and it would be just as easy to fall back into that same comfort now, if it weren't for his brother. Sam smiles and takes her hands back. The moment passes, and they continue along the trail, quiet again.

The next day is muggy and overcast, the sky a flat, distant gray. In the morning, the air feels heavy, sluggish. Even the Hummingbirds are hushed through breakfast.

Campbell sends Nick and his shadow out to place an order of frozen food at the Smith's Ridge market. They take the old Camp pickup and stop at Lobster Point on the way back, where Nick turns the truck down a dirt trail through the brush. They jerk and rattle downhill to the foot of the dam, a flat, muddy shore. Here, the rush of water falling over the spillway muffles the sounds of Camp, the laughter and splashes carried across the lake. Sam steps out of the truck and wanders to the water's edge. She lights a cigarette.

The little shack at the head of the pool is not as decrepit as it looks from above. It has an industrial-looking steel door, padlocked. Hefty concrete channels direct the flow of the stream through the base of the building; Sam can hear the shush and splatter of it echoing through the foundation. She wonders what happens, or happened, in a fish hatchery, what it looks like on the inside.

"How 'bout it, freckles?" Nick calls behind her back.

Sam laughs. That afternoon at Sardine Flat has become their secret, a dark, private joke. It was a sort of tipping point, she knows now—it's easy to let one secret bleed into another. She walks back across the mud and sits on the tailgate beside him, and they share the rest of the cigarette.

Nick is a clumsy kisser. The stubble on his jaw leaves blotchy red rashes on her face and throat. In the back of the pickup, they knock knees and bump heads and laugh childishly at each other. Sam likes the way he looks at her when he props himself up on his elbows. She likes the silliness of it, the ashy breath and smiles. She tugs his T-shirt over his head and the lanyard around his neck comes off with it. The keyring falls to the truck bed with a clatter.

"Do you . . . ?" His eyes trail over her. The end of his question wanders off. He has a hand under her shirt, his belt buckle undone. A blanket of dead pine needles prickles against Sam's back.

Sam shrugs. They could—there is something crass and intriguing about the idea of it, here in the dirty truck bed under broad, sober daylight. Then again, she thinks, sex has a nasty way of changing everything, nudging the scales from silly to serious. She isn't sure she wants this to become real. As she leans in to kiss him again, a staticky buzz from the cab of the truck makes them both flinch.

Nicky. Campbell's voice leaps out at them. *Nick, you there?*

They hold their breath, waiting. A few seconds pass in silence before he turns his attention back to her.

The radio buzzes again. *Nick, pick up.*

"Christ." He huffs as he shoves himself upright. On his knees, he slides open the rear window of the cab and reaches through to find the radio. Sam sits up, hastily tugging her shirt back into place. The truck groans with their movement.

Nick locates the radio and drags it back through the window. "What's up, boss?" He has his back to her. Between bony shoulder blades, Sam notices a long, jagged white scar.

The radio crackles. *Where are you? You need to get back here.*

"We're on our way."

Is Sam still with you?

Nick's brow furrows. He looks at her anxiously, and Sam frowns back.

"Yeah. She's right here. We're just coming over the bridge." He shrugs. "What's going on?"

Hurry up, come straight back to the office. Campbell's voice through the static is biting, urgent. *Both of you.*

"All right. Be there in five."

For a second or two, they look at each other. Nick sniffs and wipes at his nose. "I'm sure it's nothing," he says, moving to buckle his belt.

"Are we going back?"

He freezes, belt extended in one hand, and blinks at her. "What—Do you want to . . . ?"

"No." Sam clears her throat. "We, uh, we should get going."

She watches him carefully scoop up his keys and hang them over his neck. The little black tube on the keyring settles into the well of his chest; it rises and falls with his steadying breaths. He catches her looking at it. "Relax. I'm sure it's nothing," he says again. "I probably just double-scheduled someone, or something. You know how he gets about that."

The change of pace has her dizzy. Sam ties her hair up. Not sure what else to say, she asks: "Where'd you get that scar on your back?"

His laugh is dry, affected. "I don't know. Always had it."

Nick stops the truck again at the top of the trail. They get out and lean against the front bumper to share another cigarette, wordless, gazing out over the water under the gray sky. On the far end of the lake, the ski boat turns circles, buzzing like a wasp. Cheers and whoops ring on the stiff air.

They park beside the barn and hurry up the trail to the office. Heavy voices drone inside—Sam can hear them through the screen door as she follows Nick up the porch steps. She steps into the room behind him, and a sudden, tense silence strikes her like a wall. Richard Byron is here, leaning against the surface of the desk with his arms crossed.

Campbell stands up rapidly. "Where the hell have you two been?" The anger in his face is bizarre, entirely out of character. Scattered around the room, the rest of the assistant directors stare blankly at them.

Nick blinks. He looks like he has been struck motionless. "We stopped for a minute. What . . . ?"

"When I tell you to come, you *come*," Campbell spits through gritted teeth. He pinches the bridge of his nose beneath his glasses and shakes his head, wincing. Restrained, softer, he gestures at Sam. "Come here, kid."

She steps toward him, feeling the heat of everyone's gaze. Her thoughts run wild. She wonders if this is about her—about her and Nick, maybe. Did someone see them at Lobster Point? Or is it her fault the horse died, after all? Campbell reaches out and places his hands on her shoulders. Something horribly sad in his look sinks into her, fills her with dread.

"What's going on?"

Richard Byron clears his throat. Still under the weight of Campbell's hands, Sam turns to him. He uncrosses his arms, shifts his stance, and runs a hand through his hair. "I wish we didn't have to tell you this, Sam, but you need to know." His eyes meet hers, and he sighs. "Poppy Warbler is dead."

week six

Sam

HE LEADS HER AWAY FROM the office with a hand on the back of her neck. The clouds overhead are breaking. A broad sunbeam cuts free from the sky and strikes across the surface of the lake, sparkling in the spray of the ski boat. They step down from the porch and follow the trail toward the mess hall.

"Do you understand all that?" Byron asks her. Slow and clear, the way she might talk to her campers.

Sam nods. "So, she's not really dead."

"Technically, no." He sighs. "But, practically . . . Well, she's gone, Sam. Her heart gave out. Her body just quit. There is no bringing her back." He pauses and clears his throat. His hand lifts from her neck to wipe a speck of something from his lip, a bit of falling dust or a fleck of spittle. "I think she wasn't honest with us about the state of her health when she applied to the program. She never should have been cleared for the consciousness transfer at all. Her body couldn't take it."

"But her brain is fine."

"You could put it that way. She is still conscious, and her consciousness is still here, with the camper. For now. We can keep her supported for the time being, but . . . I can't say how long that's going to last. She's comatose, essentially. Everything is gone but that one little sliver of being. And we have no control over that sliver."

They are starting down the mess hall steps, now, toward the lawn. All around them are shouts and laughter, splashes, the buzz of the boat's motor. Horses clop in single file along a trail not too far off. They pass the announcement benches and settle onto the picnic table under the bell tower. Byron sits outward, facing the lake, with an arm propped up on the table behind him. He is so much calmer, Sam thinks, than the last time they talked like this—measured, professional.

Sam struggles to find her voice. This is too much to understand. It occurs to her now that if there is a line between science fiction and reality, they have landed on the wrong side of it. The sky sinks down onto her; the air is too thick in her lungs. A staticky hum rings in her ears. "Can't you just grow her a new heart? I mean, you grew her a whole new body."

He smiles. "It doesn't work like that. I am not her healthcare provider. Neither is Phoenix Genetics."

"But . . ." She examines the grass between her feet. "She's here, now. She's fine, right? I mean, she's at archery right now."

He looks at her steadily. Watching, patiently waiting for her to finish her thought.

"So, she doesn't have to die, does she? Just because her other body is gone—"

"Right." Byron stops her. Again, he smiles. "That's what I thought you were going to say. That's where this whole thing gets a little sticky." His arm on the table is wrapped around her. One hand pats her opposite shoulder. "You have to realize—it's not her *other* body. It's her body. It's her. The kid here at Camp is just . . . Well, let me put it this way: you know why we always call them 'campers,' right?"

Sam shakes her head.

"We always do. Even before Camp, before the consciousness transfer, when they're just pieces of meat. We refer to them as 'campers.' We don't say that word, that other C-word. You know why?" He pauses, then answers himself. "Because they are not alive. They are not conscious. Cloning human beings is illegal—that's not what our campers are. They're just empty bodies. When they're here, when they're conscious, they're still not *really* conscious. The consciousness still belongs to the client. Now, in this situation, the client is gone, medically speaking, and the camper is still here. Do you see what I'm getting at?"

"Yeah. I think so." Sam nods. The motion is a strain, her head heavy on her neck.

Byron leans closer to her. His eyes, she realizes, are bloodshot. *Self-medicated.* "It's not our job to create an afterlife, Sam."

Again, Sam nods. The truth of what he is saying, the reality of it all, is lagging, trudging through thick mud to reach her. Poppy. Her camper, whose plump cheeks were still smudged with sunscreen when she last saw her an hour ago. Gone—but not really. Not yet. "So, what? What now? Are you going to kill her?"

A bitter, dark laugh escapes him. "No, sweetheart. No one is killing children here."

Children. A third C-word, Sam notes.

Byron looks up, searching the cloudy sky. After another heavy sigh, he says, "If Poppy makes it through the next few days, chances are she'll make it to the end of the summer. I need you to do two things, Sam. I need you to take care of her, watch her. Look out for headaches, nosebleeds, anything unusual. If her condition changes in any way, we may see some physical signs in the camper." He pauses, then goes on deliberately: "*And* I need you to make sure this does not leave Camp. If word gets out about this, it won't look good on us. We're already taking heat from Hugo Baker being here. You keep an eye on the other counselors, okay? If anyone is thinking about talking, I need you to stamp it out. Fast."

Sam isn't sure how she is supposed to stop secrets from leaving Camp—she isn't sure how secrets would ever leave Camp in the first place. No one has seen their phone in weeks. She agrees, hot and uncomfortable with his arm around her. "What happens at the end of the summer?"

"At the end of the summer, she'll go back to the facility. Just like the other campers. The consciousness transfer will be withdrawn. After that, it's up to her family and doctors. Not us. Okay?"

"Okay."

"You know . . ." His voice drifts, suddenly lighter. "A couple summers ago, I built a little cabin out there." He nods sideways, toward the trees on the other side of the lawn. "Up the hill. There's this perfect little fishing hole. It's far enough from Camp that I don't get in the way, and far enough from Smith's Ridge that they can't find me if they need me." A deep chortle bubbles in his throat, a coughing laugh. "Sometimes, when things get really crazy, I feel like I could go out there and just *disappear*. You know that feeling?"

"Yeah," Sam answers honestly.

He blinks, and the faraway gaze drains from his expression. "I don't, though. I can't. Because I'm responsible for all this." A gesturing hand indicates everything he is responsible for, swaying vaguely toward the grass, the lake, the sky. "We have responsibilities we can't dodge, Sam. You and I both. Especially now." Byron clears his throat and nods to himself. "I want to set up regular meetings with you, okay? Let's keep each other in the know on this whole thing. That all right with you?"

Wary, all the more confused, Sam nods.

"That's a girl. You're the best counselor we have, you know. Honestly, if Poppy Warbler wasn't already your camper, I'd have Gus switching around cabin assignments right now so she was. I trust you, understand?"

The way he says the word *trust* sends a cold sensation down Sam's spine, as if he has poured a handful of lake water over her head. It makes her think there is more behind that word. Much more. *Trust* is the door to a room full of dark, ugly secrets, and Richard Byron plans to unlock it, swing it open, guide her inside with a hand on the back of her neck.

He leans toward her. Sam doesn't think to move away. Byron kisses her on the cheek, lingering just long enough for her to feel the wiry scratch of his beard against her jaw. Her skin prickles—with a nauseous sort of jolt, she recalls laughing, stubbly kisses, hardly a handful of minutes ago. The hum in her ears grows louder. Then he claps her firmly on the shoulder. "Well, I've got to finish debriefing with the ADs. You just take your time, okay? Get yourself oriented before the lunch bell rings."

"Okay."

As he is leaving, she stops him. "Chard," she says, and winces—they aren't supposed to use the nickname to his face.

He laughs. "Yes, Sammy?"

"I just . . . Why drag it out? Why don't you send her back to the facility now? Not that I want her to go, but . . ."

Byron chews on his lip and pockets his hands—playful, boyish. "She paid for the whole summer," he says, then turns and carries on toward the mess hall steps.

By dinnertime, everyone knows. The news travels in a hushed, blanketing buzz. Sam hovers over Poppy for the rest of the day, watching her for a change, for some kind of sign. Nothing is different. She is herself, just Poppy, wild hair and scabby knees. She throws a fit over the chicken nuggets at dinner.

Sam manages to avoid talking to anyone about it until after campfire, after she has finished the bedtime story and finally turned out the lights. She leaves the cabin in a hurry, without her flashlight. As soon as the door clicks shut behind her, she is violently sick. She is going to vomit. She dashes off the porch and stumbles over the dark trails to the lawn. Bracing herself against the cool stone of the bell tower, she chokes, gags, but all that comes forward is a loud, dry sob.

Someone followed her. Light footsteps pad quickly closer on the lawn, then a warm set of arms wraps around her. Rosie sinks onto the grass with her, and Sam lets herself be held. The ropes have been cut, the floor has dropped out from under her feet; she is in free fall, grasping at air.

"I didn't sign up for this," she gasps.

"Yes, you did," Rosie tells her. "You did, and so did I. So did she."

It's a sobering reminder. Sam runs her hand over the grass beneath her, digs her fingertips into the earth. She could leave. Resign, run away, go back to Paris. She chose to come, and she could choose to leave. It's only summer camp.

Rosie, as if following her thoughts, whispers, "You're not going to quit, are you?"

Sam looks up at the sky. The pain in her stomach is slowly settling. She imagines it, for a moment, but it passes in a rush. It would be impossible. Life outside of Camp is too far away. "No." She shakes her head. "I'm here."

Logan

AFTER A WEEK, HUGO BAKER and Donna break up. No one knows exactly why. When they ask, Donna shrugs and says, "He was starting to creep me out."

Rumors say they kissed. Other rumors say worse.

"I bet *he* broke up with *her*," says Milly. Logan knows, by now, that she adores the drama. Without it, she would have nothing to make fun of.

During morning announcements, Hugo sits behind Logan. He tugs her braid. "Hey, horse girl."

Logan looks up from the bracelet she's weaving. It's the most complicated she has made yet: black and white with a blue-and-gold double *X* pattern. Aside from a few loose stitches, it's perfect. "What?"

"Who are you making that for?"

"I don't know." Logan can feel the rest of the Ravens staring at her.

"Can I have it?"

No boy has ever asked her for a friendship bracelet before. It sounds ridiculous, almost vulgar. He might as well have cussed.

"Umm. I guess."

Hugo's counselor snaps down the bench at him. "Hugo! Quit talking to the girls."

"Okay, *Smellias,*" says Hugo, and everyone giggles. When Logan looks forward again, she catches Donna's jet beam gaze.

The summer is almost halfway over. The Fourth of July went by in a blur of powdered donuts and sunburnt shoulders. Next will be the midsummer dance, on Wednesday night. Logan has hazy memories of the dance from her last stay at Camp, when she was littler. She remembers throwing up on her counselor's toga after eating too many popsicles. Now, she isn't sure if she should be looking forward to it or not. Dressing up in costumes and dancing seems like little kid stuff—anyway, she doesn't know how to dance. She can't jump around and scream like a Hummingbird, not anymore.

The theme of the dance is decided by the Falcons and Eagles together, as the two oldest cabins. They announce it in a badly rehearsed skit at breakfast on Monday morning. At the end of the skit, a tall blond Eagle named Stephanie stands on her chair and screeches: "Boys versus girls!"

A clattery silence falls over the mess hall. "What?" someone shouts back.

"Boys versus girls!" Stephanie, still standing on her chair, rolls her eyes. "On Wednesday afternoon there's gonna be a huge Capture the Flag game: boys versus girls. Then you come to the dance dressed as a boy, or a girl!"

Campers murmur at their tables. "I don't get it!" yells one of the Pigeons. "Does that mean boys dress as girls, and girls dress as boys?"

"No, just—" Stephanie grumps and crosses her arms. "Wear what you want."

"I'm gonna be a girl!" cries a Hawk. The rest of his table snickers.

Logan shares a frown with the other Ravens. With the announcement over, chatter and the clamor of plates and silverware pick up again. A counselor, passing the Ravens' table on her way back from the coffee pot, stops to mutter to Sadie: "Who signed off on that?" Logan is sitting directly across from her. She perks up at the quiet exchange.

"I don't know. Guess everyone's a little preoccupied, right now," says Sadie. The other counselor frowns knowingly and continues on her way.

Milly is in an uproar for the rest of the day. "Boys versus girls?" she wails. "That's the dumbest thing I've ever heard. What, are we supposed to just wear our normal clothes?"

Logan looks at Milly, her dirty T-shirt and short locks, her square shoulders and bony face. In her normal clothes, it's hard to place Milly on one side or the other. She stops short of saying so out loud. "I don't know. Capture the Flag sounds fun, though. Do you think we should go?"

"Uh-huh. I'm gonna play for the boys' team, so I can kick Stephanie's ass for picking such a stupid theme."

"Milly! You can't play for the boys' team."

It's afternoon activity, and they are on their way down to the barnyard. Logan has less love for the barn animals than she does for the horses, but it's a quiet place to pass a lazy, hot afternoon. Socrates the goat is particularly entertaining—he has buck teeth and sideways eyes and likes to eat carrots right out of her hand.

Hugo and Max are at the barnyard, too. This is the first time the four of them have signed up for an afternoon activity together since air rifles, since they freed Spark. "Hey, Millipede." Hugo shoves Milly hard in the shoulder. She shoves him back. He glances sideways at the counselor, then smiles at Logan, privately. His cheeks are flushed strawberry red with their shared secret. "My partners in crime," he whispers to her.

There are a few other boys at the activity—Hugo's posse of Falcons—and a cluster of giggling Bluebirds, who perch on a hay bale and whisper amongst themselves. The counselor, Kyle, lies on his back on another hay bale with his sunglasses on. The boys chase the chickens for a while, and Max helps Logan feed Socrates. He doesn't say much to her. She is still a little mad at him for embarrassing her at the beach. They haven't talked about the Pike Falls trip they are supposed to go on, alone, later in the summer.

About halfway through the activity period, a miracle strikes: the counselor leaves the barn. He says that he has a stomachache and is going to the kitchen for a ginger ale. He does look a little woozy. No one has ever been left unsupervised at an activity before—it feels like they have an obligation to get up to something, break some kind of rule. One of the boys suggests throwing rocks at the goats, but Logan quickly shuts that down. Another boy looks at her and Milly, thinks, and asks if they want to play Truth or Dare. It isn't a game the boys would ever play on their own, Logan understands, but an intriguing option because they are here, and they are girls.

Milly and Logan shrug at each other. "Okay."

They sit in a circle on the hay-strewn floor. The Bluebirds watch, silent and worried, from a distance. Logan is next to Max. Across the circle from her is Hugo, his legs crossed, leaning cockily over his kneecaps.

"Who wants to start?"

"I will," says Milly. "Henry. Truth or dare?"

"Dare, dude, duh."

"Do a backflip off the hay."

The boys love that. "Do it, pussy!" Hugo howls, smiling.

Henry climbs up onto the stack of hay bales. For a moment he just stands there and brags, then he turns his back to them, leaps, and tucks. He slips on the landing and falls on his butt; still, it's impressive. Logan laughs and claps with the rest of them. Boys, she is slowly realizing, aren't really all that complicated. They don't make her nervous the way girls do. This is easy.

"Okay, Todd. Truth or dare."

"Truth—but make it *dirty*."

"Okay. So, you get a blowjob from the hottest girl in Camp, but first I get to punch you in the head. Would you do it?"

"Dude, stupid question. I'd let you punch me in the *balls* if it was Sharon. Or Stephanie."

Logan laughs. Their dirty jokes are plain and wide; compared to the nasty, prickly things the girls say in the dark of the cabin, this is nothing. The Bluebirds looking over at them suck in their lips and whisper behind their hands.

"Logan. Truth or dare."

Logan hesitates, playing with the bracelets on her wrist. She definitely can't do a backflip. "Truth," she decides.

"Okay. Who do you like?"

The boys watch her intensely. She picks at her fingernails. "No one." As she says it, her eyes land on Hugo Baker. She didn't mean to look at him—it's just that he is straight in front of her—but they see. They don't let her get away with it. Henry shoves Hugo and shouts with delight.

"*No* one?" he says. "You don't like no one, you like him! You looked at him!"

Hugo's cheeks go pinker. He laughs, looks at her quickly, then wrestles Henry under his arm. Mortified, Logan melts into the ground. She wishes she had said *dare*. Now it's her turn to ask, and she has to take their attention away from herself as quickly as possible, so she turns to Max. "Truth or dare?"

"Dare," he answers, scratching at his hand beneath his cast.

Logan nods and looks around the barn. She needs to think of something, fast. Something big. Her eyes land on the skinny ladder against the back wall, and without pausing to consider it, she says, "Climb up there!"

The boys gasp. Milly gives her a surprised look. Logan realizes, too late, that she has said something horribly mean—he can't climb with his arm in a cast. Max stands up in the same instant, looking almost brave.

"Wait," she reaches toward him weakly. "Wait, no, never mind. You don't have to."

The boys have already taken the idea and run with it. "That's the counselors' place, right?" Henry asks, excited. "Yeah, do it, Max! Tell us what's up there! Elias says they have a pool table *and* a soda machine."

"Taps said they have slides and a ball pit."

"Do it, Max!" says Hugo. "You can do it!"

Max doesn't look at Logan as he turns around. He marches straight past the hay bales, to the back of the barn, and places his one good hand on a rung of the ladder. To her utter horror, he begins to climb. He goes very slowly, using only the tips of his fingers of his cast left arm. Logan has to look away. Milly and the boys cheer him on.

Max reaches the top of the ladder and disappears through the trapdoor. Footsteps stomp slowly over their heads. "It stinks up here!" His voice is muffled when he shouts down to them. "There's a fridge. And . . . *whoa!*"

"What is it, Maxie?" Hugo calls up.

His feet thud back toward the door, then his head appears. His face is red, his hair hanging down. "Beer!" he exclaims. "A *lot* of beer!"

Kyle is crossing the barnyard with his soda just as Max's feet touch the barn floor again. When he steps inside, all of them are sitting politely on the hay. Milly balances a chicken feather on her lips, attempting to blow it upward and catch it again. Max flops onto a hay bale and pretends to nap.

When the bell rings, they leave the barn in a hurry. The Bluebirds skirt ahead of everyone else, all atwitter. Behind them goes the jeering pack of boys. Milly and Max fall back; she quizzes him frantically him about what he saw in the counselors' fridge ("But how *much* is a lot? Was it in cans? Bottles?") That leaves Logan walking alone with Hugo Baker. Stiff and a little sweaty, she wonders if she should speed up or fall behind with Milly.

He nudges her with his elbow. "Truth or dare?"

Logan looks at her toes. "Umm. Dare."

"Okay. I dare you to give me that bracelet you're making."

She giggles. "Okay."

"Now your turn."

"Umm, okay. Truth or dare?"

"Truth."

"Okay, how about . . ." She thinks fast—What would the other boys ask him, or Donna? "Who do you think is the cutest counselor?"

"Sam's pretty," he answers. "But she's also kind of a bitch."

That is a big word, a stinging word. A grown-up word. It sends an electric tingle down Logan's spine. They've started walking faster. Milly and Max are far behind them now.

"Truth or dare?"

"Truth."

Hugo grins at her. "Do you like me?"

Logan doesn't know what to say. Her face is hot. He laughs, bubbly and high. "You don't have to answer that," he says. "It's okay."

They reach the lawn and stand at the edge of the trail, facing the grass. Hugo stops walking, so Logan stops, too. He squints, like he's thinking hard about something, then reaches out and grabs her arm and pulls her off the trail, into the trees. Dead pine needles crunch beneath their feet and stab at Logan's ankles. "Come here."

"We're supposed to stay on the trails."

"Just come here." He tugs her until they reach a broad tree trunk, a few feet off the trail, out of sight of the lawn. With her back to the scratchy bark, he reaches out and puts both hands on her shoulders. He looks her in the eyes. Logan's stomach does a backflip as high and wild as Henry's off the hay. "Truth or dare?" he asks quietly.

"Dare?"

"Cool." Hugo smiles. He tips forward in a jolting way, like someone pushed him from behind. His mouth lands on hers, quick, lips pressed flat together, then he leans back again. Logan reels. A lot of strange things have happened since she got to Camp at the start of the summer, but this, out of everything, simply cannot be real.

A raspy laugh shatters the air. They both turn their heads back toward the trail. Milly and Max are standing there; she howls and bends double, pointing at them. Max looks stunned. "Yuck!" Milly laughs. "I think I saw *tongue!*"

Hugo tells her to shut up. His whole face is red, from his chin to the tips of his ears.

They walk into dinner together, holding hands. Logan's palm is slick with sweat—his sweat, she hopes, and not hers. Her heart thunders in her mouth. As they cross the mess hall, campers stare from their tables. Counselors slowly lower their coffee mugs, mouths open, watching them pass. If music were playing it would have screeched to a stop. Logan is soaring, swimming inside her brain. Hugo doesn't let go of her hand until they reach the Ravens' table. "See you later," he says, wiping his palm on the front of his jeans.

"Bye." Logan hardly recognizes the pitch of her own voice. She sits down to dinner. There is a moment of shocked silence. Everyone at the table, Sadie most of all, stares at her. Then the Ravens burst into a frenzy.

Sam

"Do you want to?" he asks her.

The question makes Sam laugh. It sounds so clunky, out of place. "You ask?"

"Shouldn't I ask?"

Sam shrugs. No one she knows asks, at least not out loud. They know she wants to—or they expect her to stop them if she doesn't.

Sex at Camp isn't all that different from anywhere else in the world. Sam understands it; she knows the complications and the missteps and the sticky, tangled feelings. Sex is not at all private, but public, and political. It's a game, like anything else. They keep score, they draw lines and track their numbers, show them off discretely like a hand of cards. They weigh and measure each other against those hands. Sam knows the rules. The game has always been easy for her.

It's raining. Rainstorms in the mountains never come with a warning, and they never come lightly. The clouds swooped in over the ridge and broke open like floodgates within a half hour. Sam was supposed to be lifeguarding this morning, but now she is here, in the guest cabin with Nick, watching fat raindrops plop from the roof outside the open window. The guest cabin was his idea. When he unlocked the door with his lanyard of jangling keys, the little tube between them tapped against the lock, flashing in the gray light. Later it fell against her bare skin. It was cold and unexpectedly heavy. It settled in the well of her chest as he leaned over her. When he realized he was still wearing the lanyard, Nick laughed, apologized, and tossed it carefully to the floor.

They lie on the bare futon and watch the rain outside. The sky is lightening. Chances are the storm will evaporate as quickly as it appeared; they won't have to cancel the Capture the Flag game in the afternoon, or the dance in the evening. Sam is oddly bitter about it. She wills the clouds to darken and the rain to fall harder, the break from the routine to continue. Calloused fingertips run along her side.

"You're really beautiful, Sam."

"I know," she says. After a strained pause, they both laugh. "Sorry. I know that sounds shallow." She rolls to face him. "I just mean, I know what I look like."

He smiles thinly. "You don't want guys to compliment you on your looks, you mean?"

"No, it's not that. Guys will say what they say. I just already know what I look like." Sam chews over her own words, then adds: "That probably comes across pretty bitchy, doesn't it?"

"No. I don't think so."

She would not have been so brash with someone else. Something about him makes her feel reckless, like she can do anything, say anything. Him, or the place they're in. Their surreal world, where rain appears out of the blue and dead girls lisp through missing teeth. Where murderers and bear turds and ghost stories all somehow lump together into the same vague threat. In light of all that, everything is just about as irrelevant as anything else.

"So," Nick clears his throat, changes the topic. "The murderer and the wife were holding hands at dinner. Did you see that?"

It sounds like the punchline to a bad joke. Sam laughs. "Yeah. Sadie's pretty torn up about it." Sadie has been distraught, actually. She has taken on the prepubescent Gill couple as her personal mission, a desperate chance to prove that true love exists. As it is, chaos apparently trumps true love—the girl has a crush on Hugo Baker instead. "Can you imagine being her? Waking up at the end of the summer and realizing who you were holding hands with?"

She thinks he will laugh. He doesn't. He grimaces up at the ceiling, running a hand absently over his bare stomach. Sam follows the trail of his fingers from ribs to hip. There is something undeniably funny about this, lying here in the rainy gray light with him, exposed, every freckle and belly hair out in the open. She can hear campers shouting from the archery range a few yards away. "No," Nick says sincerely. "I can't imagine waking up at the end of a summer like this, at all."

Sam rests her cheek on the back of her hand. She looks up at him and wonders how much he knows, that she does not. She wonders—a little maliciously—what kind of information she can gain from this. "What *is* that like?" she asks slowly. "When they wake up?"

He sighs, a rush of air through his nose. "I think it's awful, actually. I talked to Chard about it once. He said . . . Well, basically, imagine the hardest comedown from the most amazing drug you could take. They go to sleep thinking they have their whole lives ahead of them. Then they open their eyes, and it's fifty years later. That's why Chard's never done it." He pauses, chews his lip. "That's why I'll never do it."

"You don't think the high is worth the comedown?"

Nick shakes his head. "I think it's like anything else. The only way to get over the comedown is to get the high again. And Camp is a little more expensive than heroin." He smirks.

Rain patters on the metal roof over their heads. The smell of it through the window is earthy and sweet. It's almost time for the lunch bell to ring. Soon, in another minute or two, they will have to get up and put their dusty T-shirts back on, go out to face their weird lives again. Sam thinks over what he said. Something is stuck in her brain like food in her teeth; she picks at it curiously. "So," she begins, then falters. She doesn't want to push him too far. "Never mind."

"No, what is it?" He rolls and turns a hard gaze over her. One hand on her hip tugs her closer. The thought suddenly strikes Sam that if they were to compare hands, she might come out on top. He is older than her, but shyer, colder, slower to act. Maybe that's why she feels so bold with him—between the two of them, she might be the one holding all the cards, after all.

"You said they go to sleep. Is that how it happens? After Camp, I mean?"

A few pattering seconds pass before he responds. "You mean, how do they get back to their bodies?"

"Yeah."

Nick's eyes shift. He squirms against the cushion. "I don't know that much. But there's one easy way to do it, right? I don't know how, exactly, but I know it's quick and painless. And they don't remember it when they wake up."

Sam nods. She thinks back to Richard Byron on the picnic bench a few days ago, laughing at her. *No one is killing children here.* Her curiosity drives on. She nods toward the cabin floor, where the little black tube lies, cold and ominous, next to their clothes and radios. "What's that thing on your keychain?"

He looks pained. His grip on her body tightens. "You know, don't you?"

She doesn't say anything. She wants him to elaborate.

Nick sighs. "They're not people. You know that. They're not really alive. If something were to happen, like with Max on the horse, but worse . . . we can't just let them suffer. We have to send them back."

"What about Poppy?" Sam asks before she can stop herself. "What if something bad happens to her?"

Days have gone by, and Poppy Warbler is still very much her usual self. A train wreck, but a living one. Nothing has changed, at least on the surface. If no one ever told her Poppy Warbler is dead, Sam would have no idea. That doesn't change the fact that she cannot stop thinking about it. She watches Poppy obsessively. Compulsively, she needs to keep an eye on her, to put a hand on her head, on her little round belly; to make sure she is here, she is real.

"Something bad already did happen to her, Sam." Nick seems to have reached his limit on answering questions. He sits up on the futon and runs his hand through his hair, checks the rain through the window. "There's nothing we can do about that."

Sam sits up, too. "Is there not?"

"No." His sharp eyes widen. The balance between them totters and then flips again, and Sam is looking upward. Nick reaches for his T-shirt. "There's not."

Logan

THE RAIN COMES OUT OF nowhere, just before the start of morning period. After a little confusion and reshuffling of the schedule, the Ravens are sent to crafts with the Sparrows instead of water skiing. They sit in the musty-smelling crafts shack and squish wet clay between their fingers, listening to the plunks and pitter-patter outside. Anxiety over the dance being cancelled floats like static on the air.

The cabin is divided. Ever since Logan kissed Hugo Baker, Donna, Joy and Mei refuse to talk to her. The rest of group is on Logan's side. This is all very new and exciting—more exciting than the kiss itself, which, Logan thinks, was hardly worth the hype. She has never been the center of any kind of drama. Out loud, she says she hates all the fighting and wishes everyone could get along, but inwardly she is glowing.

"What are you going to wear?" Liz asks.

Logan shrugs, focused on her weaving. Her blue-and-gold X-pattern bracelet is almost finished. She told everyone, just loud enough for Donna and the others to hear, that she will give it to Hugo today. "I don't know. Do you think we should all be boys?"

"Screw that." Milly slams a fist into her clay ball, splattering pasty droplets. "I'm going as a *man*."

Liz laughs. "Ooh, you're right. Let's get all the ties from down at campfire."

"And draw on beards!"

"And chest hair!" Milly and Liz giggle and squirm on their stools.

Logan finishes her stitch and holds the bracelet up for them to see. "What do you guys think?" she asks loudly. "Is that long enough for his wrist?"

Liz coos over the bracelet, but Milly sees what Logan is doing. She shoots her a hard look—*knock it off*, her face says. Logan lowers the bracelet but not her voice. Milly doesn't know anything about boys and bracelets, anyway.

The rain lets up by lunchtime, and the Capture the Flag game is on. The Ravens braid each other's hair and draw thick black lines on their cheeks with Sadie's eyeliner. They cuff the sleeves of their T-shirts, like boys, and giggle as they flex and pose in the mirror. The battlefield is set up behind the ropes course, a flat stretch of forest divided into two sides by a line scuffed through the pine needles. Red T-shirts are tied to stumps on either side, and jails are marked off with sticks.

Rosie and Sam captain the girls' team and Elias and Jeremy lead the boys. They huddle up, chanting and cheering and thumping their chests across the line. Pudgy little Poppy, the Hummingbird, wild-haired and missing both front teeth, growls and screeches like a goblin at the boys.

Sam waves her arms to bring their huddle in tighter. "Let's wreck these guys," she says in a mean whisper.

Rosie crouches in front of them. "Remember, ladies: anything boys think they can do, girls do it better."

"Girls do it better," Sam repeats.

They chant back: "Girls do it better!"

The sky is gray, the air is humid, and the light beneath the pines is dim and serious. They're testing the speakers for the dance back at the bell tower; drumbeats thunder through the trees. The game begins with a shout from Rosie, and the boys and girls take off running. Logan can't remember ever taking a game so seriously. It's all-out warfare, and she wants to win. At one point she sneaks deep enough behind enemy lines to see the boys' flag.

Exhilarated, she catches her breath, waits for her moment, then leaps from her cover and sets off at a sprint. She is nearing the flag, can almost touch it, and then—*whack!* She tumbles to the dirt.

Logan looks up from her back and shoves her glasses into place to see who tagged her. It's Hugo. He laughs as he bends down to help her up. There is her bracelet, the newest addition to the collection on his wrists. "I'm sorry!" he says. He doesn't look sorry.

Across the playing field, the counselors are distracted. Rosie has tackled Elias to the ground. Caught up in the violence, Logan smacks his hand away. She helps herself to her feet and marches herself to jail, fuming.

Now she is determined to win. Free from jail and back on their own side, she, Milly, and Rosie plot out a new strategy. The clouds overhead have grown heavier quickly; it looks like the rain is on its way back. When the drops start to fall, they smear the paint on the campers' cheeks and blur the dividing line drawn in the dirt. The needle-coated ground grows slick.

Logan sneaks behind the trees again. Safely hidden on the boys' side, she signals to Milly and Rosie through the rain. They lead a charge of girls across the line, shouting fearfully. With the boys distracted, Logan bolts for the flag.

She has it in her grasp. Cold raindrops splatter the lenses of her glasses. Logan sprints, faster than she has ever run in her life. Her heart thrums, pumping pure adrenaline.

"Hey, up there!" She hears the call and the stampede of feet behind her. She is nearly there. As she sprints the last few feet, she glances to her side, up the hill.

Logan's lenses are smeared with water and flecks of dirt. Just like the night she looked out the infirmary window, a distinctive shape between the trees catches her eye: a shadow, long and limby, peering at her through the rainy haze and branches. A high fear strikes her heart. As she squints to pin the figure down, she stumbles and falls, face-first into a carpet of wet needles and leaves. Her glasses go flying. Gleeful shouts roar up around her—she made it across the line.

The girls' team barrels in on her. It's all wet hugs and hair tousles and squeals. Logan holds the flag proudly over her head. For a second, she glances distractedly up the hill, searching through the pine trunks—but there is nothing there. It was just a trick of the rain and shadows. She waves the red T-shirt in the air and hollers: "Girls do it better!"

Even in all the excitement of her victory, Logan can't help but notice something else weird on the border of her attention. Poppy has been knocked down by a bigger boy. She lies in the dirt, her body shaking with what looks like tears. Before anyone else can reach her, Sam comes tearing away from the crowd of girls. She slides to her knees at Poppy's side and picks her up. Poppy flops like a doll in her arms. She is laughing, not crying—the full-bodied, breathless cackle of a little kid. It's strange, Logan thinks, that Poppy's counselor doesn't laugh with her, or even smile. She hugs her tight and throws Rosie a dark look over her head. The scene doesn't make any sense to Logan, but she has no more than a few seconds to consider it before the game is back on. The flag is replaced, the line redrawn, and another round begins.

In the end, it's a draw: two captures for the boys and two for the girls. The rain stops and the clouds finally clear. Muddy and scraped, still trembling with fury, they leave the battlefield for dinner. Loud and exaggerated recaps can be heard from every table.

The bell tower is strung with twinkle lights and streamers for the dance. Music booms from massive speakers set up on the hillside. Logan, Liz and Milly pilfer baggy shirts and ties from the props closet behind the campfire stage. They draw on smudgy mustaches with the same eyeliner pen they used for the game.

Hugo turns up in a strapless red ball gown. "Borrowed it from Elias," he tells them, adjusting the too-big bosom. It keeps slipping down below his nipples.

Before Logan can figure out what she is supposed to say to Hugo, he disappears—with Milly. They sink into the crowd of bouncing kids and Logan can't find them. She ends up standing next to Max at the snack table. He isn't wearing a costume, just his usual shorts and blue T-shirt and a little pink bow clipped in his hair. Katie put it there, he explains.

"Where'd they go?" Max shouts over the music. Logan looks sideways to see him holding out a popsicle for her. She shakes her head.

"I don't know." After an awkward pause, she looks at him again. She should apologize for making him climb the ladder, she thinks. Even if he did embarrass her first. "Hey, listen . . ."

Max fumbles the popsicle he is unwrapping as he turns to her. She doesn't have time to finish her thought, though, before Hugo and Milly are back. They both smile mischievously; they look like thieves with pockets full of treasure. They have a plan. "You guys want to go see something?" Milly whispers.

This plan is different, not like freeing the horse. It's worse. They want to break the rules just to break the rules. Logan's heart flutters nervously. She doesn't really have a choice. Being friends with Milly means jogging to catch up or staying behind—and she doesn't want to stay behind. Not if Milly is taking Hugo with her. Max, still holding two popsicles, one unwrapped, agrees with a silent nod.

They creep off at the start of a loud pop song. The counselors are standing on the benches, tossing their arms around and shouting the lyrics, not seeing anyone but each other. Sneaking through the dark is as thrilling as sneaking through the trees into the boys' territory. Hugo trips over his ball gown and the rest of them stifle their giggles behind their hands. Milly murmurs about bears and ghosts lurking in the moonlight. They enter the barn through the wide doors and bumble for the light switch, grunting and stepping on each other's toes. At last Hugo finds it. With a great buzz, industrial light bulbs overhead flicker to life, painting the place in bright, warm yellow. The goats shout in surprise.

"Hey, Socrates!"

"Milly, shut up!"

"It's all right," says Hugo in his full speaking voice. "No one's going to hear us down here." He dances across the barn floor, shaking his long dress and wiggling his eyebrows at them. "Come on. Last one's got to chug a full one."

Logan climbs the ladder behind the rest of them. It's higher than it looks, and scary—but that is hardly justification for being left behind. As soon as her head pokes through the doorway, her heart sinks. The place is awfully disappointing: a dusty attic that looks a lot like her grandparents' garage. There is no pool table or soda machine, just some old couches and the stink of feet. A rope ladder dangles in the center of the room, leading up into the rafters. Grown-up spaces, like kissing, must not live up to all the mystery and whispers.

Milly is already at the fridge. She tugs the handle delicately, an explorer at the door to an ancient tomb.

"It's a different kind than it was last time," Max says, awed, peering over her shoulder.

"That was only, like, two days ago. Did they drink it all?"

"They must be alcoholics."

Hugo reaches into the fridge. "Here, Maxie, catch!" He tosses a can behind his back at Max, who misses it. It falls to the floor with a solid *thump*. The can spins and hisses and a fountain of beer sprays upward. Hugo laughs.

"Hugo!" Max cries. He leaps back from the sticky spray. The bow slips from his hair.

"Relax." Hugo tugs at his dress, which has slipped from his chest again. "They won't know it was us."

"Who are they going to think it was?" Logan asks.

He shrugs. "A ghost. Who cares?"

They open two cans and sit on the dusty floor, passing them back and forth. Beer, it turns out, tastes like aluminum and dirty straw. Logan grimaces and takes little sips, wondering worriedly what it will feel like to be drunk. Her eyeliner mustache leaves black smudges on the rim of the can.

"You know what?" Hugo smacks his lips. He sits with his legs spread wide, so they can see right up the red dress. He is wearing shorts, Logan sees, then quickly looks away before anyone can accuse her of staring. "They're not just alcoholics. They're all sex addicts, too."

"*Sex* addicts?" Milly snickers. "What's that supposed to mean?"

"I mean, all the counselors are *doing* it. With each other. All the time."

"How do you know that?"

"You know what we found in Elias's locker?" Hugo shifts his weight to his knees, leaning forward to reveal something very important. "A condom. If he's just leaving them around, that means he probably uses lots of them."

Logan waits until Hugo's attention is diverted by the beer before she mouths to Milly: *What's a condom?*

I don't know, Milly mouths back. They share a shrug.

When both cans are drained, they start to get sillier. Hugo stands to waltz around the room, humming to himself. Milly fixes the bow in Max's hair. All of them are red-faced and laughing, but Logan waits, still, for something to happen to her. Her mouth tastes terrible, and she is getting steadily more nervous by the second. She wonders if she is the only one worried about getting caught. As if he can read her mind, Max suddenly pauses in the middle of his sentence. Panic overtakes his expression. He presses a finger to his lips and gestures downward.

Someone is coming into the barn. Logan hears footsteps and two adult voices, loud and snappy.

"Hide!" Hugo heads for the rope ladder in the middle of the room. Max dives for cover behind the couch against the farthest wall, Milly after him. Logan jumps to her feet. She hesitates, stutter-steps, then follows Hugo up the swaying ladder. He catches her arm and helps her up.

They are in a dark crawlspace, on a squishy nest of unrolled sleeping bags surrounded by piles of boxes. It smells like leather and rubber and dirt. Logan lies down flat on her back beside Hugo, listening, struggling to hold her breath in check. The counselors are climbing into the loft. Their words become clear as they reach the top of the ladder, first one, then the other.

"Would you just listen to me?"

Hugo's hand reaches out to Logan's shoulder. "*That's Elias,*" he breathes.

"I am listening to you," says the other, higher voice. Logan recognizes the lilt of it—Rosie. "And I'm telling you, you're wrong."

"How can you say that? You don't have proof. No one has proof."

"I don't *need* proof. He's rich, he's white, he's powerful. He's guilty."

"That is so biased. I mean, shit, that's just prejudiced!"

"That's not how prejudice works, idiot."

Logan hears the tinny clank of a can kicked across the floor. She winces. The counselors' argument pauses, their voices soften. They start debating who might have left the beer on the ground.

In the dim of the crawlspace, Hugo's hand has shifted from one shoulder to the other so that his bare arm stretches all the way across her chest. She turns her head slowly, careful not to crinkle the sleeping bag beneath them. He is on his side, looking at her.

"Must've been Germ," says Rosie's voice. "He's wasted."

Logan gasps. Milly was right—they *are* alcoholics. They get *wasted* during the Camp dance. This is shocking and somehow wonderful news, the very grimiest of gossip. Logan raises her eyebrows at Hugo, who smiles. He wiggles just the tiniest bit closer to her. Dust motes dance in the sparse yellow light between them.

"Whatever." The refrigerator door opens with a soft suction sound. There is a heavy clink of glass, a slosh of liquid. "Here. Cheers."

Hugo squirms closer. His breath is hot on Logan's face. From what she can make out, his expression is serious. From below them comes a gulp and a gasp, a clunk. Hugo rolls forward and plants his lips on hers. It isn't a gentle, quick kiss, like before—this is something else entirely. His entire mouth engulfs her, his nose knocking against her glasses. Logan can hardly breathe through the rusty straw taste of beer. She lies frozen in surprise and sudden panic.

"I'm not done making my point, by the way. I mean, if you need to think he's innocent just to get through this summer, fine. Whatever. But that's a garbage opinion in the real world, and you know it."

"You're still not hearing me! He's a good kid. He is. If he's a good kid, is it that crazy to think he might be a good person?"

Hugo's body weight shifts over Logan, pinning her down. The only thought that manages to shove its way through her buzzing head is that she should try to kiss him back, but she doesn't know how. His tongue—his *tongue*—squirms like a slug against her teeth.

"I don't care if he's a good person or not! He's a murderer!"

They both freeze. Hugo lifts his head and frowns down at her. Logan shifts away, frantic to catch her breath, and the sleeping bags rustle beneath her. Silence falls in the loft. She stiffens and sucks in her lips.

"Oh, hang on. Is someone in here?"

"Hey!" Elias shouts. "Someone up there?" A thud makes them both jump; he has thrown something at the bottom of their crawlspace.

They stare at each other. Hugo clears his throat. He makes his voice very deep. "Uh. Yeah." Logan closes her eyes and shakes her head. This is it, she thinks—they're done for.

A pause stretches, then the counselors laugh. "All right," says Elias. "We're out."

"Who is that?"

"Probably Datie and Kane. I mean, Katie and Dane." Elias laughs coarsely. "It's still working hours, you animals!" he shouts. Hugo opens his mouth to reply again, but Logan throws a hand over it, silently begging him not to push their luck.

"Here, give me that," says Rosie's voice below them. Another gulp, another clunk, then the fridge opens again. "Let's go."

Logan slides farther away from him on the sleeping bags. They wait in silence until Rosie and Elias's voices have left the loft, tracking them back down the ladder and across the barn floor. They are still arguing.

When Logan drops down from the rope ladder, Max and Milly are already standing. They both look stunned. Milly's jaw falls slack. "You guys," she laughs, "what the *shit* was that?"

Logan tenses. She wishes everyone would stop swearing so much.

"Did you hear that?" Max asks. His fingers are digging anxiously at his left wrist under the fading blue plaster. "She said 'murderer.' Who do you think they were talking about?"

Hugo Baker lands on the loft floor next to Logan. His hair is all askew. The ball gown has fallen to the middle of his stomach, twisted around backwards like on a cheap plastic princess doll. His lips and chin are smeared with black eyeliner. Mortified, Logan quickly reaches to wipe her own mouth. Max cracks a smile; Milly yelps with laughter.

They walk back to the dance as quickly as they can without running and reenter the crowd in pairs: first Hugo and Max, then Milly and Logan behind them. No one seems to have noticed they were gone. The rest of the Ravens are clustered in the crowd, dancing goofily with a group of boys.

Logan feels sick. The lingering taste of beer and Hugo's mouth are a sticky, pasty goop under her tongue, churning in her stomach. As they stand at the edge of the party, watching their friends dance, Milly leans toward her. She still looks so funny in her tie and mustache. "You know what?" she asks through the side of her mouth.

"What?"

"Beer kind of tastes like farts, doesn't it?"

The two girls look at each other and gradually crumble into giggles. Logan can hardly believe what they have gotten away with.

•••

THERE IS A TRADITION AT Camp: every summer, after the dance, the oldest cabins listen to a scary story on the lawn. Tonight, Dane is telling it.

Logan, Milly, Hugo, and Max sit at the back of the group apart from the rest. They share smug smiles—they know things no one else knows now. Dane is probably drunk, they whisper. After this, he'll be somewhere with Katie. They snicker. It's like the four of them own the world.

Everyone asks for the same story. They've all heard different versions over the course of the summer, and they want the full thing, the real deal. Dane agrees reluctantly. He asks them if they are sure, if they won't be too scared. This story is especially scary, he says, because it's true. Girls in their boy costumes whimper and slink together; boys in their girl costumes sniff and straighten their backs.

"Danny McGee was a camper here at this camp, just like all of you," Dane begins, "a long, long time ago . . ."

Logan looks at Hugo, who is listening fixedly. She looks at Max, who looks back at her. He gives her a crooked smile.

In the last version of the story she heard, Danny McGee wandered off the trails and simply disappeared. Dane's version is clearer on what happened. It wasn't a bear or a beast that got to him, but other campers.

"Danny was a little different from most kids. The other campers picked on him."

He has a good voice for storytelling, low and broody. The story plays out in detail. One night near the end of the summer, at a campout at Lobster Point, some boys tried to play a prank on Danny. They chased him onto the dam, then built a campfire on either side. He was afraid of heights. They thought it would be funny to make him stay the night out there. When he begged them to let him come down, they shouted, *So, jump! Jump, Danny, jump!* So, Danny jumped.

Dane pauses for a long time. The warm twinkle lights have gone out behind him. In the darkness, the forest creaks and groans. "A lot of people say Danny McGee never really left Camp Phoenix. Sometimes, late at night, you can still see his shadow walking around, just off the trails."

Logan leans forward, clasping her chin between her knees.

"Sometimes you'll hear him coming up behind you. You'll feel him, right over your shoulder. But when you turn around . . . there's no one there. We can't really be sure what he wants. If you ask me, I'd say he's still looking for the kids that bullied him. They're all old men by now, but Danny doesn't know that. He's just watching, waiting until he finds someone that fits the mold."

"Then what?"

Dane shrugs. The moonlight rolls on his shoulders. "I don't know. If you were Danny, what would you do?"

Hugo squeezes the back of Logan's hand. He looks past her, down the line of them. "Make them *jump*," he whispers.

Sam

POPPY LIES CURLED IN HER sleeping bag. Her eyelids are heavy, sinking downward. Magic marker smudges, the shadows of a button nose and whiskers, streak gray across her flushed face. Regardless of the theme, the Hummingbirds decided they would dress as kittens for the dance. Katie helped them make felt ears and tails in crafts and Sam colored their faces. Poppy's tail, the glued seams ripped and bleeding fluffed white cotton, lies next to her on the pillow.

"What was your favorite part of the day?" Sam kneels at her bunk. She reaches out to smooth a wisp of hair behind her ear.

"Dancing," Poppy whispers.

"You had fun at the dance?"

"Mmhmm."

"I saw you out there. You're a good dancer."

"I'm gonna be a dancer when I grow up. And a singer, too."

Sam laughs. She lets her face fall to the flannel sheet, her hand resting on Poppy's hair. "Yeah," she says when she lifts her head, "I bet you are."

The rest of the girls are asleep already, snoring into their pillowcases. They are greasy and dirty, dry and chapped and sunburnt. They are happy. No one has cried all week, not even Rachel. Sam pats Poppy's cheek as she stands up. She flicks off the light switch and is sitting on her bunk, tying her shoes in the dark, when she hears Poppy rustle and turn in her sleeping bag.

"Sam?"

"Yeah?"

"I love you."

Sam drops her shoelace. "Good night, Poppy."

Rosie and Elias are already waiting on the trail outside. The two of them are bickering about something; they have been bickering about something all night. Their matching costumes cut bizarre, puppet-like silhouettes in the moonlight. With tools from the crafts shack, they managed to splice together a pair of each of their shirts and sweatpants, vertically, so they are both wearing half-and-half: girl on one side, boy on the other. Elias has one side of his hair up in a taut pigtail and Rosie has half of hers tucked into a low bun. The full effect is honestly remarkable.

"God help me," Rosie had sighed as she posed in their bathroom mirror. "Promoting the gender binary like it's the nineties."

"But you look good," Sam told her.

Rosie sighed again, defeated. "I do look good."

Between her office work and meetings with Richard Byron and her preoccupation with Poppy, Sam had no time to put together a costume. She wound up dressing all in orange and hanging an old warning sign from the boathouse over her neck: *DEEP WATER: No Swimming Beyond This Point.* "Are you a girl or a boy?" campers asked her. She answered: "Boy? I thought it was girls versus *buoys!*" The joke went largely underappreciated, though it got a hearty laugh out of Gus Campbell.

"You're such a pig," Rosie is saying as Sam comes toward them on the trail. "No one even sounds like that. Name one girl who sounds like that."

Elias, squinting up at the sky, carries on with his embarrassingly pornographic impersonation until Rosie smacks him and he chokes on his own laughter. "You do," he taunts her.

"I do *not.* Who told you that?"

"Small camp," Sam says, butting between them. "Sound travels."

"Shut up, Sam."

They're all a little drunk already. The midsummer dance, for one reason or another, is more of an event for the counselors than the campers. It's the one night of the summer that stands out from the rest—a milestone, in a way, a night worth celebrating. No one wants to drive, so they stay in the parking lot, sprawled on tailgates and hoods, drinking and gossiping like teens after prom.

Sam's place at Camp is changing. Tonight is another brutal reminder of it. Since the news about Poppy spread, the other counselors treat her differently. They look at her differently: with pity, sometimes, and sometimes with something like contempt. Despite herself, she feels like she's somehow at the root of the tragedy. Not the cause of it, exactly, but the epicenter; while everyone else can look away, Poppy Warbler's death revolves around her. Her special treatment this summer doesn't help—the private meetings, the radio on her hip. If only they knew, she thinks, that Richard Byron specifically asked her to spy on them. If only they knew about Nick, the secrets he whispers in her ear. They look at her like they do.

Rosie would tell her to stop feeling sorry for herself. Sam shakes herself out of a sleepy trance and sits up on the hood of her car, ignoring their chatter across the windshield behind her. Fishing for an escape, she glances across the lot. Nick is leaning against a bumper with Dane and Katie, picking at his beer label. Sam attempts to catch his eye but realizes she is far beyond the borders of his attention. She slides off the hood, mumbles about needing to pee, and stumbles toward the barnyard.

There is a smelly little outhouse behind the barn. When Sam steps out of it, she sniffs and wipes at her eyes, choking back the lump in her throat. She walks back around to the front of the barn and jolts, surprised to see someone sitting alone in the doorway. He appears surprised by her, too.

"Oh. Hey." Taps frowns at her. His back is to the light, his shadow stretching across the mud in front of him. He has a beer can in one hand and the bulge of another in his sweatshirt pocket. He squints, looking her up and down. "Having a bathroom cry?"

Sam nods. At the moment, she can't find a reason to be embarrassed. Taps gestures for her to sit beside him in the doorway. He offers her the beer in his pocket with an impish little smile. Sam takes it gratefully. She blinks and dabs at her eyes with her sweatshirt sleeve.

"What's going on?"

"Nothing." Sam laughs, reaching down to peel a fleck of dried mud off the toe of her shoe. It's the truth; she can't point to anything in particular that drove the tears, just the stink of the outhouse and a drink too many. "Really. It's just, like, a weekly thing, now." She snorts.

"I get that." Taps nods. "You sure you don't need me to beat someone up for you? I mean, I know Nicky can be kind of a jackass."

She freezes, unsure how to react. At his knowing smile, she breaks and winces. "How do you . . . ?"

"I saw you guys going into the guest cabin today. Wasn't snooping," he clarifies quickly. "I was on my way to meet someone there myself, actually. You guys beat me to it."

Sam sucks her teeth and shrugs. Of all the people to know, she supposes Taps is not the worst. He has never been much of a gossip. She opens her beer with a crack and a fizzle and looks out across the barnyard. Then she turns on him, frowning. "Wait. *You* were meeting someone at the guest cabin?"

He smiles wryly. One hand taps out a gentle beat on the wood slats beneath them.

"So, someone with keys to the guest cabin?" Sam prods him when he doesn't answer. "Come on. You know mine. Tell me yours."

Taps shrugs. "Well, you're not dumb. Figure it out. There are five ADs. You're banging one, and two of them are banging each other."

"Oh." Sam understands thickly. She runs a quick count on your fingertips. That leaves only Gabe and Amy. "Huh. I wouldn't have thought she's your type."

Taps chuckles. "*She's* not," he says around the mouth of his beer.

"Oh." She looks back at her open fingers and manages to catch his point just before it sails over her head. "*Oh*. Shit. I mean, I didn't know that." It's a pleasant surprise, actually, that there are secrets at Camp she knows nothing about, still some gossip that can shock her. "How come no one knows that?"

His sleeves are tugged up over the palms of his hands, the beer can clasped between them. It crinkles as he fidgets. "We don't talk about it. He doesn't think it's a good idea."

"Why?"

Taps sighs. "Honestly . . . he says Chard wouldn't like it if it got around to him."

Rosie's outrage rings in Sam's head. *Like it's the nineties*, she groaned. "So what? What's he going to do? He can't fire you for who you're with."

The beer can crunches louder. Taps's fingers clench. "He owns the Camp. He owns the town. He can fire whoever he wants for whatever he wants." He pauses, and they both drink in gulps. Then he goes on. "Phoebe and I went to the same high school. Did you know that?"

Sam shakes her head.

"Yup. Grew up together. She was always a weirdo. I mean, blue hair, anime, rainbow high-tops . . . the whole thing. She changed her whole vibe to come to Camp. But she was still kind of *off*. I mean, didn't you notice? Then, soon as something goes a little wrong, *whoosh*." Taps runs his hand through the air like a soaring bomb. "Guess who's gone? I'd bet you anything, if he knew, it'd be the same thing with me. Gabe would probably be all right, since he's an AD—he's, you know, in the inner circle. But I'm still replaceable." He brushes off her gaze with a forced shrug. "He wants the kids to think everything's normal, you know? And he gets to decide what normal means."

His frankness settles heavy around them, thick as snow. Quiet and dense. "You sound so . . ." Sam laughs. She has no reason to be laughing. ". . . *Chill* about that. Aren't you mad? Don't you want to be able to be yourself?"

Taps shakes his head. "Richard Byron," he says, speaking up to the moon, "is from another generation. The dudes from the other generations make the rules." He drains his beer and twists the can between his hands, clamping it down to the size of a hockey puck. Then he nods, satisfied with his work. "That's the way it's always been."

Another minute of quiet commiseration passes between them. Sam finishes her beer. She wipes at her eyes and nose again, and he helps her to her feet to rejoin the party.

•••

SHE WAKES UP TO THE sound of birds. Before her eyes open, still half in a dream, she is thinking of Poppy. The sharp pain of her splitting lips drives her into consciousness.

Sam blinks and sees daylight. She looks up at a bare wood ceiling—not the ceiling of the Hummingbirds' cabin. She sits up and finds herself in a bed, in a cramped attic bunk room. Gray, early morning sunlight streams through the windows.

"Oh, God. Oh, no." Her head is swimming, the creeping tendrils of an intense hangover blooming behind her eyes.

"Hmm?" Nick rolls over beneath the single flannel blanket beside her. The sheets are peeling off the corners of his mattress. "What time is it?"

The other bed in the room, Sam sees with relief, is empty. Fuzzily, she remembers: at the bottom of a bottle, she caught him by the back pocket and they snuck off. Dane, Nick's roommate in the office bunk room, was sleeping with Katie in the guest cabin, so they came back here. The room is stuffy, heavy with the smell of men and dirty laundry and sleeping bodies. Nick's guitar is propped against the wall, his clothes folded neatly on his shelf. He is shockingly vulnerable sleeping next to her, naked and crusty-eyed. For a bitter, blaring moment, she looks at him and lands somewhere between love and repulsion—they aren't actually so far apart, she thinks.

She has to close one eye and squint to read her watch screen. "Five fifteen. Ugh."

"You're fine," he mumbles into his pillow. "Campbell comes in around six."

Sam struggles to lift herself off the mattress and stumbles into her clothes. "Shirt . . . shirt . . ." she mutters; lost, a drunk vagrant, bumbling through the streets of Paris in search of bottles in the gutters. "Where's my shirt? Hey!" She throws a balled sock at Nick. "I can't find my shirt."

He sits upright, blinking, and grabs for something on his shelf. "Here." He tosses it at her.

Sam holds the shirt up. It's enormous, navy blue, bold white text printed down the front: *GOD IS A LESBIAN*. She laughs through a hiccup. "Is this yours?"

"Dress code violation. You can keep it."

Sam scrambles into the T-shirt. It hangs to the center of her thighs, and the fabric smells musty. She stands in the doorway, holding her shoes, and looks back at him. What is appropriate here? A kiss goodbye? Some intimate words? A middle finger? She gives him a gruff half wave from the doorway, and he waves sleepily back. "See you later, Red."

She shuts the door as quietly as she can behind her.

At the foot of the office stairs, Sam pauses. She looks up. The human figure standing over the coffeepot is as horrifying and somehow unsurprising as swooping death itself. Richard Byron stands poised mid-step, mug raised halfway to his open mouth. They look at each other. Sam's head whirls; for a moment she thinks she can talk her way out of this—there has to be an excuse—then she sees herself as he must. Hair tangled, eyes glazed, socks and shoes in hand. There is no mistaking what she is doing here.

The look on Byron's face shifts seamlessly from shock, to embarrassment, to a shameful sort of delight. "Oh." His gaping lips curl upward. "Oh, *no*."

"Oh no," Sam echoes. She looks down at the borrowed shirt, then back to him. "Chard. I can—" Explain, she is going to say, but falters. She cannot.

His eyes roll upward, peering through the ceiling slats into the bunk room. Pondering. He sips at his coffee. "Huh. Really?" Watching her thoughtfully, he steps across the room and sits in Campbell's desk chair. One ankle crosses lightly over the other knee. After another sip, he nods toward the front door. "You were on your way out?"

Sam nods. "Yep. Yes, I was."

"Miss Red?" She turns, halfway through the screen door. His smile is amused, verging on adoring. "Stay on the trails."

Sam hurries away from the office porch, then pauses, hesitates, and changes direction. She may as well stock the gold in the creek now and have an excuse in case anyone else catches her out of the cabin. Halfway through her hike up the trail, she stops, dashes into the trees, and hurls herself over a decaying stump to vomit into the pine needles. What comes up is clear and sloshy. Tiny hammers batter behind her eyes. Her nose and throat burn.

At the gold-panning claim, she stands and stares into the bushes across the creek. "Hey!" she calls into the wild. She wants to see the bear again. She hollers for it, begs it to appear, to run to her, to eat her. "Come on!" She picks up a rock at her feet and hurls it across the water. It falls short, landing with a quiet splash. Nothing moves in the bushes. There have been no signs of the bear in weeks. It must have moved on or died. It may never have existed at all.

It's still early, well before the wake-up bell, when she gets back to her cabin. The campers are sleeping soundly. Sam stoops to put a hand on Poppy's forehead—warm, safe, full of life—then tiptoes out to the bathroom. Outside, one of the showerheads is already running. The bathroom mirrors are dripping with steam. Rosie's half-boy, half-girl shirt is piled sloppily on the concrete floor alongside the stitched pair of pants. With another wave of anxiety, Sam wonders what she knows, if she caught her sneaking away last night.

"Rosie?" She steps closer to the running shower, then stops. She can hear a familiar bickering, hushed voices through the splatter. Another pair of the same stitched pants hangs over the edge of a sink. "Rose?"

"Hold still."

"It's not working, they're not going away. Hot water is supposed to help."

"It's not hot water, it's *cold* water."

"Stop it, I'm freezing. Don't make it cold."

Two pairs of bare feet are visible below the curtain, toe to toe. In a rush of disbelief, Sam strides to them and throws the sheer plastic aside. They both jump. Rosie's eyes are completely off-kilter. Elias's blond curls are plastered to the sides of a red face, his neck and chest spotted with tremendous, tennis ball-sized hickeys. He sways and squints at her through the steam.

"Hey." Elias points a pruned finger at Sam's chest. "That's my shirt!"

week seven

Logan

GOLD-PANNING IS THE WORST ACTIVITY at Camp. The gold is fake. Everyone, even the little kids, knows the gold is fake. They shuffle around in the cool water, slipping on algae, searching for snakes and crawfish in the reeds. A hawk turns circles in the sky overhead, screeching at them. It's a hot morning. Logan wants to plop down and sit in the creek like in a bathtub, splash the water over her face and armpits and dunk her head to rinse her hair.

"It might be real," Milly says, hopeful, holding a sparkling nugget up to the sunlight.

"It's not real." Logan shakes her head. "The other day, I saw a finch with a chunk *this big*." She makes a sizable hole with her thumb and forefinger. "You know how much money that would be worth if it was real? They wouldn't just let some kid keep it."

Max slips and stumbles. He grabs her shoulder, nearly pulling her over. Logan grunts.

"Sorry!" He grimaces. "I can't get my cast wet."

"Get out of the water, then."

"But it's hot."

"Max, be careful!" Taps shouts. He sits on the creek bank with his sunglasses on, his bare feet in the water. "Anyways." He turns back to Donna and Mei, who lounge on the rocks beside him, not really listening. "What was I saying? Oh, yeah. In the pioneer days, people came from all over just to get a shot at panning this creek, right here. It's the richest creek in the world. It all comes from snowmelt, way up in the mountains . . ."

Logan stands still in the water, watching him talk. Next to her, Milly crouches, shifting through the stones and slime. Her clothes are soaked.

"Why do they all do that?" she mutters. "Why do they lie to us like that?"

Max, too, glances toward his counselor. Very carefully, he bends down to scoop up some water in his hand, then sprinkles it over the top of his sweaty head, holding his cast arm up high in the air. He shakes his head, drops flying. "It's not lies," he says thoughtfully. "Just . . . stories. Like the Danny McGee story."

"The Danny McGee story is true."

"How do you know that?"

Logan frowns. In her head she sees the ghost, the tall shadow hiding in the trees. Looming through the branches in the silvery moonlight. The more she thinks about it, the surer she is that it's the same ghost from Dane's story. It has to be. It was too real to be a coincidence. "I just know," she says.

As Taps tells his story, another counselor comes hiking up the trail to the creek bank: Sam. She has a little cardboard box in her arms, which she places delicately on the ground next to a tree trunk. Then she stands back and waves Taps over to her. She has her sunglasses on, too, and her face is red and haughty. Her hair is in a high, sloppy bun. Logan looks her over. Her stomach twists in a weird way as she watches Sam lay a hand on Taps's arm.

"I don't know," Max carries on. "I don't know about him being a ghost and all, but I guess the whole thing with the bullies, and him jumping off the dam . . . that could be true."

Logan ignores him, watching the counselors carefully. Something important is going on. Sam leans in and whispers into Taps's ear; her expression is serious. Then Taps smiles. "Nice," he chortles. "Okay."

Milly stands up in the creek, shaking the slime off of her hands. She looks past Logan at Max. "You really think there could be kids that are mean enough to make another kid jump off the dam?"

Max frowns at her. "You wouldn't get it. You're a girl."

"What the hell is that supposed to mean?"

She says this too loudly. The counselors snap their heads up from their quiet conversation. Milly draws air through her teeth. "*Oops . . .*"

"Hey," says Sam, "watch your language."

"Okay, sorry."

Logan waits until Sam has finished her conversation and turned away, disappearing along the trail again. In her bare legs, her T-shirt as long as a dress, she doesn't look like a counselor. She looks like someone who just rolled out of bed and stumbled into the forest. Logan turns to Milly and whispers, "Sam's kind of a bitch, right?"

Milly reels back from her. "Jeez, Logan. That's kind of mean."

"Yeah, Loges," says Max. "Since when do you talk like that?"

Logan shrugs. She starts bending down to look through the creek bed again, but something stops her. She turns to Max. "What did you just call me?"

A funny look crosses his face. His hair is wet. Murky droplets trail down his forehead and leave streaks through the dirt on his skin. "I don't know," he says. Apparently giving up the search for fake gold, he turns and shuffles his way out of the water.

Hugo catches up with the three of them when they reach the lawn before lunch. He strides across the grass toward them, peppy and smiling. He has a thin, untied friendship bracelet in his hand: white and pink, heart pattern. "You guys have headaches today or what?" he greets them, eyebrows wiggling.

"Why would we have headaches?"

"Because of the beer!"

"*Shh.* Jesus, Maxie. Keep your voice down." Hugo bounces lightly on his feet. He thrusts the bracelet in his hand at Logan. "Here, this is for you."

It isn't very good. The stitches are crooked and disordered. Still, he—Hugo Baker—went out of his way to make her a bracelet. A pink bracelet, with hearts. Logan squirms with embarrassed glee. She can't figure out the right response. As her tongue trips numbly over the words, Milly interrupts them, tugging on Logan's shirt to get her attention.

"Hey, who's Mr. Campbell talking to?"

They all turn to look. The Camp director stands at the foot of the mess hall steps, not too far from them. He is talking quietly and seriously with another older man, a tall man with a beard and dark gray hair. The man has his arms crossed, one foot propped up on the bottom step.

"I don't know. I think I've seen him before." Logan shrugs. "He's in the mess hall sometimes."

"Yeah," says Hugo. "He lives in the town, or something. Elias knows him. Why?"

Milly stands still, staring hard. "I don't know. He looks like someone I know."

All four of them watch the man and Mr. Campbell quietly. The director shakes his head, the other man nods, and they both roll their necks and shove their hands in their pockets. The man with the beard scans the crowded lawn. He looks right at the four of them, then pauses. He is smiling. He says something to Mr. Campbell and points straight toward them. Logan can't hear his words, but she could swear she sees her own name on his lips: *Logan*. She looks away in a hurry.

Max meets her gaze. His eyes flick back toward the steps, then he looks at her again. "Logan," he says slowly. "What's your last name?"

"Adler. Why?"

The funny expression shimmers across his face again. He looks like he is trying to dig something out from between his teeth with his tongue. His lips purse and twist, then he shakes his head. "I don't know."

The bell rings for lunch and their conversation drops. Hugo reaches out for Logan's hand, and everything else in the world falls away.

Sam

"I don't know." Rosie's eyes are dead behind her sunglasses. She shakes her head and flops her hands dully at her sides.

They sit on the lifeguard dock in swimsuit tops and shorts, keeping a passive eye on the splashing campers and talking in low voices. The sun beating down over them is relentless, and Sam feels sick, dizzy and uncomfortable in her skin. She feels like she woke up in the wrong body; this one is too big, clumsy, shaped all wrong. Every once in a while, they have to stop their conversation to shout at a rule breaker.

"Henry! No flips off the dock!"

"What do you mean, you don't know?" Sam eyes her. "You can't just not know."

"I don't know." Her hair is wet and loose, clinging in lumps to her suntanned shoulders. She is beautiful and reckless and defeated, a comic book heroine, fed up. "I don't know, okay? It just happened. We were drunk, and we were walking around, and I don't know where *you* disappeared to." Her attention drifts to the shore. "Sharon! No running!"

"And?"

"And I *don't know*, Sam." Rosie smacks the dock with an open palm. Her lips hang open for a moment, thoughtful. "It definitely happened in the boathouse. Also . . . maybe again, in the shower this morning." She winces. "I think we were quiet."

"There's no way you were quiet."

"Shut up. Seriously, for the rest of the summer, just shut up. It's fine. I'm *fine*." Rosie rubs at her temples. A gag chokes in her throat; she swallows it, shakes her head, and holds up her index finger at Sam. She scoots forward on the dock and slides into the water, disappearing below the dark surface.

Sam watches her go. Her fingers are trembling. Something about the idea of Rosie and Elias together, hilarious as it is, has her disgusted in a lonely, selfish way. She slaps a palm across her chest and glares at the lakeshore. "Sharon! I see you running one more time, I'm sending you to crafts!"

When Rosie climbs back onto the dock, she wrings out her wet hair, dries her sunglasses on her towel, then turns to her sharply. "Your turn, now. What happened to you last night? How'd you end up with El's shirt?"

The T-shirt is a damp lump beside them on the dock. Sam has been wearing it all day—changing somehow fell behind in her priorities. She clears her throat and launches into the story she prepared.

Rosie listens, her face inscrutable. Then she laughs. "You and *Taps*? Where?"

"In the air rifle shed." It isn't a difficult lie to come up with. There are only so many people, so many places. The pieces can be shuffled around like a board game. *Colonel Mustard and Miss Scarlett, in the air rifle shed, with a fifth of vodka.* "My shirt got . . . you know, dirty, so we went down to laundry. This was in the lost-and-found pile. Stewart!" She turns back to the water, grateful for a diversion. "Get *off* the buoy!"

Rosie laughs. Gently, at first, then louder. She lifts her sunglasses to meet Sam's eyes and unravels, feverish. Sam picks it up. Soon all the campers at the lakeshore are frowning in confusion toward the lifeguard dock. They laugh until tears are streaming from their eyes, until the sky is spinning over Sam's head and her lungs are aching for air. She feels, despite her headache and the guilt of lying, suddenly gleeful. For a brief, bright moment they could be anyone. Any normal twenty-somethings, at their normal summer job, giggling over the normal antics and regrets.

The ecstatic moment is cut short by the buzz of Sam's radio. She quits laughing and leaps for it—every buzz could be news about Poppy.

Sam?

"What's up, boss?"

AD meeting in five. I'll send someone down to swap you out.

"Oh." Sam watches Rosie. Her bright look has faded. "Yeah, okay. Be right up." They look at each other. Rosie turns to the swimmers in the water. "Sorry."

"No, go ahead." Her voice is strained, the bitterness behind it thinly veiled. Sam stands and tosses the T-shirt back on, then clips the radio to the waistband of her shorts. As she straps into her sandals, she wishes she had told Rosie the truth about where she was last night. She wants to tell her about him, about them, to pick apart his words and looks with her, to laugh over her mortifying encounter with Richard Byron in the office. How would Rosie look at her then, if she knew? How much stronger would the bitterness get? What would they whisper behind her back each time the radio buzzed? The most she can muster is a weak, sorry smile as she walks off the dock.

She gets to the office just before the start of the meeting. Dane looks up at her when she walks through the screen door, and her anxious heart shudders—he must have found something in his room: a sock, her shirt, a corner of foil wrapper—but he laughs, and says: "Dope shirt, Sam."

She nods and moves to get herself a cup of coffee from the back of the room.

When Richard Byron walks into the office, he claps her briskly on the shoulder. "Afternoon," he says without looking at her directly. Campbell comes through the door after him, then Nick—who, to Sam's dismay, also pats her on the shoulder as he passes in the exact same casual manner.

"Afternoon."

Byron raises an eyebrow at her over his coffee cup.

"Nicky, you seen your brother today?" Dane snickers. "Looks like he fought an octopus."

"And lost," Katie adds.

Nick nods, pouring his own coffee cup. "I did see that."

"We're trying to figure out who did it to him. Wait"—Gabe gasps—"was it *you*, Sam?"

"No!" Sam says, and Nick inexplicably snorts with laughter. Again, Richard Byron looks pointedly at her.

"All right, enough," Campbell grumbles. He sits heavily at his desk, rubbing his eyes. "I don't want to hear that. Don't make me hear that."

They smile at each other. "Sorry, Dad."

The meeting is nothing special, just a midsummer check-in. There are some routine issues with the activities and cabins. A boy in the Pigeons is having bedwetting problems; they need to restock the spare sleeping bags. No one says a thing about Poppy. There isn't much to be said, Sam supposes— nothing has changed. She is still as dead as she was a week ago. Campbell looks over his checklist, tutting under his breath. "Oh, Nick. Sometime next week I want you to let Sam write a schedule on her own. Okay, Sam?"

"Sure."

"Great. That's all from my end. You got anything, Rich?"

Byron leans against the back wall of the office. He puts a hand in his pocket and rolls his neck. His gaze touches on Sam briefly. "Just keep up the good work, that's all. I know it's been a tough one so far. I'm proud of you all."

As everyone files out, he waves Sam over to his side. She lingers back and leans against the thin wood panels beside him. For a second or two, he says nothing. He watches Campbell and Nick leave the room together. They stop to talk on the porch, just outside the screen door.

"How is Poppy?" Byron asks her in a low voice.

"Fine." Sam squirms on the spot. She feels like there is another shoe left to drop. If he is going to fire her, she would rather he do it now, and quickly. Then she will rush to Rosie on the lifeguard dock and tell her everything. Maybe she will even be dragged away in a scene of dramatic heroism, spitting, cursing the world.

"Good. Nothing weird? Nosebleeds? Overly exhausted?"

"Nothing I've noticed."

"That's good. She's been pretty stable over on the other end, too." He clears his throat, sips from his mug, then bobs his head at the door. His voice drops still lower. "You know, Gus would have an aneurism if he knew you spent the night out of your cabin. You—his golden child." He chuckles. "How long has that been happening?"

Sam looks at Nick through the screen. His hands are on his hips, hair rustled up by the breeze, chatting cheerfully with Campbell. "Not long."

Byron looks forward, too. Another sip of coffee—Sam can smell it, burnt and muddy, too long in the pot. He shakes his head good-naturedly. "Nicky was the first one to say he liked you for the shadow job. Last summer. We were down at campfire, and I saw the way he looked at you. I didn't think anything would come of it. He's so professional about those kinds of things, you know." A tiny smile plays on his cheeks. "Maybe he could use a bad influence."

The rhythm of these conversations has become familiar to Sam. She knows he will ramble his way to his point, taking his time, amusing himself. "I don't know," she says, just to say something.

He turns to lean on his shoulder against the wall, facing her. An oaky cologne mixes pleasantly with the smell of his coffee, strong and soothing. "He's told you some things, hasn't he?"

Sam nods.

"Do you know why I hired you?"

She hesitates, thinking back to what Nick told her in the office weeks ago—a lifetime ago, really—about the doctors and teachers, the failed early summers. Is he referring to that, or to her, specifically? She glances out the screen door again. "Sort of," she says.

"So, you get it. It's sort of a dance, these summers. There's an art to it. Everything becomes a part of the bigger picture." He sips from his mug, coughs. His eyes run up and down her. "Don't worry, Sam. You keep my secrets, and I'll keep yours. That seems fair to me. I do have a little job for you, though."

"Okay."

"Max and Logan Gill. I want you and Nick to take them on their campout next week." Byron smiles at her. "You're exactly what they need. I want you to go on the trip and enjoy yourselves. Go be kids. Don't be careful while you're up there. Do you understand what I'm getting at?"

A wall has come down. For a fraction of a second, the authority, the esteem, is gone, and Sam is looking directly into the depths behind it. In an instant, it hardens back into place.

"Monkey see . . ." he says, then shrugs. "Well, you know."

Sam folds her arms across her chest. She can feel the weight of him looming over her, a timbering pine, on the brink of crashing down. He could crush her like a bug in his fingertips. "Yeah."

Byron nods, smiles briefly at her again, and rises off the wall. He drains his mug and crosses toward the sink in the back of the room. "I can't say that's a Camp-appropriate shirt, by the way."

"Oh, yeah. Sorry."

"Speaking of appropriate, tell your friend Elias to put a scarf on, will you? Kid looks like a leper."

"Okay."

He leaves the office. Sam watches him ruffle Nick's hair as he passes him on the porch. She fingers the hem of her ridiculous T-shirt. Her head is pounding. For a moment, she closes her eyes and spins behind them and wishes he had just fired her.

Logan

MAX'S CAST COMES OFF PARTWAY through the sixth week of Camp. Logan sees him showing off a shrunken, pale left forearm at the Hawks' table. Nurse May gives him a tidy black wrist brace, smaller and much cleaner than the blue cast. He is practically unrecognizable, a new man.

They leave for Pike Falls on Friday morning after breakfast. Logan meets Max and the counselors at the office. In her hiking pack is a single change of clothes and her swimsuit; her compass, water bottle, flashlight, and toothbrush; a pad hidden in a rolled pair of socks—just in case.

Sam is coming on the trip, and Nick, one of the older counselors. Logan doesn't know him beyond the occasional speech at announcements or song at campfire. Some people say he's Elias's brother, but she has never been able to tell if it's a joke or not. They do look alike, a little, although Nick is taller and dark-haired and a lot less fun. He gives her a bag of food to carry in her pack: protein bars and powdered oatmeal packets for breakfast tomorrow morning. Max carries ham-and-cheese sandwiches and apples.

To get to the trailhead, they have to drive over the bridge and through town on the other side of the lake, then a long way down a dirt road, deep into the forest. Normally this is done in the Camp bus, but since it's just the four of them on this trip, they get to take the little red pickup truck that's always parked at the barnyard. There are only two seats in the truck, the counselors tell them, so someone will have to ride with the bags in the open back. Max grips his healed arm protectively.

"I'll do it!" Logan jumps to the opportunity. "Please!" she adds, so Max can pretend he is letting her have it, just to be nice.

"How about boys up front, girls in the back?" says Nick. "Max can help me navigate."

On their way out of Camp, they pass the barnyard and stables. They're empty, to Logan's disappointment. Sitting in the rattling back of the pickup with the wind and dust in her hair is the coolest she has felt all summer. They drive through the trees, past Lobster Point, up and over the bridge beside the dam. It must have been a thousand years since Logan looked down on the spillway from this height the first time, on her way into Camp from the doctor's office. She closes her eyes and watches the light flash red to black as the shadows of the trees rush over them.

"What's the name of the town?" She has to shout over the roar of the engine and rushing air.

Sam glances at her. She was gazing off, wearing that half-awake expression the counselors always have, apparently very deep in thought. "Smith's Ridge."

Logan watches Sam. She sits with one knee up, an arm propped over it. Her tank top swoops low; her chest is flat and sun-spotted, ridged with bones. *Pretty*, Logan realizes, must mean something different to boys and to girls. For girls, prettiness is constant. Always on, always checked, adjusting braids and batting eyelashes. Boys see pretty in a single broad scoop, all or nothing. There is a special talent to it, she thinks—being pretty to boys.

The town is empty. Like a ghost town. They pass through it quickly and the shady forest swallows them up, then the road gets rougher. Dust kicks up and sticks to their lips and eyebrows. Sam tells Logan riddles as they sway and bump up and down in the truck bed, trying to hold themselves steady.

Their hike begins up a steep slope. The air is still and stifling. It's quiet; all Logan can hear are their own footsteps and heavy breaths, and the occasional rustle of a chipmunk or bird in the scrub bushes. She starts to pant and sweat. Misery sets in and her shoulders ache under the pack. This wasn't supposed to be so hard. Eventually, though, the ground levels out and the landscape changes around them. They cross a high meadow spotted with wildflowers. In the distance they can see snowcapped peaks. Dragonflies and chubby bumblebees float between the sprigs and green buds at their knees, heavy, swollen with sunshine. Max, who was huffing and puffing along the first part of the hike, breaks into a happy, light stride, his braced wrist swinging free.

The counselors slow their pace. Nick shows them different plant species, points out animal tracks and names the peaks around them. Every so often,

Sam winks at Logan and Max and picks up a heavy rock from the trail, then stuffs it into the top of Nick's pack while his back is turned. The trail winds around and gently upward, over boulders and fallen logs, beneath trees a century old. Logan's imagination carries her away—they are a family of nomads, wild people, scouting their way toward their next adventure. They sing campfire songs as they go.

Around midday they reach the campsite: an open, needle-coated stretch of ground with a blackened ring of rocks for a firepit. The men's room and women's room are established on opposite ends, behind bushes and trees. They eat their sandwiches and change into their swimsuits. Logan feels instantly lighter, like she could run the rest of the way. Without the packs, they finish the trek up a pebbly incline and arrive at the top of Pike Falls.

The waterfall itself, like the barn loft, isn't as magical as Logan envisioned. It's more of a trickle than a thundering flow, over smooth boulders and slime. That's because of the drought, Sam says. The fact makes Logan uneasy; she didn't know about a drought. She can't remember when she last thought about the weather or the world outside Camp Phoenix at all. They clamber down into the ravine and look up, cool mist on their faces. It takes some splintering courage and heckling from the counselors for Logan to jump into the pool. She comes up gasping and kicking. The water is icy cold.

She and Max climb and slip and tumble and splash each other. They shiver as they compare goosebumps, arm to arm. Something in Max has changed. With his shoulders thrown back and his hair on end and his arms outstretched for balance, he wanders the algae-slick rocks. He is bigger here, away from Camp and the other boys. Not older, exactly, but bigger. He smiles at her through chattering teeth.

"Look," he whispers, and points sneakily up toward the sunny rocks, where the counselors lie tanning. Logan looks and catches it with a delighted gasp: Nick's hand on Sam's back, close to her butt, the lightest touch. Maybe an accident—maybe not. She shivers and grabs onto Max's arm, laughs so hard she almost falls.

They get back to their campsite sunburnt and starving. Dinner is bean-and-cheese burritos and smoky-tasting hot chocolate, heated over the fire in a little metal pan. Afterward, Nick leads them up a short trail to an open lookout. The sun is setting. They step out of the trees, and the ground drops away below them. Logan never imagined so much world could exist in a single view—forest and mountains and streams, miles and miles laid out like a picture at their feet. She stretches one arm out, aiming to reach down and leave a handprint across the surface of the Earth. The sinking sun douses it all in golden orange.

Nick cups his hands around his mouth and shouts out loud. The yell makes Logan jump; it thunders out and is lost in the hugeness of the landscape. Sam smiles wildly, then she copies him. They shout louder and louder, one after the other, howling and whooping. At first Logan laughs, bewildered—this is as absurd as his hand on her back—but Max opens his mouth and he shouts, too, so she tries it, lets her breath tear free from her lungs. Soon they are all screaming and stomping and beating their chests. Their voices rise like bubbles, floating away from the cliff, trapped forever in the atmosphere.

When they leave the lookout, Logan can't stop smiling.

Darkness falls quickly. There are marshmallows to be toasted and stories to be told around the fire. It gets colder. They huddle up on logs and hold their hands close to the flames. Logan can feel the warmth leaching away through her sunburn; she tugs her sleeves over her fingers and hugs her knees to her chest. They beg the counselors for another rendition of Danny McGee. "The *truest* version," she pleads. "Tell us *exactly* what happened."

Sam smiles, sneaky, like she's telling herself a joke. "It was a long time ago, you guys. I wasn't born yet. Nick wasn't even born yet," she teases him. Nick—plain and boring, Logan always thought—looks like a different person when he laughs at her. A weaselly curiosity nudges Logan, watching the grown-ups. She wishes Milly were here to smirk and speculate with her. "All we know is what people have told us."

"Did you go to Camp when you were a kid?" Max asks suddenly.

Sam nods. "Of course. When I was your age. How else do you think I'd know the story?"

"Were you a Raven?" asks Logan.

"Uh-huh. And a Magpie, the year before that."

Max sits next to Logan on their log. He has his hood up, so she can only see the ridges of his eyebrows and nose, rimmed in red firelight. He rolls his marshmallow-toasting stick between his palms. "When was that?"

"When I was eleven," Sam answers.

"I mean, what year?"

"Max," Nick cuts in with a choppy laugh. "If you want Sam to tell you the story, you're going to have to let her talk."

Logan nods. "Tell us the truth," she says. Only half of her is joking. She believes in the Danny McGee story as much as she doesn't believe in it. Like when she was littler and had her first suspicions about Santa Claus, she is straddling the line. "Do you really think he's a ghost?"

Sam shrugs. She picks up her marshmallow stick and prods it into the glowing coals. "I don't know, Logan. I really don't want to scare you. Sometimes, though . . ." She flips the stick upright. Its tip is red and smoldering, a tiny trail of smoke swirling from the top. Sam holds it close to her face. She is cast in a dream-like glow from beneath her chin, shadows crawling over her hair. ". . . No. I don't know." Her voice falls to a whisper, like she is talking to herself.

"Sometimes what?" Logan breathes. She leans her elbows on her knees and holds her chin in her hands. The fire is hot on her face.

Sam glances at Nick. He frowns, like he's warning her, and she nods. Her lips twitch before her words come out, to show that she is choosing them very carefully. "Let's put it this way. There's a reason we always tell you guys to stay on the trails. We don't know what, and we don't know why. All we know is that, as long as Camp has been around, bad things have happened to campers who wander off." Sam shakes her head. Her voice lifts. "But that's enough of that, I don't want to scare you guys. Anyway—whoops! Look at the time, Nick."

He looks at his watch. "Oh, shit! We'd better go."

Logan knows the swear is intentional. He is trying to act like he's treating them like grown-ups. She and Max have heard the way the counselors really talk to each other—they can't be fooled.

"Go?" Max repeats. He lifts his hooded head anxiously. "Go where?"

The counselors are standing, zipping up their windbreakers and shuffling through their packs. "You guys didn't think we were spending the night out here with you, did you?"

"What?"

Nick scoffs. "Come on, guys. It's a campout. Time to learn some survival skills."

"*What?*"

They shoulder their packs and tug their beanies over their ears. Before there is time to ask another question, they are gone, with a final shout over their shoulders: "Make sure you put the fire out! We'll see you back at Camp!"

Max looks at Logan. She swivels, searching for the counselor's retreating figures, but she can't see anything beyond the reach of the firelight. A nervous moment stretches. "They're . . . kidding, right?"

"Yeah." Logan nods. She hopes she sounds brave. "Of course they are. They'll be back in a second."

Seconds tick into minutes and the counselors do not return. For a long time, they watch the fire. Max's leg bounces against the log. The flames sink low, and the embers smolder black and red and angry. "They have to be joking," he says softly. Somewhere among the trees a branch cracks, and they both jump. "They *have* to be joking."

More time passes. Not sure what else to do, they put more sticks on the fire and decide to unroll their sleeping bags next to each other, for safety. They agree to accompany each other into the woods to pee, standing one at a time with their backs turned and their hands over their eyes. "Cover your ears, too!" Logan tells him as she crouches.

They scrunch down in their sleeping bags on the hard ground. By now they have worn out the subject of whether or not the counselors are playing a prank on them. They agree—more or less confidently—that Sam and Nick are probably hiding not too far away, keeping an eye on them. Testing them, Logan suggests. Just to see how they might react.

"Or . . ." Max says, and Logan giggles.

She thinks of that light little touch, of Hugo's words in the barn loft. Hot breath. Slimy tongues. "Yuck," she says out loud.

It's cold. The fire has burned down to coals, and they're out of sticks. The darkness is getting thicker. A breeze rustles through the trees and seeps into the fibers of Logan's sleeping bag. She shivers.

"You think Sam was just trying to freak us out?" Max asks. They lie with their heads together, on their backs, looking up at the stars. Trillions of them. More like dust than pinpoints. Logan still has her glasses on; she nudges them up on her nose and braces her hands behind her head.

"You mean, the whole thing about how bad things happen to kids that go off the trails?"

"Yeah."

"Yeah." She doesn't believe herself—not fully—but this would be a bad time to admit to being afraid. Somewhere in the darkness, a bird calls. It's a lonely, musical sound. Logan wonders what kinds of birds are up at night, and who they might be calling to.

A few minutes go by, and her thoughts have started to wander when Max speaks up again. "Truth or dare?"

Logan considers. "I don't want to get out of my sleeping bag. So, truth."

"Are you and Hugo going out?"

"Yes." Hugo asked her to be his girlfriend two days ago while they were sharing a pedal boat on the lake. *Girlfriend* is a weird word to describe herself by. It leaves a sticky-sweet taste in her mouth, like cherry lip balm and bubblegum. She likes to whisper it under her breath when no one is listening, getting the feel for it. She doesn't want to talk about that with Max. "Your turn. Truth?"

"Yeah, sure, truth."

"Okay, umm . . . Do you have any brothers or sisters?"

"I think so."

"You think so?" Logan pushes herself up to look at him through the dying firelight. She can only see the top of his shaggy head, his bent elbows and wrist brace. "What, you don't know?"

There is a pause. Then Max says, "We've been at Camp for a long time." Logan isn't sure if it's supposed to be an explanation for his strange answer, but she lets it go. "Truth?" he asks her.

"Truth."

"Where do you think we go when we die?"

Logan blinks up at the stars. The branches around them shiver. The bird calls again. "Jeez. That's a big truth." She closes her eyes, and on the backs of her eyelids she sees the red glow of the coals. She sees Max hitting the branch, and Spark galloping through the trees, and a bloody pair of sneakers half submerged in water. She opens her eyes again. "I don't know what you want me to say. I don't know."

"I don't know, either," he says. "But what do you think?"

"Well, what do *you* think?"

"Truth?"

"Truth."

Max rolls in his sleeping bag. Logan turns, too, and they face each other, braced on their elbows in the dirt and pine needles. His face is streaked with sticky grime and firelight and shadow. He looks like a monster, like he did after his fall. Logan fights the urge to look away. "I think," Max says slowly. "I think I saw something, once. When I got hurt. Remember, I went to the hospital?"

Logan nods.

"I had this dream, when I was there. It's . . . sort of hard to explain. I was at this hospital, and then I was asleep, and then I was . . . it's like I was floating. I don't know. I know it sounds weird. But it was just for a second—I was floating down this hallway. It was really bright. And there were doors on both sides, and every door had a name on it. And I looked over, and I saw my door. My name."

"It said *Max*?"

"It said, *Gill, M*. Last name, first letter. Like a roll call."

"So . . ." Logan hesitates. "So, what?"

"So . . . I don't know. I think that has something to do with it. I think, if I tried to open that door, I'd see where I'm gonna go when I die. But I didn't. I just kept floating." Max squirms and folds his arms down. He rests his chin on the top of his braced hand, and his fingers scratch soft, thoughtful patterns into the dirt. "Does that sound crazy?"

"Yes," Logan says, and she laughs, even though nothing is funny at all. His words are hard to comprehend. They tap against her brain, trying to burrow in, but she blocks them out. She'd rather talk about ghosts, about the counselors making out, anything else.

"Well, you want to hear something even crazier?"

"I don't know. Are we still playing?"

"There was another door there, too. Right next to mine. Same last name, different letter. It said, *Gill, L.* I don't know who that is."

Logan rolls onto her back again. She decides to take her glasses off. The clear view of all the stars in the sky is suddenly too much for her. "It was just a dream," she tells him. "Anyway, you're thinking too much. You shouldn't be thinking about all that stuff. Death and stuff. You're just a kid."

After another long pause, Max asks her, "Are you sure?" His voice is hollow and dreamy.

Logan isn't sure what he is asking. She pulls the mouth of her sleeping bag tight to her chin and clamps her eyes shut. "Good night, Max," she says, just to stop him from talking. She isn't really going to fall asleep. It's too cold.

Max's sleeping bag rustles as he turns over. He reaches back with one unsteady hand and pats her awkwardly on the top of her head. It feels silly, and it makes Logan smile behind her closed eyes. "Night, Loges."

Sam

THEY SIT AT THE EDGE of the ravine, on her sleeping bag, looking down at Pike Falls flowing into the black pool below. They cannot stop laughing. Sam has never seen Nick laugh so hard; his face is crinkled, tears in his eyes, head thrown carelessly back at the stars.

"We're being cruel, aren't we?" she asks through staggering breaths. "Should we go back?"

Nick shakes his head. His chest trembles as the roar pitters down, carried away on the rush and splatter of the falls below them. He sighs, hiccups, and passes her the wine bottle. Remarkably—endearingly—he had it stowed in his pack all day. "They're fine," he says. "Here. Your turn."

"Okay." Sam holds the bottle to her lips and blows into it absentmindedly, producing a hollow, airy ring. "I think you never had a drink until college."

He laughs inwardly. "That's wrong."

Sam frowns and tips the bottle back. The wine is cheap and sweet, warm against her lips. "What, after college?"

Nick reaches out to take the bottle from her. "Before. I was pretty young, actually." He squints at her. They both have their knees up, legs zippered together, hunched close against the biting chill. "I think you hate your middle name."

Sam takes the wine back. "You're good at this."

"Just lucky."

They've been playing the game for a while now, tossing their guesses back and forth, each a bit heavier than the last. It's silly, flirtatious. Away from Camp and alone with him for so long, Sam realizes she hardly knows who she is looking at, or how she should feel about him. They abandoned the campers in the forest together to do this, exactly as Richard Byron told her to.

"What do you think about all this?" she asks Nick presently, nodding toward the trail behind them. "Them, I mean. Why would they do this to themselves? Did they really think meeting as kids was going to make them fall back in . . . or, you know, fix things for them?"

He reaches distractedly for the wine bottle, looking up at the stars. "I'm not sure that's why they did it. I don't know. It's interesting though, isn't it? The whole idea of going back in time, to be kids together. Like, fuck it—let's put your soul and my soul in a jar together, shake it up and see what happens." He thumbs the neck of the bottle. Sam catches an absent sort of recklessness on his face when he blinks away from the sky. "They're not the first to try it. We've had other couples."

"Did it work for them?"

Nick shrugs. "Who's to say what 'working' means. None of them ever came back." He takes a swig from the wine and passes it back to her. "He told me he has a crush on her. Max. In the truck. Well, he didn't say that exactly, but I knew what he meant. He wanted to know why girls always go for the wrong guy." He snorts. "Poor kid. Wrong guy, indeed."

"What did you tell him?" Sam marvels at how simple it is for him to pick the brains of the boy campers. Girls can't be maneuvered so easily; girls are suspicious, too aware of the world.

"I told him he should just be himself. Be nice to the girl. I told him, the nice guy always gets the girl, in the end."

"You shouldn't have told him that."

"Why not?"

"That's not fair to her. Girls don't owe boys anything just for being nice to them." This is what Rosie would say, Sam knows as she says it. She wonders if she is being honest, if she is speaking her own mind, or just sponging into the personality of someone she admires. She wonders if it makes a difference.

Nick shifts forward and rests a hand on her thigh. Sam leans into the touch. "Fair enough," he says after a pause. "But he's not a boy, remember? And she's not a girl." He shrugs. "Anyway, that's not my choice of words.

Chard told me to say that to him, if I had the chance."

A breeze picks up, and Sam shivers. She pulls her hood over her head.

Every trail of thought she goes down lately seems to lead her to Richard Byron. He has his hands in everything she does—even this night, the laughter and the hand on her thigh, the taste of the wine on her tongue and her own curious attraction to him. Byron is there in all of it. They are dolls in his dollhouse, and he is looking over them, picking them up, smashing them together.

"Why," she begins, slowly, carefully. "Why did he send us out here, you think? He caught me that morning, and he knows . . . but do you think it actually makes a difference? For them?"

Nick shrugs. "It might. I've always said Chard should've been a movie director or something. He does that every summer. Tweaks things, sets up little scenarios to make it all more memorable for the campers."

"For the campers."

"Yeah, for the campers. What do you mean?"

"It just feels . . ." Sam chews on her lip, a shred of dry skin. "I don't know. Like he's screwing with us. Like he's setting us up, the same way we're setting them up." Again, she nods behind her, toward their campsite down the trail, where she assumes Max and Logan Gill are shivering with cold and fright around the dying fire. "Does that sound crazy?"

Her words rest between them for a moment. They both sip from the bottle in thoughtful silence. A bird calls somewhere in the trees. Then Nick says, quietly, "Don't do that to yourself. You can't start thinking like that. I know it's tempting. Because we're so cut off from everything else, and we know what the campers really are, it's easy to think . . . but you can't. We're not like them. If we were, we'd know it."

"Are you saying they know it?" In the darkness, away from Camp and brave with wine, it seems like a perfectly reasonable question.

Nick nods matter-of-factly. "They know it. Of course, they know it. They don't lose their memories in the transfer, you know. Those kids"—he shrugs toward the trail—"know exactly who they are. Just like they know we didn't really abandon them back there. Just like they know there's no such thing as ghosts. The only reason the whole thing works is that they want to look the other way. We make it easy for them."

"We keep telling them ghost stories," Sam whispers.

"Exactly. And they love them. Because a ghost isn't as scary as . . . you know."

As Poppy Warbler, she wants to say. A ghost isn't as scary as a washed-up pop star in a hospital bed, empty, living out her final days in a manufactured body. Dead and living, child and adult, here and gone. A constant reminder that they are all going to get old and die sooner than they believe. Nothing is scarier than that.

Sam drains the bottle in her hand. Despite his warning, she can't help but let the question spiral. In another life, older, miserable, what would she want? Without a doubt, she knows it would be this: wild air, stars; cold fingertips running along her ribs, making her shiver. She tips into him and they fall back onto the sleeping bag together. It would be easy to look the other way. Goosebumps. Breathy kisses. Little gasps and giggles. The sleeping bag slips beneath them, and Sam's back scrapes against gritty rock. Clumsy, rough, nothing too serious—when she is older, she thinks, and Camp is far behind, this is what she'll want to remember of it.

They zip back into pants and jackets and lie on the sleeping bag for a minute or two, shivering. Sam's back stings. Nick's fingers trail over the back of her neck, catch in her tangled hair.

"What *is* your middle name?" he asks her.

"Renée," she says. "For my aunt." For a funny half second, she tries to bring her aunt Renée's face to mind and fails. She can only remember hating the name.

•••

BACK AT THE CAMPSITE, THEY find the campers curled on their sides, facing a pile of hot ash in the firepit. It has been fascinating, watching the two of them together. Maybe it's only because she knows what they are to each other, but Sam could swear they move and speak in similar ways, like twins. They both have sweet, rounded faces and downcast eyes; both ask questions in high, nervous voices and purse their lips while they're thinking. As Sam stoops to stir the ashes in the pit, Logan Adler-Gill suddenly looks up at her. She blinks blearily. Her red-framed glasses sit beside her in the dirt.

"You're back?" Her voice is thin with exhaustion.

"Yeah." Sam smiles. "Glad to see you survived."

The girl squirms down in her cocoon-like sleeping bag. "You guys are assholes," she says from behind closed eyes. Sam spits out a shocked laugh.

The next morning rises sticky and bitterly cold. They are all dirty and sap spotted. The hike back down the mountain takes half the time, and they load up into the truck—girls in the back, boys in the front, like before—with a good chance of making it back to Camp by the end of the morning activity period.

Sam braces herself against the wall of the truck bed with her knees raised and her arms propped up behind her. She notices Logan copying her, holding herself in the same way. As they begin the bumpy drive, she watches the camper curiously. Logan's features are soft, endearing: mousy brown hair and ungroomed brows, glasses precariously balanced on a button nose. Cute, Sam thinks of her. Incredibly relatable, too, in the self-conscious way she carries herself, the way she watches and imitates, careful not to cross a line. Sam asks her if she had fun on the trip and she nods sleepily.

Not wanting to push too hard, she asks, as gently as she can, if she and Max get along. Logan nods and says that they are friends. "*Just* friends," she clarifies, as if she can read through Sam's question. She adds cockily: "I have a boyfriend."

"Oh?" Sam steadies herself against the side of the truck bed. They both bounce and rock unorthodoxly with each bump in the road. She knows who Logan's boyfriend is. "Do you like him?"

"Mmhmm." Logan fiddles with the friendship bracelets on her wrist.

Sam presses on, for no real reason other than fulfilling her own curiosity. "Is he nice to you? Your boyfriend?"

She nods at her bracelets. When Sam asks if he has ever hurt her, she looks up, surprised. Loose hairs billow across her face in the rushing air. "Why would he hurt me?"

"Boys can be jerks, sometimes. That's all."

"Hmm." Logan twists her lips and prods her glasses into place with her index finger. "He pushed me down, once, in Capture the Flag. But that was before we were going out."

Sam is struck by how young this girl is, how innocent. With a jolt, she realizes there are as many years between the two of them as there are between her and Nick. Then, with a gentler shock, she remembers that is not true at all.

She can't remember what Hugo Baker looked like, exactly. When she thinks of him, she sees Elias's camper, the thirteen-year-old boy. She has an unsettling image of that kid at the crime scene. Blood-splattered, knife in hand. His childish face turned down in a violent sneer, looking over the body at his feet like he just pushed her down in Capture the Flag. "Can I tell you something, Logan?"

"What?" The girl looks at her warily.

Sam flounders. This is none of her business. This is not a kid, not a troubled little girl—this is just another rich, bored woman searching for an escape. "Just be careful. If he ever does anything to you, anything you don't like, promise me you'll come tell me about it, okay? I won't get you in trouble. Either of you." As she says this, she feels the stinging welt on the small of her back and wonders who she is to tell any girl how to behave with boys.

Logan gives her a dismissive frown. She has an attitude. "Okay," she says. She looks at Sam like she wants her to know she has no idea what she's talking about. She is right about that much.

week eight

Logan

COMING BACK TO CAMP PHOENIX after the Pike Falls trip is like coming home at the end of a long, exhausting journey. They were only gone for about twenty-four hours, and Camp isn't really home—but it *is* home, in a way. Logan's real home is far away and fuzzy in her memory.

She sits with Milly on the mess hall steps before lunch and tells her about the trip. She tells her about the way Sam talked about Danny McGee's ghost, how nervous and careful she was. She tells her about the counselors leaving them at the campsite.

"They left you alone?" Milly is stunned. "Just you and Maxie?"

Logan nods. "Yeah—and get this." *Get this* is something Donna says a lot. Logan rolls her eyes in the way she has adopted from her, too. She doesn't care; Donna isn't around to catch her being a copycat. "This morning, on the way back, Sam was trying to ask me if I *like* him! Just like Sadie did."

"Huh. Do you?" Milly raises her eyebrows.

"*Milly!* You know I'm going out with Hugo."

"Yeah. How could I forget." Milly makes a face like she smells something rotten. She slumps forward on her stair, her elbows on her knees and her chin cupped in her hands.

There is a little voice in the back of Logan's head that likes to whisper things, nasty things. Things she shouldn't be thinking. It has been getting louder. *Jealous*, it says now.

She is sick of Milly's constant need to be different from everyone else. Her dirty clothes and gravelly laugh—Logan wishes, all at once, for a different best friend. A friend whose hair she could practice braiding. Milly's hair looks like no one else's in Camp, and she'll never be able to braid it. She reaches out to touch the short locks and Milly flinches away.

"Why's your hair like that?" Logan snaps. She can't stop herself. "No one else has hair like that."

Milly's look is stabbing. "No one else at *Camp* has hair like mine," she says, "because practically no one else at Camp looks like me."

Logan rolls her eyes and shifts away on the step. Milly always needs to be so different.

In afternoon period, she goes by herself to the lakeshore to meet Hugo. He smiles when he sees her and gives her a quick hug, his arms stiff around her shoulders. He wants to take out a fishing pole from the boathouse. Logan decides not to take one herself. It seems more appropriate just to sit on the fishing dock and watch him untangle his line and cast it out, over and over. The lake is calm and mostly empty; a few other boys fish from the shore or in rowboats. A lifeguard looks over them with glossy, disinterested eyes. It's scorching hot. Flies buzz around them, landing over and over in the sweat on Logan's forehead.

"Do you think the ghost is real?" she asks him.

Hugo shrugs. "Maybe." He is busy with his line. He talks a lot about fishing, but he doesn't seem to be too good at it, Logan notes to herself.

"What about the murderer?"

He laughs. She likes that bubbly laugh of his.

After a while, the heat and the flies are too much for her. She gulps down the rest of the water in her bottle and walks off the dock to refill it.

The faucet is in the boathouse, back behind the sailboat racks where the moldy life jackets get piled. It's cool and dim inside. Logan watches the clear trickle flow from the faucet into her water bottle. Just as she is thinking about what she should say to Hugo next, an eerie chill creeps over her. The hairs on the back of her neck prickle up and goosebumps spread over her arms. She is sure there is something—someone—standing right behind her.

"Boo!" Hands close over her throat.

Logan drops her water bottle. No scream comes out of her; she's terrified into silence. Someone is laughing, a bubbly, boy's laugh. "Hugo," she sighs, turning.

His hands drop from her throat to her shoulders. "Did you think I was a ghost?"

"Yeah, actually, I did," Logan admits. She was fully prepared to see the black shadow looming up behind her—Danny McGee in search of his bullies.

"Don't be an idiot. There's no such thing as ghosts." Hugo's smile fades. His hands drop from her shoulders to her hips. He pulls her waist into his. Logan dimly recognizes the look from the barn loft: extremely serious, like something important is about to happen. She isn't sure she is ready to try kissing him again, but his hands are on her hips and his face is closing in, and he is her boyfriend, after all—this is what they're supposed to do.

First, it's just a quick peck on the lips, like when they were playing Truth or Dare. That makes her smile. Then he looks nervously around the boathouse and tugs her farther behind the sailboat rack toward the life jacket pile, where no one would be able to see them if they came inside. The shadows are deeper back here. Logan lets her body go weightless as he guides her. He presses himself up against her. She panics and reminds herself to open her mouth and breathe through her nose, like she once heard Mei telling the other girls.

Is this really what everyone is so obsessed with? This is what grown-ups do for fun? Logan despairs behind her closed eyes. Making out is gross and suffocating, and it stinks. If this is adulthood, she wants no part of it. She doesn't know how to stop him.

Hugo grips her tight, pushing her backward. They fall clunkily onto the pile of life jackets, damp and reeking of lake water and mildew. He is laughing, like this is a good joke, so she laughs, too. She really does like that laugh of his. Then he lunges for her again, and she falls onto her back. He is on top of her, heavy, holding her down. A spongey cold soaks into the back of her hair and shirt. Hugo grunts in an ugly, animal way. Logan's eyes scrunch shut. In the shadows of the boathouse, she sees blue waves and anxious red splotches.

Panic wins. She wants to stop. She tries to pull away from him, but her head is pressed into the wet foam. She shuts her lips tight and clenches her fists and waits for him to stop kissing her. For a moment she thinks he might not stop at all, but then his head is off hers and she is looking up at him in the shadowy light. One bony knee digs into the center of her thigh. He looks confused. He opens his mouth—Logan assumes, to ask her what is wrong—but nothing comes out.

"Hugo," she wheezes, "I—I can't breathe."

He moves so his weight is off her, but keeps his arms around her, holding her in place. The life jackets shift and slide, tectonic plates beneath them. Her glasses are crooked. Still so serious, he looks her in the eyes. "Come here."

She can't possibly come any closer than she already is, Logan thinks, but quickly realizes he isn't talking about all of her. He means her right hand, which he grabs by the wrist and pulls toward him. To his lap. He presses her palm to the front of his shorts.

"Hey!" Logan snaps her arm back. Sharp fear and hot embarrassment twist through her.

"It's all right." Hugo's eyes are heavy, half closed. He grabs her wrist again. "Come here." Logan doesn't know what to say. She isn't exactly limp and weightless anymore, but he is so much stronger than her.

"I don't know how," she manages.

"That's all right. I'll show you how." He wiggles, causing a life jacket to slide to the ground with a sandy *flop*. Logan looks frantically up at the ceiling. He guides her hand. "It's okay. You're my girlfriend. We're supposed to do this." His forehead presses into hers. His breath is hot on her face, fogging her lenses. "Come on. Donna did it."

It's ugly and alien and hot against her skin. Logan tumbles in her head. They're old enough. Donna did it for him. Adults do it. She thinks of Sam— cool and confident, messy hair, skinny arms stretched out against the truck. She does things like this, too, for the boys who touch her back like it's something to worship. Numb, she lets him steer her hand. The voice in her head is back, but it isn't whispering anymore. It shouts at her: *Grow up. You have to. Donna did it.*

"Wait. Wait—I don't want to."

He ignores her.

You have to.

Someone calls Hugo's name. One of his friends. "Hugo! Dude, come here!" More boys' voices join the chorus. They're right outside the boathouse, at a run, their feet stamping. "Hugo! Henry caught a fish!"

Hugo flinches and lets go of her. In a quick, hopping motion, his shorts are back up and buttoned. It's like nothing happened at all. He looks at Logan, pink-cheeked and smiling as he catches his breath. The tips of his ears are bright red. Affection and confusion and embarrassment and terror bombard her from that smile. "I love you," he whispers before he turns and runs out of the boathouse. He says it quick, easy, like a grown-up.

A minute or two go by before Logan stands up from the life jacket pile. Her legs feel weak and shaky. She holds her right hand awkwardly at her side, like it's coated in paint or blood and she has to be careful not to touch anything until she washes it. Stepping out into the sunlight, she looks toward the fishing bench and sees him. Hugo Baker is surrounded by a group of boys, all of them crouched with serious faces, like him. "Kill it, dude!" they shout, "kill it!"

Hugo has a rock in his grip. He kneels in the grass by the dock. Logan sees something flopping, a shimmery tail. He lifts the rock and brings it down hard. The other boys cheer.

"Hit it again!"

He slams the rock down again. The fish flops, the boys shout, and he bares his teeth. Hugo holds his trophy up for everyone to see. His arms are slick with guts and scales.

"You're the man!" they howl. They shout his name; they can't get enough of him. "Hugo *goddamn* Baker!" The lifeguard looks on dully from her rowboat. Logan's feet begin carrying her away.

She finds Sam at the Hummingbirds' cabin before dinner, brushing the tangles out of Poppy's hair. Logan doesn't want to be a baby, but Sam said she wouldn't get her in trouble, or Hugo. Her palm and fingers are still burning, and her mouth feels dry. When she looks at Sam, she feels an intense longing for someone else, someone older, someone who has all the answers. She can't remember what her mom looked like. They've been at Camp for so long.

At first, she isn't sure what to say. Boys can be jerks, Sam said; he might do something to hurt her—but he didn't hurt her, not really. She chews on a fingernail, then says, "I have a question."

The counselor nods. It's like she already knows what she is going to say. She sends Poppy out of the cabin and sits Logan down on her bunk. "Tell me everything," she says. Logan does.

Sam

AS THE SUMMER DRAGS TOWARD its end, Camp is engulfed in a sweltering heat wave. The afternoons become unbearable. Even her early morning walks to the gold-panning claim have Sam sweating. With the heat comes the bugs: mosquitos in swarms at dusk and dawn, fat flies crawling over skin, wasp nests like land mines waiting to be stumbled upon. Campers and staff swamp the infirmary with bites and bumps and heat rashes. The horizon is growing hazy. There is a fire somewhere on the other side of the mountains, Campbell tells them. Uncontained, and growing.

The heat has everything running slower, looser. The heat, and the fact that they are passing the seven-week mark, impossibly tired with the finish line still just out of sight. Their tightly knit schedule has begun to fray at the edges. Counselors lounge in the shade, nursing hangovers, and forget where they're supposed to be. Campers wander lost in the middle of activity periods. Prank wars and food fights erupt, swear words fly unchecked.

Poppy is as loud and demanding as ever. Sometimes Sam forgets why she is supposed to be keeping such a close eye on her. In the back of her slipping mind she begins to suspect, among other things, that Richard Byron made the whole thing up. She spends her morning walks fantasizing about crossing the lake and sneaking into the facility to see for herself what is really going on behind the door marked *Warbler*.

Maybe while she is there, she muses, she can hold a pillow over Hugo Baker's face.

Not six hours after their conversation in the truck, Logan Adler-Gill came to her with tears in her eyes. "Made me touch it," she told her. The conversation made Sam realize she isn't as far from twelve as she thought; she remembers *it*—the haunting idea of it, the hilarious, horrifying mystery.

She used to look at the Hugo Baker case more or less passively, neutrally, but she has no doubts about it anymore. The kind of boy who does a thing like that becomes the kind of man who believes he can get away with anything.

She has complained to Nick and Campbell, but the most they will offer is sympathy. There is nothing they can do about it, they tell her. There is no proof of anything inappropriate. Whatever happens between two kids in a boathouse is no one's business but the kids'.

In a last-ditch effort, Sam decides to go to the boy's counselor. She knows Elias is as attached to Hugo as she is to Poppy, and she can't blame him for that, but he could talk to him. He could try to encourage him to stay away from girls like Logan for the rest of the summer. Maybe, at least, he will listen to her, and Sam will feel a little less powerless.

During free hour in the afternoon, she asks Rosie to keep an eye on the Hummingbirds and treks across Camp to the boys' cabins. Their world has gone dead and dry. Spiny bramble pricks at her ankles and lizards skitter across her path. She arrives drenched in sweat and irritable.

A handful of boys sits sprawled on the Falcons' porch in cuffed shorts, their scrawny chests bare and sunburnt. They are playing a roulette sort of game: facing each other with spread legs, one at a time tossing a pebble blindly up into the air between them and closing their eyes as it falls back down. "Don't cover your balls!" they shout, squirming in place. "Nobody cover your balls!"

"Hello, boys." Sam leans over their porch railing.

Hugo Baker flashes her his charming, little boy's smile. "Hi Sam. You wanna play rock-balls?" He shows her the pebble in his hand.

"No, thank you. Is your counselor here?"

"Eli-*as!*" another boy shouts toward the cabin. "*Girl!*"

"Great." She walks up the steps and wedges her way through them, all too aware of the raised eyebrows and dopey grins behind her back.

Elias sits on his bunk in the back of the empty cabin, in only his underwear, plucking at his guitar and singing fixedly to himself. When he sees Sam coming through the cabin door, he jolts. His fingers slip and the guitar brays, loud and off-key. "Dude. What are you doing here?"

Sam steps down a row of cluttered, unmade bunks toward him. The cabin stinks like old socks. Musty towels and pebbles and half-carved wood shanks are scattered over the floor. "I need to talk to you," she says, "about the murderer."

Elias's eyes narrow, and he lowers the guitar from his lap. "You shouldn't call him that."

Sam sits beside him on the bunk. She tells him, in a low voice, about Hugo and his girlfriend. Elias nods. He isn't going to care, she knows immediately, watching his expression. He is unimpressed. Bored, if not even a little proud. He scratches at his naked chest and wipes his nose on the back of his wrist.

"You have to say something to him, El," she pleads. "I know he looks up to you."

"Well, what do you want me to say? Look," he sighs, "don't overreact because it's him, all right? As far as we should think of it, he's just any other kid."

"He's *not* just any other kid," Sam says through her teeth. Outside, the rock *thunks* to the porch. The boys shout. Sam looks at Elias and knows the conversation is going to be pointless. She is digging for help in all the wrong directions—every man she knows was a boy once.

"Anyway." He leans back on his elbow, picking at his fingernails. "You shouldn't worry. Apparently, she dumped him. He's actually pretty torn up about it. He wants to sing her a song at the talent show to win her back. It's kind of cute, honestly."

Sam stands from the bunk. The heat is suffocating, heavy, bearing down on her. She can't think straight. She gazes absentmindedly around the cabin and lifts her shirt hem to dab the sweat from her face. Elias's stare drills into her back; she turns to see him smirking.

"Nice rug burn, kiddo. You get that in the air rifle shed?"

She rakes her eyes over his bare body. Bony kneecaps, scraggly little chest hairs. There is a hole in the elastic of his briefs. She is furious at him, for some reason she can't quite nail down, as if the heat and the haze in the air is all his fault, radiating from his smug grin. "You're one to talk," she snips. "If either of us is getting a slutty reputation this summer, it's not me."

Just before she reaches the cabin door, he stops her. "Hugo has night terrors. You know about that?"

Sam nods.

"You know what he says, every time? You know what he wakes up screaming?" Elias's face swells with emotion—possessive, adoring; a parent's look. "He says, 'I didn't do it.'"

"Well, he says that all the time, doesn't he? Out there?" Sam gestures beyond the cabin porch, across the lake. "I guess if you repeat something enough, it gets into your subconscious."

"I think he's innocent, Sam."

"I don't care."

She lets the door fall shut behind her, satisfied at having the last word, and steps past the boy murderer sitting on the porch. His cheeks are flushed, his face alight with childish excitement. He whispers a delighted dirty joke to his cabinmates as Sam walks away.

Campbell calls an emergency meeting after dinner, during evening activity. The assistant directors and Sam gather in the mess hall. Richard Byron is elsewhere, busy. Two pressing issues have come up. The first is that they have been blackmailed. Campbell recites the email he received out loud; it's short, and so horrendously cheesy that Sam catches Dane biting his lip to keep from laughing.

I know about the little dead girl. Pay me for the rest of the summer, or I'm telling everyone.

Phoebe's threat is not the problem. Even a credible threat would not be a problem, not for Richard Byron, not for Phoenix Genetics. Sam knows that—they all know who they are and what they work for. The problem, according to Campbell, is that Phoebe somehow found out about Poppy. Someone violated the terms of their summer contract to get in touch with her.

"She was friends with Greg, in the kitchen," Gabe suggests. "I saw them hanging out a few times. He can get Internet up in town, can't he?"

"What about Taps?" asks Katie. "He knew her from home. Right, Sam?"

Sam shrugs. "Why does it matter? She can't actually do anything."

"Because," Campbell sighs, exasperated, and runs a hand over his bald head. "Because rules are rules. Poppy isn't the only high-profile client here. Camp Phoenix is supposed to guarantee confidentiality. We let one thing slip, and next thing you know, something gets out about Rachel Settler, or Hugo Baker—"

The words come hiccuping out of her before Sam can stop them. "Maybe some gossip *should* get out about Hugo Baker!"

Katie shoots her a sideways, warning glare. Campbell lurches in his seat. His eyes are wide, his kind face hardened. Sam's chin sinks toward her chest. "We talked about that, kid," he tells her firmly. "You have to let it go."

The second pressing issue of the evening, to Sam's utter shock, is her own promotion. The mood at their table takes a sharp upward turn, and Campbell proudly tells her that, in exchange for her shadowing work and the burden of Poppy's situation, he has decided to officially change her title and pay for the final weeks of the summer. "You'll still be with your cabin, of course," he explains, "but I'll get you your own set of keys and have you trained in some supervising work. I"—he nods across the table, at Nick—"*we*, just thought it wasn't fair, how much we've asked of you this summer. You should be getting something back."

Sam beams. For a moment, she is flattered. They each hug her in turn as they leave the mess hall, Campbell warmly, Nick stiffly, Dane nearly collapsing her ribs. It feels good, but she knows something is wrong. This is too close to Phoebe's blackmail attempt. Sam is the dead girl's counselor. She has been inside the facility; she saw the decision-making play out after the horse accident; she knows what the murderer did to the wife. Sam puts the fake gold in the river every morning. To get something back is to stay in her place. This is wrong, and she can choose to acknowledge that it's wrong or stay flattered. Either way, the decision has been made.

The next morning, in the office, she signs her new contract. "Welcome to the team, kid." Campbell pats her on the back. "You happy?"

Sam nods and smiles. He leaves to find a set of keys for her, and she is left standing directionless in the center of the room, watching Nick work on the schedule board.

"Hey," she says to him. She finds nothing to follow it up with.

"Hey." He looks distractedly up at her. "Oh, hey. I need to borrow Poppy at free hour today."

"What? Why?"

"Nothing. We're working on something. Don't worry." His smile melts as he watches her expression. He glances at the screen door, still jittering from Campbell's exit. "Hey, by the way. We should be careful now."

"What?"

"You and me." He gestures at the space between them. "I mean, with the promotion. He asked me about it, and I sort of stuck my neck out for you. If he found out . . . You know, we should just be careful."

Nick has a habit of bringing up uncomfortable subjects in the daylight. It's starting to wear on her. "I didn't ask you to stick your neck out for me."

"I know. I wanted to." He rises from his chair and steps across the room toward her, leans in to kiss her. Then he hesitates, as if she said something to stop him. "What?"

"Nothing. What, you?"

Nick shrugs. They are on entirely different tracks, passing each other in opposite directions. Waving as they go by. "Listen, Sam."

"What?"

His eyes fall to the office floor, then back to her. He forces his hands into the pockets of his shorts. "If something is going on with you and Taps, it's . . . I mean, I get it. It's Camp. I can't be mad at you for hooking up with someone else."

Sam blinks at him, for a moment completely lost. Then she sputters. A glob of spit from her sudden laughter hits him in the chin, and she apologizes frantically, both of them scrambling to wipe it off at the same time. "There's nothing going on," she tells him on the other side of the confusion. "Taps isn't interested in me, I promise."

"What?"

"He has a thing with Gabe. They're trying to keep it quiet. I thought you knew."

"I don't know anything." Nick shakes his head.

The prickly barrier she was holding against him softens. Sam closes the space between them, her fingertips resting against her new contract on the desk. "I'm not planning on hooking up with anyone else," she adds quickly. "Just so you know."

Nick fidgets with the lanyard around his neck, looking awfully proud of himself. It isn't such a stretch to see a quiet, pubescent boy behind that smile, sharp-eyed and shy, desperate for attention. Every man she knows was a boy once. She wonders, in Hugo Baker's shoes, how he might have behaved.

At night she dreams about the white-tiled hall. She searches for Poppy's name along the doors, but she can't find it. The place becomes a maze; she turns corner after corner and only finds more hallway, more doors. More names. The lights flicker and darkness seeps through the arched ceiling, dripping down to fill the hall and bury her, drown her. Just before she wakes up, Sam remembers whose name she is actually looking for on all those copper plates. Not Poppy's, but her own.

Logan

SOMETHING WEIRD IS HAPPENING TO Camp Phoenix. Nothing big, nothing exciting, but something like a haze in the hot air has them all flipped upside down. Like time has crinkled up and skipped ahead without anyone noticing, everything is suddenly different.

Milly isn't Logan's best friend anymore. She doesn't know when it had happened, but it did. Hugo Baker isn't her boyfriend—that happened right after her talk with Sam in the Hummingbirds' cabin, the very next morning. She wrote him a note, folded the friendship bracelet he made her into it, and gave it to Max to give to him. It was the boldest thing she has ever done. That same afternoon, she went to the ropes course and crossed the fifty-foot tightrope. The ease of it amazed her; she has spent her entire summer terrified of something that took all of five steps to complete.

Donna and Joy and Mei hang around her. Liz and Annie hang out with

Milly. No one is mad at each other, but no one is exactly happy with each other, either. It's too hot for anything, friendship or fights. In the late-summer heat, all the flowers have died, all the brush has turned brown, and the sky is a smoky gray. Somewhere not so far away, something is on fire. Somehow, this is not the same place Logan arrived at seven weeks ago.

The talent show is coming up. Sadie, bright and desperately cheerful as ever, is doing everything she can to encourage the Ravens to sign up for it. She even offers to cover their slots on the cabin chore chart if they participate. They roll their eyes at her. Talent shows are for babies or people with real talent; there is no in-between. During free hour, Logan and Donna sit outside and laugh at the Magpies practicing tuneless routines on their deck. They push each other like it's a competition—whoever can come up with the nastiest comment wins.

"Look at Gracie's fat little knees."

"Did you see that dumbass jump Emily just did?"

"I can't even hear what they're singing—they sound like dying pigs."

They giggle and fix their ponytails and roll up the cuffs of their shirtsleeves. They know they are being mean. It feels good to be mean. Anyway, the Magpies can't hear them.

On the day of the talent show, Logan signs up for an afternoon horse ride with Max. He says he is ready to try it again now that his cast is gone. Their friendship has been easier since the Pike Falls trip. The other girls never tease her for hanging out with him—there is nothing to tease about. It feels nice just to go to the stables, to see the horses and smell the muck and dander and dog around behind Elias, bothering him. Logan doesn't even mind riding Daisy.

"I've been thinking," Max shouts back at Logan over his shoulder. He is riding a sturdy old gelding named O'Leary. His helmet is fastened tight, rivulets of sludgy sweat seeping from the brim. "Maybe the murderer and the ghost are the same person."

Logan laughs. "You mean, Danny McGee is a murderer?"

"I mean Danny's *ghost* is a murderer." Max wiggles in his saddle. "Remember what . . ."—he glances up the line of lumbering horses, toward Elias, who is too far to possibly hear them, anyway—". . . *he* said? About someone being a good kid? He said, if he was a good kid, he might be a good person."

Logan nods. "And Rosie said, 'He's not a good person—he's a murderer,'" she recites. She remembers the night of the dance. Still, it feels so long ago. Months, or more.

"Right. So, maybe . . . I mean, just hear me out." Max smiles. He knows he is being silly. They are playing a game, the same way she and Donna play by making fun of the Magpies. "Maybe Danny is the kid they're talking about. What if, every once in a while, he, you know, *picks off* a camper—someone he thinks deserves it?"

She considers that, chewing on her upper lip and tasting sweat and grime. "And the counselors all know about it. But there's nothing they can do about it."

"So, they tell us the story," Max carries on, growing giddy, "to warn us."

"Because if they tried to talk about it like it was real, we wouldn't believe them." The giddiness rises in Logan's voice, too.

A Pigeon riding in front of Max whips around at them. "What the hell are you guys talking about?" he lisps. Max and Logan giggle at each other. They tell the kid to mind his own business. Silly. They're just being silly.

On the walk back from the barnyard toward dinner, they pick up the conversation again. Max looks happy, gesturing excitedly as he talks. He shoves his shelf of dark bangs out of his eyes in the same ticking sort of motion as Logan adjusts her glasses on her nose. Their theory is gaining ground, picking up momentum. "He goes after bullies, but it could be anyone!"

"But he has to get the kids when no one else is around."

"Like if they're sneaking out?"

"Or alone in the infirmary."

They pause and shiver and laugh. They have both spent nights alone in the infirmary. They're starting to spook themselves with their own story. Logan pokes at the idea carefully. "He hasn't killed anyone this summer, right?"

"Not *yet*."

A nervous squeal escapes them both. They are moving slowly along the trail; everyone else has already passed by them on their way to the lawn. Logan realizes Max is holding her hand. Fingers cuffed, not laced—it feels very normal.

"You know what else?" he chatters on. "Hugo has these nightmares all the time. He'll start screaming in the middle of the night. We can hear even it from our cabin. *I* bet it's Danny haunting him."

"Why would Danny haunt Hugo?" Logan frowns.

"Well, because he goes after bullies."

She drops his hand. "Hugo's not a bully."

Max stops walking. He looks at her and the smile melts from his sunburnt, rounded cheeks. He is a half inch or so shorter than her, Logan notices, standing so close. She thinks he is going to say something else, but he doesn't. He leans forward and kisses her on the lips.

"*Max!*" Logan jerks backward.

Suddenly as silent and sullen as that far-off morning when he lent her his lip balm, Max rocks back on his heels and frowns froggishly. Logan turns to jog away, leaving him behind her on the trail.

•••

THE TALENT SHOW STARTS OUT about as uneventfully as she expected. A few little kids toss yo-yos and strum out-of-tune guitars. Jaeden and Jeremy play host, cracking bad jokes and leading the same cheesy old campfire songs between each act. Logan keeps her eyes on the fire. She is far away. When the Magpies' routine begins, she forgets to cast Donna the narrow-eyed grimace she has been planning all afternoon. Farther down the Ravens' log, Milly laughs her gravelly laugh.

Only one act is surprising enough to lift Logan from her trance. Toward the end of the show, when the stars have already appeared above them, Nick sits on stage with his guitar. He usually plays with Elias. This time, the person sitting next to him, cross-legged at the edge of the wilting wooden platform, is Poppy.

He plays, and she sings. The song is spooky and sad, the melody trickling through Nick's fingers. Poppy's singing voice is high and clear and almost perfect for someone so little. A hush falls over the whole crowd and the crackle of the campfire grows louder. Logan looks at Sadie and sees tears on her cheeks. That's a little dramatic, she thinks smugly. She tries to get the other girls' attention, but everyone is focused on the stage.

The spell doesn't last long. Directly after Poppy's performance, the Falcons come on to close out the show. Music begins, booming from a staticky speaker somewhere offstage. Six boys start chanting a peppy rhythm and snapping their fingers to the beat. Just as a foreboding feeling sinks into Logan's gut, the singers appear: Elias from one side, Hugo Baker from the other. They lope together, swinging their arms, singing a sappy love song. Hugo wears the same tie Logan wore to the dance; Elias has his red ball gown on. The whole act is perfectly rehearsed—even the background singers move right on time. When they point toward the crowd, drawing out a long *yooouuuu*, Hugo's finger lands directly on Logan.

She buries her face in her hands until she can feel her heartbeat in her eye sockets. She hears the music end, the boys' feet stomping off, and Hugo shouting: "That's for *you*, Logan Adler! I *love* you!"

Laughter and wolf-whistles burst like sparks from the campfire. Someone shakes Logan by the shoulders. Everyone is howling, even the counselors. She is shattered, flustered, grinning behind her hands.

Then the laughter dies. Applause turns to gasps of shock. Someone screams. Logan wrenches her eyes open and jumps to her feet, searching for whatever they are all looking at. They crane their necks toward the logs closest to the fire, where the Finches and Hummingbirds sit. She sees a shock of blond in the dirt, a flushed chubby cheek. Poppy has fainted.

Everything becomes a blur. Logan is rushed from her seat; the counselors herd them away from the fire and stage. She looks frantically back and catches sight of Sam kneeling in the dirt, clutching a limp body.

"Is she dead?"

"I saw blood!"

The entire camp is corralled away toward the lakeshore. Little kids whimper. Counselors shout that everything is okay. She only fainted, Mr. Campbell is trying to reassure everyone, his bald head bobbing like a buoy on the sea of campers. Logan's toes get smashed in the bustle. She sees Sadie crying, harder now, for real. Someone grabs her wrist and grips it tight.

"*The ghost*," Max whispers. His breath is hot in her ear.

Sam

THEY WERE REHEARSING A SONG. Sam imagined something nefarious— blood tests, brain scans, whatever else—when Nick came for Poppy at free hour three days in a row. They were just rehearsing a song for the talent show.

She really can sing. It isn't her song, not a Poppy Warbler song. That would be a step too far. It is clearly Poppy Warbler singing, though; with her eyes closed, Sam can imagine the other person, the grown-up, the star. After the performance, Poppy sits in her lap. She leans forward on her knees, excited, laughing at the Falcons' song and dance. Then, all at once, she falls quiet. Her eyes roll back in her head, and she slumps to the ground.

Her body is hot in Sam's arms. Her pulse races, throbbing in her throat. As the last of the campers are rushed away, Sam shakes her, then slaps her hard across the face. Poppy's lips twitch.

"Sam!"

Sam can't answer; her jaw is locked tight. She grabs for her water bottle in the dirt beneath their campfire log. Behind a wedged thicket of trees, she can hear the campers clamoring, Campbell shouting for them all to settle down. She unscrews the lid of the water bottle and overturns it on Poppy's head. "Come on," she snarls. "Not now."

Nick crouches next to them. He has a hand on his keychain. Sam shoves him away.

Then, in an instant, she is back. Her heartbeat slows. She sputters and blinks. She is standing and talking by the time the talent show should be wrapping up, demanding to know why she is all wet.

"Heat exhaustion," Nurse May says. In the infirmary, she takes Poppy's pulse and temperature and offers her a fudge popsicle. "If it was any other kid, that's what I'd be telling you. Dehydration and heat exhaustion."

What she means, Sam understands, is that Poppy is not any other kid. Poppy is a ticking time bomb. Poppy is a medical marvel—two brains, two bodies, one half dead and one too young to realize; something is bound to misfire eventually. Heat exhaustion or worse, it doesn't matter. She is gone in less than three weeks.

Sam stands with Rosie in their conjoined bathroom under the flickering lights. Not crying, not complaining, just standing together. "I don't like this," she says out loud, eyeing an enormous moth overhead. It flutters into the plastic light fixture. *Thunk . . . thunk . . . thunk.* "I didn't think I was going to love her so much."

The next morning, she wakes up late and skips her walk to the gold-panning claim. Oh well, she thinks—maybe the gold's sudden absence will make it more believable. At the nurse's instruction, she is careful not to let Poppy out of her sight all day. She brings her to the office in morning period, lets her sit in the air-conditioning with a soda and a picture book. "Relax," Nick tells her under his breath. "She's all right."

They watch Poppy kicking her stumpy legs against the carpet, giggling over the book. Sam shrugs him off and focuses on her work. When Campbell comes in, he smiles at Poppy and rubs Sam's shoulders. "Richard wants to talk to you," he tells her, like a consolation.

Curiously enough, he wants to meet her at his personal office, in the facility. Sam leaves at the start of dinner. On her way out to the road in the rattling pickup, she stops at the barnyard and scrambles up to the Nest. She takes two deep swigs from the vodka bottle Jeremy keeps in the fridge, then dashes back to the truck feeling lighter. In the cab, she lights a cigarette and sings, driving with one hand, smoking, shouting Poppy's song out the open window.

She has never taken the road to the front entrance of the facility before. It's grand, sophisticated, alien in the wild landscape. Sam parks beside the porch and walks up the steps, half expecting to be greeted by bellhops in white gloves. The carved oak door swings inward at her touch. Inside is an airy lobby, clean, decorated with wood carvings and warm leather sofas. The lights are off. A woman in pale blue scrubs starts and nearly drops her tray at the sight of her. Sam explains that she is here to see Richard Byron, and she points her unsurely in the direction of his office.

The door at the end of the hall is shut. Sam hesitates, swishing the air between her cheeks, tasting vodka and cigarettes. She knocks.

"Come on in!"

She steps into a high, bright room. One wall is entirely taken up by tall windows; through them, Sam can see the slope of the ridge and the lake, the lawn, the mess hall steps. A little speck of a person sprints up the stairs, late for dinner.

"Sam Red." Byron beams at her from behind his desk. The screen in front of him is swiveled aside. Spread over the polished desktop are a stack of papers, a tumbler, and a bottle of amber liquor, half empty. The space around him is clean, modern, academic. In front of the desk are two leather seats. He waves for her to sit and Sam steps forward. This feels distinctly rehearsed— serious to the point of comedy, like something from an old, bad spy film. Sam thinks she ought to have a hand on her holster. She sits.

"Sam Red," he says again. "That's, ah . . . monosyllabic, isn't it?" He smacks his lips. His smile is crooked, his eyes red and steady. He produces another crystal tumbler and fills it, then passes it wordlessly across the desk. Sam recognizes the label on the bottle. The same bottle has been gathering dust in the back of her parents' liquor cabinet for years, too expensive to touch.

"Thanks."

He nods. "I heard about last night at the talent show. Our little dead girl." He says this like a joke; he is using the words of Phoebe's blackmail intentionally. "How is she?"

"Fine." Sam sips from the glass. She would like to have a taste for expensive liquors someday. If this bourbon—if it is bourbon—is supposed to be any better than Jeremy's plastic jug of vodka, she is none the wiser.

"And how are *you*? I hear we've made you an assistant director. That must feel nice." He looks her over. There is another shoe left to drop. Sam can feel it falling. She waits. "Of course, no one cleared that with me, but that's fine. That's fine." He smiles. "I approve."

"Is that what you wanted to talk to me about? Or is it about Poppy?" Sam eyes the papers on the desk. They are client profiles, she can see, but she can't make out the pictures on them. Maybe they are new clients, set to come to Camp a year from now. A world away.

"Neither, actually." Byron drains his glass and stands, leaving his chair swiveling behind him. He picks up the bottle by the neck as he walks around the desk toward her. His shirt is creased from sitting, open at the chest. "Poppy's fine, by the way. Considering. No changes on this end, I mean." He sinks into the chair beside Sam. "What I needed to tell you is that you've got to stop sticking your pretty little nose in the campers' private lives."

Sam blinks. Byron refills the glass in his hand, then sets the bottle on the desk. *Thunk.* He angles toward her in his seat.

"Don't play dumb with me, all right? You know what I mean. I'm talking about you getting all riled up over Hugo and that girl getting handsy in the boathouse."

Sam clasps her tumbler with both hands. "He assaulted her."

He snorts, loud and sudden. "Jesus, Sam. Listen, I know your generation is a little more sensitive about these things, but back when I was growing up . . ." He lifts a finger from his glass to gesture toward the window. "When both of those two were growing up, we didn't just throw words like *assault* around every time someone got a little uncomfortable. You need to settle down." He sips, smiles. "Hugo Baker is who he is, I know. But you can't let your bias stop those kids from being kids. That's what they came here to do."

"He forced her to touch him." The drink, or the exhaustion, or the sheer ridiculous of it all, has done something for Sam's courage. She sits forward on the leather chair. "That's not kids being kids. That's boys learning how to rape girls and get away with it."

Richard Byron nods. He watches her, patient and humored, a grown-up sitting through a child's performance. Sam drains her glass. He leans over the arm of his seat to refill it for her, then settles back again. "Do you know why I hired you?"

This is the second time he's asked it. Sam spins her full glass on the desk. "It has to be college kids. Young people. For the summer to be realistic."

"Yes. Specifically, though—Do you know why I hired *you*?"

"I guess not."

"It's because you're pretty," Byron says, without pause. "Gus doesn't do the hiring. I do. I have my staff reach out to hundreds of profiles every summer, then I sift through the applications myself. You caught my eye last year. Not because of your college credits, Sam; not because you're smart. Because you're pretty. You've got that classic look, that girl-next-door look. I knew how much the boys at Camp would like you."

His glass is empty. He sits upright to place it back on his desk, where it clangs against the bottle. A cold ache settles into the pit of Sam's stomach.

"I was right, wasn't I? Look at what you've done to Nicky." He laughs, cups his chin in his hand, his elbow propped against the arm of the chair. "That boy—God, I love him—he thinks the sun shines out your ass. Imagine the two of you coming back to Camp together, year after year. Managing it together.

A family business." His laughter rises, manic, unchecked. "Wouldn't that be lovely? All because I liked you first."

The liquor sits like a rock in Sam's gut. Fear like frost creeps from her chest to her fingertips. It's a fear she knows all too well, the kind that shows up late at night, brought on by eyes lingering too long across the train or footsteps coming closer in a dark alley. The fear of a scream loaded in her throat, keys clenched between her knuckles, legs at the ready to run. She struggles to meet Richard Byron's bloodshot eyes evenly.

"Do you understand what I'm trying to tell you?"

"Not really." She wills herself to sound cold and confident. He wants spite from her, and she is in no position not to give it.

"I'm telling you that you're overstepping your role here. What are you, nineteen? Twenty? I like you, and I want you to stick around, but I'm going to need you to grow up and accept reality. You need to understand your place here. You need to understand that you are living in a fucking *simulation*." He nods toward the bottle on the desk. "This!" He waves at it. "Did you like this?"

Sam nods. Byron sits forward and grabs the bottle, fills his glass to the rim, then pinches the neck and swirls the amber dregs over his eyes.

"This is mine," he says. "I paid for it. I had it trucked in from a hundred miles away. I can do this . . ." He stands up, cocks his arm back, and hurls the bottle across his desk. It hits the wall and shatters spectacularly, rattling bookshelves, shards skittering across the floor. Sam jumps. ". . . And it doesn't make a difference. No one cares. My bottle, my wall. My staff will clean it up."

When he sits again, a cool haze has come over his features. He slicks a steady palm over his hair. "You drove over the bridge to get here, right? Old Hatchery Bridge? You know why we call it that?"

"Because of the old fish hatchery."

"No!" He huffs. "There is no old fish hatchery. Do you know what a fish hatchery even looks like? Because I don't!" Byron leans closer toward her, close enough that she can smell bourbon and stale coffee on his breath. "That building under the dam—that's where the campers go when the clients are done with them. They get packed in there, harvested, dissolved. Flushed downstream. *That's* the reality. The fish hatchery is just another part of the story."

Poppy, a voice in Sam's head wails. She closes her eyes. Poppy, gone. Empty. Slowly sinking into black water. Dissolving into pieces. In a way, she always knew.

"He hasn't told you that, has he?"

"I . . ."

"Good." He smiles and shifts to the edge of his seat. One hand reaches out and pats her thigh, lingers there deliberately. His lips twitch beneath groomed whiskers. "I don't mean to scare you, Sam. I just want you to remember where you are. This is not the real world. That girl—What's her name? Brandon?"

"Logan."

"Logan." He nods. He knew that, Sam thinks. "She came here to escape. She came for the story, and that's what she's getting. A little drama, a little shame. The bad guy, the love triangle, nice kid gets the girl . . . She wakes up younger, and happier. That's what she paid for. Your job is to give her that. Play your part. Got it?"

"Got it."

He squeezes her leg. "Trust me, sweetheart. This is my world. Nothing has happened this summer that I didn't decide on." He flashes his teeth at her, brilliantly white. "Okay?"

"Okay."

He leans in closer. Sam's fists clench in her lap. She hears the door creak open and whips her head around to see—of all people—Taps, standing hesitantly in the doorway.

Byron straightens his shoulders. His hand lifts delicately from Sam's thigh. "Oh, hello." He laughs and toes a shard of glass beneath his desk. "Come on in, buddy. You'll have to excuse the mess."

As they pass each other in the light of the window, Sam and Taps lock eyes. He is disheveled, puffy, as if he has been crying. His teeth are gritted.

Outside, the sky has gotten smokier. Sam sits in the driver's seat of the pickup and gazes upward. She wonders what they are going to do if the fire gets any closer. Evacuation from Camp Phoenix cannot be possible.

Nick has taken her off the schedule for the evening, so she spends the activity period sprawled on a couch in the Nest, listening to the hum between her ears. Impulse wins over and she swigs from the vodka bottle again. By the time the bell rings for campfire, she is honestly drunk. Not so drunk she can't hold her composure, but drunk enough to be careless. Daria, squirming on her lap, whines that she smells funny. Skits and songs and bedtime stories go by in a rush, and then she walks down the trail with Rosie back to the Nest. Back to the bottle. Everything is normal, everything is fine. Sam gulps and giggles and lets herself stagger off.

She fades into awareness sometime in the middle of the night. It's dark. She is standing in the center of the dam, looking down over the rushing spillway. Someone is shouting at her. The sky spins, stars cartwheeling overhead.

"What the hell are you doing?" Rosie has her by the arm.

Sam tries to remember what she is doing. She had a purpose, she could swear. Her hands clasp a wiggly, rusted railing. The night is so warm; her hair under her wool cap is slick with sweat. "The hatchery," she tries to explain.

Elias steps behind her on the walkway and holds her by the shoulders. They drag her off the dam, onto the dirt. The rush of the water quiets. Not so far away, the light of their campfire shimmers through the trees, shouts and laughter dancing on the smoke. "Are you trying to kill yourself?" Elias shakes her, furious. "Honestly, are you?"

Sam sputters. When she looks back down from the stars, Rosie is shaking her head, explaining quietly to him that she is just drunk. She stumbles her way along the trail behind them, back to Lobster Point. In the light of the fire, she squints to focus. Faces swim.

"We found her. She was out on the dam."

"Christ, Red. Get it together."

Sam snorts, depositing herself onto the dirt. She thinks of something rude to say. Whether or not she says it out loud, she isn't sure. A lanky shadow rises from its seat and strides toward her. There it is —*the ghost!*—she has finally managed to pin it down! It crouches over her. Anxious, gangly arms wrap around her. Indignant, she shoves at his chest.

Everyone sees. In the lengthening silence, the fire crackles and the blood pounds in Sam's head.

Rosie and Elias escort her back to Camp. Refusing to let her climb the ladder into the Nest, they sit her on a hay bale inside the barn. Rosie sends Elias running for water. Fading in and out, Sam barely catches her question.

"It . . . wasn't Taps in the air rifle shed, was it?"

She shakes her head.

"Why would you lie about that? To me?" Rosie's hands snap from her hips, to her chest, to a broad questioning gesture at the barn air. "Also." She drops to a whisper. "*Ew*, Sam! Since when?"

"Pretty much all summer." Sam hiccups. The truth is going to come out eventually. This is as good a moment as any. "Since last summer, actually."

Rosie's jaw sets tight. "So that's why you got to shadow him this year, right? And now you're an AD." She shakes her head. "Honestly, I had my suspicions. I just thought you'd at least tell me."

Sam's head lolls between her shoulders. Elias returns with his water bottle in hand. He forces it into her fist, uncapped. Looking between the two of them, Sam is overcome with nastiness. "You know what? At least I have someone," she says to Rosie. A gulp of water strikes her stomach uneasily. She gasps and belches. "You got so desperate this summer, you went and . . ." She trips over her tongue, shoving an empty palm at Elias to indicate the end of her sentence.

Elias looks rueful, then confused. "Wait, what?"

Rosie has on a mean, sharp glare, a look Sam knows well. She has never been its victim before. "I'm gonna tell him."

Sam's stomach lurches. "Go ahead. I'm gonna throw up."

She doesn't make it far. She is crouched in the mud just outside the barn doors, heaving, when she hears a voice call out behind her. "Hey!" Elias barks. His shadow, long and haunting in the yellow light, cuts across her back.

Sam doesn't turn. "Yeah?"

"You're a shitty person."

She retches and spits. "Yeah."

The shadow lingers. "You okay?"

"Uh-huh."

"Go to bed. I'll see you tomorrow."

"See you tomorrow," Sam says weakly.

She bumbles her way back to the Hummingbirds' cabin with the creeping sensation that someone is watching her, just over her shoulder. Each time she turns to look, she finds herself entirely alone.

Logan

THE HAWKS PUT ON A skit about the life and death of Danny McGee at campfire. It's silly. Their counselor, Taps, stars as Danny, and the Hawks play the bullies. At the part of the story when he is supposed to jump off the dam, they all start singing to the tune of *Old Lady Leary:*

> *Late last night, while we were all in bed,*
> *Danny McGee took a fall and now he's dead . . .*

Taps hovers worriedly at the edge of the stage. On either side of him, the boys chant.

> *Fire, fire, fire!*
> *Water, water, water!*
> *Jump, Danny, jump!*
> *Aaaah, splat!*

Danny McGee leaps and lands on his face in the dirt to the cheers of his crowd. Logan can hear Milly on the other end of their log murmuring that the whole thing is pretty morbid. For the rest of the skit, Taps runs around draped in a sheet, picking the boys up and carrying them off stage one by one.

"It was all my idea," Max says proudly the following day. "I wrote the song, too."

"You didn't write it. You just changed the words to *Old Lady Leary*."

It's morning activity period. The Ravens and Eagles are playing a soccer game against the Falcons and Hawks. Logan has felt sick and sludgy all morning; she can't stop worrying about the smoke in the air, imagining the insides of her lungs lined in black tar. She sits on the sidelines next to Max, watching the game.

Hugo sprints up and down the length of the lawn with his shirt off. He stares right at Logan as he runs by. Since his performance at the talent show, he never seems to stop staring at her, like he is constantly waiting for her to say something.

"Do you still like him?" Max prods her.

Logan rolls her eyes. She slides away from him on the grass. Hugo, she notices, sees this. He slows down to a sideways saunter as he passes them.

After the game, she stands in a clump with the other Ravens, debating whether or not they have enough time to dash back to the cabin and change out of their sweaty clothes before lunch. Logan is laughing at something Mei said when her attention is drawn to the middle of the lawn. Hugo and Max are supposed to be helping the other boys collapse the foldable goal posts. They stand close to one another with their arms folded over their chests. Logan hears her own name. ". . . none of your business," she hears Max say. Then Hugo catches her eye and waves her over to them. She crosses the lawn, and Max's face grows panicked. "No, wait!"

Hugo looks cocky as Logan approaches. He still has his shirt off; it's wrapped like a towel around his neck. His hair is slicked back from his forehead with sweat. He looks like a greased-up gangster, like someone from a movie. "So, you guys are going out?" He waves a hand between her and Max.

"What? No!"

Max's eyes are cast down at the grass. He refuses to look at her.

"Well, that's what he just told me." Hugo scoffs. "See, I knew you were lying, dude."

"That's not what I said!" Max raises his head, ignoring Logan. "I didn't say we were going out *yet*."

"Yet?" Logan repeats. Still, they both ignore her. The boys have eyes only for each other. She spins and sees that the lawn is emptying. The other Ravens have started off toward the cabin to change. She wonders if she should sprint to catch up with them.

"You're a liar." Hugo's jaw twitches meanly. "Why would she even want to go out with you?"

"Because, I'm the good guy. *I'm* the nice guy." Max glances swiftly sideways as he says this, like he wants to be sure Logan is listening. "You're just an asshole."

"I'm Hugo goddamn Baker." Hugo laughs, his cheeks flushed red. "Who are you, fatass?"

Logan stands frozen in place, wishing she had left the scene when she had the chance. Max looks like he might hit him. "You think you're so cool. Everyone thinks you're *so* cool." He is on his toes, as straight as Logan has ever seen him stand, to meet Hugo's eyes. "But you're not that cool in the middle of the night, are you?"

Hugo grunts. His smile melts. "Shut up."

"We can all hear you in our cabin. Every night. *I didn't do it, I didn't do it, it wasn't me!*" Max's voice goes high and whining. "What are you dreaming about, Hugo? What didn't you do?" Somehow, now, he is looking down at Hugo, lumbering over him.

"Shut up!"

"Because, if you ask me, it kind of sounds like you did it!"

"I said shut *up!*" Hugo lunges forward and shoves Max in the shoulders. Not too hard, but hard enough to knock him off his tiptoes.

Max catches his balance. There is a flash of embarrassment in his face, and his eyes narrow. "Fuck you."

It happens too fast for Logan to see. In the blink of an eye, they are on the grass, grunting and spitting and hitting. She shouts and leaps back. "Hey!" she cries out loud—either to get the boys' attention or the attention of someone, anyone around, to come and stop them. The counselors are far away, filling their water bottles.

The boys roll and Max sits straddled over Hugo, pinning him down. He reaches back with his good arm and hits him hard in the face.

"Max!"

He hits him again. Logan sees blood, a flash of red over tumbling white and tan and green. She dives forward and tries to catch Max by the arm, but Hugo's kicking feet launch her backward. From her back she sees a short bob of hair sprinting toward the tussle. Milly must have been watching the whole time—she comes dashing in to help Hugo.

"Knock it off, Maxie, get off him! Get—ow!" Milly takes a flying elbow to the eye. "What the *shit*?"

"Milly?" Max sits upright, and Hugo takes the opportunity to slug him hard in the stomach. It's only then that a counselor arrives.

All four of them are marched to the office. They sit on the porch in the hazy sunshine, silent aside from the occasional whimper and groan. Hugo has bloody tissues stuffed in each nostril, and Milly's left eye socket is swollen and glassy. Max still looks woozy after vomiting on the lawn. Logan is just miserable. They listen to the happy, clattering sounds of lunchtime from the mess hall down the hill. Behind the closed office door, Mr. Campbell and a few older counselors are deciding what should be done with them. They were hastily questioned by Dane, then handed ice packs and told to wait. This is unfair, Logan thinks. At least she and Milly should be allowed to leave.

Footsteps crunching over the trail toward them make Logan turn. It's Taps—coming for Max, she assumes—but he only shoots them a little smile and steps inside, closing the door behind himself. A minute ticks by, then another. It's so hot, Logan thinks she might faint. The voices in the office pick up. Someone is shouting. They all lean curiously closer to the door.

"Do you think they forgot about us?" Hugo whispers, straining through his plugged nose.

Logan chews on her lip. "I hope not." She cannot distinguish the words from inside, but something tells her the shouting has nothing to do with them. She catches a name she hasn't heard in weeks: *Phoebe*.

The door flies open and Taps steps out. Behind him, Logan sees angry adult faces. He stomps across the porch and down the steps. Then he stops, turns on his heel and comes back. He crouches in front of the bench where Max is sitting. There is something sad in his face, something nervous—a look a grown-up should never wear.

"Who hit first?" he asks Max softly.

"He did," says Max. Hugo doesn't argue.

Taps smiles. He reaches out to grip his shoulder. "Listen, buddy. I have to go. Something . . . came up. I have to go home. They're gonna move one of the other counselors in with our cabin, okay? Can you tell the other guys for me?"

Max nods.

"Thanks, dude. I'm gonna miss you. Really." As Taps walks down the porch steps again, Nick appears in the office door. He has his hands on his hips, frowning. He looks at Taps, and again, it isn't a grown-up look at all. They look at each other like something horrible has happened. The world has flipped upside down. Taps stands on the trail. He shakes his head. "I'm done," he says. "I'm done with this." He stomps back toward them, up the steps, back to Max. Nick watches them with a hand stretched halfway out, as if Taps might pick his camper up and run away with him, like in their campfire skit.

"Taps?"

"Max, buddy, listen to me." His voice is quick and hard. "I have to tell you something. None of this is real. You know that, right?"

"Taps . . ." Nick's eyes go wide.

"Listen. You know where you are. You know *who* you are, Max." Taps has a hand on the back of Max's head, bowing their foreheads together. "You're an adult, you're forty-five years old. This is your wife." He swings his head along the bench, from Logan to Hugo. "This guy is a murderer. You're adults, you're all—"

"Christian!" Nick seizes Taps by the shoulder and drags him back, away from the bench.

Now Taps is shouting. Logan looks on. Everything is shimmering in the smoky heat. They are trapped inside a snow globe, shaken up in ash and glitter.

"You're adults! This isn't real, it's a dream! It's a fancy dream, Max! You're asleep, you're over there, across the lake!"

As Nick struggles to get his arms around Taps, Dane comes bursting through the door. They shove him up against the side of the building, shushing him, trying to cover his mouth. Taps keeps shouting around their hands. The words make no sense. His voice is clear and high, streaming over them.

"None of this is real! You're in a fake body, all of you! In a couple of weeks, they're going to kill you to wake you up! They're gonna kill you, Max! And Poppy, Poppy Warbler—"

Hands close over Logan's ears. Someone is lifting her, dragging her off the bench and across the porch; she is tossed to the carpet behind the office door. The rest of them follow. Mr. Campbell slams the door behind him. The air conditioner roars inside. Logan sits up and sees Max staring back at her, and Hugo, his eyes huge, his face bloody.

Outside, the shouting is muffled. She can still hear it. *None of this is real.*

"Don't listen to any of that, kids. Don't listen. He's sick."

It isn't the air conditioner. It's something inside her head. Louder, louder it whirs and hums. Max reaches toward her on the carpet. He is saying her name. She falls back against Milly's side.

Max. Max has a beard and gray-flecked hair. Max sits at his drawing desk in the window. Max holds the baby to his chest in the dewy morning. Max kicks the kitchen table and slams a plate, and he cries, but he never shouts.

None of this is real.

She can see Max, and she can see herself. She is looking down at her from above. She is naked, lying in a hospital bed. Logan grips her head between her hands. "No," she says out loud. The tears are cool on her hot cheeks—she didn't know she was crying.

Mr. Campbell picks her up and lifts her in his arms. She falls against his shoulder. "Easy," he says. "Easy. You're all right." He rocks her like a baby. The lights in the ceiling are screaming at her; her head is shattering. Logan sobs, but she doesn't know why.

When Nurse May arrives, she hands her a glass of cold water and a little blue pill. "Take this," she says. Logan shoves the medicine into her mouth and swallows, and everything melts away.

week nine

Logan

THEY HAVE TO STAY THE night in the infirmary. It isn't really fair—Logan and Milly weren't even involved in the fight. As far as she can remember. The heat has them all woozy and tired, and they're quiet as they eat their dinner together at a folding table on the infirmary porch. While the rest of the world is at campfire, Nurse May reads to them from a wordy chapter book.

There are three bedrooms in the infirmary. Logan and Milly are assigned to the one with a bunk bed—Logan on top and Milly on the bottom, like back at the cabin. Max and Hugo each have their own room. Logan took a long nap in the afternoon, and now, as strange and sleepy as she feels, she is sure she won't be able to fall asleep. She rolls and wiggles on the creaky top bunk.

"I'm sorry you have to be here," she says out loud, not sure if Milly is awake to hear it or not.

After a pause, Milly says, "It's okay. It wasn't your fault. Anyway, my eye looks kind of cool."

Logan laughs. "Yeah, it does."

"What were they fighting about, anyway?"

"Me, I guess."

From the bottom bunk, Milly sniffs. Logan can hear the starchy rustle of her infirmary sheets. "Logan?"

"Yeah?"

"My name's not really Millipede. It's Camilla."

Logan smiles. "I'll still call you Millipede, if you want."

"Okay. Thanks."

There is more to say, but Logan doesn't know how to say it.

Eventually, steady breaths below tell her that Milly is asleep. She waits, thinking, wondering if sleep will find her. She can't get comfortable. Earlier she took a little blue pill to calm her nerves, and it has taken the tracks right out from under her train of thought. She is scattered, dizzy, and a little afraid. After some time, she sits up, puts on her glasses, and climbs as quietly as she can down the side of the bunk bed. The nights have been so warm lately. In just her cotton shorts and tank top, she tiptoes barefoot for the bedroom door.

She steps out into an outdoor corridor. In front of her is the bathroom, and beyond it the infirmary itself, where Nurse May is sleeping—soundly, Logan hopes. On either side of her are the other bedrooms, all in a line under a single sloping roof. Logan hesitates. She looks up at the crescent moon. It casts a sharp glare of silver across one of her lenses; she stands still for a moment, turning her head this way and that, watching the beam dance. Then she steps toward the door on her left.

After three soft taps, she hears a mattress creak. Padding footsteps. The curtain in the window is decorated with cartoon squirrels. As Logan watches, the squirrels are shoved aside and a pale face peers out at her. *Hi*, he mouths. Logan smiles back.

Hugo opens the door, just a crack. His pajama pants are printed with dancing bears in a checkered pattern. "Hey. What are you doing?" In the soft light, Logan can see how his nose has swollen. Little purple lines like war paint bloom beneath both of his eyes.

"I can't sleep," she admits.

He opens the door wider and lets her into the room. They tiptoe together back to the bed—the same bed Logan slept in before, the night she had her period. Hugo climbs in first and holds the blanket open for her to lie down next to him. They face each other, on their sides, hands stuffed beneath the pillows. Logan rests her folded glasses on the bedsheet. They whisper.

"Are you okay?"

He nods. "Mm-hmm. It doesn't hurt too bad." Logan knows he is acting tough. She saw him whimpering on the office porch, the bloody tissues crammed into his ballooning nostrils.

"I'm sorry. About all this."

"Why? It wasn't your fault."

"I don't know."

Hugo Baker smiles at her and wiggles down into the mattress. His hand on the pillow stretches out and stops just short of touching her. His hair has grown long over the summer. It sticks out at funny angles from his bruised face. "I meant what I said, you know," he whispers.

What he said on the campfire stage, he means. The same thing he said in the boathouse. It sounded silly, at first, but now Logan thinks she understands: he didn't mean it the way adults do. Adult love is complicated. It has rules attached, like work. Love, she thinks, is supposed to be pure and whole and accidental, and lying here in the darkness, with their heads together and their knees touching and the bears dancing on his pajama pants, she can't imagine anything more clear and true than this very moment, being twelve.

Her memories of the afternoon are sticky. Taps was angry. He said things to them that they weren't supposed to hear. Things about Max. Things about her, and about Hugo. She could recall his exact words now, if she wanted to. She doesn't want to. They flicker in her head, on the brink of disappearing into foggy oblivion. Logan deliberately pushes them over. There is no time to worry about sticky things, things that make her stomach hurt and her skin crawl with flies. More pressing issues are at hand.

"Listen," she says to Hugo. "I think we're all in danger." She watches the whites of his shifting eyes as she tells him the theory she and Max cooked up: that Danny McGee is a murderer. A killer ghost.

"Makes sense. Yeah. That's why they're all so scared to talk about him. I bet he goes after someone every summer."

"He's trying to kill Poppy, I think."

"When she fainted?"

"Exactly. He almost got her."

It all makes sense. She remembers one thing Taps said, the last thing that got through to her ears before Mr. Campbell's hands closed over them. *Poppy*, he said. *Poppy Warbler*. Something about the story, as it is, still doesn't fit quite right. There is a missing piece. It clicks into place, and she gasps.

"You know, in the story, he's trying to get revenge on his bullies. But . . . what if it's different than that? What if they weren't bullies, the kids that trapped him on the dam?"

"You mean, they were the good guys?"

"Maybe Danny was the bully. Or *worse*. Maybe he wanted to kill kids back then."

"And even after they got rid of him, he's still trying to do it."

"It's not about revenge. He's just a murderer."

"Murderer," Hugo repeats. "Yeah. That's a better story."

They gasp and giggle together. Happiness pours over Logan. The facts are shuffling themselves into order in her head. "I don't think it's a story. He's real. I know he is. I've seen him. He's real, and he's after Poppy."

The ghost is real, and the ghost is the murderer, and the counselors know. They have been hiding it from them all summer. Because every summer, he wants to kill someone, and this summer, he wants Poppy. That's why they were so scared when she fainted, why Sam sprinted so fearfully when she fell in Capture the Flag. It all makes perfect sense. Logan speaks these thoughts out loud to Hugo, letting them flow through her, bolstered by the cover of darkness. She believes every word that passes her lips. She isn't telling a story, just channeling the simple truth.

Hugo takes it all in. "Well, if he's real, and he's going after a Hummingbird, we should do something about it. Shouldn't we?"

Logan nods. They are playing make-believe. Just being kids. It doesn't matter—the game feels too good not to lose herself completely in it. "We should find him."

"And trap him."

"And kill him." She lets her head drift on the pillow, her eyes falling slowly shut. She is so tired. "Kill him," she says again, "for real."

Sam

"CAMPBELL WANTS ME TO SHOW you how this works."

Nick sits on the edge of his bed. Sam faces him, cross-legged on the other bunk—the mattress is bare, now, and the shelves beside it are empty. Dane has moved into the Hawks' cabin. Nick brandishes the black metal tube on the end of his lanyard. He shrugs the looped cord off his neck and passes it to her. She takes it hesitantly.

"Don't worry. You'd have to be really stupid to hurt yourself with it."

Sam nods. At the moment, she does feel stupid. She is halfway dressed, straps sliding from her shoulders, strands of hair stuck to the sweat on her brow. Whatever she came here to say to him, to confront him about, fell dead behind her lips when he kissed her. It's so much easier to look the other way. Now he sits here in his bare chest with his jeans still undone and looks at her with a blank, adoring smile. He looks at her like she is something pretty.

Sam clasps the little black cylinder. It's cold in her fingertips.

"Press that button on the side," he tells her. "There—you kind of have to dig your fingernail in." She does, and a slim band of metal peels away from the tube on either side. A notched wheel circles it, near the top. "Now—carefully—turn that gear. Four clicks to the left . . . now three to the right . . . and four to the left again. Good."

The top of the tube springs open in three parts, like flower petals. Inside is a tiny silver nub. The needle is tucked in its casing, its point hardly protruding enough to pierce skin.

"There. Now, don't touch it, okay?" Nick reaches out to take the tube—the needle—back from her. He holds it gingerly at half an arm's length from his face. "It's spring-loaded," he explains. "You just hold it up to the skin and press it down, and it'll inject." He gives the flower-petal top a nudge and the cylinder folds itself back together. The carefulness fades from him as it does. He gestures over his body with it. "Upper thigh, inside wrist, or side of the neck." Nick lifts his chin and prods the lethal little tube against his throat. "It shouldn't take more than a minute. That's it."

Sam nods. "Four to the left, three to the right, four to the left," she murmurs, committing it to memory.

"Good." He smiles at her as he hangs the lanyard over his head again. "There's only two in Camp. I carry this one, and Gus keeps the other one downstairs. You'll never have to use it, you know. You should just know how, now that you're an AD. Just in case."

"I won't use it on Poppy."

Nick's face falls dark. "I wouldn't ask you to."

Sam stands and turns her back to him to finish getting dressed. She is late—she should be helping Katie take inventory at the crafts shack. He asks if she wants to go into town with her later, after lunch. "I know you hate hot dog day. We could go find some real food." He says it casually, like they have options. As if there is some new, niche café in town waiting to be discovered. Like there is anything in the entirety of Camp or Smith's Ridge that Sam isn't sick to death of eating. She busies herself with the straps of her sandals.

People know, now. It was bound to happen eventually. The whispers tore through Camp on a riptide, somewhere between rumor and truth. Considering everything else, Taps's sudden firing and the smoky sky and the heat wave smudging and smothering them, it passed in day or two. No one seems to care what's real or gossip anymore.

"Sam? What's up?"

She looks up at him. He has his arms folded across his chest, his face flat. What he thinks of her, she can only imagine. "What happened to Taps?" she asks at last.

"Is that what you're upset about?" Nick shifts on the edge of his mattress. "Look, I know you guys were friends, but rules are rules, right? He told those campers . . ."

"I mean before that. He was fired before he said anything, wasn't he? What happened there?"

"It was Chard's decision. He thinks Taps is the one that told Phoebe—"

"So, whatever Chard decides goes, right?"

"Yes." He nods. "You know that."

Sam watches him, swallowing a thousand different thoughts. Nick Borowitz is all rhythm and rule, routine and respect. That was why she was attracted to him in the first place. For a moment she can see through his eyes: the world is clear and hard, each new truth an obstacle lined up to knock down. It must be nice.

"Those kids are screwed up," he tells her. "He probably ruined their whole summer. The bottom line is, Taps did a bad thing. Even if he wasn't the one that talked to Phoebe, nothing justifies what he did."

Sam picks up her own keychain and loops it over her head. She fingers the radio at her hip and stews over what final words she can toss back at him. He beats her to it.

"Hey. You're too caught up in it." His voice falls flat against her back. "This isn't real life. It's a job. A couple more weeks and it's all going to be over. You'll be back in Paris."

Sam hovers with her hand on the doorknob. "Are you sure?" The very idea of a life in Paris is ridiculous, imaginary. For all Sam knows, she could jab herself with the needle around his neck right now and wake up a different person, in a different world. Just like them.

Nick doesn't offer an answer. She leaves the room, jogging down the steps into the empty office.

Later, during free hour, she helps the Hummingbirds put on a fashion show. They wear underwear on their heads and swimsuit tops and windbreaker sashes. Sam steals glitter from the crafts shack and dusts it over their hair and cheeks. They strut down the aisle between their bunks in an uproar, bellies heaving with delighted laughter.

Poppy wears a long gown, navy blue. *GOD IS A LESBIAN*, it says. The hem of the shirt sweeps up dust and hair clumps along the floor slats. Her hair is up in crooked pigtails, her face bright pink with excitement. When she talks, her tongue slips through the gap where her two front teeth should be. One little nub is growing in already.

"*Late last night*," she trills, "*while we were all in beh-hed!*"

Sam scoops her up and holds her in her lap. Poppy laughs, and her whole body quakes and squirms.

Sometimes, she thinks about running. She could take Poppy in the middle of the night. They would be halfway across the country before anyone noticed. They could go back to Paris together; she could raise her as her own daughter. They would lie low, live in a little apartment, sing and cook and read and take on a whole new life.

Of course, it's a silly fantasy. She has to grow up and face reality. Poppy is tied to a dying body across the lake. Her life is in Richard Byron's hands. For all Sam knows, hers is, too.

She doesn't know what is going to happen when the summer ends. She can't quite get a grip on what is real anymore. She holds the wiggling, laughing little body in her arms and feels the warmth of her, the rushing blood beneath her skin. She presses her lips to her temple and measures the heartbeat racing there. Outside, the smoke in the sky is growing thicker. The wildfire is closing in on them. Anxiety sits behind everyone's eyes, unspoken. It feels like disaster is just around the corner, and they are all biding their time with other worries until it arrives. Sam is ready for it. After everything this summer, it might as well happen. Maybe when the fire comes, it will wake them all up.

Logan

It's FUNNY HOW SOMETHING THAT starts out as a game can become real so quickly. As soon as they're out of the infirmary, Logan and Hugo begin spreading their version of the Danny McGee story like a fever. Logan tells it to the Ravens late at night with her flashlight under her chin, all of them tucked like bundled babies in their sleeping bags. Hugo tells it at crafts at the barnyard, and again on the lawn while waiting for dinner. It only takes a day or two for their version to become the truth.

As they tell it, Danny McGee was lonely and mean, a bully. As soon as he arrived at Camp Phoenix, the other kids knew there was something wrong with him. He picked on everyone, or else he lurked in the shadows, watching. He didn't know how to be nice. The only one who ever took pity on him was a little girl, a loud, pudgy Hummingbird with blond hair and missing teeth. She tried to make friends with Danny when no one else would.

Danny loved the Hummingbird very much. She was his only friend, and he wanted to keep her forever. One night, he stole the girl out of her cabin and told her they were going on an adventure. They snuck out of Camp together to Lobster Point. Danny wanted to cross the dam and run away into the forest on the other side, but the little girl realized she was being kidnapped and started to scream.

Luckily, the Falcons were camped out at Lobster Point that night. They heard the Hummingbird crying and came to chase Danny away from her. While their counselor ran to get help, they trapped him on the dam and lit a fire on either side so he couldn't get away. Danny McGee refused to accept his fate.

"So he couldn't be caught and taken to jail, Danny decided to jump." Hugo always finishes the story in a spooky, floating voice. He's a good storyteller. "That way, he knew he could stay at Camp forever and never be lonely again. He's still here now, today, hiding in the trees. Looking for friends. If he picks you, he kills you—and you have to stay here with him."

"It's a good story," the Ravens tell Logan, visibly frightened.

Logan shakes her head. "It's not a story, you guys. That's what really happened."

They laugh at her the first time she says it. A little less loudly the second time. Why not? Logan thinks to herself. Why shouldn't their story be real? The more she thinks about it, the more sense it makes. Everything strange that has happened to her this summer can be explained by the story. The ghost is as real as anything.

One morning, they wake up and can hardly see out the cabin windows. The smoke has fallen from the sky and landed on the ground. It's thicker than fog and smells bitter; the little bit of sunlight streaming through is an ugly reddish orange. Camp looks fake, like a painted scene.

Mr. Campbell announces at breakfast that most of the outdoor activities will have to be canceled. He jokes that they can't risk anyone coughing up a lung. At least, his voice makes it seem like he's joking—the worried look behind his glasses does not. The activities that aren't canceled make a short and boring list. The Ravens and Hawks are sent back to the mess hall in morning period to play acting games and cards. It all grows old fast, and they wind up sitting in circles on the floor, back on the feverish topic of Danny McGee. The counselor tries to shut Logan up, to make her stop telling her story—that gives her a cool satisfaction. If they don't want her to tell it, it must be true.

She ignores Max through the whole period. She still can't forgive him for breaking Hugo's nose, or for whatever he said about her at the soccer game. There is something else, too. She doesn't want to look at him. He is a creeping shadow at the edge of her attention. If she looks, she will see something she doesn't want to see, she will slip and fall and not be able to get up again.

At lunch, Logan keeps a close eye on Sam. She watches how she treats Poppy, constantly holding her hand or letting her sit on her lap, clutching her close. She doesn't handle any of the other Hummingbirds that way. None of the other counselors handle their campers that way. It's obvious that something is wrong.

She sneaks out of the cabin at the start of free hour. In the smoky orange air, she is braver, invisible. She is an astronaut exploring a strange new world. Hugo meets her at the bell tower. They walk together, free and alone like they own Camp and everything in it. They whisper, loud and bold: Who's going to stop them? At the lakeshore, the smoke in the sky is so thick they can't see the top of the ridge on the other side, only a striking beam of bright red light on the horizon. Logan thinks it's just the sun breaking through the smoke, but Hugo is sure that it's firelight. The top of the ridge is burning, he says, in quiet awe. Logan suddenly remembers Spark and swallows a hot dose of worry. She desperately hopes the horse has run far enough by now.

They sit on the shore between parked rowboats, tossing pebbles into the water. Neither of them has any clue what time it is. "We should go back to our cabins soon," Logan says.

Hugo shakes his head. "Let's not. Let's stay out here. No one's even gonna know we're gone."

He is probably right, she realizes. With all the smoke, the sleepy late-summer blur, Sadie could carry on the whole day thinking Logan is right behind her. The lakefront activities have been canceled. They could stay here between the rowboats until nighttime. It's a creepy, comforting thought.

"What are they going to do if Camp burns down?" she asks out loud.

Hugo shrugs. He flicks a little gray pebble between his fingers. It lands with a satisfying *plink* and ripple. "Send us home, I guess."

"Home," Logan repeats. She wonders what Hugo's home is like. The lake laps at her bare toes, gray as the sky and warm as bathwater. At the beginning of the summer, it was bone-numbingly cold. "Let's keep walking. Maybe we'll find him."

"Find who?"

"You know who."

They get up and walk on, away from the lakeshore, past the campfire stage and then back uphill. They avoid the trails and trudge between the trees, dry leaves and needles ankle-deep beneath them. It's slow-going and a little painful, but new, different. For a while they can be far away from Camp, far from everything they know. They arrive at the ropes course and run across the wide dirt clearing.

"Remember when Max fell? It was right there, by that tree."

"Uh-huh. I remember you crying like a baby." Hugo punches her.

Onward, upward. In the distance, the bell chimes for afternoon announcements. They reach the air rifle range.

"Remember when we were scared of bears?"

"I was never scared. I told you, I'd shoot a bear right in the face. *Pew, pew.*"

They tug at the door to the locker where the guns are kept, but it's latched tight. To Logan's annoyance, Hugo keeps working at it, his face determined.

"What are you going to do with one, anyway? You can't shoot a ghost with an air rifle."

"Maybe I can." He grunts and pries at the locker door. The rusty metal screeches.

"Come on. It's locked. Let's go."

"Where?"

Logan shrugs. She is light-headed and wild. Probably from all the smoke. "Anywhere."

They go sightlessly through the trees. When they reach the creek, they decide to follow it upward. Minutes pass, then what must be an hour. They wonder out loud if anyone is looking for them back down at Camp and giggle at the prospect of it. They talk about walking on forever. Eventually they have to reach a town, Logan thinks out loud. They could steal some food and supplies and set out into the true wilderness. Find Spark and live forever in the forest.

"What about the fire?" Hugo plays along with her.

"It's still far away. Someone will put it out before it gets to us."

"I think we're walking towards it."

They pass the rocky lookout point, where Max once offered her his lip balm. A little farther on, the stream is wider and the path along its edge is thinner. They walk in and out of the water, stumbling over slippery rocks, leaves sticking to their wet sandals. It seems like Hugo was right: they are getting closer to the fire. At least, the smoke around them is heavier. It's hard to see anything. The air smells charred and toxic, and the sun is an evil red orb hanging over the roof of branches. Logan coughs.

"Look!" Hugo stops and grabs her by the arm.

"Where?"

"There!"

She squints through the shade and smoke. Up ahead, the stream flows from a wide pool. Like something from a dream—or a nightmare, maybe—she can make out the shape of a rickety building between two tree trunks. It has a tiny front porch and a screen door, swung open. "Is that a house?" she whispers.

"I don't know. It looks abandoned."

"Creepy."

Hugo steps forward, but Logan tugs him back. His foot slips from the creek bank and he stomps with a splash into the water. "Hey!"

"Sorry!" She winces.

He steps back onto solid ground, shaking pebbles from his wet sandal. "Come on, let's go check it out."

"I don't know. I don't like it."

"Don't be a pussy."

"I'm not! I just . . ." Logan trails off. She strains her eyes forward and feels her body tense. Her heart flutters. There is movement up ahead. Sharp, human movement. The distinctive creak of a footstep on a wood porch reverberates through the air like a gunshot. Hugo whips his head around and they both stare toward the shack by the pool.

Someone is standing there, looking at them. It's not a shadow. There is no mistaking it for a play of the light through the branches or a passing deer or a leaping squirrel. It's a human body, tall and looming, hands on its hips. The thick smoke and shadows and the burnt light warp and twist it, but it is there—it's real. Logan hears Hugo's breath draw deep and fast into his lungs. His hand clamps hard onto her wrist.

"Say something," she hisses through her teeth.

"You," he mutters back.

Time stretches and the figure on the shack porch does not move or make a noise. It only sways, just slightly. Eventually Logan clears the lump in her throat. "Hello?"

"Hello," a gravelly voice says back. Logan twitches and steps backward. It was not a kid's voice, but deep and strained. The figure is faceless in the smoke.

"Are you him?" Hugo asks, his voice high.

It moves strangely, tottering in place. "Him?" A rumbling laugh sends a shiver down Logan's spine. It somehow rings from all around instead of from a single point, like the trees themselves are laughing at them. "Sure. I'm him."

"No." Logan shakes her head. "You're too old to be him. Who are you? Do you live here?" When there is no reply, she lowers her voice. "It's just some crazy old man, Hugo. Let's go." She pulls at his arm.

"Hugo?" The voice spikes. They both freeze. Logan's heart hammers. "Hugo Baker? Is that who that is? And little Logan Gill."

"*Adler*," Logan breathes. Her stomach churns.

Hugo hovers hesitantly, like he wants to step forward across the creek. Closer to the shack. Then, thinking better of it, he leans back into Logan. His face is frightened, the pink of his cheeks somehow brighter in the dimness. "How do you know us?"

The whole forest laughs again. "Where exactly are you two going? You running away?" The questions flow in a slow-moving stream, a sticky trickle, with no breaks between them. It sounds inhuman, like whatever is speaking to them only just learned how.

They share a terrified glance.

"You know too much, don't you?"

In a stroke of bravery, Logan answers. She steps slowly backward as she does, ready to bolt away in case it suddenly comes after them. "We know about you," she says unsteadily. "We know who you're trying to kill."

"Uh-huh," the ghost laughs. "Who's that? Who am I trying to kill?"

A twig snaps under Logan's foot. Hugo's arm is pulled taut; he isn't moving with her. "Poppy. Her name's Poppy."

"Poppy. Poppy Warbler," the thick voice drawls. Its arms lift and fold. Like a tree decaying at the roots it sways, then stumbles forward, down from the porch of the shack. Laughter, high and crazed, swoops over them. "That's done, kiddo. Poppy Warbler is dead." The ghost is headed for the edge of the water.

"Hugo!" Logan tugs him harder.

Hugo is frozen to the spot. "Who *are* you?"

"Who do you think, Hugo?" There is a splash—the ghost has reached the stream. A head lifts. Logan can almost make out the face. Arms raise. A mouth opens. "Boo!"

Hugo leaps into action. He shoves Logan forward as he turns. "Run!"

They run. They sprint, tumble and fall, pick each other up and run on. Soon they reach the lookout point, and the gold-panning claim; they find the familiar trail and come to a stop, heaving. They are soaked with creek water from the knees down, scraped and bleeding. Hugo's cheek, still bruised from his fight with Max, has a fresh new cut from a whipping pine branch. He huffs and spits.

The fear in Logan's chest is overtaken by a quick, bright rush of joy. "He's real!" she shouts. "I told you we'd find him!"

"Was it really him?"

"It had to be. He knew our names."

"He called you . . ."

"Forget it." Logan shakes her head and nudges her glasses up on her nose. "That was the ghost. That *had* to be the ghost."

They look at each other. Hugo seems to want to argue, but he nods. "It . . . *had* to be," he says slowly. Then his eyes grow bigger. "Poppy."

"Poppy!"

They dash down the trail, back into the heart of Camp. To the office, they decide; Nick or Dane or Mr. Campbell will help them. It's still afternoon activity. Everyone is stuck indoors, telling stories or playing games. The few counselors they pass look at them lazily as they sprint by—either no one realized they were missing, or no one really cared. Beneath her panic, Logan is disappointed.

They reach the office porch and take another moment to pant and spit. Logan steps in first, swinging the screen door open in a burst.

Four sets of eyes stare at her: Sam's, Nick's, Mr. Campbell's, and another man's, a stranger. All of them stand with their arms folded across their chests, frozen in mid-conversation. The stranger is wearing dirty pants and long sleeves and a grease-stained ball cap. His face is withered and smudged with dirt. He looks stunned at the sight of Logan, and Hugo behind her. The sudden artificial chill of the air conditioner makes her shiver.

"Logan?" Sam steps forward. "What's up?"

"Where's Poppy?!" Logan shouts, spraying a speck of drool. She wipes at her chin. "Is Poppy okay?"

"What? Why?" Sam looks up at Mr. Campbell, who frowns. "What activity are you supposed to be at?"

Hugo has moved his way inside the room. "Is she dead?" he cries. "Is Poppy Warbler dead?"

Mr. Campbell stoops and grabs Hugo by the back of the neck. "Who told you to say that?" he asks quietly.

"The ghost of Danny McGee! He's real. We just met him!"

"He said he's gonna kill Poppy!"

"No, he said he already *did*!"

The man in the hat laughs, loud and bewildered. "What's going on? Who are these two?"

"Ah, nothing." Mr. Campbell's smile looks forced, not like his usual big grin. It makes him look different, wrong. "Our campers can get a little wrapped up in the ghost stories here, that's all. Sam, why don't you take Logan and, ah—" He pauses, coughs. "Why don't you take them up to the infirmary? They're probably a little dehydrated."

Logan shakes her head. "No, please. I don't want to take another pill."

The dirty man frowns worriedly at her.

"Logan, hon. Why are you so worked up about Poppy all the sudden?" Sam's concerned face makes Logan's heart sink. She feels suddenly silly, like a little kid who forgot she was playing make-believe. She looks toward Hugo. His eyes are twitching all around the room, and his hair stands up on end—a wild boy. "Danny McGee is just a story. I promise."

Sam walks them out onto the office porch with a hand on each of their shoulders. She tells them, in a too-sweet tone like Sadie's, that they will go to the mess hall and get a soda, and everything will be all right. Partway along the trail, the hand on Logan's shoulder burns red-hot. She throws it off.

"We're not kids!" she snaps at Sam, who tilts back and looks her over in surprise. "Stop lying to us! Tell us the truth. Why do we have to stay on the trails?"

The counselor's expression is hard to read. Her eyes are dull, lined in gray. She straightens up and puts her hands in her pockets, looking quickly between Logan and Hugo, and sighs.

"Because of the ghost."

Logan nods. Hugo looks satisfied; he reaches out and squeezes her arm, just above the wrist. "It's not just a story? He's real?"

"It's not just a story. He is very real. If you really met him, you know. You're lucky to be alive."

"What about Poppy? Did he get her?"

"Poppy's fine." Sam shakes her head and turns to lead them along the trail again. "He's never going to get her."

Logan and Hugo share a smile. They nod to each other and follow Sam, beaming, victorious. Finally, they know the truth. They are the only campers who know what's really going on at Camp Phoenix.

week ten

Sam

KUHN AND WICKER FOREST SERVICES is a privately contracted logging and wildfire team. The best in the business, according to the print on the doors of their trucks. They've come from three states away to reach Smith's Ridge.

Wicker doesn't make an appearance at Camp, but Kuhn sits in the office for hours, sipping black coffee and negotiating pleasantly, as if the world around them is not burning as they speak. His eyes, bright and beady, are glued to Sam beneath the brim of a dirty ball cap.

"State's doing what they can to contain it, but you folks are pretty damn far from the nearest populated area. No one pays much attention to what happens out here, to be honest."

"So." Campbell, with raised eyebrows, taps against his desktop to drag Kuhn's attention back to himself. "What can we do?"

"Nothing much." The fireman shrugs and lifts his mug to his lips. "We'll get out there and start clearing a perimeter. Smoke's nasty, but it won't kill you."

"We can't evacuate. It can't get near us."

"I understand that, and it won't. Not this one. But you should know, you're going to have to rethink that policy eventually. Shit gets worse every year. A place like this won't last forever—that's just the reality." Kuhn swishes the dregs in his mug and winks across the room at Sam. "Can I get another refill, angel?"

When Hugo Baker and Logan Adler run screaming into the office, Sam is nearly relieved. It's hard not to laugh; the campers are scraped and muddy and wailing like they have seen a ghost—wailing, in fact, about the ghost they've seen.

"Is Poppy Warbler dead?" Hugo looks more like a frightened boy and less like a murderer than Sam has seen him yet.

In the confusion, Sam catches a look on Kuhn's face: deeply disturbed and morbidly curious. He leans toward the campers, squinting, searching for the seams and zippers in their flesh. At Campbell's tense look, Sam grabs them by the shoulders and marches them out.

She can't say what happened to them. In all likelihood a counselor is behind it; her best bet is on Jeremy, who has taken to spiking his morning coffee and chain-smoking joints on his free periods. He must have said something about Poppy a little too loudly in front of the campers and had to cover his tracks with the ghost story. Whatever happened, both Hugo and Logan—already fragile enough after Taps's outburst—seem to be under the impression that they have met and spoken with the real-life ghost of Danny McGee. The silly story she started herself has grown into something monstrous over the course of the summer.

Their faces are glazed over, ecstatic. Drunk and sloppy with excitement. They hold hands as they follow her to the mess hall. Watching them, Sam thinks of Elias. Maybe he is right. Maybe Hugo Baker is a good kid—or a kid, anyway; maybe good and bad aren't so simple. Kids do terrible things. In another life, if someone had stopped this boy, told him no; if he learned not to take everything he wanted; he could have been another man.

Anyway, Sam concedes to herself, he's only a boy now. There are no lessons to be learned, no better adults to shape. Logan smiles like a toddler with his hand in hers. Sam gives them each a soda and delivers them to crafts, leaves them with a finger pressed to her lips. *Don't tell anyone.* Whatever it is they think they know, they nod, assuring her that they won't.

The smoke from the forest fire has transformed Camp into a hellish wasteland. Sam can hardly see five feet in front of her along the trail. The dull sun casts the world in a peculiar, apocalyptic glow. They have flipped into another dimension, split the fabric and slipped between realities. Back in the office, Nick and Campbell are alone, talking across their separate desks. The way they pause and look up, half smiling, when she walks in makes her wonder self-consciously what they were talking about.

"Kuhn left?"

"He wasn't too interested in sticking around once you were gone." Campbell grimaces and gestures toward the door. "So? What in the hell was that all about?"

"I don't really know." Sam explains her exchange with the campers as well as she can. "I guess they overheard something about Poppy, but they're sort of taking it in their own way."

"Oh, good lord." He runs his palms from his head down his brow, sliding his glasses out of place. "What do you mean, their own way?"

"The ghost."

"The *what*?"

Nick leans across his desk toward Campbell. "They're deflecting," he says, in a tone that suggests the comment is not meant for Sam. Campbell nods knowingly.

Sam sits heavily in the chair Kuhn abandoned and crosses her legs, folding her arms over her chest. Her foot twitches sporadically in the air. "They seem . . . happy," she says. "For what it's worth."

"They're in a state of extreme distress."

"Aren't we all?"

Campbell casts her a disapproving look. He takes off his glasses to rub his eyes—comically small, watery and bare. "I don't know what the right move is here. We'll just have to keep a close eye on them until Richard's available."

"Where *is* Chard? Shouldn't he be here?"

"He's busy."

"Busy?" Nick laughs. "He's on a bender up at his cabin. Sam's an AD now, remember? We don't need to lie to her."

"Christ, Nicky. You don't need to be so blunt with her, either."

"You don't have to say *her*, I'm right here."

They both look up at her, surprised. Outside, the bell chimes for dinner. Sam rises from her seat.

"I'm sorry, Sam," says Campbell slowly. "This summer has been . . . You shouldn't have to be . . ." He falters.

Sam glances between the two of them. An empty, haunting sort of fear rattles her. It feels like crossing a tightrope only to realize the belay was never attached, like growing up and learning that adults don't have all the answers, either. No one is steering the ship; they've been lost at sea this whole time. "It's fine," she says.

On her way out the door, she catches Nick's eye. He looks uncharacteristically apologetic. It's over, whatever it was. Or maybe not. Somehow, it isn't up to either of them to decide.

The Hummingbirds will not stop singing the latest version of their favorite campfire song. Deb, who has grown more confident in the past weeks, conducts them through dinner. "*Late last night, while we were all in bed . . .*" Her mouth is rimmed red with tomato sauce.

"*Fire, fire, fire!*"

"*Water, water, water!*" Maggie F. brandishes her water glass triumphantly, slopping an ice cube onto the table.

"*Jump, Danny, jump!*" they shout. "*Aaaaah, splat!*" All seven girls pound their fists on the tabletop. The spaghetti dish trembles. They giggle, showing off the food in their mouths.

"Okay, now I'm fire, fire, fire—no you're fire, Rachel—I'm water, water . . . Sam! Sam, are you watching?"

Sam smiles. "I'm watching. Let me see it again."

After campfire, she volunteers to cover Sadie's spot on the patrol schedule. She has been staying in more often; she is tired, and the overdrinking and dirty jokes and judgment have lost their fun. She sits alone on her cabin porch and looks out over the quiet smoke and starlight. A bizarre sense of peace has come over her. Even as everything buckles and twists and comes undone around her, she feels strangely serene. Maybe stress has an endpoint, she reasons, and she has finally found it.

About an hour before curfew, as she makes her way back down the trail from a stroll around the cabins, she hears a pair of voices from the Chickadees' porch. Sam pauses and peers around the corner of the cabin. In the weak light, she sees a silvery blond head, bent low. She hears a murmur, then a giggle she is sure she has never heard Rosie make before. As she watches, the two shadows wrap together, rocking back and forth. Sam smiles and turns back up the trail before they can spot her.

Her radio goes off early in the morning, around the time she should be waking up for her walk to the gold-panning claim. Campbell is calling the assistant directors to meet in the mess hall. They arrive bleary-eyed in their sweatpants and messy hair, murmuring about an apparently wild night. Richard Byron waits for them there. He is calm, tidily dressed, composed aside from red and swollen eyes. They gather around him at a table in the back of the mess hall. He smiles at Sam and tells her how nice it is to see her; how happy he is to have her included in these meetings. They are all so tough and resilient, he says, and the finish line is just around the corner.

"This smoke is obnoxious, but it isn't going to kill us," he says, echoing Kuhn. "Last I heard, we're not in the fire's direct path. It should clear out by the end of the week."

That seems logical enough, Sam thinks. Nothing can really touch them here, politics or storms or disasters. She can imagine any number of ways for the summer to end—in smoke and confusion, in collapse, but not in flames.

When she tunes back in, they are talking about Taps. "He's been paid in full for the summer," says Campbell grimly. "Last I heard from him, he got home safe. That's the end of it."

Sam chances a glance across the table at Gabe, whose face is an empty slate.

"It's not, actually." Byron drums his fingers over the tabletop. "We have his mess to clean up. Hugo Baker, Camilla Meyer, Max Gill, Logan Gill." He counts each name on a fingertip, gesturing broadly.

"Adler-Gill," Sam corrects him.

"Probably soon to be just *Adler*," Nick adds. Sam nearly laughs. He casts her a flicker of a smile across the seats between them. "What are your thoughts?"

"My thoughts are, it could be worse. These things happen. What matters now is that they're still enjoying themselves. That's our priority." Byron leans back in his seat, scratching at his beard. In the dim, shadowy light of the windows, he appears older and wiser than usual, almost stoic. Sam watches him and wonders if she dreamed up the afternoon on the other side of the lake, the bright room, the bottle shattering against the wall. "What matters is what they're looking back on a week from Saturday. If they're still immersed enough in the experience, a little crack in the paint won't mean much to them. In the end."

"A week from Saturday," Dane mumbles. He has been leaning back in his chair so the front legs hover upward; he lets them fall to the wood floor with a *clank*. "Is it really that soon?"

"Someone should be watching them," says Campbell. "I don't know what Hugo and Logan were doing wandering around by themselves in the middle of the day yesterday, but that can't be happening."

"It's not the wandering we need to worry about. It's the talking. I think we can get those four happily through to the end of the summer, but if they start talking . . . if they break through again and start telling other campers . . ." Byron huffs and waves a hand, indicating that the end of his thought is too much of an inconvenience to speak out loud. "I agree with you, though. We need to keep a close eye on them."

"What if we take them on a campout?"

Nick grunts, bobbing his head toward the smoky windows. "I don't think *out* is a good idea right now."

"A camp-in?" Amy suggests. "We can isolate them. Come up with a project or something. Keep them busy."

"Play some games."

"Tell stories," Sam adds. Richard Byron turns a glowing smile on her.

By the time the wake-up bell rings, they have laid out a loose plan. They will keep the four distressed campers together in the guest cabin, supervising them in shifts, until everything Taps told them on the office porch has passed into meaningless memory. Until the paint has dried. Or, until they crack again—in which case, they will have to be sedated and sent back across the lake to their summers' end.

"I don't understand," Sam says aloud, hardly aware that she is speaking. "How can they just forget and move on? He told them everything. Do they just . . . not want to believe it?"

After a quiet, tense pause, Nick answers her: "Would you?" The rest of the group glances uneasily between the two of them. Sam shakes her head, and the question dies there.

His mind made up, Byron sends them off with the chime of the bell. Sam lingers for a moment in the mess hall, looking at him. He is talking to Campbell, their heads bent together and their voices low and serious. When he looks up at her, whatever she was planning to ask dashes from her mind. He doesn't wait long for her to say anything.

"How is Poppy, Sam?"

"Fine."

"Looks like she'll make it through to next week healthy and happy, huh?"

"Yeah."

He straightens up in his seat, shifting his weight and attention toward her. "You do understand, don't you, that next week is the end of the road?" he says soberly. "The campers aren't designed to last longer than a few months. You *do* know that every day she spends wired into the consciousness transfer is money out of my pocket. Right?"

Don't do anything stupid, he is telling her. As if he has read right into her daydreams.

"I'm sorry to say it so bluntly, but that's the reality of the situation. You know that, right, Sam?"

Sam nods. She hesitates, then realizes she has nothing to say. She leaves the two men to their discussion and walks back to her cabin.

Logan

THE COUNSELORS ARE SCARED. LOGAN can see it in their faces. They constantly tell the campers, all day long, not to worry about the smoke, but there is plenty of worry in their own high voices and fidgeting fingers. When adults get scared, they tell more lies. They tell them the fire is still far away, but suddenly there are strange men in big trucks and dirty pants littered across Camp. They carry chainsaws and axes.

"Cool!" Hugo gushes over the firefighters.

Logan finds them creepy. She doesn't like the way they laugh and tease each other and try to talk to all the kids. She thinks if they are here to fight off a fire that might kill them all, they should be more serious about it.

The night after their encounter with the ghost of Danny McGee, Logan hardly sleeps. She tosses and rolls in her sleeping bag, listening to the branches and crickets outside the window. Listening for footsteps. She wants to tell Milly about what happened to them, but she can't seem to find the words. Thoughts rush and tumble in her head, worry over worry, and when she finally falls asleep her dreams are bright and vivid. The next morning, she is so tired she feels like she is still dreaming. The smoky darkness doesn't help.

At breakfast, Mr. Campbell approaches their table and quietly pulls Sadie aside. Logan strains toward their whispers but can't hear anything. Sadie nods. Then he clears his throat and waves toward her and Milly, asking them to come with him.

They follow him out of the mess hall and wait outside while he dashes back in. He returns, to Logan's surprise, with Hugo and Max in tow. "You guys," Mr. Campbell says to the four of them—excitedly, even though he looks so tired and droopy—"are a special group. You're going to be helping me and some of the counselors out with a really special project."

"Why us?" Hugo asks immediately.

"Well, aren't you all friends?"

They look at each other. Logan pushes up her glasses. Max sniffs and swipes at his hair. Milly shrugs.

"Don't you want to know what the project is?"

Logan glances at Hugo, who stands with his chest pushed out, squinting with suspicion into grown-up eyes. Slowly, she nods. "Okay."

The project, it turns out, is not very special at all. After a few more quick bites of breakfast, Katie comes by to swoop Logan and Milly from their table and bring them back to the dorm, where they pack an overnight bag. She leads them to a little cabin up the hill, next to the infirmary. Logan had never noticed it before. Inside, the place is cobwebby and smells like mildew. There is a living room with a few old chairs and a couch that pulls out into a bed, a bedroom with another pullout couch, and a few shelves stacked with old photos and nonsense. Their project is to paint a mural on the back wall of the cabin—for visitors to see, supposedly. Logan can't help but wonder what kind of visitors they're talking about. The firemen are the first strangers to show up at Camp all summer.

Dane arrives with the boys, their packed bags slung over their shoulders.

"Why are we staying the night?"

"For fun," says Katie curtly. They stand outside the cabin, ankle-deep in spiny brush, staring at the peeling wood-paneled wall. She hands Logan a bristly paintbrush. "We're having a camp-in. It's going to be fun."

It is fun. First, they coat the wall in a chunky layer of white. Then Katie sets them loose with their imaginations and all the colors they want. For an hour or two, Logan actually forgets about the smoke and the fire and the ghost. They laugh and wipe paint on each other's clothes. Counselors come and go. Nick brings them lunch, and they eat it on the cabin porch, peeling the dried paint patches off their arms and legs. A breeze picks up and the smoke is suddenly thinning; a bright beam of sunshine reaches Logan's face and warms her skin. She closes her eyes and turns her chin up to it, drinking it in. In that sunbeam, she feels a flash of what summer was until now. What it should be.

They stay at the little cabin all day, through dinner. During campfire time, Elias shows up with his guitar. He plays, and they beat on benches and boxes and sing along.

> *The more we get together, together, together,*
> *the more we get together,*
> *the happier we'll be.*

With each verse, they get louder. Singing turns into shouting. Like at the lookout above Pike Falls, they stand and jump and beat against their chests.

> *'Cause YOUR friends are MY friends,*
> *and MY FRIENDS ARE YOUR FRIENDS . . .*

Logan stomps against the floor, feeling the beams creak beneath her, hoping they might break open and let her through. She shrieks into Milly's face, and Milly shrieks back:

> *THE MORE WE GET TOGETHER,*
> *THE HAPPIER WE'LL BE!*

They grip each other's arms and swing each other around, flinging their bodies onto the open futon and cushions scattered across the cabin floor. They howl like wolves. They laugh until Logan thinks she might puke.

"Rage!" cries Elias over his guitar. "Rage, children!" From the doorway, Katie shakes her head at them.

At night, they lie in their sleeping bags on the dusty floor. They fought over who should get the futon, boys or girls, so the counselors folded it away and laid out camping pads for them all instead. They flip and rustle and whisper in the dark. Katie and Dane are outside on the porch. Logan can hear their voices through the walls. *Datie and Kane*, Elias called them once, that night in the barn loft.

"We saw him, yesterday," Hugo whispers as quietly as he can. "He lives in a cabin in the woods. He's not a kid, like he was when he died. He's an old man."

"How do you know it was him?" Milly asks. Max is silent, thoughtful.

"You would've been sure, if you'd been there. It wasn't human." Hugo's hand reaches up in the dark, twisting at the wrist, grasping toward the ceiling. He looks a little like a ghost himself.

They don't say much else about it. Max and Milly might not believe their story, but they have to be thinking about something, silent and awake as they are. No one says it out loud, but Logan knows they all feel strange. It can't be a coincidence that Camp has locked them all away together. No one else has been given a special project, no one else has had a *camp-in*. She stews over the possibilities. Maybe they're being punished for releasing Spark. Or for the beer during the midsummer dance. Or the fight after the soccer game. Maybe they are here to prevent them from telling other kids the truth about Danny McGee—or maybe to protect them from Danny himself, who knows now that they're on to him.

Sometime in the middle of the night, she wakes up and rolls over to find Max lying close next to her on the floor. He is wide awake, his eyes two wet glimmers. The memory of Pike Falls rushes over her, the smell of crushed leaves and river water, the chirping crickets and bitter, cold night air. She breathes his name, but he doesn't answer.

The next day dawns and nothing has changed. Curtains of smoke, glaring sun. They have breakfast in the cabin. In morning period, Sam arrives, and she brings Poppy with her. They paint the wall. Poppy proudly shows them her brand-new tooth. She cries when her picture doesn't come out the way she wanted, and Hugo helps her fix it. The way he wraps his arm around her shoulders to comfort her reminds Logan of the afternoon they met, all those weeks ago.

Dane and Nick drive them out to Lobster Point and let them splash in the warm water. It feels good; they push and dunk each other and end up swimming. Logan floats, pretending she's a crocodile. With only her eyes and nose above the surface, she looks flat across the lake like a murky pane of glass. From this angle, the dam isn't so scary. She can't see the water rushing over it or the steep drop on the other side. It's just a concrete barrier, a soft gray line between here and there.

They finish the mural after dinner. The cabin wall is coated in pictures, splashes of color and handprints and looping signatures. It doesn't look particularly good, all in all. Maybe that's why they painted it in a place no one will ever see.

Time passes slowly, and they get bored. They read from chapter books and listen to Dane's stories as the sun goes down. Logan wonders what the other Ravens are up to. She wonders where Poppy is, if she is safe. She listens for ghostly footsteps. The counselors leave them with the lights still on to sit outside on the porch.

"Tell me again," Max says after a long silence. He lies stretched out on the futon. The book he has been reading rests facedown on his chest, open to his page. The way he props one arm behind his head makes him look almost like a grown-up. "About the ghost."

Logan tells him. She might be exaggerating what they saw and heard in the woods, but she desperately wants him to believe her. When she is finished, Max nods and picks up his book again. Milly speaks up next. "Guys. Why are we here?"

They look at each other and chew on their lips. No one has an answer.

•••

"LOGAN. *LOGAN.*"

Logan's eyes snap open. It takes her a moment to find herself—she is lying on the floor, on a camping pad, in the dusty cabin. "Hmm?" She sits up, her sleeping bag crinkling.

Max holds a finger to his lips. He crouches by her pillow, wearing his hoodie. Next to him, Hugo leans over Milly.

"What's going on?"

The boys shush them and motion for them to stand. They tiptoe out the back door of the cabin, into the smell of burnt air and fresh paint. It's lighter here, moonlight streaming weakly through the smoke. Logan blinks and adjusts her glasses to get a look at them. Not so long ago they were beating the life out of each other; now the two boys grin excitedly back and forth. "Look," they whisper. "Look what we got."

Four long air rifles are leaning against the new mural, black smudges in the artwork. Logan stares at them for a long, sleepy moment before she figures out what they are. "We bent the locker door open. With a big stick," Max says proudly.

"What the shit?" Milly gasps. "What do you guys think you're doing?"

Hugo beams at her. "We're going after him. All four of us. We're going to set a trap."

They talk about it for some time in quiet voices. Katie and Dane are sleeping in the back bedroom of the cabin. If they heard the things the four of them are talking about, Logan thinks, they would have them sent home the very next day. Milly looks at Logan with a face so serious it's almost sad. "You really, really saw him?" she asks her with those serious eyes. "You *know* he's real?"

Logan nods. "He's real. I know it." A shudder runs down her spine as she says it. For once, she is in charge, and Milly is the one doubting the adventure. Milly is the one who will have to jog to catch up.

They never really had a choice. The four of them, the dam, the ghost—it's the only way, the last thing they need to do before the summer ends. Logan feels like she is walking the tightrope again. She has to keep pushing forward. She can't stop. She can't look down, or she'll fall.

Back inside, they tie their sneakers and flip their hoods over their heads. They shut the back door carefully behind them. The air rifle is cool and solid in Logan's grip. Like masked robbers, they sneak along the trails, backs hunched, guns cradled to their chests. Someone laughs in the distance. The counselors are all out of their cabins, doing whatever it is they do at night. Logan leads the way up the Hummingbirds' porch steps. She knows Poppy's bunk is the closest to the door; she saw it while she talked to Sam. She pushes the door silently open. While the other three stand guard on the porch, she crawls inside and crouches at the foot of the bed.

"Poppy," she whispers. The blond head rolls over. She blinks up at her, sleepy and confused. Logan holds a finger to her lips and smiles behind it. "Hey. You want to go on an adventure?"

Sam

SAM. YOU THERE?

Sam lifts her head. She is lying on the Nest floor between Rosie and Elias. They've been lying like that for close to an hour, drifting, not talking. Quiet conversation trickles around them. The beer in her hand is half empty and warm.

She reaches for her radio. "I'm here."

You need to tell everyone to go to bed.

The conversation dies. Everyone in the Nest pauses to look at her. Bottles lower slowly from lips.

"Why?"

Tell everyone to go to bed, then meet us at the guest cabin, please. Katie's voice crackles into the silence. *And bring Elias.*

Elias sits up at the sound of his name, his eyes puffy and sleepy. He is wearing his old contraband T-shirt—Sam gave it back to him a few days ago.

It was a weak gesture of apology. The crinkled word *GOD* glints white over his sweatshirt zipper. He frowns, and Sam shrugs back.

"Well," she says out loud to the group. "Go to bed, I guess."

The three of them wait until the Nest has cleared, then they finish their drinks and climb down the ladder, shutting off the barn lights behind them. For the first time in days there is a visible moon in the sky. In its dim light they hurry across Camp, listening to the ruffled mutters of the other counselors branching off toward their cabins ahead of them. Katie and Dane step down from the guest cabin porch to meet them on the trail. Their faces are glazed with exhaustion. Katie's lip trembles as she tells them.

"What do you mean, *gone*?" Sam rubs her eyes, for a moment entirely convinced she is dreaming—half drunk, asleep on the Nest floor. "Where did they go?"

"I don't know, but . . ."

"But what?" Her heart sinks. She knows, just by the guilt and pity in their looks, whose name is to follow.

"We checked all the cabins. Poppy's not in her bed."

"What? Why would they take Poppy with them?"

"We thought you guys might have an idea." Dane nods between Sam and Elias. "Anything weird Hugo said, El?"

Elias shrugs. "Not to me. How long have they been gone?"

"I don't know. We thought they were asleep, and we left for, like, a minute."

Sam squeezes her head between her palms, trying to make sense of it. Four preteens and Poppy, vanished into the smoke. The murderer among them. *Is she dead?* he asked, frantic and scrambling, a scared little boy. It reads like a riddle she is too tired to solve. "What do we do?"

It's Rosie who acts first. She steps up on the trail, and Sam understands with a sinking weight in her stomach how utterly misplaced her own promotion was. It should have been someone else, if things were really fair—it should have been Rosie. "Let's start looking. I'll go check Hummingbirds again. Someone go down to the lake. If we don't find them in an hour, one of you should call Campbell." At Dane's look, she shrugs. "The longer you wait, the madder he's going to be."

They split up. Dane rallies the other assistant directors, and they search through Camp as discretely as they can. Elias checks his cabin; Sam checks the Ravens'. They look through the boathouse, the crafts shack, the game room. Flashlight beams shimmer through the branches, hoarse whispers calling, haunting the dark spaces between them. A fruitless hour goes by. Just after midnight, Gabe finds something that sends them all over the edge of panic: in the shed at the air rifle range, the storage locker has been broken into, the metal door bent backwards on itself, lock still intact. At that, they decide to call Campbell.

"Not like they're going to hurt anyone with BB guns," Elias mutters.

"It's not that, dipshit. It's the fact that whatever they're up to, they thought they needed to take *guns* with them."

"Maybe they're just running," Sam suggests. "They know. Maybe they're just trying to run away."

"What about Poppy?"

Sam shakes her head. Her lips twist and pinch, exhaustion tugging at her eyes. "They know about her, too."

Campbell's voice over their radio channel is as furiously alarmed as anyone could have expected. Dane chokes back giggles; Katie smacks him. With the call over, there is nothing left to do but wait. Sam excuses herself from the huddle and wanders, alone, to the office. She is thinking about coffee, and maybe a quiet minute alone.

The lights are on, she sees from the trail. Sam steps inside to find Nick sitting at his desk—she thought he was still out looking with everyone else. His hands are folded over the desktop, his head resting on them, like he is sleeping. His hair is shaggy and overgrown from the summer. At the rattle of the screen door, he sits upright, startled. His eyes are rimmed in red. Sam pauses in the doorway. The fluorescent overhead light is jarring in the surreal hour.

"How 'bout it, freckles?" A sad smile twitches over Nick's face. He wipes his nose with the back of his wrist. Unfathomably, he is crying.

"Hey." Sam crosses the room toward him. Reality wavers just slightly as she moves, as it has so often lately. "You okay?"

"Yeah." He swivels in his seat and reaches for her. Sam lets him. His arms wrap around her waist, pulling her into him, resting his head on the soft part of her stomach.

"I'm sorry," she says. She runs a hand over his hair.

Nick blinks up at her. "Why?"

She doesn't know why.

"Listen." He lifts his head from her belly and brings his hands around to her hips. "You know that scar on my back? The one you asked me about a while ago?"

Sam nods. Whatever has him in this state clearly has nothing to do with the runaway campers. It's something else, something personal—one beam has slipped and the whole house is tumbling.

"The thing is, I have no idea where I got it. I've been thinking about it. I know *something* happened, and it was when I was a kid, I think, but I just can't remember." Nick shakes his head wildly. His grip on her tightens. "I know that next week, when all of this is over and I get home, I'll remember again, but I can't right now." He gulps. "It's like that every summer."

"What do you mean?"

"Every summer," he goes on, tugging her closer to him, his knees on either side of hers, squeezing her. "I forget little pieces of who I am. It's like, I'm someone out there, and I'm someone else in here—and those people aren't even the same. And I always wonder if that's how the kids feel, too. I've been sitting here thinking about it, and I can't see why not. I don't see any reason to think we won't wake up next Saturday and our lives will be almost over."

Don't do that to yourself, he told her, once. *You can't start thinking like that.* Sam looks down at him and finds herself strangely pleased. Here she stands, stronger, holding him together. "I feel that way, too," she tells him. They look at each other. Maybe the two of them are like Logan and Max Gill, after all—old and beaten down and desperately trying to rekindle something they lost, something they never really had to begin with. Maybe they are Poppy Warbler and Hugo Baker, once great and past their prime. Maybe they ought to get up and start running.

Sam drops to her knees at his chair, trying to think of something clever. Nick sniffles. He grips her face in both hands. His eyes run over her, like he is going to say something, but Sam cuts him short by bringing her palm down hard against the front of his chest. *Thump.* Nick recoils and lets go of her. He blinks, then laughs. Sam smacks him again. He does it back, crooking his elbow at an awkward angle to tap against her sternum.

Thu-thump. Thu-thump. Thu-thump. They must look ridiculous. Sam feels the smile spread over her face. They laugh like they've won, like they've finally figured it all out. *Thu-thump. Thu-thump. Thu-thump.*

Nick pulls her upright and they stand like that, a foot of space between them, swatting each other's chests and laughing. He steps closer and kisses her, and Sam kisses him back. Her head spins sleepily. It's supposed to be this way, she thinks. If he is right, if they are just like the campers, then nothing really matters, anyway. They can do whatever they want. Can, and should. He lifts her onto the desk, shoving papers and scattering pens. Sam hooks her legs around his waist and fumbles with the buttons of his flannel shirt. To hell with the missing kids, to hell with all of it. Nothing is real.

The clatter of the screen door breaks them apart.

"Are you *kidding* me?"

Sam turns. Campbell stands at the office door in plaid red pajama pants and a hooded sweatshirt. *Emerson High Junior Varsity Lacrosse.* He holds one hand to his forehead, eyes wide, nostrils flared. Close behind him, Elias is red-faced with horror.

Sam scoots sheepishly off the desk. A single loose notecard flutters to the floor beneath her. As Nick opens his mouth to explain—or apologize— Campbell shakes his head and holds up an open palm toward them. Sam can see the anger roll in a lump down his throat. "Okay," he begins. "Okay. I'm going to turn around, and I'm going to come back in, and *this* is not happening." After spitting the last few words, he pivots and slams the screen door behind him. Elias jumps out of his path.

Nick clears his throat and rebuttons his shirt. Sam winces guiltily at Elias. *Sorry,* she mouths. He frowns like he isn't sure whether to laugh or scream.

Three loud stomps mark his progress across the porch, then Campbell is back. He blinks quite a few times before speaking. "*You.*" He points an accusatory finger at Nick. "Stay here. Sam, come with us. We're going to drive up the road and see if we can't find them." At that, he turns and leaves again.

The Camp pickup idles just outside, rumbling, its headlights casting solid beams through the smoke. A dark figure sits in the passenger's seat—Sam doesn't need to see his face to know who. She clambers up onto the open tailgate beside Elias. He looks at her, his face half lit in grayish yellow. His voice is barely audible over the truck's engine.

"We'll find them. You know he wouldn't hurt her."

Sam nods. "I know he wouldn't."

"Sam!" Nick comes loping down the office steps. He reaches the back of the truck and shoves his outstretched hand into hers. The panic, whatever momentary lapse had come over him, is gone. He smiles his old, thin smile. In her hand is his worn black lanyard, the keyring with its jangling keys and the little metal cylinder between them. "Just in case," he says quietly. Then, louder, toward the driver's side window: "Try Lobster Point! We took them swimming out there today."

The dam, Sam thinks—of course. The truck's horn blares, Campbell telling Nick to get out of the way. He gives her arm a grateful squeeze and steps back. The truck jerks into gear. As they roll away, Sam hangs the keychain around her neck and tucks it beneath her sweatshirt, where the needle sits cold and hard in the well of her chest, rising in tune with each nervous breath.

They drive slowly all the way there. Elias and Sam shine their flashlights along the sides of the road and shout the names of the campers. In the lull between shouts, she can hear the men talking, their voices a steady drone. She wonders how many times something like this has happened to them, if they are scared.

The truck pulls off the road at Lobster Point and parks just beside the pile of ash left from their nightly bonfires. Sam and Elias slide off the tailgate. "Hugo!" Elias calls, tossing his flashlight beam around the trees.

"El." Sam grabs him by the elbow. "The dam." Now that they are here, it seems so obvious. "The story."

Elias nods. Richard Byron, in jeans and a heavy flannel, steps down from the passenger's-side door. He is alert, bright, shining over them. "What story?"

Sam leads the way from the campsite toward the water. The last time she walked this trail she was stumbling, drunk; the memory hits her with a surge of hot embarrassment. It strikes her as funny, how a serious situation can dig out the most prickling, menial feelings. She hears the rush of water, rounds a thick trunk, and then she can see the lakeshore, and the dam, a thick strip of black across reflective, calm water. She sees them first, frozen in the beam of her flashlight. Then she hears them. Five little figures stand on the concrete wall, shouting over the rush and splatter of the spillway. She picks up her pace.

A heavy hand thuds into her shoulder from behind. "Turn the light off," he hisses in her ear. Sam does as she is told. All four of them approach the edge of the dam, a slippery hill where dirt meets concrete. The kids are shouting, indiscernible. Byron takes the lead, stepping out from the shadows of the trees with spread arms.

"Hello!" he calls out to them. He stands still at the end of the dam.

Sam can see them more clearly now as her eyes adjust to the absence of the flashlight beams. She sees the rifles in their hands. She sees rounded cheeks and gaping mouths, and a little glare of moonlight reflecting off owlish lenses. For a second, she stands back and finds the scene horribly beautiful.

"It's him!" the kids yell. One of the taller shadows reaches out and grips the littlest; Sam hears the clear, high shriek she knows so well. A shock of blond hair swings. She thinks to run for Poppy, but Richard Byron is blocking the path onto the dam. He holds her back with one steady arm.

"Kids! Come on back here!" Campbell calls from behind them. His shout is somewhat broken, quieter than it could be. Elias stands still and silent.

"Hush," Byron whispers over his shoulder. "Give them their moment. Let them work it out."

There is some commotion out on the dam. Their voices rise. Someone has Poppy by the shoulders. Sam lets herself be held back. She could fight. She could get around him, if she really wanted to. He looks down at her in the smoky moonlight and shakes his head, and Sam stands quietly waiting.

Logan

THEY TURN THEIR RIFLES TOWARD the edge of the dam. Logan's heart races with excitement. It was a long, toe-stubbing journey out of Camp, past the glowing barn full of counselors and down the road to Lobster Point. She felt jittery and bright, shot through with static electricity, as they crossed the slippery dam walkway. They set and baited their trap. Now the ghost has arrived, just like Hugo predicted. A flicker of lights, a moment of tense silence, and a figure appears from the shadows. Logan recognizes it, tall and dark and looming. Its arms reach toward them. "Hello!"

"What now?" Max whispers. Logan hears the *click* of the safety on Hugo's gun. They hold them up like they really know how to use them.

Poppy—she has been in high spirits, happy with their adventure, up until now—lets out a little whimper. Logan puts an arm across her to protect her from the ghost. Poppy squeals.

"Hey!" Logan pulls her arm back like she bit her.

Another voice cuts through the night at them. This one is weaker, not ghostly at all. "Kids! Come on back here!"

Milly stands at the edge of the group, closest to the shoreline. She turns a confused grimace back to the rest of them. Her air rifle is still raised, butt to her shoulder, finger on the trigger.

"Wait a minute." Max lowers his gun. Logan looks at him, and something heavy sinks in her chest. "That's not him," he says. He is quiet now.

Logan squints at the figure on the end of the dam. "Yes, it is." She raises her own rifle. Her safety is on, but that doesn't matter. She is holding it.

"No, it's not. That's just some guy." Max puts one hand on Poppy's shoulder, holding her tight. As if he wants to run off into the forest with her. "We're being silly."

"No, we're not!" No one looks fiercer behind their rifle than Hugo. He has one eye closed, the other squinting into the shadows through his scope. His face is a twisted sneer. "That's gotta be him!"

As Logan watches, the ghostly figure moves closer. Hugo stands at the back of the group. When he pulls his trigger, there is a loud *pop* and she can hear the BB rush over their heads. Milly slaps her hands to her ears. Poppy screams. From the shore, where the ghost of Danny McGee looms, comes a sudden grunt and shout.

"What the *fuck*?"

Logan gasps. She lowers her air rifle. There is more than one person there at the edge of the water. She can see their black shapes shifting.

Max shakes his head. He leans down to rest his gun on the concrete at their feet, then he grips the skinny guardrail with both hands. Poppy stands between his arms. They both face outward, out toward the old fish hatchery and the dark world beyond. Logan feels sick. Her head wobbles. She grips the rail herself, the metal cool against her palm. She looks toward Milly, hoping for a dash of confidence, but Milly isn't looking back at her.

"I think I hit him!" Hugo cheers.

"That's not him," Max says, barely over a whisper. His profile, framed in murky silver, transforms as Logan watches. His eyes go dull. His chin drags down. His shoulders bow.

Poppy tilts her head up at him. "Did we get him? Did you kill him?"

Max slaps the guardrail. "It's not *him*!" His yell frightens Poppy, who shrieks again and slips out from under his arms. She shuffles to her left, toward where Milly stands. Max goes on shaking his head. "We're being silly," he says again. "This is just a game. There is no ghost."

Voices mutter from the lakeshore. Movement in the shadows. He is right, Logan realizes—nothing is waiting there but regular people. Counselors, out looking for them. They are going to be in so much trouble. She has stopped on the tightrope; she is looking down. Her head hurts. Behind her, Hugo still holds up his rifle. "Yes, there is," he insists, brave as ever. "He's here. He's here for her." He nods toward Poppy. "He's gonna come out here to try to get her, and we're gonna throw him over."

Max leans sideways against the railing to face Hugo, shouting past Logan at him. "There *is no ghost*! It's just people!"

Something shifts in Hugo's face. He looks at Max down the barrel of his gun. "No . . ." he says, slowly. "Hang on. *You're* him." He aims over Logan's shoulder, straight into Max's face.

"What?"

"The ghost possesses people!" Hugo cries, high and eager. "That's it! He possessed some old guy up at that cabin, and now he's possessing Max! *That's* Danny McGee!"

Logan looks between the two of them. She glances again at Milly, who stands behind Poppy, sunken and confused.

"You're crazy!" Max yells. Below them, the spillway roars on. "We're all crazy. We're *all* crazy!" He is screaming, now, louder than he needs to. "The ghost is made up! It's just a story! It's just distracting us from the *thing*!"

"What thing?" Milly asks. Her shadowed face is full of fear. She, too, looks suddenly older.

"You know. We all know! Taps told us, remember?" Max turns on Logan. She lifts her gun halfway, unsure. "None of this is real. Don't you remember what he said? Don't you remember *me*, Logan?"

"What are you talking about?"

"Don't listen to him," Hugo begs her. "He's Danny!"

Max does not stop. He stands tall against the rail, his body facing outward, his head turned toward Logan. She grips the rifle down low, at her waist. "I remember you," he says. "I remember everything. I do. Taps was right." He is melting before her eyes. His face droops, downward, downward, downward. "Loges, it's me. Please. I want to get out of here. Let's just go now. Let's jump, and everything will be back to normal. I want to get *out*."

"Don't listen to him, Logan!"

Poppy has started to cry. Her sobs rise and mingle with the falling water, crashing into the black far below.

"Come on, Logan. Let's get out of this place. This fucked-up place. Let's go home!"

Logan hesitates. She stares hard at Max. *Max*—like a breath of fresh air or a hard knock on the back of her head, she realizes—or, at least, she thinks she does. The thought passes in a flash, whatever it is. Fear and thrill take over. She raises her air rifle and clicks the safety to *off*. "You're not Max. You're the ghost. You're the murderer."

"No. Logan, listen."

"No!" Logan shouts. She is strong, now, growing stronger from the inside out. "I'm not listening! You're the ghost. We caught you. You want to jump, then jump! Jump, Danny, jump!"

The cold barrel of Hugo's rifle rests against her shoulder. His voice rises, gleeful. "Yeah! Jump, Danny, jump!"

"Wait . . ." Milly steps back on the walkway, lowering her gun. As she does, the tip of her air rifle smacks against the guardrail. The thrumming *thwang* rattles over the sound of the water. Logan looks at her and feels only more rage.

"Come on, Milly. Look at him. You know it's him. Jump, Danny, jump!"

Poppy stops crying. Her face falls soft and curious; Logan can see it in the gap between Max and the rickety railing, still swaying from the force of Milly's gun. As she watches, Max looks out at the smoky night air. His fingers, curled on the guardrail, peel slowly upward. Until this moment Logan didn't even realize—he isn't wearing the wrist brace anymore.

"Jump, Danny, *jump*!" Hugo shouts on.

The rail is level with Max's waist. He bends down slowly and crouches under it, then stands again on the other side. It isn't real. This is still just a game. Nothing is really going to happen.

Still, she chants at him. "Jump, Danny, jump!"

Max's hands are off the railing. He twists his head to look back, and Logan catches a spark of something—his eyes are smiling again, his face is back to normal. He's just playing along. He is going to say something.

"Jump, Danny, jump!"

A flash of blond, like a gust of wind, rushes across Logan's middle. Poppy has joined in the game. She shouts along with them. Her little arms reach under the rail. It's just a step and a stomp, and a shove, like in Capture the Flag. She is strong for someone so small. Max's hands jerk up and outward, but there is nothing to grab.

Logan holds her air rifle to her chest. Max tips forward quietly, and gravity takes him. For the second time this summer, she watches him fall.

Sam

FOR A MOMENT, SHE HAS a choice. The campers come running back along the dam, shouting, their toy guns dragging forgotten at their sides. Poppy is first. She must have been the first to look away and start running. Richard steps sideways and allows Sam to sprint out onto the cement ridge; she catches Poppy and lifts her up. Standing with her clung tight to her chest, she looks backward up the trail.

The truck is still parked at the campsite. The keys are in the ignition. She could run. She could take Poppy and go. Distracted as everyone is, they won't know to chase her.

The other three campers reach them, wild-eyed, screaming Max's name. Sam knows, now, who went under the rail. In the darkness she could only see a shadow waving its arms. Elias clutches his shoulder where the BB hit him. "Hugo!" He snatches the boy by the hood of his sweatshirt, yanking him from the edge of the dam and onto the dirt. Hugo falls on his back. He looks up, fearful.

"Elias?"

"Sam?" Logan is at her side. She stammers. "I . . . He . . ."

"Where is Max?" Campbell barks. He tears the air rifles from the children's hands one at a time. He must know, Sam thinks—he had to have seen the falling shadow as clearly as she did. Maybe he is in denial. Maybe he wants to make them say it.

Milly Meyer chokes back a sob. "He fell."

Sam wavers, her arms trembling under Poppy's weight. She could still run. She looks back up the trail. The warm body, pressed hard against her chest, digs the metal of the keyring into her skin. Frightened fingers cling to the fabric of her sweatshirt. Sam looks between Campbell and Byron, and in an instant the moment passes. She kneels and manages to pry Poppy off her. "I'll be right back, okay?"

Poppy shakes her head, reaching to grab her again. She whimpers. Campbell crouches to pull her into his own arms, presses her head against his shoulder. As he shushes her, Sam turns and takes off running.

The trail to the bottom of the dam is steep and poorly maintained. Sam stumbles over roots and rocks. She should have gone back up to the truck and taken the road around to the old hatchery, but it's too late now. Halfway down, the path smooths out and she breaks into a cautious sprint. The black pool is shallow at the base of the wall. Misting droplets blur her vision as she splashes forward. Not unlike Pike Falls, the flow spilling over the dam is much more impressive from below.

The body is half submerged. He lies on his back, looking up. Sam reaches him and kneels at his side. Her knees hit stone with a weak splash. Max's legs are twisted unnaturally beneath him. He must have landed exactly where he is now, in about six inches of slimy water. Two feet to his left, he may have hit deeper water, may have made it out with just another broken bone. His eyes are open. His chest rises and falls, fast and quivering. He sees her and gasps out loud.

Sam moves robotically. The lanyard is off her neck, the needle in her hand. She digs her fingernail into the button on the side. Her hands are steadier than she would have imagined. "One, two, three, four," she counts under her breath. "One, two, three. One, two, three, four." The mouth of the metal tube furls open.

The boy's body shakes. In the darkness Sam sees him in pieces: the whites of his eyes, the muttering lips, the ripple of a tremor in his cheeks. His features float up to her, disconnected, inhuman.

"You're going to wake up," she says out loud. "I promise. You're going back home." She holds one hand against his damp brow and with the other presses the needle hard into the side of his throat. A slight *click* ticks against her palm as the spring releases.

Max looks at her. His jaw clenches, and he nods. His eyes fall shut.

It takes a minute or two for the shallow breaths to stop. Sam waits, watching.

She wonders if this looks the same in every circumstance, the moment a person leaves. If it makes any difference that Max is not going far. Across the water, headlights shine on the old fish hatchery. She hears the slam of the truck door, splashing footsteps approaching.

Richard Byron crouches beside them. His hand closes gently over Sam's, taking the keychain from her fist. With two fingers he reaches out and measures the last few feeble heartbeats in Max Gill's neck. After a long, quiet moment, he sighs. "Okay. Good." They stand together, and Byron lifts the sopping, broken body. With some difficulty he heaves the boy over his shoulder. His other hand strokes Sam's hair. They walk back to dry land slowly, together.

In the gleam of the truck's headlights, Byron pauses. His face and shirt are soaked, rivulets of watery blood running over him. He nods sideways toward the concrete shack, the old fish hatchery that was never a hatchery at all. "You want to come?" he asks her. The question is sincere, though his voice is gruff, huffing beneath the weight of the body. "You want to see?"

He isn't being morbid. He isn't just inviting her to watch him dispose of the camper, but to show her how it all works. To let her into the inner workings of his most prized possession. Sam understands, and considers. She shakes her head. Cool droplets roll like tears from her brow. She doesn't want to stomach it, not tonight.

He nods. "All right. Take the truck, then. I'll take care of this."

"Okay." Sam hears her own voice like a stranger's.

Byron grunts and shifts the burden on his shoulder. "Get those kids to the infirmary. May will give them a sedative. Tell them Max has some injuries, but he's fine. Tell them he's on his way home."

Sam nods. She doesn't wait to see him opening up the door to the old fish hatchery. She climbs into the driver's seat of the pickup and pulls away.

•••

THE SUN RISES RED IN the smoky sky a few hours later. Sam sits on the steps of the infirmary porch, a cup of muddy, burnt black coffee in her hand. Inside, Poppy and the preteens are safely snoozing. They won't wake up for hours. When they do, their world will be bright and simple again, albeit foggy. Sam is tempted to ask Nurse May for one of the little blue confusion pills herself.

Elias drains his coffee cup. He sits beside her with an ice pack taped against his bruised right shoulder—the BB hit him in the soft spot just below his collar bone, hard enough to leave a considerable mark. They have long since worn out the jokes about him getting shot on the job, and by Hugo Baker, no less. They sit in quiet commiseration, watching the sky lighten, listening to the trill of the birds.

"What's the weirdest thing you can think of right now?" he asks her, toying with the mug in his hands.

Sam considers. "Sleeping in my bed, probably. Going to class. Calling my mom." She snorts. "What about you?"

Elias shrugs. "I think I'll ask Rosie to marry me. If the world doesn't end before next Saturday, we'll elope somewhere. Get a couple of desk jobs. Have a kid, name her Poppy." He frowns at the sunrise. "What do you think about that?"

"You're right. That is weird."

He laughs, scratchily, behind closed lips. Sam snickers back. After a while she stands, stretches, and starts down the infirmary steps. She has to move; she cannot sit still in her head for another minute. They share an understanding smile before she turns away. Sam leaves him with his ice pack and his weird ideas and meanders off toward the guest cabin. She hasn't had a chance to see the finished mural yet.

She is standing in the brush, just uphill from the back of the cabin, when Nick finds her. He looks relieved. Dark hollows beneath his eyes punctuate a ragged smile.

"He made it through," he says, as soon as he is close enough to reach her, with a whisper. It's still too early to speak out loud.

"Hmm?"

"Chard just called. Max is up and talking at the facility."

"Oh." Sam nods. She swirls the last of her coffee, lukewarm between her palms. "That . . . took a while. You think he stopped somewhere on the way?"

Nick steps toward her, shaking his head. He wraps his arms over her shoulders and pulls her into him. "That's a big question."

They stand together in silence for some time, looking over the new mural. It's hardly beautiful—Sam imagines it will be painted over again during pre-Camp setup week next summer. Hasty, sloppy pictures are splattered patternless over a white backdrop. The longer Sam looks, the more details she can make out. A pine tree with a spindly trunk. A shark. A brownish lump on four legs that might be a bear, or a goat, or a horse. *Millipede Meyer was here*, painted in looping purple scrawl, and just above that, a heart encasing the initials *HB + LA*. Toward the bottom of the wall, at about Hummingbird height, two squiggly stick figures hold hands on a flat line of grass. One is carefully labeled: *Poppy*. The other, *Sam*.

"Did you see that one?" Nick asks. Sam follows his pointing finger upward, to the far-left side of the mural. There, a little black figure stands on a gray wall. Green waves are painted below, and on either side, flames. A lump settles in her throat. They both stare at the painting.

"He's a real person," Sam says quietly, half to herself. "Danny McGee. He's a guy I knew when I was a kid. I just used his name for the story. I wish I'd told them it was just a story."

Nick rests his chin against her shoulder. "It doesn't matter what name you give it. There's always been a ghost at Camp."

"What do you mean?"

"Someone's always telling some version of the same story. This one just got . . . out of hand."

She thinks over the dark moment, the tumbling shadow. She heard them chanting: *jump, Danny, jump*. It was viscous, religious. Childish. Max went under the rail on his own, but in the end, there must have been a nudge. She saw the swing of his arms, the tilt of his body. She would like to blame Hugo Baker, but the words won't rise to her lips. In the end, it doesn't matter. They were only being kids. The fall was a natural consequence of the summer, of innocence, and Richard Byron was right to keep them from stopping it.

Max fell as a kid, running from a ghost. There are worse ways for a summer to end. Whatever they were doing out there, holding guns and chanting, they were doing it for the same reason they loved the story so much; for the same reason they sing campfire songs and cross high tightropes and holler from clifftops; for the same reason they came to Camp Phoenix in the first place.

For that same reason, Sam turns away from the painting of Danny McGee and leans into her own ghost.

"Come on," Nick says, turning her toward the trail with a hand on her back. "We can still get a couple hours of sleep before breakfast."

week eleven

Logan

THE CAMERAS LOOK NOTHING LIKE any camera Logan has ever seen. They are big and black and clunky, with dials and buttons and thick round lenses. They must be old, she assumes—Camp Phoenix must have been using them for decades.

Everyone gets a camera. There are ten pictures loaded inside. Ten pictures they can take of whatever they want, then give back to their counselors to give to the director. The pictures will be printed and sent to them at home. To remind them, the counselors say, of the fun times they had here.

On the last day of Camp there are no activities. Everyone runs around with their heavy cameras strapped over their necks, trying to use their ten pictures wisely. The firemen are gone, and so is the smoke. The sun shines yellow in a blue sky. Camp is bright and beautiful again, just in time for them to leave it.

Logan takes a picture of her bed, with Milly sitting on the bottom bunk, making a silly face. She takes a picture of all the Ravens on their front deck. She takes a picture of Elias in the stables, frowning at the saddle he is scrubbing, and another of Sam and Rosie making faces at each other on the lifeguard dock. She gives her camera to Milly, who takes a picture of her and Hugo on the mess hall steps. She sits between his knees and he hugs her around her shoulders. They are laughing when the shutter clicks.

She would like to take a picture of Max, too. As much as they disagreed this summer, he was her friend, and she would like to have a photo to remember him by. Max went home early. Sam says the fall off the dam broke his leg and two ribs. An ambulance came to take him to the hospital, and from there he went straight home.

Milly says Max fell. She says they were being dumb kids out there on the dam, and in all the excitement of their make-believe, Max just lost his balance. She doesn't believe in the ghost anymore. Hugo remembers it differently. He says that Max was truly possessed by the ghost of Danny McGee, and when he jumped, he killed the ghost inside him once and for all. He says Max is a hero. He says that, if their places were switched, and he knew the ghost was in *him*, he would have jumped, too.

Max didn't jump. Not really. In the end, he wasn't going to. Logan knows that, and she is sure Hugo does, too, but they don't talk about it. There are some things no one ever needs to talk about.

Whatever happened, exactly, they don't get into much trouble for it. After another night in the infirmary, life goes back to normal. Hugo has to help repair the locker door at the air rifle shed. Mr. Campbell tells them they shouldn't talk about the ghost of Danny McGee anymore. It's a story, he says, and nothing else, and the more they talk about it, the more they are going to scare themselves and the other campers. Logan asks if he is going to tell their parents about what happened—if not about Max's fall, at least about them stealing the air rifles and walking out of Camp in the middle of the night. Mr. Campbell shakes his head and gives her a funny smile. "We'll see."

Despite all the warnings of being on thin ice, Logan does break the rules one last time. Two nights before their last night, she sneaks out to meet Hugo at the lake by the fishing dock. He brings his sleeping bag, and they wrap it around their shoulders. They stay out until the sun comes up, pretending to be grown-ups.

"I'm going to be in big trouble when I get home," he tells her, quietly, as they lie dozing on the grass.

"Why? Because of the thing with Max?"

"No." Hugo shakes his head. He looks up at the stars, and Logan can see them shining on his eyes. "Something else. Something that's not my fault."

He won't tell her what, exactly. Won't, or can't. "Well, you're not home yet," she says.

They talk about writing or calling, but it doesn't make much sense. Neither of them knows their address or their phone number. They will find a way to see each other again, Logan imagines. Something tells her Hugo Baker will always be a part of her life.

The final campfire is quick and silly. A few people go on stage to show off their favorite songs and skits one last time. Nick and Poppy perform again, like they did at the talent show. They sing a different song, a happier song. This time, everybody cries. Even Logan, to her own surprise—she lifts her fingers off her cheek and laughs when she finds them wet. When they finally stand up to sing the final good night song, though, the tears have all cleared, and everyone is giggling. The coals in the firepit burn low and red.

Look up to the moon, moon, moon,

Hug every rock and tree,

I will take care of you, my friend,

If you take care of me.

She promises Milly and all the others that she will be back at Camp Phoenix again next summer. They'll be Eagles. This is not a goodbye, they swear to each other—just a see-you-later.

They leave Camp the same way they arrived, on the white bus with the bird's nest logo on the side, in groups. For most of the morning they sit on the lawn in the sunshine, waiting for their names to be called. Logan hears her name in the middle of the day. Hugo is already gone. She hugs everyone, Milly last and longest. "You're my best friend," she tells her, funny as it feels to say out loud. Milly smiles back.

There are seven or eight other kids on the bus with her. Katie drives. She drops them off at the side door of a big log cabin. A doctor in a white coat greets them there. She says she will give them all a checkup and then send them upstairs, where their parents are waiting.

The doctor leads them down a long hallway, into a cramped room cooled by a blasting air conditioner. The floor is white tile, and the walls are blank. "Wait right here," she says cheerfully and leaves, shutting the door behind her.

Logan blinks. She looks down at her arms, tanned and scraped and stacked with woven friendship bracelets. Confused, she turns toward Oscar, the Finch, who has taken a seat on the floor. Just as she is opening her mouth to ask him what he thinks is going on, a loud whirring fills her ears.

Sam

CAMP PHOENIX IS CLOSING. THERE is going to be an investigation. They have made it through one fire only to fall right into the next.

The case against Richard Byron's company was opened already, a few years ago, after someone complained of immoral treatment of clients. There wasn't enough evidence to take any real action at the time. Until three days ago, that is, when Phoebe Jackson, Christian Rodrigues, and a man named Tom Kuhn approached the case detective together. Byron was notified that his camp will have to be shut down while the investigation takes place. If anything comes out of it, he could end up with charges of cloning a human being, and abuse. Not child abuse, of course—no one involved with Camp Phoenix is a legal minor—but abuse of his power, a breach of contract with his clients. It all comes down, Campbell says, to the little blue pills: memory-altering drugs administered without consent.

Campbell tells this to the assistant directors in the office after the final campfire. They are toasting the end of the summer with champagne in coffee cups when he breaks the news to them. They should keep this quiet, he says, even after their summer contracts are up. Until the case goes public.

He doesn't think anything is going to come of the investigation. Richard feels confident, he tells them, and so does he. "We'll be closed for a summer. Maybe two. Then everything will be back to normal. If anything, an investigation that comes up clean is going to look good on us."

"But it is all true," Sam says to Nick in private, later that night. "Poppy was technically a clone. For half the summer. And they all took those pills."

Nick laughs. "No one's saying he's not guilty. They're saying he's going to come out clean."

"Will you come back and work here? When it opens again?"

Without a shred of hesitation, he nods. "Chard won't always be around to run the place," he says. "Camp is good. It's a good idea, and people need it. Someday, when someone else takes over, it won't have to be so ugly and secretive."

"When you take over, you mean?" she asks him. Nick smiles. He squeezes her hand and changes the subject.

Sam isn't around to watch Poppy board the bus back to the facility the next morning. She says her goodbyes to the Hummingbirds quickly, after breakfast, then runs off to help Rosie and Elias box up supplies in the boathouse.

She chooses not to think about it. She knows, as it happens, that the light is going out in Poppy's eyes. Her body will be wrapped in plastic, piled into a van, shuttled down to the old hatchery, while up at the facility the machines keeping her alive quit beeping. Sam can look the other way. It's over, and she is tired. There was never anything she could do. Poppy Warbler vanishes from the world on the last morning of Camp exactly as Sam knew her: pure, wild, and young.

The funny thing about the end of the summer is how easy it is, how quickly it all wraps up. What took them a week to set up in early June takes a single afternoon in late August to take down again. They work feverishly, laughing, shaking off the summer. Old mannerisms and references slip back into place; the wall comes down as the magic of Camp is swept away. By the time they are done—all the guns and the bows and the crafts boxed away, the boats locked in the boathouse and the boots and saddles packed up—the campers are gone. Camp is empty again, exactly as they found it eleven weeks ago.

Pizzas and coolers of drinks are laid out on the lawn. Campbell wanders from group to group with his plate in hand, saying his goodbyes, urging them—with a little twinkle in his eye—not to party too hard tonight. He catches Sam at the picnic table as the rest of them are splitting up for a frisbee game. "Richard couldn't be here," he says quietly. "He asked me to tell you goodbye for him."

Sam looks into his kind face. She wonders how much he knows. "Anything else?"

"We'll be in touch. Things are going to have to be quiet, for a little while, but—" A frisbee sails over their heads, and Campbell ducks. They both laugh. He pats her arm, smiling, and Sam is struck with sadness for the first time today. "We'll be in touch."

Night falls and Campbell quietly disappears. They sit around the campfire, telling stories, drinking, laughing. In the early hours of the morning the fire burns low, and the group breaks apart, stumbling back to empty cabins. Sam finds herself alone with Rosie, Elias, and a bottle of bad tequila. They sit at the shore with their toes in the mud, watching the stars ripple on the surface of the lake.

She tells them about the investigation. She is sick of keeping secrets, sick of trying to obey her better judgment. Neither of them seems surprised to hear it.

"You could help, you know," says Rosie. "After everything with Poppy. Everything with Max. You could actually get the place shut down."

Sam doesn't answer. She is thinking about Poppy, and about Max. She takes a deep swig from their bottle and comes up gagging.

Elias laughs at her. "I'll see you, won't I? Thanksgiving? You'll be a big hit at Nana's house, you know."

It takes Sam a moment to understand. For half a second, she lets herself imagine it: sweaters, nervous laughter, a grand family home. Hands on thighs beneath the dining table. She shakes her head. "I'm not coming to Thanksgiving, El. I'm going back to Paris."

Elias kicks at the starlit water. "That's a shame. You'd be good for him."

Sam takes another long drink and smacks her lips. Looking out at the ripples across the water, she giggles and decides she would like to go for one last swim.

Her hair is still damp when she wakes up at dawn. Rows of empty bunks stretch in front of her, the mattresses crinkled and stained. It's a sad, spooky sight. Sam sits upright and rubs her eyes. Nick mumbles behind her. She laughs at him, large and utterly out of place on her little bunk. After a dizzy moment, she rises, throws a sweatshirt over her head, and pads barefoot across the cabin floor. She crosses the outdoor bathroom and nudges open the Chickadees' door on the other side. Peering down the row of bare beds, she finds them tangled together and fast asleep in the bunk beside the front door. Sam smiles to herself.

Rosie blinks and looks blearily up when Sam touches her. She is wearing—to Sam's delight—the old blue T-shirt Elias had on last night. *GOD IS A LESBIAN.*

"Looks better on you than me."

Rosie glances down at the arm wrapped around her chest. "Ugh." She grimaces. "What time is it?"

"Early." Sam crouches next to her bunk. "Listen. I'm taking off. I don't want to wait for everyone to wake up." In truth, she can't stand the idea of the drawn-out goodbyes, the promises of staying in touch.

"I get it." Rosie nods.

Sam suddenly cannot think of what to say next. She smirks at the two of them. "Is this going to be something?"

Rosie laughs breathily, a rush of air through her nose. "God, no." Even as she says it, Elias twitches and flops over beside her.

"Sam?" His voice is groggy with sleep, eyes squeezed shut as if in pain.

"Yeah?"

"Get the hell out of here."

"Okay." Sam laughs. She should tell them she loves them. Instead, she tousles his hair, leans forward and kisses Rosie on the cheek. It's better, she thinks, to hold onto a little regret and hope for a chance to see them again.

She packs fast and poorly. Nick walks her to her car. The little black sedan is alien to her, now, something from a stranger's life. They linger stiffly in the parking lot, tired. He kisses her in a hollow, routine way.

"Will you be back? Next summer?"

Sam looks at him. It's impossible as ever to read behind his eyes. "There isn't going to be a next summer."

"You know what I mean. The next summer there is."

"I don't know." Sam adjusts the weight of the bag on her shoulder. She tips backward, away from him. "I can't think about it now."

"Okay."

She wants to tell him to come see her in Paris. She wants to ask him to find her—he doesn't even have her phone number. She wants to tell him that if she leaves this place to find herself in another life, if the whole summer has been a dream she paid for, after all, she will be glad to have spent it with him. She says none of it. She kisses him again and sits in her car before she can watch him walk away.

•••

SAM IS ON HER WAY back to Paris when she hears the news. It's after sunrise, the tail end of a dreary red-eye flight. She has just touched down for a three-hour layover and is waiting, half asleep, for the *fasten seat belt* light to switch off. The woman in the next seat—red lips, tidy bun—scrolls through her phone, eagerly consuming everything she missed while they were in the air.

"Oh, my God." She turns to Sam, wide-eyed.

Sam is in no mood for small talk but knows she can't ignore her. They still have another twenty minutes at least to be stuck next to each other. "Hmm?"

"Poppy Warbler died!" the woman gasps. One hand flutters to her heart, the other scrolls frantically across her screen. "Oh, no. I can't believe it. I used to love her."

Sam gazes out her window. "Me too. How did she die?"

"In her sleep, I guess. She was at that camp . . . You know, the one where they turn you into a kid? Gosh, that place just creeps me out. Anyway, I guess it was a heart attack or something."

"Wow." Sam nods. She offers her a sympathetic smile. "I'm sorry to hear it."

Back in Paris, she falls into a normal life. She has a new apartment, and new classes, and a new group of friends to run around with, getting into the same old trouble. She is young, and very much awake. On the day Hugo Baker is convicted for murder, she tries to call Elias. He doesn't pick up. She forgets to try again. At Camp, her life in Paris felt impossibly far away. Now, the opposite is true—the summer is like a worn-out memory of an old dream.

Sam watches from afar as the investigation against Richard Byron and Phoenix Genetics plays out on the public stage. It becomes the newest trending scandal. For weeks, even in France, it is all anybody talks about. Then, like anything else, it goes stagnant. Months pass and Sam doesn't know what has happened to her old job. She doesn't bother to check.

One gray December morning, on her hurried walk to class, a shout from behind makes her freeze in the center of the sidewalk.

"Poppy!" The voice is clear and flat, distinctly American. "Poppy!"

Sam looks around until she sees them: a family of tourists, hustling across the street in their raincoats and hats. A woman shouts from the back of the group. "Poppy, wait! Slow down!"

For a silly moment, she nearly expects to see her. Unstrapped sandals, wild blond hair. Scabby knees and missing teeth. Running too fast through the streets of Paris, of all places, with a sloppy craft project in her fist. Of course, it isn't her. As Sam watches, the woman catches up with a dark-haired girl in a pink beret. She is tall and awkward-looking, probably about fourteen. The girl rolls her eyes and waits for her family to hurry up. Sam fights the urge to shout out to her.

"Poppy," she mumbles once the family has moved on up the street. She shudders, like she has seen a ghost. Sam shakes her head, and the feeling passes. She pulls her coat tighter around her neck, turns on her heel, and picks up her pace. She is going to be late for class.

Logan

Dr. Camilla Meyer, the plaque outside the building reads. *English Literature. Room 23.*

It's a nice building, red brick and ivy, at the heart of the university campus. The hushed patter of students' voices echoes in the halls. Logan climbs to the fifth floor to find room twenty-three. She forgoes the elevator, telling herself she is working in her cardio for the day. The truth is she is nervous.

The old Black woman who opens the door might be Milly—she also might be anyone. Her face is beautiful, gracefully succumbing to age, her eyes kind but distinctly sharp. She wears her gray braids swept back into a regal bun. The woman looks Logan up and down. Then, with a flash of a smile, she pulls her into a rough hug.

"My God, look at you." Milly holds her at an arm's length. She is still shorter than Logan. Her voice has a little gravel in it. "You're old."

Logan laughs. She follows Milly into her office. They sit on soft armchairs, facing one another, and trade a few strange pleasantries. Dr. Meyer teaches a lecture or two each semester and advises students in her spare time. The office feels homey and well lived-in, and she has a sunny view of the campus out her window.

"I guess I should be retired. God knows I'd rather be doing something than just sitting around, waiting to die." Milly chuckles. "I'm an author, really, by profession."

"Of course you are. I know your name." Logan smiles at her, shaking her head. She can hardly believe who she is looking at, the words she is speaking out loud. "I didn't realize until I woke up, but I knew you all along."

At that, the old woman laughs. Logan knows that laugh—scrappy, raspy, and lively. "We didn't realize a lot of things until we woke up, did we?"

From her purse, Logan pulls an envelope of photographs. Milly takes hers from the drawer of a side table, and they exchange them. The photos came to the house about a month ago. In the same envelope was a long and wordy letter about Phoenix Genetics' integrity and their value of the Gills as clients, a promise that their services will be available to them again as soon as possible. A heap of corporate backpedaling in the face of their fresh public scandal.

"Oh, look at this one." Milly sighs, squinting at one of Logan's photos. Logan rises from her seat to identify it: a snapshot of the Ravens, standing on their cabin porch with their counselor. The image quality is poor and grainy, not unlike her memories of the summer. More likely than not, that is intentional. All a part of the experience. "Look at Sadie. Jesus, she's just a kid."

"Yeah." Logan shakes her head, still smiling. "We were awful to her, weren't we?"

"Downright little bitches," Milly chortles. She flips the picture to the bottom of the stack in her hands and examines the next. It's of herself, on their shared bunk. Sticking out her tongue. The next is of their table in the mess hall, Donna and Joy posed like models on either side. Another of the lake, clear and flat. The next of a boy and girl on the mess hall steps. He is hugging her from behind. Their faces are blurred, moving in a bout of sudden laughter. "Oh." Milly raises her eyebrows. She wears a familiar, know-it-all smirk when she hands the photo back to Logan.

Logan nods slowly. She studies the photo, as she has many times already. Still, she struggles to wrap her head around the fact that the girl in the picture is her—let alone who the boy is.

"He went down for it, didn't he?"

Again, Logan nods. She has been following the case passively. "More or less. They said there was 'no intent' in the end. Still, six years is significant, for someone like him."

"You think he did it?" Milly always has been blunt. She stares through her, and Logan feels her cheeks flush like a child's.

"I . . ." She hesitates, tiptoeing around the right words. "I don't know. I heard he was charged with sexual assault, years ago. At the very least, I think that could be true. And that's enough." This is difficult to force out, sticky in her throat. "Max kept talking about trying to get involved in the trial. He thought he could give a character testimony or something. It was all over before he could get ahold of anyone, though."

"Oh, Maxie!" Milly bursts with scratchy laughter. The mood between them brightens. "God, that should've been the first thing I asked you. You're really *married*?"

"Fifteen years." Logan brandishes the ring on her finger. "Our kid turns five next week." She fumbles through her purse for her phone to show Milly pictures of her family. The old woman's face lights up with glee. She hovers her fingers over the screen, zooming in on Emma's face, then Max's.

"I cannot believe it," she repeats.

"Do you have a family, Milly?"

She nods. "Three boys. All grown now, of course. I was married for a little while there." She shrugs. "She was too good for me. And she knew it." There is a light pause as Logan puts her phone away again. They both turn back to the photos in their hands. "Are you two going to be all right, then?" Milly asks eventually. "You and Max?"

Logan hovers on the edge of her answer. Before she left the house this morning, she caught Max watching an old clip of Hugo Baker's sentencing. He had the screen paused on his mugshot and was sitting still on the couch, one arm propped behind his head. Just staring at it. "We will be," she says. "It's going to take time."

Max was standing in the entrance to her room when she woke up. He was the first thing she saw, cross-armed, in normal clothes, leaning on the doorframe. Her head was still spinning. *Max*. He had been awake for a week already. The fall from the dam killed his boy self on impact, of course. When he talks about that night—though he rarely does—he says it was a simple matter of closing his eyes and opening them again on the other side. Logan knows there is something he isn't telling her. That's fine. There is plenty she isn't telling him, too.

The two women sit talking for a long time. They talk about their lives and their shared, surreal summer. They talk about Poppy Warbler and the investigation over human cloning. They talk about waking up and the headache of reality. Everything they saw or did or overheard in the past summer takes on a much darker tone, in retrospect. At the same time, though, it all has the fond glow of childhood memories.

"We really thought we were going to kill a ghost," Milly cackles, tears in her eyes. "With BB guns. How stupid could we be?"

"Oh, give yourself a little credit." Logan shrugs. She is slightly embarrassed; talking to Milly about the summer is a lot like her college years, like talking about a drunken night the morning after, recounting all the ways she made a fool of herself. "*We* weren't really there."

"What do you mean? Of course we were."

Logan fidgets with her wedding band. She has found it difficult, lately, took look down at her lap, at her pale, aging hands. Though it has been years since her vision surgery, she occasionally reaches up to adjust the glasses on the bridge of her nose. "That wasn't really us," she says, trying to keep her tone light. "I mean, we came away with the memories, but those kids . . . they were their own people. We're not them."

Dr. Camilla Meyer frowns at her. "Is that how you justify it all?"

"What?"

"Logan." Milly sighs, shaking her head. She takes the photo back from Logan's hand and holds it up to her. She points at the girl's blurred face. "If you really think *that* girl was her own human, with her own soul . . . well, then, the boy she forced over the dam that night was, too."

"Yes," Logan answers steadily. She has been through this debate in her own head a thousand times. "So was the boy who gave her her first kiss."

"You'd rather be guilty of murder than of being chummy with a murderer? That's what you're saying?"

"I'm saying none of us are guilty of anything." Logan draws her lips tight across her teeth. She has held strong to this belief with Max; she will hold strong to it with Milly, too. "They might have had some part of our heads in them, but those kids weren't us. We don't have to answer for anything they did."

"Convenient." Her smile is wry, knowing. "But I can see where you're coming from."

Another hour passes, and eventually Logan has to leave. There will be traffic along the drive back home, and Max will be waiting up when she gets there. She gives Milly a long hug. As a final thought, almost impulsively, she apologizes for the way she treated her that summer, driving her away for the sake of popularity.

"Don't worry about it," Milly laughs. "It wasn't you anyway, right?" On their way out the door, she lingers, then asks her one last thing. "Do you think you'll ever see him?"

"Who? Danny McGee?"

Milly scoffs. "Hugo. Will you go see him?"

"Hugo's in prison."

"Exactly. I bet he'd appreciate a visitor." She nods toward Logan's purse, where she buried her envelope of photos. "I bet he'd like to see that picture."

Slowly, Logan allows herself to smile. She is coming to a curious realization: Milly is an author. She and Max both work in publishing, and Hugo, of course, was once a legendary filmmaker. They made their livings with stories, all four of them. Maybe that was what got them into so much trouble that summer. Maybe that was what brought them together and drove them out looking for adventure. Maybe that was why they were all so convinced the ghost was real. "Not now." Logan shakes her head. "I couldn't do that to Max, after everything. I have to focus on our life—our real life—for a while."

"The place is going to open up again, you know." The old woman leans in the doorway, looking up at her, a spark of mischief in her eyes. "We'll have another chance to go back. You think you'd do it?"

Logan knows for a fact that there is nothing she would not give to go back to Camp Phoenix. To be that girl again. She would go this very second if given the chance. "Maybe." She shrugs. "Like I said. I need to focus on my real life, for now."

"For now." Milly nods. Logan knows she can read right through her. She wishes she didn't have to leave. "So, see you later, then?"

Logan smiles. "Yeah. See you later."

ACKNOWLEDGMENTS

I had a weird idea while I was working at camp one summer. Seven years later, thanks to the help and support of so many incredible people, I finally get to see that idea become a real-life book.

It never would have been possible without my agent, Emmy—they were the first person to take a chance on me, and I am forever grateful for the opportunity they gave me. I also owe a huge thanks to my publisher, Robert J. Peterson, for helping me polish this story, and to Dale Halvorsen for a brilliant cover.

This book is really for everyone who supported and inspired me throughout this long process. For my friends who never stopped encouraging me. For my parents, who met at summer camp. And, of course, for that camp, and everyone I've spent my summers with there.

Above all, thanks to my husband, Maciek, who has always kept me hopeful, and who never complained when I kept the light on in our one-room apartment to stay up writing all night.

ABOUT THE AUTHOR

QUINLAN GRIM IS A WRITER, traveler, and freelancer from Northern California. She has a BA in Philosophy and an MA in Global Studies. She currently lives in California, where she spends her time reading, studying, and working as a content writer. Fiction is her first love, and she's particularly fond of spooky stories in woodsy settings reminiscent of home in the Sierra Nevada mountains.

CPSIA information can be obtained
at www.ICGtesting.com
Printed in the USA
BVHW080914151222
654214BV00011B/845

9 781955 085106